FAKING IT

Merry —

Great chatting to you!

Stephen

FAKING IT

[signature: Stephen Berger]

STEPHEN BERGER

Copyright © 2008 by Stephen Berger.

Photo credit: Debra Steinberg Photography Studio

Library of Congress Control Number: 2008904125
ISBN: Hardcover   978-1-4363-4117-2
                Softcover   978-1-4363-4116-5

All rights reserved. No part of this book may be reproduced or transmitted in any form or by any means, electronic or mechanical, including photocopying, recording, or by any information storage and retrieval system, without permission in writing from the copyright owner.

This is a work of fiction. Names, characters, places and incidents either are the product of the author's imagination or are used fictitiously, and any resemblance to any actual persons, living or dead, events, or locales is entirely coincidental.

This book was printed in the United States of America.

To order additional copies of this book, contact:
Xlibris Corporation
1-888-795-4274
www.Xlibris.com
Orders@Xlibris.com
47953

Dedicated to the loving memory of Casey . . .

Chapter 1

She wakes me up from a peaceful nap. Sprawled on the bed, belly up, with my legs apart, and old gym socks covering my cold feet that are pointing toward the ceiling. My faded jeans and thirty-five-year-old sweatshirt tells the world where I went to college.

It is cool, a damp cool. Her warm breath on my left ear and her moist tongue close by. I open one eye at a time, not expecting any surprises. I touch the soft blonde hair, and her large round dark eyes meet mine. "Yes, Fern, I know," I gently whisper into her sweet face.

She responds. Her bark resonates throughout the lobes of my skull. Her puffy tail wags like a windshield wiper on a very wet night. She jumps off the four-poster bed with all four stubby legs landing at once. No way am I attempting that; it's one leg at a time sliding to the wood floor for me. Standing, I stretch my arms upward to regain circulation. Deep breaths confirm I am alive.

The rain drums against the windows of the bedroom. It is time to go out. Walking in the rain is good for both of us. It will work out the cobwebs, clear the dust from my brain and from her coat. Walking down the old gentrified steps, down two stories to the lobby of the Charlestown brownstone, demands I be awake. She is waiting on the landing with the blue cloth leash in her mouth. I check my left pocket for the jiggling of keys and open the two wood doors to the wet cool outside world.

The well-lit park across the street always delights my senses. Fern prances up the concrete steps to the enclosed area commemorating Bunker Hill. As she drags me to all four corners of the manicured grass, marking each as her own, my baseball cap is a success against the rain. She deposits; I clean up and dump the waste in the trash bin. What a team. Wait, who is in charge here?

Carefully, we take one wet stone step at a time, down past the wrought iron gates to the concrete sidewalk. Staying in sync with my four-legged friend, I go back through the wood doors at the condo into the warm entryway. The smell of stale cigar smoke is absorbed by the old wood stairwell. Leash in mouth, Fern waddles up the staircase, and I follow.

A quick, warm shower motivates me to make plans for the evening. No shave, but clean nonetheless. Toweled off and dry, dinner is served. To her. Do I make the move and go alone to the local tavern? Do I need to be with other humans now? The desire to make do with what the fridge has to offer and settle in for a mindless evening of TV is pulling at me. I let it go. Off for a lonely walk to the tavern. I find my way through the narrow wet streets of Charlestown, through the park, watching the different dog breeds playing and their owners socializing amongst themselves. Down steps and down the hill to more narrow streets. I find Main Street, walk two blocks, and the Warren Tavern appears, blended in with its corner location. This neighborhood pub has served the community since the Revolution. They say Paul Revere and General Washington had a few beers at this old oak bar. The difference is they weren't watching the Patriots. They were the Patriots. Real confrontations were being planned so we wouldn't be paying taxes to the present Queen Elizabeth. Scary thought.

The tall dark-haired woman smiles at me from behind the podium. No lecture, just a question, "How many?"

"One." I am not comfortable saying that number.

"The bar is full. Would you like the main room or the room to your left?"

I glance at the crowd in the main room. Old oak floors and thick ceiling beams, wonderful fireplace, and a loud buzz of conversation from the many couples and their friends. I see a small corner table in the room behind her. I point to it. "I'll sit over there."

She gives a quick, friendly smile, and I follow her black outfit to the cozy corner. My wet jacket and Red Sox hat occupy the second seat. I ignore the half-curtains that need replacement. But if they were new, they wouldn't belong.

Somehow finding comfort in a chair of all wood, I survey the room. The left corner has a long table occupied by three generations, the latest addition in a high-chair and well-behaved. Directly in my view is one-third of the packed wood bar. People are animated and the slow stream of those leaving is being instantly replaced.

The three people sitting in the right corner table appear to be in their fifties. My age. Two men, one woman—all look to be dressed in remnants from an old L.L.Bean catalogue. Their conversation tries to be private, but it's not accomplished in this room. They seem educated, conservative in their body language, and focused on one subject. Their old parents, dead and alive, dominate what they say to each other. "Would you like a drink before ordering dinner?"

The Boston accent abruptly takes me away from my table snooping. The waitress is cute, in a teenage-trying-to-be-adult kind of way, and has short curly blonde hair and a forced smile of insecurity.

"What's on draft?"

She starts reciting a long brewer's litany. I forgot that New England has more local beer than Delaware has restaurants. I stop her at the word *Sammy*. For those not in the loop, *Sammy* equals Samuel Adams Lager. My head swivels like a periscope evaluating the local sights. A short blonde woman with dark eyes is staring at me from the bar. I cannot help but notice her. Her hair smartly cut, her eyes dark and round. Not quite a diagnosis of hyperthyroidism, but healthy dark and round. My Y chromosome directs me to survey her body. Probably a gymnast who was expelled from her team because her figure was too feminine. Two X chromosomes expressing themselves.

Sammy arrives in a tall curved glass. My lips barely touch the frosted rim when I hear, "Have you decided?" There are so many decisions to be made, the least of which is what to eat.

"Do you have any fish on special?" After all, it is Boston. Listening to the choices, I decide the baked scrod is for me. I negotiate for extra vegetables and no potatoes, an extra $1.50. What a businessman I am.

Before my next sip, the house salad arrives, an assortment of green and red, nice and crispy, with balsamic vinaigrette. Good start. The corner people have their main course served; geriatric talk is put on hold. As I enjoy the fresh bread and salad, the empty table to my left becomes occupied, a couple in their thirties with a young child who is seated in my direct earshot. The little girl is maybe two years old.

Oh no. Please, no. It is happening. At the table on my left, the two adults are loudly talking baby talk to their smiling two-year-old. Superparents, I am sure they read all the right books. Probably two PhD's apiece but speaking loud baby talk like two idiots. I wish my left ear could close. The right corner comes alive after the main course is completed. Over coffee they are discussing the yin and yang of being eighty and failing.

Baby talk to my left, the cute blonde from the bar occasionally looks at me, and the final chapter's review on my right. I am seated in the middle of the cycle of life. Finally, my scrod arrives, surrounded by brightly colored steamed vegetables. Not looking anywhere except at the cooked fish, I simply enjoy the taste. It is wonderful protein for me. And wonderful distraction. The meal suits my hunger. I don't want to prolong my meal, but I want to enjoy it.

Mercifully, some sort of nutrition is brought to the two-year-old and the superparents. I am sure weeks of computer research were involved in the right food choice for the two-year-old. The food is soon all over the child and the table. The superparents smile and make sounds as they enjoy their baby expressing itself. The other table is discussing the merits of burial versus cremation.

I want a second Sammy, but better to have it back at my place in front of the television and the Red Sox. I cannot help but think of the big dark brown eyes that are sitting at the bar as well as the four-legged variety back at home. I look up from my empty plate, and there in front of me are two round dark eyes, the two-legged variety.

"This is the only seat in the place; I don't want my salad at the noisy bar. May I?"

I look up, eye to eye, eye to body. The bar is backed up, a waiting line extending into the rainy street. Saying yes is the only humane thing to do. I am so humane. "Sure, I'm just about done. I'll have coffee if you want company."

"Thanks."

Before I can move, she finds a peg on the wall, and my coat and cap are hanging. No more empty chair. She smiles, sits down, and puts both of her hands on the glass of white wine as if to gently caress each curve. The hands slowly slide down the stem. The glass slowly moves toward her mouth. The half-full glass is now a quarter full.

"Your salad." The waitress places a large bowl of greens in front of her.

"I hope you don't think I am pushy, the bar was getting claustrophobic."

"No problem." I order a mug of decaf coffee

"My name is Fern."

Amazing, the same name as the four-legged blonde I sleep with. I have to admit, sharing the table with this Fern seems natural. Almost like a real date. Like the old days. We both smile at the adult baby talk next to us. Before she joined me, I found it irritating. Eye contact is made as we share listening to the conversation about the end of life.

"My name is Adam." We shake hands, my elbow deftly bypassing what was left of Sammy. My coffee arrives in a big white porcelain mug. Fern is halfway through her salad. I feel at ease as well as a little insecure. I adjust my chair; our knees touch briefly.

"Adam, are you from around here?"

"I've lived here for about a year."

"Do you like it?"

"Yeah, it's neat; people, dogs, and a bunch of things always to do here in Boston and the nearby mountains." She looks at me as if she really cares what I say and think. I can't quite figure this out.

"I guess since you have been here about a year, you don't have deep roots?"

I have never been asked how deep my roots were. Thinking about the year I have lived here, I recognize my goal was ultimate superficiality. And I was quite successful with that goal. Do I tell this stranger about these things? Do I want her not to be a stranger? "I am not lonely." At least, I don't think I am.

My paranoia has me drinking my coffee with the handle on the left side, because I noticed a small chip in the ceramic on the opposite side. The brew is strong, hopefully decaf. Fern finishes her salad and orders a cup of tea. She pours the boiled water over the Darjeeling tea bag. She takes the tea bag out and places two teaspoons of sugar in her mug.

"I see you like things sweet."

"Only my tea."

"Do you eat here often?"

"This is my first time. Business brings me to the area."

"What kind of business?"

"I work in the international corporate marketing world. I can't tell you much more than that. Traveling is my way of life."

"Where are your roots?" Her eyes briefly flip to the bar, then the entrance, and then stare at me. She looks at her mug and a half-smile covers her white incisors.

"I travel often."

I know the line is drawn. We all have our own definitions of what is out-of-bounds. The trick is finding a person who is playing the same game as you. The table is cleared, leaving cold mugs caressed by our warm hands. I call for the waitress, her insecure smile present as she places the check on the table. She doesn't ask if refills are wanted. The line out to the wet street is demanding to fill the empty seats. There is no battle for the check. I slip the plastic card into its little pocket, and my tablemate looks at the entranceway.

There is an awkward silence as we look at each other. I hope my credit card will arrive soon. My plan is to stand up, nod, and say, "Nice meeting you." I am hoping the Red Sox aren't rained out. Part of me sends my core into a flip-flop. Why am I thinking of the Red Sox now? Mercifully the check arrives. I do the paperwork and return my plastic to its rightful home. Surprised at the silence, I stand up and am about to say goodbye.

"Thanks. Sorry, I was just thinking about work."

"Oh."

"No, I mean it. You didn't have to pay for me." She turns, lifts her weathered purse, and dives in to its recesses to produce a wallet.

Before she can speak, I do. "My treat, you saved me from being born and dying at dinnertime." She looks at me as if I am from Mars. "I can explain, but I have to go walk my dog."

"I like dogs, what kind of dog is it?"

"Heinz 57." We are standing during this deep conversation. Our jackets on, we walk out the door. The people waiting probably wonder why we are discussing ketchup. Before I know it, we are halfway to my place. I look at my new walking companion and describe the other Fern, my Fern. The rain is a slight drizzle, and the air has a renewed feeling about it.

"I just have to meet her and see what she looks like."

Am I ready for this? She wears a dark baseball cap, and a long black coat going down to her shins. The black gym shoes match the black slacks. Her head is tilted down as she walks. There is something mysterious that I want to unravel. Before I know it, we arrive at the doorstep to my place.

"Why don't you wait here while I get her?"

"Why?"

"Well, OK," and I open the door and watch her walk up the steps. "Second landing, that's me." It takes me two tries to go through the sequence of locks into my condo. I am not exactly feeling like James Bond. As soon as the door opens, the two Ferns take to each like old friends. They have to be related.

"Your place looks neat."

She must be complimenting the housekeeper. My four-legged friend grabs her leash from the umbrella stand, looks at me, and takes off down the steps.

"I can relate to her, where's the bathroom?"

I point her in the right direction while my little Fern is pulling me in the other direction.

* * *

While outside on our familiar routine, I am unsure of what is going on with this other Fern. A total stranger is in my place, and I am walking the dog. What's wrong with this picture?

I feel a bit like a fool. She could be robbing the place. Then I realize, what would she take, the furniture? She would look pretty ridiculous walking the streets of Boston with my old hockey sticks and collection of old *New Yorker* magazines. But then again, this is Boston. I look at my four-legged Fern before we climb stairs. She looks happy to be making a new friend. Why can't I feel the same?

Knocking on my own door before entering, I don't know what to expect. What I find is a surprise. She, the other Fern, has her running shoes off, feet up on the arm of the couch, and her coat thrown over the bench by the door. A Sammy ale is open and in her hand. The Red Sox are in the fifth inning, but I totally ignore the fact they are losing to Kansas City 5-1. Her body language sends me signals as if she's been here before. I wonder if I'll learn to speak that language.

"I couldn't resist checking out the fridge, may I offer you a beer?"

"How can I say no to my own beer?" Our shoulders touch on the couch. Halfway through our beer, I start to feel that tonight may be a beginning.

"You live here alone?"

"Yes." I am not about to offer my life story, it is bottom of the seventh, only down by two. It is difficult to think about what is happening at Fenway. "Have you been to Fenway?"

"No, I've never been to a pro sports event."

I don't know her well enough to offer her one of my two tickets to the ball game on Sunday. Her empty beer bottle finds its way to the wood coaster on the table in front of us. She helps herself to a second beer. As we chat, it feels like I am on my first date in a long while. Do I want to really know what kind of person she is? My first bottle of beer is half full; she finishes her second and finds another coaster. My four-legged friend curls up on her favorite rug. An occasional snore reminds me she is here.

"Time again, must be the beer." She removes herself from the couch and walks to the bathroom. The bathroom in my bedroom.

The Red Sox tie it up in the eighth while the shower is running. I don't know what is going on. The Sox win in the ninth, and somehow that is not where my attention is. The shower is off but no reemergence of my new friend. I turn the post-game show off. Silence. I walk directly to the bedroom. She is curled up under the blanket, her head on my pillow, the reading light on. She looks at peace. A feeling I lost a long time ago.

I quietly make my way down the stairs with the four-legged one. The night air feels good. What's going on here? Returning, I close and lock the door as quietly as possible. Something I have never needed to practice before. My little friend munches her treat, jumps on the couch, and gives me a quick look. She closes her eyes, out cold in a minute. I cannot disturb her.

Where do I sleep? I cannot disturb the human Fern. Both of my sleeping haunts are "Fern" occupied. I decide on my own bed. I toss my clothes into the corner of the room and, in my boxers, slip under the covers. Leaning toward the night table, I wash down the necessary capsules with my bottled water. It has been years since I have been with a woman. Her warmth and smell draw me to her. My left hand finds its way to the curve of her right hip. She moves her leg over mine.

Chapter 2

The dishwasher is in its loudest cycle. Half awake, I turn to the bedside clock; it is six o'clock in the morning. The washing machine's swirling adds to the noisy confusion. Nothing registers; that is not a sound for this hour. All I can remember is losing myself with a woman I didn't know. Its warmth was fleeting and soulless. There is emptiness next to me in the bed. Before, where there was warmth and excitement, now there is nothing. The only sounds are the dishwasher and the washing machine groaning.

I swing my feet onto the floor, pick up my khakis from the corner, and walk to the kitchen. My evening partner is gone. The place is spotless; nothing removed, no coffee made, just emptiness. My four-legged Fern looks at me, yawns, and rolls over. I am sure she knows more than I do. No note. I can't even find the beer bottles.

There is no way I can return to bed. I go to the bathroom and can't find my toothbrush. The toothpaste is missing. The towels are missing. Maybe she collects bathroom items like I collect hockey sticks. I need coffee.

* * *

Our morning walk isn't the usual mindless exercise. I follow my little friend by rote, and my confusion seems evident as I stand in front of my neighbor's door. Reality jumps at me when the woman leans over to pick up her morning *Globe* and smiles at me.

"Had a few last night, eh?"

She is from Toronto and a fellow hockey fan, but we never before have chatted at 6:20 a.m. "Yeah, the Sox pulled it out, great game." She smiles, and I find my way to the correct door.

Once inside, I make coffee, drink the orange juice, and boil the water for oatmeal. While setting the table for one, I realize nothing has been touched. The second mug of coffee clears my mind, but I am still confused.

Who is she? Why was last night the way it was? I don't think there will be answers.

The dishwasher stops. My plans are to shower and get the paper on my way to the gym. I'll empty the dishwasher when I return. The washing machine will just have to wait.

Chapter 3

The walk to the North End is always the warm-up I need. Over the bridge, turn right, and opposite the new Garden is the old warehouse that was converted to a fitness center. It has light and character. I lose myself in the weight room. Lying flat on the bench with my head on the white towel, the only thought I have is of the bar above me. All the energy I have at that moment is focused on the bar and the 215 pounds of steel plates on either side of it. The trainer spotting me is out of my sight line; the only words I hear are his encouragement. The first rep is smooth and confident, a buzz of knowing I have conquered a barrier; the second rep is concentrated hard work; the last rep is done with a little help from my friend. I weigh 152 pounds; it feels good to be stronger than my college years. I need that, another slap in the face of time. Cooling down on the treadmill, I am just in the moment. The only buzz is not last night, but my workout endorphins.

The walk home over the bridge brings me back into reality. I think of who I used to be. For twenty-eight years I was Dr. Adam Lincoln Burke. A psychiatrist to the business and entertainment stars of New York and Philadelphia. I heard it all. I heard too much. My own humanity was buried under everyone else's problems. Sure, there was a professional support group. One day I looked around, and my gut said, "I don't belong here."

My ex-wife is a corporate attorney in England, and it was time for me to take the dog and relocate, time to transition to something else. I yearned for simplicity and solitude. I was rediscovering myself in a basic superficial world of simple pleasures.

My old self, in the sixties, would have just chalked up last night to another experience and let it go. I can't do that now. Last night was an ingredient that I wasn't prepared to deal with in this transition mix.

Before I know it, I am back in my bedroom and staring at the empty bed with its ruffled sheets and blanket. The blanket I toss in the pile that will go to the cleaner, and I empty the washing machine and dump the sheets and what I was wearing into it. I just now realize that all the bathroom towels are in the pile that makes its way into the dryer.

Before hitting the shower again, I appreciate my compulsiveness in always maintaining a travel kit with toothpaste and toothbrush. That was my savior in the morning before heading out. The second shower cleanses me of last night. Drying off, it feels like my evening was a story I read in some novel. The remnants of last night will disappear after my stop at the cleaner's before lunch. I slip in my CD of Herbie Hancock and listen to his mellow jazz while I rinse the breakfast dishes for their trip to the dishwasher.

My usual rhythm is out of sync. The dishwasher is finished, clean and warm. Emptying it, I don't know what to make of the three beer bottles in the bottom row. Who washes beer bottles? No big deal, off to the recycle container. All these strange happenings are lost in my usual routine.

The four-legged blonde still with me, always one I can rely on. Once a stranger, now a roommate. Like many a lonely divorced guy, I met her through an agency. They weren't able to offer me any of her history, and she wasn't exactly the type to give away her secrets, but I was told housetraining and friendliness weren't an issue. As I rub her belly, her big eyes reflect love. I don't care about her past. Could I meet somebody to rub my belly and not care about my past?

My daily chores keep me busy, and before I know it, it is 5:00 p.m. I know because I feel the roughness of Fern's leash rubbing the back of my hand. I stopped wearing a watch when I left the world of scheduled appointments. My only schedule is meeting all the locals at the park as a pre-dinner ritual. The bulldogs all hang together, the Dalmatians ignore everyone else, and Fern and I mingle with social canines and their humans on the other side of the leashes.

"Adam, what's up?"

My tall friend Gord always has positive energy that radiates outward. I've never seen him wearing anything but jeans, a dark top, and Nike running shoes. I've known him for seven months and still have no idea what he does for a living. His American bulldog, Bowser, and Fern were good friends.

"Great ball game last night."

"Yeah, did you see the post-game show? Big Papi was really buzzed."

"No, I was sort of occupied." He looks at me with a knowing guy-to-guy smile. Bowser and Fern are off leash and moving around the grassy corner in the park. One is strutting, the other waddling. Sort of a canine version of the odd couple.

"One night this week, you want to grab a beer?" This is our weekly routine.

"Sure, give me call." We never discuss our past or, for that matter, our future.

My mindless routine reestablished, and I go through the next few weeks enjoying the sights and smells of Boston. The baseball season is coming to an end, and the approaching winter coolness has me thinking about the Bruins. I am even toying with the idea of joining a no-contact C-level ice hockey league. Why not? I am starting to feel content. It all changes with the loud, repetitive knock on my door.

The loud fist against wood, pounding, jolts me from the peace of reading the *Globe*'s sports section. "Yes, who's there?" I slowly walk to the door. Fern's ears perk up, and she moves beside me.

"Dr. Burke, we're with the authorities. It is important we speak with you."

It doesn't register, "the authorities," but the firm-sounding voices kick an anxiety level into my gut. "Do you have IDs?" I peek through the eyehole in the door and see what appear to be badges. This is a new experience for me.

I open the door. A man and a woman enter. "Leave the door open." I don't know why I said that. They quickly display their badges and tell me they are from a federal agency. They don't say which one. I just stand in place. Fern starts to growl. I stare at both of them. They stare at me. The silence seems forever.

The whistle of the kettle's boiling water for my dose of green tea ends the staring contest. I have butterflies in my gut. "I am going to turn the kettle off, then tell me who you are and why you are here." I walk to the stove without turning my back to them. Fern stays in place, staring. She doesn't move. Putting the kettle on a cold burner, I sit down and do not offer them a seat. They don't ask for one.

The man appears to be in his thirties, with a short military haircut of blonde hair that appears dyed. The dark suit, narrow grey tie, and polished black shoes on his thin frame give the appearance of him being part of a larger force. His hazel eyes are cold. The woman is short, Hispanic looking, with a rough complexion. She wears a dark blue business suit off-the-rack that comes close to fitting. Her round face is smiling at me. I can't help noticing her bleached teeth. She is missing her upper-right first bicuspid. The fur on Fern's back is looking as rigid as her stance.

"I'm Agent Hernandez, this is Agent Wright. We appreciate you letting us in, we should have telephoned first. Sorry about that."

Nobody is offering a hand for a friendly shake. "Why are you here?"

"We would like to ask you some questions."

I look at the phone. I wonder if I should call a lawyer. But I haven't been doing anything that interesting since I sold my practice. The professional, logical switch turns on in my brain. Emotions on hold, I stare at them as if they were patients of mine. If nothing else, I could teach them how to dress.

"May we sit down?"

"Sure, would you like a cup of tea?" Maybe I can get their guard down a bit, let me in to their game. I don't feel threatened anymore.

"No, thanks, let's get to business." Agent Wright is the alpha male in the room. At least in his mind he is. Agent Hernandez is still is showing the bleached teeth, which just makes the missing bicuspid space more obvious. Fern sits by my side, her stare fixed on the intruders, her tail not moving. The tall pseudo-blonde reaches into his coat jacket and produces a mug shot. He places it on the table in front of me. "Do you know her?"

Looking at the photograph brings back the memories of my one night of companionship. She looks so serious in the picture; I don't remember that expression. "I met her briefly." The photo triggered my memory of her with her eyes half closed and the scent of light vanilla from her hair.

"What were the circumstances?" Ms. Hernandez is playing at being the woman who wants to know all the gossip.

"Just a drink at the tavern around the corner. It was crowded that evening, she happened to sit next to me."

"What did you talk about?"

"The weather and the Red Sox."

"Did you have sex with her?" Mr. Subtle Tough Guy enters into the conversation.

I want to get these people out of here. I decide to flush them out with a little confrontation. "Unless you are with the Kinsey Institute, I won't answer that question." I get the distinct impression they think the institute is a branch of Harvard.

Alpha decides to take over, bad dye job notwithstanding. "Doctor, this is not an academic survey, this is quite serious."

"How serious?"

"The young lady is missing. If you know anything about her, it will be helpful."

The butterflies that have flown from my gut find their way back. "She spent the night here. I never knew her before, I only know her first name."

"What did you talk about in the morning?"

"She left before I woke up."

"What time did you wake up?"

Agent Wright is taking charge. My attitude is changing. "Six, I always get out of bed around then." A little lie.

"Any note or clothing left behind?"

"Nothing."

Agent Hernandez smiles. "Do you mind if I look around and dust for prints?"

"Go ahead." The butterflies leave, and a cold, confused fear slams into my gut. I know they are going to find nothing.

She opens her large purse and produces a smaller case, which she immediately opens. She pries around my place, taking pictures with a digital camera, and scraping whatever is scrapable. Drinking glasses, cups—whatever Fern could have touched are dusted, photographed, and cleaned. Actually, my place will probably be cleaner than before they arrived.

I have to restrain Fern; her aggressive pose is telling me she feels her space is being violated. The official twosome packs up its gear and turn to walk out the open door. Agent Wright turns and looks me in the eye.

"What was her name?"

"She gave me her first name, it was Fern." My four-legged friend immediately looks up at me for the next command.

"That's not her name." They leave quickly without closing the door.

I close the door, and every lock is turned. I immediately go to the cabinet that houses the single malt scotch. I pour the Glenlivet into the bottom of a juice glass and drink. The immediate warmth is welcome. A second sip down shifts me; second gear feels good. I have a strong need to speak to someone. If I call my ex-wife, she'll say to call a lawyer, and not even ask about the dog. I have no legal contacts in Boston. Maybe I'll call Gord and meet him for that beer.

"Gord, if it works for you, it's beer time." I hold the phone a bit away from my ear; he has a tendency to speak loudly

"Meet you at the car; it's around the corner by the schoolhouse. Fifteen minutes?"

"Sounds good." I need the company. What should I tell him? I don't know. Maybe I should find out who he is.

The schoolhouse is an old solid historic building made into condos. What hasn't been made into condos? I hear abandoned prisons are next. I give Fern her treat; she earned it. "See you in few hours." She seems to sense my need to get out. I sense her need for a nap.

Chapter 4

He is behind the wheel with the engine on when I arrive. His nine-year-old blue Toyota 4Runner is probably the only SUV manual stick in the northeast. He never leaves second gear in Boston. We arrive at our favorite pub next to Fenway. No ball game tonight, a relatively quiet time to be there. Relatively. The woodchips on the floor house generations of anything you can imagine. We order our usual artery-clogging dinner of cheeseburgers and french fries. Our frosted mugs arrive with the pitcher of beer. It is tinted green.

I don't have a clue why the beer is green. Nor do I care. "What the hell do you do?" I am so tactful.

"I was a cop in this city for eighteen years, early retirement."

"Why early?"

"I was at the wrong place at the wrong time in a drug bust. Caught a few, my left ear doesn't work."

Now I know why his voice is so loud. "Sorry."

"Don't be, my life is fine now, no complaints."

I just realized how long he has lived in the area. He bought before gentrification. His place must be worth a fortune now. Formerly a cop, now my friend, a drinking buddy, and somebody I can talk to about my little adventure.

I have been so caught up in myself; who was that woman? Missing from what? I never asked the two invaders; I was taken so off guard. How much is my friend to be trusted? I finally know what Gord is all about. He never asked me what my story was and I didn't offer. He was a cop, so what the hell. "A few weeks ago I met this woman at the tavern."

"Uh huh." He looks at me over his mug of green beer.

"We went back to my place."

"Uh, huh." He pours his third round.

"We slept in the same bed."

"Did you get a good night's sleep?" His laconic droopiness makes me think of a bored bloodhound.

"Yeah, and she disappeared the next morning."

"She take anything?"

"No."

"So what do you care?"

"I mean, there was nothing, no trace of her, she even put the beer bottles in the dishwasher and took everything she touched in the bathroom, including my toothbrush."

His eyebrows arch. He is interested; the pitcher is moved aside. "She didn't want to leave any prints, who the hell was she?"

"I don't know."

"She got a name?"

"I don't know."

"Why you telling me this stuff?"

At this point, about three tables are staring at us. They all have the same pitchers of the green beer, so it isn't the color of the alcohol that got their attention. I am used to the volume of Gord's voice. It is above the crowd noise. Time for the rest of the story to be told at my place. "Hey, it's time for Bowser and Fern to hit the park, I'll tell you the rest in the car." Bowser and Fern, sounds like a law firm.

"Sure, usual split?"

"Yeah."

Back in the security of the 4Runner, I tell the whole story.

"So where was this dynamic duo from?" His voice is smoother than his shifting gears.

"I don't know, but they had badges."

"Where were their shields from, the FDA, NAACP, AARP, AAA?"

I feel like a complete idiot.

He parks in his usual spot. I have never figured out how he always manages to park in the same spot.

We both know enough not to continue this conversation in public. We meet in the park with our four-legged roommates. Our little friends give each other the hello sniff. Switching places, they give us the sniffs.

Unlocking the leashes, the dogs find their usual spot and play and pish and play. We are both silent. Gord deep in thought, me, hoping he can make some sense of this.

The four of us settle back into my place. Our friends share the water bowl; Gord and I crack open two beers.

"I have to get this straight." The cop in him is looking at me with serious eyes. He continues, "Those two bozos come into your place, flash some shield, dust the place, take some pictures, and leave? They ask you about her time with you and how long she stayed here?"

"Yeah."

"On their way out they tell you the name she gave you was false?"

"Yeah."

"Then they said it was serious, she was missing?"

"Yeah."

"Anything you want to tell me that you didn't tell them?"

"That's it, she flew into my life, and she flew out."

"OK."

He doesn't look at me. Staring out the window, I see a side of him that is new to me. But then again, this is all new to me.

"I want you to write down the names of these two. Also, write down what they looked like—color, hair, what they wore. Whatever you can think of; I want every detail."

I go for the notebook in my study and the black ballpoint pen. When I sit down by the kitchen table, Bowser and Fern are sitting together. The only difference is Bowser has his leash on and Fern doesn't.

I hand over my completed assignment to my friend. He looks at it quickly, folds it three times, and places it in the back pocket of his jeans. He looks at me. "I'm going to see if I can track these two down; I still have contacts where I used to work."

He stands up; Bowser stretches and starts pulling the leash. "I'll get back to you in a few days."

The door closes, and I have the feeling I am in over my head. In what, I have no idea. I always thought the adventurous unknown would be cool. I was wrong.

Chapter 5

My walk to the gym in the North End is clearing my head, or, more accurately, emptying it. My goal is to not to dwell on the recent past events. The hint of winter chilling my freshly shaved face has a crisp, cleansing feeling. The cold places me in the moment.

Working my back and biceps with dumbbells creates the pain that I crave. I feel as if I am alone, ignoring the others. Ending with abs, I look forward to walking the other direction over the bridge. I merge with the schedule-keeping crowd off to their offices. Even though I fantasize, I have no schedule. I stop for a moment, staring over the metal railing at *Old Ironsides* docked as a national treasure, and promise myself to take the tour one day.

I feel a sudden impact on my right side. It is more like a push than being crashed into. My gym bag cushions the blow. Instinctively, I turn and look down to my right side. A woman is picking up her attaché case from the ground. She looks up at me. "Sorry, I wasn't looking."

She is tall, dark-haired, and in her mid-forties. Her athletic frame reminds me of someone I occasionally see at the gym. She pushes her dark hair away from her oval face, her olive skin exceptionally smooth.

"It's OK." I mumble.

I turn in the direction I came from, not wanting anything to do with another casual female encounter. After a few steps, I stop, look back, and, making sure there is plenty of distance between us, follow. The view is nice, but I want to cross the bridge and go home. I don't go directly home. I take a jigsaw route in case I am being followed. With more than a hint of paranoia, I almost jog to my place, looking both ways as I open the entrance doors.

Once inside, I don't acknowledge the first-floor smoker as he emerges from the foyer with an unlit cigar between his teeth. I look back in time to see his bushy grey eyebrows and sweatshirt from Notre Dame facing me. A quick nod receives a quicker nod from me as my keys go through their routine, letting me back into my comfort zone. I have to chill.

The telephone message machine is lit up. Pressing the button lets me know there are two messages. I boil some water for a cup of green tea.

Settling in on the brown leather chair with a cup of warm tea calms me from my self-inflicted paranoia. Fern casually looks at me from across the room. Sitting on her favorite little old rug, all is well in her world. The little red light on the telephone stand reminds me that there is an outside world. Whether I want to know about it is another story.

"I'm working on my contacts. It's been a few years, and there has been some turnover and transfers. I have a meeting with a detective I can trust from the old days. I'll get back to you."

I haven't heard from Gord in over a week; it is good to hear his message. In public our conversation is guy sports talk. I have a feeling he's enjoying getting back in the game. The second message is disturbing

"Hi. This is from the person you know as Fern. Do not talk to anybody about me. I am using a disposable cell. It is gone, as am I."

Staring at the phone, I replay it two more times. Pressing the Save button, I call Gord.

My turn to leave a message: "There's something you have to hear." Then I flash back on the investigatory two. They never left a card. I watch enough cop shows to know that detectives leave cards.

I go outside. Fern is my companion. The long walk to the liquor store is not for booze. Not that I don't need it. It is the closest place that sells both the *New York Times* and the *Wall Street Journal*. My morning will be spent engrossed in the details of the Left and the Right. I read in the study, leaning to the right, when the sound of the phone makes me place the editorials on hold.

"Hey!"

It is Gord. I put the phone down without hitting the hands-free button. "What's up?"

"I'll be over around seven tonight. Anything you want talk about?"

"No."

"See you later."

"OK." I take a deep breath. I go over to the fridge to make sure the beer inventory will meet our requirements. It doesn't. I look at Fern. I tell her that after lunch we're off to the grocery for a few six-packs. She has an empathetic look only an old friend who understands you can possess. It's all in the eyes.

Later is eight o'clock. Gord is wearing his usual outfit of jeans and a dark shirt. His uniform. No matter how much we think we change, we don't. "You eat?"

"Nope."

I place the order for the usual pizza: half pepperoni, half fresh veggies. Sitting down on the couch, Fern comes over to us and sniffs Bowser on Gord's leg. His hand lazily rubs her ears. I play the tape. I play it four times. Hearing it the fourth time, I turn it off. Both of his hands are under his chin, elbows on quads, while Fern wonders why she isn't the center of his attention. "Is there something you're not telling me?" He looks directly at me.

"No, that's it, I swear."

"Something tells me this is not just some babe screwing around making sure hubby doesn't find out."

The buzz of the front door gives me an excuse to move away from this conversation. The arrival of the pizza does not change the mood. Gord's slicked-back silver hair and small round eyeglasses give the appearance of someone in charge. At this moment, he is no longer just a dog-walking buddy. Nothing is said as the pepperoni disappears before the veggies. A few slices will wind up in my fridge for lunch tomorrow.

"What did the shields look like? I want every little detail."

My whole life I was the best student, the best researcher, the best clinician. I prided myself on the details. Now, I feel like an incompetent fool. I have no details. The surprise of the visit took away my ability to be me. Gord must realize that; his tone isn't condemning.

"Look, I understand why you feel out of the loop. I have to digest this."

We both have two beers to help the pizza along and our thoughts. He tells me he has to think this over, for me to watch my back, and don't worry. Watch your back and don't worry, how do you do that? Getting up, moving his broad frame to the door, he smiles.

"See you later, Fern."

The sound of his footsteps leaving is the last I ever hear from him.

Chapter 6

Routine. I crave the rhythm of repetition. Security in sameness covers me like an old quilt. I wonder if my quilt will ever feel the same. There is something missing from my usual walks in the park. Fern isn't the same, but she adapts to change better than I do. A part of our jigsaw puzzle of a group is missing. No Bowser, no Gord. I haven't heard from him in ten days. I just figure he is being a cop and taking the time to solve my mystery events. I have confidence in him; he's probably working on his contacts, uncovering the facts. My messages are not returned, and after two weeks go by, my concern turns to worry.

On my way back from the gym, I decide to take a different route. Change my routine. Walking a steeper path to my place leads me past the old High School Condos. I make a sharp turn, a bit out of the way, to check out Gord's usual parking spot. The 4Runner is in its usual home. Dirty as always. Looking at it closely, an alarm goes off in my head and gut. There is a film of dust on the windshield. Dust all over the SUV. The tires are a little lower than they should be; it hasn't been driven in some time.

My mind races with all sorts of rationalizations. Maybe he is out of town on this mission. Maybe on vacation, an airplane ride away. All sorts of combinations and permutations are possible. None of them explains why my calls are not returned. Do I call the police? What if he is working the case and resents me calling his former employer? I decide to give it another five days. Don't ask me how I arrive at the number five.

Four days go by, nothing from my buddy. A few canine pals from the park ask me about Bowser; I just say, "Away with his roommate." We continue our little chats and watch our four-legged companions enjoy each other. Bright sunshine, clear blue sky and the fifth day rolls onto my schedule. I clog it up with the usual mundane routine. I even go shopping at Brooks Brothers and buy two sweaters on sale. Not that I need them. I am looking for, and finding, excuses for not confronting the reality of making a decision.

Opening the door to my place, dropping the bag holding the presents to myself down on the kitchen floor, I look at the telephone stand. I grow excited seeing the blinking red light. Listening to the message is deflating. "I'll be in Boston for a conference with a client; I may have time to meet for a quick drink. Let me know of your availability within forty-eight hours."

It is my ex-wife. They did not teach warmth and understanding to her at Yale Law School. I was hoping it would be an update from Gord. I was looking forward to sharing a pitcher of beer with him and making sense of my little adventure. I can't forget that evening; tell me who she is—her name, her job. Tell me who the two people with badges were, who they work for, and why they asked me those questions.

I sit down on the leather couch with my hands under my chin and elbows resting on my quads. Not aware that I am the image of Gord deep in thought, I sit in silence for what seems forever. Twenty minutes later, I pick up the telephone. I don't have time to press a number on the phone. There is somebody pounding on the door. Fern looks up and assumes her protective stance. Getting up slowly from the couch, I walk to the door and peer through the security hole. The distorted image shows two men. "Who are you?"

"The police, we need to talk."

I've heard that before. "Give me a minute."

I need time to compose myself. I have to remember the questions asked of me by the mysterious duo and by my ex-cop buddy. First of all, I have to make sure these guys are the real thing. Gord would want me to do that. It strikes me as odd that I am thinking of him in the past tense. I open the door. The two detectives smile and walk in. The taller of the two closes the door. They look at me and make eye contact with Fern. The shorter, wider, and rounder one squats down to Fern and gently rubs her ears. She wags her tail and promptly rolls over. There goes my first line of defense. It is obvious these guys are pros. Of what, I'm not yet sure. "I'd like you both to hand me your badges and answer a few of my questions before we talk."

"Sure, can we sit down?"

I am not anxious about their presence. I am hoping they will have the answers. The tall one is buttoned down, about mid-forties, and has a mix of red and grey hair. His dark blue pinstripe suit, white shirt, and red tie work with his black-laced oxford shoes. The other fellow looks like a bowling ball. He also has a dark blue suit, but everything else about his outfit is also dark. His slicked-back black hair and pale complexion remind me of an Oreo cookie with the top layer half off. After all, he is sweet to Fern.

I study their badges. They identify themselves as detectives in the Boston police force. I write down their badge numbers and names. The sleek tall one is Detective Willard Browne; his partner is Detective Vito Castellano. They make themselves comfortable on the couch. Fern is happy with Detective Castellano massaging her neck.

"I have a corgi at home."

I didn't ask for that response. I am not looking for these guys to be friends. I return their badges to them. "Why are you here?"

The tall one answers, "An old buddy of mine has been talking to us about some people who asked you some questions. He hasn't been answering our calls; we thought you could help us out."

Now the butterfly nest in my belly is reoccupied. "OK, guys, before I answer any questions, I want to call the station house to make sure you are who you say you are." The shorter one, Castellano, looks up and smiles.

"No problem, here's the number."

"That's OK; I'll use the phone book." I am pleased with my protective paranoia. After playing with the administrative buttons on the telephone, I finally reach a human voice, the chief of detectives, Robert Stanton. He verifies who, what, and why these cops are in my apartment. Vetting complete, I look at both of them. I have the impression we are going to be spending some time together. Hoping my memory isn't becoming selective, I review the story.

Surprisingly, they don't ask me any questions. I make an appointment to meet them at the station house the next afternoon at three o'clock. They don't tell me what for, and at this point I am in their hands. They stand and move toward the door. Detective Castellano reaches into his right pants pocket and offers Fern a treat. She trots over to him, sits, looks at him with wide dark eyes, and accepts her reward. She trots down the hallway to my bedroom and munches away. I shake hands with the two detectives. "Thanks. See you tomorrow." I close the door. It doesn't strike me to wonder why Detective Castellano has Fern's favorite treats in his pocket. I don't sleep well.

Chapter 7

I am trying to get comfortable and sliding into unproductive restless sleep when it is time to get up. Turning the alarm off before it turns on, I start the usual morning routine. It is a damp, cloudy day; somehow I find comfort in that. My gym activity is brief, a forty minute quick walk on the treadmill.

Returning to my place and smelling fresh coffee is a simple pleasure. Sitting at the dining room table with a content Fern at my feet, my hands surround a warm mug half full with French roast coffee. Looking out at the park, I feel good. The feeling is because of the interesting day scheduled: the morning workout, the preparation for the station house appointment and the afternoon meeting.

I approach the appointment as if I am giving a lecture. I list each event and flesh out what occurred. I leave no fact out of the presentation. After reviewing the documents on the computer, I print each page. Upon my arrival at the station house, I am to present a well-written package to each detective plus their chief. I am going to impress the force. I cannot wait for three o'clock to roll around.

I pour a second mug and think about the phone call to be returned to my ex-wife, Jenn. I decide to phone her after lunch. That way I have a built-in excuse not to have lunch with her. Obviously, my afternoon is locked up. I have no idea why, but as the day matures, I am feeling loose and jaunty. Perhaps this afternoon's visit to the police headquarters will create some structure to the mess of the past few weeks.

It is noon, time to walk my little friend and pick up my veggie wrap down the road. They knew me well enough at Sorrell's to have the large coffee to go and the wrap waiting on the countertop at a quarter after. I say my hellos, pay, and retrieve Fern from outside the glass entrance door. After two steps, I decide to return to the shop. She looks up at me as if to say, "Why can't I come inside?" The little shop has large windows and total visibility to the outside. I find a clean plastic seat that gives me protective vision of Fern sitting and enjoying the attention from friendly neighbors.

It is important to eat a healthy lunch, and I can't imagine calling Jenn on an empty stomach. It all sits well on my walk back to my place. My little friend and I enjoy the walk. Up the stairs, I close the door, and watch her noisily slop down a bowl full of water. I grab a water bottle from the fridge and settle into the study. OK, time to call her and, hopefully, just leave a message. The phone rings four times, and I am ready to leave a message. Before the fifth ring, her familiar voice re-enters my life.

"Hello."

It is such a soft yet professional sound. I know its tone will change after hearing my voice. "Hi, it's Adam, returning your call."

"Yes, I am leaving Boston tomorrow morning; I could see you between seven thirty and nine thirty tonight."

"Where?"

"The usual hotel in Copley Square."

"See you at the bar."

"Fine."

Two hours should be enough time to catch up on the financial reports.

Wearing one of my new crewneck sweaters, white button-down shirt, and neatly pressed khakis, I am ready to present to the world of Boston police. This may sound ridiculous, but it feels really cool telling a cabbie to take me to the downtown police station. As I step out of the cab, I can feel the respect the driver is giving me as I pay him. It is nice to have that feeling of authority again.

It is precisely three o'clock, and I am totally ignored. I announce my arrival to the policewoman on duty and receive nothing but a nod.

At 3:22 p.m., Detective Castellano appears. His red tie stands out from his dark suit and shirt. "Hi, follow me."

All the caring charm apparent in our first meeting is no longer present. I follow him down a hallway that looks like an old Catholic high school. At least I think so; I've never been in a Catholic school. He opens the door to a small cinder block and linoleum room with three chairs around a cheap skinny table. His partner, the taller one, walks in.

"We have some questions to ask you."

I hope these guys are just having a bad day. I sit down on a chair with uneven legs. Is this a pilot for a new TV show, "Boston Cops?" I open my leather case, present three neat folders, and slide them across the desk. The detectives ignore them.

"We have some pictures for you to look at."

I have the distinct feeling this is not going to be fun. They push aside my offerings and place a folder of their own in front of me. The neat tall detective is staring at my eyes. Castellano appears to be in charge.

"Open the folder. Please."

The word *please* was an afterthought. I gingerly pick it up and open the manila envelope. I pull out three pictures. I feel cold. I feel empty. I feel sick to my stomach. It is Gord. He is lying on his back and is ghostly pale. There is a hole above his right eyebrow. I look at the detectives. I am scared.

"Do you know who this is?"

I tell them all about my relationship with Gord.

"Can you tell us where you have been for the last seventy-two hours?"

I get it; I'm a suspect. The only one to confirm my whereabouts would be my dog.

"We would like you to follow us; we need you to identify the body."

The last time I was near a dead body was in medical school. This is a friend, a drinking buddy, a confidant, the person clearing up the loose ends for me. Before I know it, I am in the room with a covered body. With a detective on either side of me, the technician pulls back the sheet. It is Gord, and I feel it is my fault. I am angry. I am weak.

I don't remember how I got there, but I am seated at a different desk in a private room.

"He was my friend, my partner for eleven years."

Now I know why Vito is doing all the talking. "I spoke to him five days ago about what was going on, he was following a lead." My cold hand holds a plastic cup of water. I spill some; my hand is shaking.

"Don't worry; we know you didn't do this. Since speaking to him, we had you watched, and we checked your phone records."

I am relieved. And sad.

"Once again, tell us what you know."

I go through my litany, and Detective Castellano presents a book of mug shots. There are no familiar faces.

"We'll call a cab for you; go get some rest. We'll contact you."

The cab ride home is like sitting in a cold room; the room is warm, my body cold.

I am in the shower, the second one of the day. No matter how hot the water is, I feel cold. I wash my short hair again and just sit down. Sitting on the tiled floor of the shower, I don't want to move. Finally I get up, turn the water off, and dry off. My clothes are in a pile in the corner. They go to the cleaner tomorrow.

With fresh clothes on, I find myself sitting at the kitchen table where not too long ago I was drinking beer with my lost friend. My now dead friend. Fern sits next to me and leans against my leg. The warmth of another living creature slowly brings me back to the here and now. Somehow, she knows how I feel. I lift the juice glass to my lips and taste the last drops of the scotch. Placing the glass down slowly, I determine that I need to get out and not smolder in my oncoming depression.

I have to go to Copley Square in an hour to meet my ex-wife. I can't believe I am actually looking forward to it. I decide to tell her nothing of what my life is like now, what is going on. Not that she will have any interest.

Chapter 8

It is eight o'clock, and I am alone, nursing a scotch at the bar. The hotel has that busy, luxurious, cosmopolitan air about it. Watching the well-dressed crowd going about its business is good distraction. I glance at the clock above the bar; it is eight-fifteen. I turn to my right and see Jenn walking from the elevator. I'm not the only head turning to look at her. Confident elegance sums it all up. Her dark hair just right, she is dressed expensively to highlight her small athletic frame, with just enough jewelry to be not noticed. She looks younger than I remember. Is it the makeup, the surgeon, or my memory? Her hazel eyes have a way of wanting you to never look away.

Staring at her as she walks toward me, I pick up my cell phone and dial my upstairs neighbor. I make arrangements to have Fern taken care of through lunch tomorrow. She gently slides into the barstool next to me.

"Adam, so good we can get together for a bit." Living in England, she picked up a bit of the accent. "My client is a bloody fool, but he pays the fare."

I still haven't heard "how are you" or "sorry about the time mix-up." I know her well enough to know that isn't going to happen. It is my turn to talk. "You look good."

She orders a glass of red wine. "My flight leaves tomorrow afternoon."

There is a tension between us that is drawing us together. We both order salads and grilled salmon. Staying at the bar makes it easier for a second red wine. I am still working on the scotch.

"You look a bit pale."

I am not going to relive the day. I need to escape. "I've been inside for a few days, catching up on my reading." I receive a look that tells me she knows I am not letting my world open up. We eat dinner without much comment. The unspoken tension is mutual. The need is mutual.

I have heard sex with your ex can be quite intense.

Chapter 9

Waking up at six-thirty, I am surprised to be the only occupant in bed. The surprise lasts for two shallow breaths as I hear Jenn's voice on the phone. She is in her robe and sitting facing the large window with the view of the Charles River. Her attention is on the computer screen on the round table and the stack of papers next to her briefcase. She turns, looks at me, and points to the right. A large silver pitcher of coffee is part of the breakfast personal buffet she has ordered. She lifts her ceramic cup and smiles. Against my instincts, I fill her cup.

My early chore completed, I head for the shower. A new toothbrush waits on a ceramic dish. Freshly showered, in my day-old clothes, I attack the fresh fruit and croissants. After my caffeine requirement is met, I walk toward the door and turn to look at Jenn. She turns, makes eye contact, quickly smiles, and nods her head. I open the door, find the elevator, and hail a taxi. Before my head is clear, I am back in my place. Changing into fresh clothes, I realize the two new Brooks Brothers crewneck sweaters I bought are both black. I don't care; it is like I am back on the hockey club with two home jerseys.

Seeing Jenn was, well, a Jenn experience. We could coin a new term, "achievement sex." We met, achieved our goals, and moved on. The previous one-night stander did the dishes and the laundry. But Fern, or whoever she is, opened a scary door in my life. At least after last night, I know this one's name and address, and breakfast was included. Knowing Jenn and credit cards, I know I am definitely a write-off.

Wearing my new same outfit, I go upstairs to reclaim my Fern. With the leash in my hand and not attached to her, she independently prances down the steps to her domain. Waiting for her biscuit, she is no worse for wear. I decide to take a walk in the park. Alone.

"Nice day for a walk."

I turn around and see a familiar face. The smiling missing bicuspid has that smile that isn't a smile. Looking at her without revealing any expression, I am determined to find out who she is. I am no longer a passive part of this picture. I ask, "Do you want to walk or get some coffee?"

She has that steely face of someone that is on a mission. No drab, ill-fitting business suit this time around. Instead, a drab, ill-fitting skirt, blouse, and multicolored vest make her look like she is ready for a bit part in a school play. Unfortunately, the writer included me. I'd rather be in gym class. "Yes, let's go somewhere with some privacy."

I am not looking forward to privacy with her. "I know just the place, about three blocks from here." I direct her to follow me to Sorrell's, nice and open, lots of light and minimal privacy. I open the glass door and direct her to the only table open. It is in the corner with a collection of crumbs on the tabletop. Bagels and muffins have a way of telling you who's been there. We both sit down on opposite ends of the table. Neither of us says a word. Looking at the crumb collection, I stand up and walk away. Well, not away. It is obvious she doesn't care, but with paper napkins in hand, I clean the table. Now I can sit down and deal with the situation. "I'm going to get some coffee." After I say that, I realize I didn't ask if she wanted anything. I don't care; she can get her own coffee.

Not changing her expression she says, "I'll get my own."

"Fine, I'll hold down the table after I get my coffee."

Sitting down with my hot, steaming black brew in the paper cup, I glance around the room. I pick up a copy of the local paper from an abandoned table. Turning pages while she is getting her coffee, a familiar face hits me like a flying frozen hockey puck. Bowser the bulldog's mug shot is staring at me from the pets-to-adopt page. It is him all right; I know all his markings. I rip the ad out and stuff it in my pants pocket.

She sits down opposite me; I have to fight to not get a headache from looking at her vest. It's time for me to do right by Gord. "Let's see your badge."

"This is not about me explaining myself to you."

I start to stand up to leave.

"You don't want to do that."

I just look at her, sit down, and take a sip of coffee.

"First, I will deny we ever met. So don't talk to your police friends. We need to find the woman you know as Fern. If you can't help us, just back off."

She stands up, goes to the counter, and buys a raisin bran muffin. She acts as if I am not even in the café. Returning, she looks at me between bites of the muffin. As she stands with her almost-empty cup in hand, I try not to stare at the raisin occupying the space where her upper bicuspid used to reside.

As she leaves, her parting words are, "Gord was a helluva guy."

I feel a thud in my chest, a self-inflicted emotional thud. She walks away, tosses her cup in an outside trash container, and leaves my view. I look at the crumbs on the table; I have an idea; can you reassemble crumbs and get an ID? No, that's ridiculous.

Wait. I run from the table, excusing myself to the young couple with their empty mugs that I push away from the trash bin. I grab the top paper cups and take off down the street. I can hear the twentyish couple saying, "I hope my parents don't get that weird."

Finding an empty plastic bag on the street, I place the two paper coffee cups inside and quickly head home.

An interesting forty-eight hours: my episode with the police, an evening of inhibited dinner and uninhibited sex with my ex-wife in a luxury hotel downtown, and a morning with threats from a woman appearing as a badly dressed gypsy with a raisin for a bicuspid. End that with a mad dash to a garbage bin in my new Brooks Brothers sweater to salvage used paper coffee cups. It's a good thing I don't stop to explain my rudeness to the pushed-aside young couple. After all, there is some logic to my action. One of these cups has the prints of the badly dressed gypsy, I think. No prints are to be gotten from reassembled muffin crumbs, but we may have a shot with the paper cup she handled.

My agenda for the day: First, to call my police friends and give them the coffee cup. The second one is to claim Bowser. I decide not to use my phone to call the police about anything. I just don't know who else is listening.

I hail a taxi going in the opposite direction I want to go. Hurriedly crossing the street, I jump in the cab. "Central Police Station," I say those three words loudly with authority. The cabbie does a quick U-turn and is speeding and weaving through the crowded streets. I guess a well-dressed guy holding a garbage bag triggers a quick response to those magic three words. Or he just wants to get rid of me quickly.

With screeching brakes, an abrupt stop almost has me in the front seat. The cabbie runs around the car, opens my door, lets me out, and slams the door closed. I reach into my pocket to get my wallet out to pay him, but he is already a half mile away.

I don't have a clue. It isn't something I am going to give a lot of thought; after all, I saved twelve bucks.

I stand at the front desk, and as the bleary-eyed policewoman looks up, I exclaim, "I need to see Detective Castellanno; I have a break in the case!" She barely moves her head as she drones into the speaker phone and pages him. I only wait fourteen minutes until the detective rolls in front of me.

"What do you got?"

Castellanno is not one for mincing words and not one for soft and fuzzy greetings. At least not when there are no cute furry pets present. In his usual dark outfit, someone must have told him it might have a slimming effect. It doesn't work. I explain to him what happened and what I did. His expression reminds me of the look I received from the young couple at the trash can.

"You gotta be kidding."

"What do you mean? You get prints, find out who it is, and we move on to solve the case."

"Not quite that easy. Look, we'll get forensics to see what they pick up on these cups. If we get a computer match, we'll call you."

I have the distinct impression that he thinks the process is hopeless. He walks me to the front desk.

"We'll be in touch."

I nod to the policewoman at the front desk. I think she moves her head. Maybe she is a mannequin; perhaps it's just another way to reduce overhead. I hop a taxi but decide not to go back to my place. Reading the address from the newspaper section stashed in my left pants pocket, I direct the driver to the Animal Rescue Center. I don't know what to expect. I never have been to an animal shelter. Fern and I met through an agency connected with the medical school at the University of Pennsylvania. I am afraid that once inside I will come home with at least four new friends. A former professor of mine did the research that proved how having a pet dog can reduce your blood pressure. All is well and good, but four dogs would have to send my blood pressure way upstairs.

Once inside, I feel as if I am in a well-scrubbed hospital: beige tile floors, off-white walls, and a desk in a hole in the wall. The young lady behind the institutional desk gives me all the information I need. I do enough paperwork to clear me with the CIA.

"You are looking to adopt Bowser?"

"Yes, I knew him, the owner of Bowser. He was my neighbor. He passed away." When good memories end with one big bad one, the bad memory lingers. With the pain.

The woman behind the desk is in her twenties, not a line on her face. Her light brown hair is cut short and black framed eyeglasses keep her from the world of direct eye contact. Probably not a bad idea considering her line of work.

"Bowser is in a foster home. We will contact you after we process your papers."

Checking my pedigree is an intimidating concept. I thought it was supposed to be the other way around. Once back in my place, Fern is all over me. It might be the curiosity of the smells of her fellow canines. I am in a waiting limbo. Not something I do well. In my days of practice, I kept a tight schedule. The world that I occupy now has its own schedule, if indeed there is one.

I am waiting to see if Fern is going to have a roommate, waiting for the police to contact me with the latest information, and waiting for the next unforeseen event. A week down the road, Fern and I have a new roommate. Not the one I expected.

Chapter 10

"It sucks, but I figured you wouldn't mind the company." Castellano and an overweight corgi are outside the door at the street in front of my condo.

He is on his cell, me, on the kitchen phone. There they are on my side of the street asking both of us to come down to talk. "Fine, I'll meet you in the park."

Fern already had her midday walk and isn't her usual bundle of energy. This time I bring the leash to her. Spotting the human and canine pudge balls is not very difficult. I can't even describe the way they walk.

"Hey, thanks for coming down. Nice day huh? Meet Bentley."

Somehow I knew he didn't travel to this part of the city to introduce me to his dog. Fern looks at Bentley, Bentley at Fern. Then the sniffs begin. Castellano and I wait for the verdict. The tails wagging signal joy and acceptance. The ice is broken at ground level. We stroll around the park, relieved that there is one less stress to deal with. I stop, turn to his bulk, and ask, "OK, what is it?"

"We need to stay at your place for few days."

"Why?"

"My wife and I are having our differences; we agreed to take some time off from each other. I got custody of the dog. It's only temporary; I don't want the guys at the force to know about this."

"How did I get this great honor?"

"You got the room, you have a dog, and it makes sense."

"The dogs get along."

"Deal?"

"For how long?"

"Three, four days."

This should be interesting. I walk with him to his car. It is a vintage auto; that is, if you consider a two-tone Chevy wagon from the early '80s vintage. The faded blue on blue with well-worn white wall tires somehow completes the picture of Vito Castellano and the chubby corgi. A Bentley in a Chevy wagon. Only in America.

Vito grabs a suitcase from the back of the wagon, and the entourage heads to my place. Once inside, I direct him to my study with the foldout bed. All the other logistics I'm sure will work themselves out. I check my phone messages; there is one message. It is the animal shelter saying everything is a go for me and to pick up Bowser tomorrow morning.

Tomorrow is beyond comprehension: a bulldog, a fat corgi, my Fern, and a very large Boston detective all living with me. This is all because I slept with someone I didn't know, who didn't want me to know her, and who disappeared. Not too long ago, I was happy in my superficial existence. Now it's superficial chaos. Or maybe not so superficial.

Just chaos.

Evening rolls around, and the gang is settling in. Everyone claims their part of my turf. Vito occupies half the couch, while Bentley rolls over on his back looking at his belly and leans on the couch underneath Vito's outstretched arm. I'm at the kitchen table, with Fern lying on her favorite rug looking at the gang. She likes the company. Dinner time, takeout is the requirement. "Look, I have all the local menus, take a look and let's order out dinner." My turf, I'm in charge.

"No problem, I don't need to look. Feel like Italian?"

"Sure."

"How about a big salad, some pasta, and veal parmesan? I know a place that will even include a bottle of Chianti."

"Here's the phone."

"That's OK, I'll use my cell."

He dials, and the conversation is totally in Italian.

"We're good, dinner in about forty-five minutes. Why don't you set the table, and I'll feed our little friends. Where's their food?"

"Leave that to me." I wasn't about to let this guy take over my routine. He produces a dish twice the size of Fern's food bowl; it is ceramic and colored red, white, and blue. Halfway up the sides are little American flags. I feed our four-legged companions, and somehow, they know which dish is their own. Bentley looks at me with expectant eyes after wolfing down his dinner.

"That was an appetizer for him; I fill the dish up to the rim."

No surprise he has a fat corgi. "He's going to lose weight; I fill it to the flag, that's it."

Vito looks at me. I have that sense he fears I will reduce his portions also. Dinner arrives, more than I eat in two days. There is no bill. He refuses to take money from me.

"I have an arrangement with some great restaurants in town. While I'm here, food is not an issue."

I realize it has been a stressful time for him; I don't criticize the volume on his plate. Chatting afterward, it feels as if we were old friends who share a few secrets. No talk about the case, just discussing the Celtics and Bruins. I tell him about picking up Bowser tomorrow. He offers to pick me up on his lunch hour and complete the Bowser deal with me. There are certain subjects on which we seem on the same wavelength.

Twenty-four hours later, there I am with three dogs and a fat detective living with me.

* * *

We are quite a sight at the park. My three little friends, all together, receive stares and smiles. Other than that, my day only needs a few adjustments and tweaks. Maintenance and neatness require more work, but the free dinners from interesting restaurants make up for that. I do ask why they are free, a wide-eyed smile and nod tells me not to pursue that line of questioning.

Halfway through our sushi take-in dinner, Vito looks at me through his chopsticks and surprises me with, "We may have something."

The wasabi is clearing my sinuses as he casually mentions the possible progress in the puzzle of the last few months of my life. I say nothing, swallow the spicy tuna, and wait. His droopy brow creases as he negotiates the eel from the plate to his mouth. I have a feeling something profound is to follow the eel.

"There's a match on the prints from one of the coffee cups you gave us with the woman you have been describing. I want to check it out after we eat. I have a picture for you to look at."

The green tea ice cream can wait. "Let me check it out now." The cold sake we drank is fighting my rising pulse. I pour more sake into my juice glass. Vito has a large California roll between the sticks. He isn't going to drop it for a perp ID. I have to watch him dip it in the dark wasabi-laced liquid and roll a slice of ginger surrounding the roll of rice, avocado, and fish. The family of canines is in assorted positions viewing this spectacle with me. On completion of the dining ritual, Vito looks at me with a benign look of contentment and offers what I didn't want to hear.

"I'm in too good of a sushi rhythm to leave the table now. My papers are all in my room. I'll show you over tea."

Last night he was wolfing down a cheese steak sandwich like he was in South Philly; tonight he is the elegant diner of Japanese cuisine, enjoying the esthetics and sensation over a prolonged time frame. For the record, I had a salad last night. I have no choice but to boil the water for the green tea. I clear the table and serve the tea. Nothing is said. Was he formulating his strategy for this presentation, or is all his energy in his stomach digesting dinner? Somehow, I think it is the latter.

I watch him slowly move his bulk toward my ex-study. He comes back a few minutes later with a picture of the woman with the missing bicuspid. It is in color; the glare of a bright blouse surrounded by her typical nondescript outfit makes me want to close my eyes.

"That's her, part of the dynamic duo who barged in on me. Yes, she is the one who blindsided me in the park and made the reference to Gord."

Vito looks at me and shakes his head up and down twice. He picks up the photo and puts it back in his case.

I need more information. "Well, who the hell is she? What is this all about?"

"Her name is Isabella Lopez. The drug trade is what this is all about."

The *Miami Vice* theme song is resonating in my head. I try to be cool. "Yeah, that doesn't surprise me."

"This will; it isn't coke or anything on the street, its counterfeit medications. A whole new level of dangerous doses finding their way into people's homes."

Of course, I've heard of counterfeit medications, but somehow I thought of it in the third person. These bad drugs have been around for a long time in countries like India, China, and places in Africa. The drugs even find their way into homes in Canada, and people rejoice at their cheap capsules, not knowing why they are so cheap. It's accepted in Canada where patients with tumors on their kidneys wait months for an MRI. Whether their medications have any quality control never enters their socialized minds. The cold weather must affect their thought processes.

What usually happens is that pill-making machines are bought secondhand on Internet auction sites. Labels can be copied with available printing technology. Sometimes crooks will open shell companies in various states and obtain medicine by stealing, misrepresenting themselves as middlemen, or buying prescriptions from Medicaid patients. Billions of dollars are spent on drugs that are bought and sold back and forth on this grey market. Of course, then there are the vials of water labeled as drugs. The people behind these deals are, at a minimum, accessories to murder who are clearly slipping through the system. I had a feeling this Isabella woman was a sleaze, but this level of evil is scary.

I peer over to the night table in my bedroom where two bottles of capsules are sitting. In those capsules is my ticket to a normal life. The capsules control my seizures. What if I received a fake shipment? I would be in the hospital as a patient with a serious problem. The truth would be unknown; I would just have taken bad meds from bad people. I must help this investigation.

"I understand how tricky this is; finding these people may be difficult."

Vito sips his hot tea. He is in deep thought, about to open this mysterious door a little bit more. "There's not much glamour in this type of investigation, our resources are limited."

"Let me help, I'm tired of being on the sidelines."

"There's a lot of grunt work to be done, we'll meet with you to get it going."

My thoughts are in overdrive. "Do you think we can find a link to Gord's murder through this Lopez lady?"

"It's too soon, too easy to be led down that path. Let's concentrate on getting facts. If this Lopez lady is still in Boston, she's not going to slide away from us."

I wonder how my long-lost vanilla Fern fits into this picture. I try not to think of her. It isn't easy. Looking at Vito and the menagerie of four-legged buddies sprawled in various poses in my living room helps to calm me.

The calm before the storm.

Chapter 11

It was so many years ago, it seems as if it was in another life. I was a young intern at the University of Pennsylvania's Medical School. The usual scene: long hours, almost knowing what I was doing, and a touch of arrogance about me. It was nice to be away from the classroom and textbook learning. I was finally in the real world. I enjoyed the emergency room work, the pace of excitement and tension. I survived on pizza and Coca Cola. In my mind back then, healthy food was for granola heads. Though I was seeing a nurse who was into everything that was natural. Her name was Christine, and we would meet in empty exam rooms at least twice a week.

The discovery, the joy of natural behavior—our sex had no commitment; it was just a mutual tension breaker. I don't think we had a conversation that lasted more than a paragraph. We never saw each other outside of the hospital.

I'll never forget a Thursday afternoon in October. I was on call the night before and had three hours' sleep. By the time 4:00 p.m. rolled around, I had absorbed six cups of black coffee. Signing out at 3:40 p.m., my anticipation of seeing Christine was all that was on my mind. The elevator couldn't move fast enough to get me to the fifth floor. Our favorite room was available, and she did her pre-sex due diligence that included never forgetting the pill. I chose to be "natural." Oh, the days pre-HIV.

At 4:15 p.m., Christine was with me on the gurney. She sat up, removed her blouse, and her beautiful round breasts were waiting for my caresses. I placed my hands on her and remember nothing else.

* * *

I am in the emergency room strapped on the gurney. I have no idea what is happening. A familiar woman is standing next to me while a young Asian man dressed in white is asking me questions. My pants are wet. I am embarrassed. I am being asked all sorts of questions, and I am confused.

I am so tired. Maybe I just fell asleep in the hallway, and they thought I needed to have a bed. I don't know.

"Adam, Adam look at me."

It is Christine. She is on my left and standing, holding my hand.

"Look at me, look at me. You had a seizure."

Not me, that's for patients in textbooks. I cannot lose control. This is a bad dream.

"Adam, this is Chris . . . you will be fine, try to relax. The neuro team will see you soon. I found a private room for you. I'll stay with you."

Atypical, nonspecific, seizure syndrome was the diagnosis. It can be controlled by medication. The trick is finding the right one. Carbatrol became my ticket to a normal life. The hardest part was learning that I wasn't Superman. It took me years to recognize that everybody has their own kryptonite. It was at that point that I decided to devote my studies to neurology and psychiatry. I wanted and needed to know as much about the mind as I could.

Oh, the last I heard, Christine is married with three kids and lives in the suburbs. I heard she is very heavy.

Chapter 12

I hardly have a beer anymore. I drink Chianti with Vito. I'm getting to like Vito, though Chianti stains my teeth. So I bleach more often.

I have a stake in finding the bad guys. Bad medication will screw up many people. I could be one of them. And I want to find who killed my friend. Looking at Bowser is a living memory of Gord. Vito tells me that a task force is being put together for this case. This case has raised some flags; the police have a particular interest in solving it. They have a murder and the appearance of a person who is in the counterfeit drug trade. Somehow, there seems to be a connection.

I'm not sure of my exact role in this operation, but my involvement does excite me. My isolation is shattered by living with a fat cop and three dogs. A difficult adjustment I wasn't planning on. Soon I will be thrown into a new world of law enforcement. I wish there were an internship available on *Law and Order*.

It is time to go the gym and have my morning ritual of exercise and mind-numbing activity. Without it, it is difficult to clear my mind. Just too much in such a short time. I am losing the ability to find time just for me. No matter what the weather, my walk across the bridge to the gym in the North End is special: watching people going in both directions dressed in all sorts of outfits, staring straight ahead, and seemingly moving at the same pace. My dark green gym bag slung over my right shoulder gives me a feeling of importance as I weave through the walkers. I try to think of my goals for the morning workout.

The old loft modernized into a gym is wonderfully bright due to the massive old windows. I position myself on a treadmill to warm up before hitting the resistance work. Today is back, biceps, and abs. I always like the way that sounds. Mindlessly looking through the window, I increase the pace on the treadmill. Looking at the corner where the Dunkin' Donuts and the New Garden face each other, I notice a familiar face.

The sleek dark-haired, olive-skinned woman is walking toward Friends Street. I remember our bridge encounter, well, collision. She has some kind of a pouch and mat slung over her shoulder. She turns at the Dunkin'

Donuts, nods at the cops with their cups of coffee, and enters the gym building. Before I know it, she has signed in at the front desk and is on the treadmill next to me. I don't have any time to be neurotic about it. I turn to look at her.

"You look familiar."

Her voice has a quiet, mellow quality. She is wearing black tights and a red and white floral tank top. Her breasts are barely legally covered; modesty is not an issue, apparently. Her black hair is pulled back and joins in a braid floating down her back. Her olive skin is beginning to glisten as she jogs on her treadmill.

"Yeah, we collided on the bridge a while ago." I talk while trying to stare blankly at the window. Somehow, no matter how paranoid I was that day, if she'd have had this outfit on, I would have stayed for a chat.

"Oh yes, so sorry."

She is apologizing again. She can't be that nice. "Nothing to be sorry about, the bridge was crowded."

"Well, I must prepare. I am just warming up. I am teaching a class in fifteen minutes." There is no urgency in her voice. Actually, it is calm and soothing. I am losing my edge just talking to her. I need a little aggressive hostility to move those weights. I wonder what class she teaches. I ask.

"It is a yoga class. You must join us sometime."

Not quite. I don't own any tights, can't touch my toes, and meditation is not my thing. "Thanks, I'm happy with my workouts."

"Your jaw muscles are so tight when you are here; your tense appearance indicates internal stress. Oh, forgive me; it is not my place to tell you about yourself. You find out with the practice of Pratyahahra."

She gently steps off the treadmill, smiles, turns, and walks through a door that goes, I guess, to the yoga room. Are there rooms for yoga?

Walking back across the bridge, I can't help but wonder about her. She is different than any woman I have met before. She seems so at peace with herself. What was the language she spoke at the end of our conversation? I'll find out next time.

I will find out when yoga classes are given. Just curious. As I leave the gym, I take an activity schedule from the front desk.

Chapter 13

The bright orange and yellow blouse lights up the drab room. The room is part of a two-bedroom apartment in the government-sponsored projects next to Charlestown. The windows look out onto a huge metal crane leaning over a field of dirt. Isabella Lopez lights her second cigarette of the morning.

Isabella misses the palm trees of her native Florida. She misses the sunny heat and good Spanish food on every corner. But she knows this is America; good hard work will get you lots of money. She will never sell her body but cares little what other people do to theirs. When this round of business is finished, she will head south where she can drive her red Hummer to the large house she lives in alone. When she wants company, she decides who, what, what for, and on what terms. Living in this place serves her purpose; no one looks twice. She looks like she belongs here. The hell with them is her opinion on smiling neighbors. She doesn't need anyone's friendship.

The door opens, and her current partner and lover walks in. He is sweaty from his five-mile run; his thin frame and matted-down hair complete the picture of a typical jogger. He can run anywhere in this town, and nobody looks twice. Even the layer of dyed blonde hair growing out isn't worth a second look. Nobody looks in a big city.

He glances at her, walks to the two windows, and opens them as wide as they permit. "I'm not breathing that crap."

"Hey, I'm cutting down, trying to stop." She speaks with no sincerity intended.

He doesn't care whether she quits or not; he just doesn't want the smoke around him. He can wait until the deal is done, and they go their separate ways.

Isabella tosses the cigarette butt out the window, smiles her aerated smile, turns, and says, "I met with our interfering doc today."

"Did you scare him?"

"I mentioned his dead friend. I don't think he wants to wind up like him. He shouldn't get in our way."

"He better not, we don't need any complications." The man known as Agent Wright is, in reality, a former college athlete, Sam Colchine. Sam was a track star at the University of Miami. He loved the attention, the buzz of being special, and the avoided classes. He lasted two years. Now, he gets his buzz doing big money deals by buying Medicaid patients' drugs for a few bucks and then reselling them to shady middle men who dilute and re-label the medications. He piles the boxes of drugs in the trunk of his rental car not caring what temperature they should be stored in. All he cares about is the cash.

"It better work; another body and half the police department of Boston will be breathing down our necks."

Taking out Gord was a rare non-drug high for him. When that job was completed, he used his disposable cell and left his partner in crime a message, "Take a bath."

When Isabella heard the message, she was scared. She may be killing people with her watered-down drugs, but she never sees their faces. She took a bath, drank some vodka, and waited for her thin partner. She knew what he would want when he got back. He returned with a glazed look in his eyes and grabbed her by her waist as she was drying herself after the bath. She felt nothing from his touches. She is not looking forward to a repeat performance.

They agree that the thousand dollars cash payment to their informant at the police station is worth it. This informant is in a good spot; she sees who comes and goes. Now they just have to find the woman known as Fern.

Chapter 14

I am starting to feel comfortable with this arrangement. I know enough to stay away from my former study and the bathroom in the hallway. I have the cleaning service come twice a week. I don't think Vito cares one way or another. I do. Bentley is starting to lose weight since I've been monitoring his food portions. I can't say the same for Vito. The canine crew is now marching at the same pace. Vito always joins us for half the trips. His excuse for leaving is that his beeper goes off. I never hear it.

My first meeting with the new task force following the case is in two days. I am looking forward to it.

I haven't seen the yoga instructor at the gym recently. The fact that she crosses my mind is interesting. She seems an exotic mystery to me. It occurs to me that I don't know her name. One afternoon I find myself in the local Barnes & Noble checking out books about yoga. I really can't relate to what I am reading. Maybe I am reading the wrong books. I can't wait to ask her. Walking back to my place, I can't shed what I read; that yoga is essentially a journey inward. I wonder if I have the courage for such a journey.

Chapter 15

Every group has its own name for fate. There seems to be some force that eventually places you where you want to be. The trick is to be smart enough to do the right thing at the right time. Take the plunge. Don't look back. The past is no longer an option. I am feeling comfortable in the energy around me. Each day is an adventure. My previous life is losing its need to be a frame of reference for me. In my own way, I am on a journey. The present journey is sitting in the passenger seat of Vito's Chevy. Bouncing through the streets of Boston convinces me he's never had the car serviced. I am afraid to look at his tire tread. At the same time, I realize that Gord's car is not on the street.

"Do you know what happened to Gord's 4Runner?"

"Yeah, it was impounded by the department. Until this is over, it's part of the investigation."

"Just wondering." It is upsetting to think about certain events of the recent past. I still haven't had a one-on-one talk with Bowser.

A block from the station house, Vito pulls over to the curb. Actually, he pulls partially over the curb. I open the door, step on the sidewalk, and look at his vehicle put in a position of discomfort. At least it looks like it's in discomfort.

Vito wedges out of the wagon, closes the door, and doesn't make a move to the meter. "I got it."

An interesting statement since I never carry change, too noisy and dirty for me. He has a bemused look as he reaches into his black jacket pocket and pulls out a parking ticket. He places it under the passenger-side wiper blade. Wiping his hands on the sides of his pants, he ambles toward the station house. I know not to ask any questions. I assume parking is his divine right.

Following my roommate into the building, we pass the usual policewoman sitting behind the main entranceway desk. Vito gets a quick nod. I receive no head movement but notice a raise of the left eyebrow. After all, I am on the bottom of the hierarchy in this world. I notice her make a quick note on a small piece of yellow paper and place it into her purse.

The coffee room is exactly as I had imagined it. I watch enough cop-show late-night reruns to not be surprised. But I am surprised by how good the coffee tastes.

"You thought you'd drink mud here, eh?"

Turning to my right, I see a tall thin black man dressed in a three-button gray suit. I can tell it is an expensive suit, and the dark blue-on-blue striped tie and polished black shoes lend an air of dapperness to the picture. His shaved head completes the look. "Frankly, yes." I can only be honest with him; this is his turf.

"I have high standards in everything I'm involved with." If he is part of this investigation, it should be interesting.

"I'm Lamar Harrington; I've been assigned to organize this task force."

He holds out his right hand; his fingers could wrap around my hand twice. I feel like they do as his firm handshake has my knuckles greeting each other. It is a painful greeting. Vito comes in for his coffee with three sugars. I watch him at home. I buy sugar once every three years. If Vito stays with me much longer, I'll have to add sugar to the shopping list.

"You guys meet each other?"

Before I can answer, Lamar speaks, "Yes, we met. We're waiting for the other team member, and then we'll adjourn to the conference room."

I never expected to hear the word "adjourn" in the police station.

"Hey, I spoke with her; she'll be ten minutes late," Vito chimes in.

I can see Lamar's eyes twitch at the word "late." I follow the sinewy tall and the short round detectives into the institutional hallway. We make a right turn and enter a brightly lit modern conference room. I am amazed. It is furnished in upscale "cops room to go" style with a wood conference table surrounded by solid wood and leather chairs. The leather on the chairs is a contrasting dark brown. A fancy bean-grinding coffee machine sits atop a black granite countertop with an inset white ceramic sink. It has everything a good kitchen has, all the appliances. And they look new. One wall has a plasma screen, another a giant chalkboard. There are flat-screen computer stations by every seat. Our tax dollars at work. Working hard.

Vito sits down at the head of the table, wearing a big smile. I look at him and wonder why he didn't just move in here.

"Too bad they don't let dogs in here."

I guess a good detective is a mind reader. Lamar sits down at the other end of the table from Vito and sips his black coffee. He looks deep in thought. The door flings open, and I jerk my head to see who the lucky late member of the task force is. Vito doesn't move; he has one hand on his cup, the other reaching for a pen from his shirt pocket. Lamar's expression doesn't change, noticeably; he is sitting very upright. Is it upright and uptight? I have to learn not to be a shrink. Let it go. Let it play out.

A woman walks in the room quickly and brusquely flings the door closed. It is the head from the front desk. I guess she was saving her energy for this moment. Looking at her, the only one not in uniform, is not easy: tightly pulled-back brown hair, medium height, and a tight officious look about her. I don't trust her. Lamar is the first to speak.

"Leslie is here as part of our support team. She will be in-house and available to all of us. Her role is to coordinate information, collate it, and have it available to us at a moment's notice. No matter where we are and what time of day it is."

She looks like a sneaky librarian to me. But these guys trust her.

Lamar continues, "She will still be at the front desk, but her priority is our investigation. She has backup on the front line."

"Front line?" That's what I put on Fern's shoulders to prevent ticks. It dawns on me; I will have to coordinate all the treatment and vet appointments for my flock. Who checks to find out if the dogs' drugs are the real deal? There is silence in the room. Lamar is staring at me. I don't know it until he says, "You look deep in thought. Do you want to share your thoughts with us?"

"Getting all these things organized will be a challenge."

"Not for us, we've been down this road before. You are going to have to think beyond your old professional box. We hope to get an energizing perspective from you."

It seems to be said in a threatening way. Though I realize there is nothing he could do to threaten me. Lamar has the floor.

"Today will be spent reviewing in-house facts. We will be sitting here until I'm happy with the day's accomplishments."

It just hits me, I have a new job, and I'm not being paid. I am eager to see the facts they have on Gord's death. I am also eager to actually see Vito work. Our dog walker is going to be getting overtime these next few weeks. Before I know it, lunch is brought in, fresh coffee made, and I find myself cleaning the mess on the table. Leslie is in and out, barely acknowledging my existence. Lamar does most of the talking.

"We have one murder, one missing person, and the door opening up on the counterfeit drug market. We want to see if there is a tie-in. It would seem so with the ID of this Lopez woman at Adam's apartment looking for the missing Fern woman. Somehow, that woman is a threat to the Lopez person. We haven't figured out who her partner was at Adam's house, but we will. The Lopez woman came back to threaten you, Adam, we have to use that."

I just look up at the corner ceiling tile; I don't want to give away my ignorance. As late afternoon arrives, I am ready to leave. Vito picks up on it and makes an offer I can't refuse.

"Look, you got homework to do. Why don't you pick up the papers we need you to study and touch base with us in forty-eight hours?"

"Sure, my head is spinning from this session today. Where do I get these papers?"

"They'll be at the front desk."

As I stand up to leave, it is like I don't exist; Lamar and Vito are discussing warehouses and their contacts inside. I hear some names of large wholesalers and national drug-buying groups mentioned as I exit. I start to wonder where my drugs are coming from.

At the front desk, Leslie hands me two information packets. "Thanks."

"They want this back by Thursday. You have to return it all to me. Sign here."

I wonder, if she wasn't wearing a police uniform, would her personality be different? Appearance does make a difference; we all know that. "Here?" I am trying to have a conversation with her. She only points to the dotted line, gives me a standard pen, and nods.

Better to use my energy to get a cab. That's easy; they are always in front of the station house. The ride home is a contemplative one. It makes me realize that I am going to be putting some time into this project. I will write down my schedule for the next few days. Get order, some logic, and some space for myself. Getting out of the cab, I notice the dog walker with our collection of canines. They all seem happy and social.

Settling into the couch, I take the large envelopes loaded with information and place them on the tabletop. I will wait for the dogs to get home before studying them. I flip on a Miles Davis CD and close my eyes. I have to find time to talk to the yoga instructor. I need distraction. I want to be selfish. But I will not let myself wander into an afternoon nap. If I do, I know I'll feel like my mind is in a fog. I have no idea what a "power nap" is. For me, it is opening a door to a mind of sludge.

I make a pot of coffee. I love the smell of the fresh brew. The computer and the telephone are a shutout for messages. I have no excuse but to read the documents. It feels like I am doing homework; well Vito did call it my "homework." The course is Investigation 101. I select the biggest mug I own and fill it with fresh hot brew, my fifth cup so far today. I have labeled the two packets A and B. I love organization. A sense of control is always comforting even if it is not true control.

The first packet contains a history of the drug counterfeit business. It is one hundred and eighty-four pages long. The last three pages are references. I push that over to my left. The second packet is a shorter grouping of information. It has the names and possible connections of the people involved in the crimes being investigated. There is a hypothetical time line of events. My name appears a number of times. Lamar wants me to digest this second package of information and put my immediate impressions in writing. This is all a hell of lot to do in forty-eight hours.

I pick up the first history packet, take my first sip, and start reading. Halfway through the mug of coffee, the phone rings.

"Hey, did I wake you?" It is Vito.

"No, just starting on my class assignment."

"Good, you looked like you were gonna zonk out in the cab."

I didn't know he cared or, for that matter, was that observant. "I'm fine; I've studied a few times before." I sound defensive.

"Anyway, look, I'm going to be working late tonight. You're on your own for dinner," Vito says.

"See you whenever, you got the keys."

It feels good to be alone for a bit. I freshen up my mug and drink enough to get through fifty-five pages of the history of fake drugs. Trust me, not close to a best seller. My collection of canine friends is itching for a walk and dinner. I take care of them, and now it is my turn. My walk with the canine crew is the easy part; the next part requires some thought. I need to get out tonight. I leave the lights on for my gang awaiting the return of Vito and walk down the stairs, not knowing where I am going to eat dinner.

Walking through the park, I wonder if I should I go back to the Warren Tavern where the adventure started. I am going in that direction but do not follow the right fork to the Tavern. I am not ready to revisit what I am still living. Taking the left fork, I find myself walking toward the bridge to the North End. The cool night air, hunger, caffeine buzz drive me at a brisk pace. I remember the Greek restaurant is just around the corner from Sorrel's and is the last stop before heading over the bridge. Why not?

The wind kicks up, making me wish I was wearing a scarf. Soon enough, I enter the modern glass-and-metal restaurant. The servers are all dressed in black shirts and pants, male and female alike. The bar has an S shape to it. I sit on the top of the S near the corner. It isn't crowded, but I decide to go ahead and eat dinner at the bar. I order a glass of Greek white wine and study the menu. Before the bartender can start reciting the list of specials, I point to the grilled fish and vegetable platter. I don't care what fish it is as long as they take the bones out. It should feel good to nurse the wine along with thinking about nothing, just feeling the pulse of the crowd entering the restaurant. But it isn't really working to down-shift my brain from firing in overdrive. Maybe a second round will help.

"I'll have a second one, thanks."

"Do you mind if I join you?"

The athletic olive-skinned lady of yoga sits next to me, facing the bartender. She smiles and turns to her left with her right hand out to me.

"Aleni Patrackis, we met at the gym over the bridge."

"Collided on the bridge."

She laughs.

"How memorable."

Somehow I have the feeling this is the beginning of something memorable also. "You're Greek, you've been here before?" Boy that was a stupid question. It must be the two wines and all the recent events affecting my judgment. I feel like a fool. Her expression doesn't change however.

"My uncle owns it. I used to work here when I was younger."

I just look at her and smile. She turns to the waiter and asks, using his name, for a dish in a language I don't understand. It is a reasonable guess that it is Greek. I tell the bartender to hold off and bring both of our dinners together.

"Are you meeting anyone?"

"No."

The first good news I've had in a while. She drinks sparkling water. We toast to no more bridge collisions. The ice is broken.

"I was thinking about taking a yoga class."

"You can collect the information about the class times at the front desk. There are different levels. It will be a good experience for you."

"I'll check it out."

The food comes. My fish is wonderful. She eats some kind of spinach pastry with vegetables. We don't speak to one another during the meal; instead, her animation is directed toward the assorted people who periodically join us to chat. They escape into their own language. There is serious-sounding talk with laughter thrown in occasionally. I finish my meal and nurse my drink. I stare blankly ahead.

"I'm sorry, they are old friends, and they come and leave in such a rush."

Somehow, whatever she says has a caring quality. She looks at me directly and stands up to leave.

"Hopefully, I will see you in one of my classes." She is gone.

My head is spinning on my walk home. Once home, I take care of my four-legged friends and myself, organize my papers and try to mentally file the events of the day, on top of those of the last few months. I briefly look at the documents I brought home. I use my bedroom as the new study. All the papers are in viewing distance from my bed. I lay down to think. Please stop thinking.

Chapter 16

My eyes open. I am confused. My muscles are spent.

"Just stay put, everything is OK."

I am on the floor next to my bed. My watch says five in the morning. Vito is talking to me. He is standing up.

"I understand. I've been through this before."

I have no idea what he is talking about. I look at him. What is he doing in my house?

"My little sister has seizures; I know what this is all about. Just listen to me."

It's been two years since my last nocturnal seizure. I thought they were part of somebody else's history. I feel weak, scared, and insecure. At least I didn't wet my pants.

"I know, I know." This is all I can mutter. The presence of Vito is more comforting than my ex-wife's was. She couldn't deal with anything that wasn't on schedule and presented itself badly. I guess if I previewed my epileptic seizures at her convenience and dressed well for the moment, we'd still be married. It doesn't always work that way.

Vito helps me up and checks me out for bumps and bruises. The left side of my tongue is chewed up a bit, but nothing that needs any attention. My legs are exhausted, like running a marathon without the training. My upper body is relatively strong. Mentally I feel insecure and angry. I thought I was done with this stuff. Just take the meds and move on. My medical training taught me otherwise, but I never look at myself as a patient.

Vito tells me about his sister, her history, and how it brought his family together. She's under control with medication and neurological care by the team that I had some part in training.

The worst part is the feeling of dependency. The last thing I want is to be out of control and dependent on anything or anyone.

"Vito, I'll be all right in a few days, it takes me about forty-eight hours to rebound from one of these things. I'll rest and eat the right food."

"Look, I'll tell the gang back at the station you caught the flu bug and that you'll be out a few days. Believe me, I understand, this doesn't leave the room. You got reading to do anyway. I'll get the dog walker to pick up your times."

I've learned it happens. It takes me time to digest this and work to not feel sorry for myself. It's good that Vito was here. I am due for my yearly neurology exam at Penn in Philly in three months. It can wait. I'm OK. It's my mind and body telling me it is time to downshift, regroup, and think. Then, OK, go forward. I just have to come up with a better way to slam into neutral than Mother Nature is dictating right now. Yoga with a beautiful Greek lady sounds worth a try.

* * *

The next two days are just as expected, tired in an emotional and physical manner. I recognize the mild depression that I am fighting. Vito insists we talk about it. He is right. Like I said, we all have our kryptonite; just deal with it.

The excuse is there to read all the documents. The quagmire of information about counterfeit medications reads like a textbook. The grey areas are huge for middlemen both large and small. Some billion-dollar medications must have a rigid sequence of events in transmission to maintain effectiveness. One middleman, for example, looking for a shortcut and not concerned about temperature-maintenance protection from light can reduce or eliminate a drug's potency. Crooks looking to turn medicine over quickly are harming people.

It isn't upbeat reading. I am not looking forward to perusing the other envelope. That one is a review of the roster and timing of people involved in this event. Seeing Fern's name brings back our evening together. Maybe some people can share an evening together and just forget it; I can't. I try to forget her, but it isn't happening. I also can't figure out what she is all about. None of us can come up with her connection to the pharmaceutical industry. At least that's what I think until I read the contents of the second envelope. Various pieces of information seem to surface, just bits and pieces. Facts come out about various people. Facts, when you have enough of them, put pieces of the puzzle together. I even remember the facts of us together, the way she looked, her smell, her taste.

But the mystery must be solved. The discovery of meaning is solving the mystery.

* * *

Time has a way of healing everything. Here I am, three days after my brain fired off on its own, and I am running on a treadmill. I haven't been back to the police station and don't miss it. Maybe I should just leave all the investigation to the pros. Something tells me it's too late for that.

I have been working on thinking about nothing, which was my original goal before spending the night with the beautiful blonde lady. I still want to find out what she is all about. My empty mind is not going to last long.

"I didn't see you in my class this morning."

Turning to my right, Aleni is on the adjacent treadmill. "Haven't been feeling very strong lately, also working kinda hard."

"Those are reasons to practice yoga." She had a way of talking that makes it seem like we've known each other for quite some time.

"I'll try a class."

She smiles and leaves her treadmill for the lockers. Well, I really have to find out about this stuff called yoga. I guess if nothing else, it has to help stabilize blood pressure. I have the schedule of classes at home; I'll check it later. Am I checking out yoga or the instructor?

Walking back over the bridge, I feel it is time to start preparing my thoughts for the guys back at the station. I decide not to write a paper since it didn't go over too well the first time. I do wonder if an outline of my ideas should be given to the woman at the front desk. Weren't we supposed to coordinate our information through her? I'll leave her a small outline of who Fern may be and what her motivation might be. I'll keep it on the generic side, nice and simple. My thoughts are that Fern is independent, gathering information about bogus medications.

In her brief time with me, Fern went out of her way to not reveal any of her past. She obviously went out of her way to make it difficult for me to trace her. If I flip the mirror, it seems that she was using my place to hide for the night. She tried to blend in at dinner in a crowded pub and then went off for the evening with me, someone who had no local history. Was there anything to our night together? Only a second time together will answer that.

As an independent, gathering information about bad medications, Fern could be a threat to the Lopez lady and her accomplice. Why else would the Lopez lady question me about her? Maybe Fern is not working independently, but with some undercover force. Shouldn't the cops be able to find that out? I jot these thoughts down on the computer and send out on the secure line to the information coordinator. Leslie Redpath immediately receives my thoughts on Fern at the station house. It is printed out and placed in Lamar, Vito's, and my folders. Nobody notices the extra copy put in her purse.

Our next task force meeting is midmorning on Monday. Unless new information suddenly arises, we are free to forget for the weekend. Sure.

I go through the pile of papers in the kitchen pass through. The only one to survive the garbage besides the bills is the yoga schedule. I organize the bills and place them against the wall by the phone. The only remaining paper is the yellow schedule. I look at it and am ready to toss it. Then I see who the instructor is on Saturday morning. Oh well, why not. The ringing of the phone brings me back to the present.

"Hey, how are you feeling?"

Between the ringing phone and Vito's voice, I am officially in the immediate now mode. "Hey, I really have to thank you for being there for me." I have given some thought about my seizure recovery and realize it could have been worse if I had been alone. Vito was a security blanket for a quicker rebound. Part of me doesn't like to recognize that.

"Yeah, just to let you know, I won't be back to the place until sometime Sunday. We're following some leads and need to keep our contacts cookin'."

"No problem. Oh, I e-mailed my thoughts to the Redpath woman. It should be in your file."

"Sure, see you Sunday."

"Yeah."

My body is feeling stronger, and the emotional well is refilling. Not quite full, but each breath reminds me who I am. I scramble three eggs for dinner, and include yesterday's green beans on the side. Nursing a cold bottle of ale, my thoughts are of the new adventure tomorrow morning. I can't believe I am planning on going to a yoga class. I realize how early I will be getting up to take care of everything before I walk over.

I don't have a clue what to wear.

Chapter 17

Sam Colchine pays for the pizza, while Isabella sets the table. He turns and places the box in the center of the table. She places a pile of paper napkins in the center that Sam pushes aside. As he grabs a slice out of the box, she closes the fridge with a bottle of Budweiser in each hand.

"I'm getting tired of living like this." He speaks between bites and chugs the Bud.

She eats her two pieces of pizza silently, using a knife and fork. It still isn't presenting an elegant picture. "You want to talk about her note now or now?"

Sam isn't one to compromise; it's his way or no way. So far it's worked in his world. Some tomato sauce from his third slice finds its way onto the sleeve of his blue sweatshirt; he doesn't notice it. He is busy opening his second beer. "I'm done eating, we can talk now."

She doesn't care if he is finished or not.

* * *

The pickup is pretty standard. Isabella sits at the bench in Soldier's Park facing the waterway. The Redpath lady, wearing a generic beige raincoat, briefly sits next to her facing the opposite direction and, after reading the paper, stands up and leaves the sports section rolled up on the bench. Isabella picks it up, places it under her arm, and walks away. This plays out like a 1950s spy movie; nobody would believe that this is how an occasional bit of information can be transferred.

It is so simple, and the easier the method, the less chance for a screw up. Isabella knows well enough to wait until she returns back to their place to open the paper. Hopefully, Sam isn't there; she likes to have her own time to digest the information. It is not to be.

"The shrink doesn't know much more than we do." Sam isn't looking at his roommate; his interest is on the leftover pizza stored in the fridge. Isabella is wrapping the trash that is on its way to the garbage bin.

"Yeah, this woman seems to follow us, and we don't know who the hell she is. Hey, maybe we're looking at it wrong. She could have info for us and wants piece of the action."

"We know she's not working with the Boston cops, our inside lady confirms that every day. Hell, they are as confused as we are as to what's her piece is in this."

They both are quiet, listening to the sounds of the cars over the close bridges. When she first came up from Miami, the cars kept her up every night. Now, it is background noise.

"She always shows up looking at some part of a deal we are working on. Then before we make any contact with her, she vanishes."

Sam lays out the brief history of this woman they know as Fern. He can't confirm who she is, and all his contacts give him blank looks instead of an answer about her. He is getting pissed and worried. Loose ends are dangerous for them, especially when getting close to wrapping up a big deal. The only person who has come close to them was this guy named Gord. An odd picture: a cop out on disability and living in an $800,000 condo. Nobody seemed to see how Gord managed that; it didn't fit together. He was a nice, quiet member of the team, a presence up north, just enough under the legal radar and just enough above the law enforcement information to have a niche within the network of middlemen. He knew how to deal with the men who had rap sheets of crimes from drug smuggling to truck hijacking. Dealing with the suits and their shell companies was part of his package. Too bad he tried to blackmail them for a bigger piece of the pie.

Chapter 18

The USS *Constitution*'s masts are directly in her sight. It is good to know her vision is not impaired. Catherine is lucky; her eyes have no difficulty adjusting to soft contact lenses, no matter what the color. And she has no difficulty in adjusting to changing her name; it is actually sort of fun: Jacobs to Jones. The harbor is in her view on her right, and beneath her is a collection of very expensive boats of various sizes, some with sail, and some without. Boston proper is across the bay and the town houses of Charlestown to her left.

Ms. Crosby Jones checked in to the Marriott Residence Inn yesterday at midday. The location is excellent for her purpose. She is within walking distance to all the characters in the story she is living. Her history as an independent person set in accomplishing her goals is well established. Top athlete and scholar, her years at Cornell helped her prepare to be self-motivated. Her sports achievements were only in activities that relied on her individual ability. Tennis, swimming, and distance running gave her physical and mental strength. Living in a large university environment taught her the outward social skills needed in the business world.

As a young defense attorney, the competitive nature of her work appealed to her. She never thought of the character of her clients. For that matter, she never thought of the character of her boyfriends. They all just served a purpose. Her time as the Miami DA rounded out her legal experience.

At thirty-six, breast cancer was not in the picture. Unfortunately, it was in her picture. She knew the best professionals in Miami, so her treatment was under the top doctors' care. She had the full package of treatment with minimal surgery. She was lucky; aesthetics were able to be managed. The run at chemotherapy was successful and humbling. Part of the package of toxic chemotherapy was a drop in her red blood cell count, causing serious anemia. The medicine called Procrit was prescribed to counteract the drop in red blood cells. The brand name is Epogen.

She picked up the vial at the drugstore on a weekly basis. A nurse injected it, and it worked. Her count went up and she felt better. She looked recovery in the face. Catherine reached her goal; she has recovered and is off all medication. It has been four years, and everyone is optimistic about her chances for a healthy future.

She never returned to the practice of law. Catherine's issue was with figuring out who she was. She was given a second chance at life, and she wanted to find a purpose for it. She found it when overhearing her oncologists talk about falsely labeled medications harming a patient of theirs. They told her about a patient who was suffering from post chemo anemia and not responding to Epogen. Luckily, a nurse discovered a false label on the vial. The patient had been receiving water. Catherine went to the proper authorities to offer help with this issue. Her requests to help were ignored. Dealing with the state agency was like swimming in molasses. If she was going to swim, it would be on her terms. Never one to wait for others to perform, she decided to go out on her own. She uses her experience and network in the law enforcement world to track down the makers of bad drugs. She gets the evidence and presents it to the politicians in power. The results follow. Now she has a purpose.

Reflecting while looking at the outside view, the charm of Boston is left unnoticed. She is more interested in her latest transition. Walking to the mirror above the sink in bathroom, she can't help but smile. She is no longer the striking blonde with big dark eyes. The extremely short combed-back shiny black hair is a wonderful contrast to her blue eyes. The table by the sink also houses clear black-framed eyeglasses to be worn over the contact lenses. Her new wardrobe masks her athletic figure and will pass her off as being just a bit behind the times. Nobody will look twice at her.

She decides on room service for dinner. "Yes, this is Ms. Crosby Jones in room 519. I will have a grilled chicken salad and white wine sent up, please. A California chardonnay is fine. Twenty minutes? That will do."

She thinks of Adam. He was at the right place at the right time. He made her hiding easy. His was a safe house with the bonus of an evening of pleasure thrown in. She knows it would have been nice to stay for breakfast, but her new life doesn't leave room to stay for anything simply pleasurable. Happy with her appearance, she places a drop of vanilla essence on her neck and thinks about her plan for tomorrow. A knock on the door brings her back to the present.

Chapter 19

Since this is the first time I planned on going to yoga class, I have to establish a system. It has been a long time since I had plans for an early Saturday morning. The alarm is set for 5:30 a.m., and the outfit I thought was yoga friendly is laid out the night before. I waken ten minutes before the alarm and turn it off. I barely slept the night before. I shave, shower, and put on my short black tights, dark blue running shorts, and old tee shirt that announces the Albany River Rats as the Eastern League Ice Hockey champions of seven years ago. I cover up with old grey sweats from Penn and make coffee.

My routine is taking care of the morning needs of my canine buddies. They are a bit in slow motion as their schedules are bumped up an hour and a half. They still have no problem enjoying the first meal of the day. Nor do I. As I walk over the bridge, I notice that it all seems to be moving in slow motion. Fewer people to avoid and very few grown-up outfits worn. I arrive twenty minutes before class and, being a yoga rookie, ask where it is held.

The young lady at the desk tells me how to get to the yoga room and asks for my check. It had never entered into my mind that there would be a fee for this adventure. I smile and ask the young lady behind the desk, "I don't have a check, how much is it?"

"Fourteen dollars for the class, do you need a mat?"

I am totally not in this loop. "Sure, are the towels the usual two dollars?" I settle the mat and towel fee and give her the cash.

She smiles and points me toward the mat selection. I grab a purple mat and a white towel and head to the yoga room. I notice a row of shoes in front of the door and sweats and jackets hanging on pegs on the walls. I figure out the protocol and enter the room with shoes and sweats off. The hot air instantly hits me. I don't have water, and my last fluid was two cups of strong black coffee. Looking around, there are nine women in halter tops and tights of various lengths. They look like former Olympic gymnasts. This should be interesting.

I unroll the mat and place the towel at the top position. The instructor's back is facing me as she kneels, sitting upright, and staring straight ahead at the wall. I notice her light highlighted hair tied back. It is not my new friend, Aleni. The disappointment builds inside me. I realize now that I am there to try and further my contact with Aleni. I sit down and stretch. The room is filling up in a hurry, and the mats are being placed pretty close next to each other. The instructor turns and mouths the words "one minute."

I feel a light tap on my left shoulder and turn. It is Aleni placing her mat behind me. She also hands me two blue plastic blocks. I smile and place the blocks next to my mat. I have absolutely no idea what they are for. The instructor's name is Lisa. She begins by having everybody stand and breathe in unison. We then bow up and down together. This stuff is easy; at least there are interesting women to look at.

One hour later, I think I may need to call 911. I am dehydrated and in total muscle pain. My positions are weak, and my ego is deflated. I feel like a fool. My present fantasy has nothing to do with those female forms in the room with me; it is about the Gatorade in my fridge.

On conclusion of class, I bolt out, well, stumble out really, dress in the hallway, and find myself on the bridge heading back home. I am moving with great difficulty. I feel like hell. Everybody is passing me; I don't even pretend I am a tourist.

"Adam, hold up." It is Aleni.

"Are you OK?"

"Not really, I'm dehydrated, exhausted, and weak. I feel a bit foolish too."

"We need to talk. Get some fluid in you, rest up, and call me after lunch. Eat a light lunch, with fruit."

If I had some energy, I would feel good about this encounter.

"Here's my card with my telephone number. Call before one." She takes off past me and turns right over the bridge.

The first call I make after climbing to my condo is to the dog walker. The dogs would have pulled me through the park, and I am in no condition for that. I slowly rehydrate with water and Gatorade. I shower again to desalinate my body. I keep the water cool. I have no appetite, but I have some yogurt and fruit. After forty minutes I feel buzzed. I don't feel bad; I feel a different kind of good. I know my muscles will be sore; they were called on to perform like never before. It makes me think just about myself and nothing else.

When I was in class, it was just the "now" that I dealt with; nothing else mattered. I am glad my efficiency is not at a high level because usually the washing machine would be in use after my shower. I reach into the washer and dig out Aleni's card from the pocket of my sweatpants. I would not have been a happy camper discovering the remnants of her card in the dryer. I'll call her in an hour. Smiling, I keep busy for an hour. I am afraid to sit down for fear I might fall asleep until the evening. I make sure the windows are open; fresh air is required.

Her card pronounces her a yoga instructor and fitness expert. Sounds good to me. I call with my energy on empty and expectations hopeful.

"Hi. Glad you called, Adam."

I didn't announce who I was. Oh, of course the electronics on the phone tell her who I am. I hope it doesn't tell her what I am thinking. "Yeah, you were right, fruit and water have gotten me back in the living."

"Why don't we meet to talk this afternoon? I have plans for the evening, how about coffee at the bookshop near the fitness center?"

"Three o'clock?"

"See you then."

I put the phone down on the kitchen table and sit on the leather couch. I lean back, and Fern jumps on my legs. Her two companions look up, and Bowser walks off to slurp some water. He comes over to the couch and rolls on his back on the floor. My left hand is on his smooth belly. The now-thinner corgi is sitting on the chair by the window, keeping guard for the gang. The little bookshop has the best coffee in town. What could be a better afternoon than coffee with a gorgeous woman?

Chapter 20

The newly adorned Crosby Jones opens the door to her suite. It isn't her dinner; it is a package from the front desk. Catherine tips the fellow a few dollars and closes the door. She can't wait for dinner before opening the package. It is wrapped in brown paper and taped together. She tears the paper off and notices the box seems professionally wrapped. She writes down the lot number.

Opening the box, Catherine finds the vials of Epogen all looking as they should, but she notices they are warm, too warm. She repackages them, places the box in the fridge, and waits for dinner. She is looking forward to continuing her research in the small bookstore in town. Tomorrow afternoon she is going to find the information she needs before making her next contact.

Chapter 21

Lamar and Vito are disturbed with the information. Surprises are something that this crew does not accept very readily. First of all, even though they are professional cops, they still don't like working on weekends. Vito is trying to figure out if his wife is seeing someone else. She is distant, doesn't like his cooking, and feels she needs some space. He knows he made a mistake not marrying an Italian. Lamar and Vito are sitting in their unmarked Ford sedan. They are waiting to find the right moment to enter #30 Monument Street. The grey building looks like the old schoolhouse it used to be. Its local history is both interesting and scary.

It was the setting of the racial problems from the past, but the new young professional couples have no concern with that. It has been redone as a fantastic condominium complex, restructuring the unique entryway, hallways, and individual living arrangements, all with high ceilings, big rooms, and big windows. Those units with a view of the Bunker Hill Monument are worth a fortune. Gord lived well in his last years. Not bad for a cop on disability. Lamar always felt there was something not quite right with Gord's lifestyle. Being a nice guy only carries you so far. Vito never gave it much thought. As long as it didn't affect him, so what? Well, it affected him now.

They have the legal papers to break into Gord's place. They are just waiting for the right moment before entering. Experience will dictate to their gut when it's time to go. They can only sit for so long. They look at each other and agree that in fifteen minutes they will enter the building. They are professional enough to do so without attracting attention.

After fifteen slow minutes, the doors of the car are flung open. Instinctively looking around, they enter the building with their passkey. Walking up to apartment 201, they nod at a young lady walking a Jack Russell terrier. Utilizing their keys and knowledge of alarm systems, they enter the late Gord's condo. It is a two-bedroom unit with a contemporary design. The only personal touches are Red Sox items scattered throughout.

A thorough search reveals nothing of interest. They do find a computer. Lamar picks up the Sony portable computer and looks it over.

"Hopefully this will give us some information about what Gord was about."

"His place is pretty generic, nothing of interest. I don't think we're missing anything."

"I'll take the computer back to the station, register it, then open it and see what's going on inside."

"Good thing you're a computer whiz. Let's take some photos and dust the place and get out of here. I'm getting hungry."

"Fine, but I need to do another walk-through and take my time doing it."

"Sure, then we'll get a sandwich and some coffee."

"Fine."

Lamar is getting hunger pangs. That's good; he thinks better that way. His eye catches an open notepad on the desk. He sees scribbles in pencil; the names Amgen, Epogen, Epoetin Alfa, Ortho Biotech, Procrit, Johnson & Johnson are legible. He puts gloves on and places the whole pad in a plastic bag and goes through the drawers of the desk. He picks up a few other pads of paper with indentations of previous writing surfacing on them. He can barely make out some words but sees "smaller wholesalers" with numbers at different angles on the pages. His mind starts to spin.

"Vito, I have some interesting stuff here. We need to talk."

"Good, we have all afternoon to do that, let's eat first."

"OK, let's file this stuff at the station house and go somewhere to eat and talk."

"Deal."

They carry their findings down the stairs as if it is theirs and nod at the young lady with the terrier as she reenters the building. The terrier stops and smells each pant leg. Probably smells Gord's place. Once settled in the car, sitting in traffic, Vito turns to Lamar and breathes deeply.

"Do you think the terrier will tell?"

Lamar pretends not to hear. "He was connected to the drug industry."

Vito lets Lamar's words sit with him for a few minutes. "You sure?"

"Pretty sure. He had implicating words written down on papers. I don't think he was talking to his stockbroker about them."

Lamar shares his thoughts, guesses, and possible avenues they can go down from here. They both are quiet with the same thought. A big disappointment finding out one of their own flipped to the other side for a few bucks. They know they don't have proof yet, but their instincts are on the same page. They all went into this profession to be the good guys; there is no place for one of them to be a bad guy. They arrive at the station house to a pretty quiet afternoon for the crew. They drop off the day's accumulation of materials with the sit-in coordinator at the front desk. Ms. Redpath has the weekend off, and the rookie young policeman filling in does everything by the book. They'll work the computer and other information on another day. They need a clean slate.

"Hey, let's go to Sorrel's for a bite." Vito already knows he is ordering the turkey wrap.

"No problem, but afterwards let's head out to the bookshop for coffee. Their café has the strongest coffee in town, the only way I drink it." Lamar has no problem with the fare for lunch, but he has gourmet taste in coffee.

That sounds good to Vito; he knows he needs something to counteract the sleepy affects of the turkey. "Deal, you drive, OK?"

"OK."

Chapter 22

The daytime soaps help fight off her boredom. Isabella finds two Spanish-speaking TV stations on cable. She smokes cigarettes as often as she can, not caring if Sam complains. It always bothers Sam. All the arrangements are made, the contacts lined up and ready to spring into action. They have the cash which will flip the boxes of drugs from one wholesaler to another. What happens after that, he has no concern. They both need each other because they know different people in the drug trade that can help them get what they want. The deal is what it is all about. The money comes in; Isabella doesn't care how.

Isabella used to be attracted to Sam. She remembers the night in Miami in a dark bar. He was younger then. They enjoyed each other for a few weeks and then realized that neither one had a regular job. One Tuesday morning before breakfast, Isabella asked Sam where his money came from.

"I know the right people who move some pills around."

"That's why we're good together; I play in the same game."

Now the game is getting old, but the money is still good. They both know the Boston deal is their last together. They were done with each other on all fronts after this.

"We got to wait a little longer for this to get pulled together; how many shows can you watch?"

She doesn't look at him.

"I need some decent coffee; I'm heading out in about an hour."

He needs time alone. Running only does so much. He is looking forward to sitting in the corner of the little café in the bookstore with a large mug of coffee with cream and one sugar. He will have the latest sports car and running magazines to keep him company. Maybe he will meet an academic woman looking for some action. There are plenty of them in Boston.

Chapter 23

The fifteen-minute walk to the bookstore is just what I need. The afternoon air is cooling me and the idea of a warm mug of coffee is appealing. I have no plans for what to discuss with my new friend, Aleni. I am hoping she will enlighten me on this whole yoga deal. I have to admit, I am a bit excited about speaking with her in a civilized, quiet scene. I walk past the Garden, two blocks down, turn left, and look forward to opening the old wooden doors to the May-September House. The word is the owners are an interesting couple.

Grabbing a tarnished brass handle, I hold the doors open for two young students and follow them in. The ambiance is added to by the brewed smell of dark coffee beans, and the randomly arranged tables beckon me to stay for a while. I've been here before when I was too cheap to buy the *Times* or the *Wall Street Journal*. Just take them from the stand, read, and return them neatly folded. At least I folded them neatly.

Looking around, I don't see any familiar faces. Wearing an old pair of khakis and blue wool crew sweater over a tee shirt has me blending in pretty naturally. My weathered running shoes are perfect for city walking. I look and feel like I belong. I find an empty square wood pedestal table for two in the corner by the section for kitchen remodeling books. I grab a big book about redoing kitchens and sit down facing the doors. I am actually finding the pictures interesting.

"May I get some advice about materials for my kitchen?"

I look up to see Aleni's white smile. I can't help but notice her dark skirt and half-opened white blouse. I never understood the protocol; am I supposed to check out the exposed cleavage or be cool and pretend that I am unfazed and see it all the time?

"Hey, I'd be happy to." Does this mean we go back to her place?

"Do you really know about this stuff?"

"It was the closest book."

"I hate to think if you sat in some other sections."

"I'm not going there. Anyway, what size coffee do you want?"

"Medium, with room for milk."

Before she finishes, I am standing and she is sitting. The line at the coffee bar isn't too bad. There is a plain-looking woman with thick dark-framed glasses arriving in line four people behind me. She is wearing a floppy oversized faded green sweatshirt and old pleated khakis. My attention is on the attraction I feel toward my new friend. I am looking forward to a leisurely afternoon in her company. Returning with two burning hands holding medium paper coffee cups, I place them on the table.

"The right one is yours, mine is full up to the brim."

"Thanks."

Once again, in reverse, I sit down and she stands up. Aleni goes to the center table where the crème and sugar and other condiments are placed. I have put the remodeling book back in the shelf by the time she returns. We both sit and hold our warm cups and stare into them.

"Always too hot, I always let it cool down."

She looks at me, smiles, and says, "Are you feeling recovered from class?"

"Yes. I see I have a lot to learn."

"That's one reason why I wanted to meet with you here. There's a book you should have."

I don't know what to say. All I am able to muster is a thoughtful look.

"It's called *Meditations from the Mat* by Rolf Gates."

"OK." I didn't know what else to say. Who is Rolf Gates? Writers always have these weird names.

"Before you leave, you should buy it. It's in soft cover."

"OK."

"It will help you understand what the practice of yoga is all about. I read a chapter just about every day."

I'm not about to get up and look for the book now; I don't want this meeting to turn into a seminar. "Thanks, I'll pick it up on my way out."

"What got you interested in yoga?"

Well, I am not going to say her butt or anything along those lines, so this is what comes out, "Flexibility training. I have nothing like that in my fitness program."

"That's important, but that's not all that it is about. I teach the class tomorrow morning at nine thirty. Join us."

"I look forward to it."

We are both halfway through coffee, and the place is filling up. The rest of our time we spend talking about how great Boston is to live in. We cover everything: local eating places, history, sports teams, and universities. We are circling. I know she has another date after this meeting; she told me earlier that she had plans. This time we both stand up at the same time. Shaking hands and looking at me, she smiles.

"Thanks for the coffee; I'll see you in class tomorrow morning. Don't forget to get the book."

She is still holding my hand. "Sure, see you in the morning."

She turns, and before I know it, our coffee meeting is a memory. I feel good. The reality is that I have a very present caffeine buzz. I use the energy to start looking around for the recommended book. I hate going to the information desk and letting the whole world know what I am looking for. I have time and energy; exploring the aisles is just another mellow adventure.

* * *

Ms. Crosby Jones is settling into a table with a large cup of coffee in hand. She is focused on one goal; it is simple. She, Catherine, needs more information about counterfeit drugs. She is going to the reference section to help locate any book that will benefit her cause. She does not see Adam seated back-to-back with her.

Adam is too entranced by the woman sitting opposite him to pay attention to anyone else. He is no longer sitting near the librarian-looking woman, not that she paid any attention to anything or anyone around her. Ms. Crosby Jones has gone to the information desk where the tall overweight fellow directs her to the section that has a wealth of boring books about pharmaceuticals. She is the only one in that section. Catherine thinks she may be the only one ever to go to this area of the bookstore. After all, the books are still in their proper alphabetically arranged order. Catherine gathers a small selection of choices and piles them neatly on her table. She had left her coffee and light overcoat behind to mark her territory.

Catherine found three factual textbooks about manufacturing and chemical composition of medicines. Her quest now is to find a book that will help give information about the bad guys who make the bad pills and those who adulterate or harm the good ones. She heard of a woman from New York who wrote a book about the drug counterfeiters. She wants to find that book.

She feels as if she is in her own protected zone in the new persona she has assumed. Wearing frumpy clothing is a new experience for her; it makes it easier to hide in this new world. She knows this is not who she is, so the disguise is going to be temporary. She thinks about what the future might bring; a company that would consult with big drug companies to keep their product safe is one thought she has. That same company could also be a liaison to government agencies with the same goals. It sounds good. Dressing like a CEO is a selfish little perk to look forward to. The idea of helping those in need keeps her fuel fired.

Anyway, time to go back to the remote aisle and search.

* * *

Lamar insists on driving over the bridge to the bookstore's café. They could have walked the ten or fifteen minutes and burned off their lunch. Vito tries to push them in that direction. Adam would be so proud of him wanting to walk some distance. But Lamar is right; they should have their service vehicle where they are. Regulations. Lamar is always right about following the rules.

With Saturday afternoon tourists, bus jams, and the challenge of Boston traffic, what should have been twelve minutes turns into thirty-five. Vito knows he can't talk to his partner Lamar about his home life. And Adam is a shrink, but he knows his new roommate wants to leave his old life behind.

He sits in the Ford stuck in traffic and wonders, since all unmarked cars look the same, why they don't stop using them. After all, who but law enforcement detective departments buy dorky-looking Fords and Chevys? Of course, in that cop TV show set in Miami, they drive white Hummers. Somehow, white Hummers driven by detectives wouldn't work even if they were H3s. Vito wonders what the two-tone leather interior looks like when Lamar brings him back to reality.

"We need to get some education about this drug-industry stuff. While we're getting coffee, we'll see what books they have on that subject."

Vito looks at Lamar with a quenched-up mouth and staring eyes. "Can't the department find an expert on this stuff and bring them in to talk to us?"

"That could be a start. Guess what, that's your job."

Vito is looking for an easy way to do this. He just looks at Lamar and feels the drink he needs now is not coffee. As expected, parking is impossible, at least legally. So they park where it's not permitted. "Now tell me, no one is going to know this is an unmarked car?" Vito looks at his partner standing tall and waits for him to open the door. It takes Vito three times as long to exit the car as it does Lamar. As is their habit, they look up and down the street before heading into the bookstore.

"You find the table, I'll get the drinks."

Lamar knows how Vito likes his java; he has plenty of time to ponder over the coffee choices as the line is long and moving slowly. He doesn't mind; that's what quality demands.

Vito is looking for a place for them to sit. The bookstore's cafe is crowded; after all, it is Saturday afternoon. Being the detective he is he scopes out the whole place. He sees two tables next to each other with half-empty coffee cups and books and clothing left behind. Typical protocol for staking claim to a table. He walks over to the table with the pile of books. He notices they all reference to the pharmaceutical industry. He'll keep an eye out to see who returns there. He may have found his expert sooner than he thought.

Two gay-looking guys stand up and leave their table by the front door. A good table, seated there he could see people coming in and out of the store without being obvious. Always thinking like a cop. After catching Lamar's eye, Vito ambles over in the shortest route to grab that table by the front door.

* * *

Sam will do anything to leave this neighborhood. It is great cover, but it is starting to smother him. And living with Isabella is now the definition of work. He needs to fantasize about old girlfriends when touching her. He is ready to find someone new to break the monotony. Walking uphill the three blocks before entering a decent neighborhood is a joy. He dreads the walk back.

Walking past the Bunker Hill Monument, he promises himself he'll take the time one day to climb all the stairs inside, another workout challenge. He never looks at the old school condo where Gord used to live; what's done is done. Gord is dead. His pace picks up crossing the bridge, and he is starting to think about what magazines he'll look for to kill time. He works at slowing his pace to prolong his time away from the apartment. He stops and takes in the sight of the Boston skyline. Nice, but nothing like the buzz he gets when breathing in the Miami air. He misses the ocean smells, the Cuban restaurants, and the excitement of knowing the right people are always nearby to keep the money rolling. He turns and walks into the opposite world of a historic Boston bookstore.

* * *

Ms. Crosby Jones walks with a slight limp. An extra touch Catherine decided to add to her new persona. There is more than a little bit of an actress in her, and frankly, she has fun creating characters. Maybe this affect will help her get access to pain meds. She is not sure how, or if she needs to, but it creates justification for her newfound limp. All this work limping will lower her blood sugar. It's nice to burn extra calories.

Catherine deposits the next book on her table and finds herself in line behind a tall well-dressed black fellow. It gives her time to decide between the double chocolate brownie and the fresh berry granola bar. Just before her turn to order, she watches the big fellow holding two large cups of coffee walk back to table by the front door. There sits a chubby white guy dressed in a black sweater and black straight-front slacks. Interesting couple.

The skinny counter girl with the bird tattoo on her left wrist looks at Catherine and asks, "Can I help you?"

That brings her back quickly to look at the sweet things on the counter. Her mind is starting to lose its concentration on why she is there. "Sure. I'll have the berry granola bar please. Thanks."

She loves brownies after sex. She wonders if things would have been different with Adam if he had brownies, not beer, in his fridge. She never thought to look in his freezer. Oh well. Holding onto to her little white ceramic plate with her healthy concoction, she limps back to her table. The only one to notice her is the tall thin man who just entered.

* * *

Sam enjoys the sights and smells of this bookstore. The eclectic group of people reminds him of the sociology courses he took in college. Looking around the room, there isn't an open table to be found. He figures, he'll get in-line for his coffee and see what is available after paying for his cup. The skinny little girl with spiked brown hair and tattoo on her left wrist fits into the eclectic mix of people on both sides of the counter. She reminds him of his days snorting coke in Miami. His Southern drug connection has the same tattoo on her wrist. He knew enough not to ask any questions about it.

"What do you care for?"

He really can't truly answer that question. "How about a large with a double shot?"

She smiles and reveals her crooked, stained teeth. His concentration is now just on watching her manipulate the espresso machine. He pays for his strong brew with exact change and, once again, surveys the room. Every table is taken. He notices two tables next to each other with books, coffee, and clothing claiming occupancy. He'll wait to see who returns before asking to share a table.

* * *

I am totally losing myself in the aisles. No matter what the subject, I pull a book off the shelf and check it out. If I'm not careful, I'll leave with a bunch of new books. Amazing how much time I am spending in the biography section. This has nothing to do with yoga, but I never realized how fascinating John Adams was. Finding my way over to the medical section, I almost need medical attention when I trip over a nondescript woman sitting on a stool reading a textbook.

"You OK?" I ask.

"I should be asking you that, you're the one on the ground." There is something vaguely familiar about her.

"I'm fine, it was a soft landing."

She looks like the librarian in charge of the city library, the type I spent my life avoiding. She stares at me through large black-framed eyeglasses, and I can't read the intent in her eyes.

"You should pay attention where you walk."

"Sorry, I'll be on my way."

There is a familiar scent that I quickly dismiss as I want to take leave of the scolding schoolteacher image. Just think, when I was fifteen years old, I had a fantasy about sex with a librarian.

To my left, two aisles down, is the sign indicating the health and exercise section of books. Maybe the yoga book is there. I have to find it, and then my Saturday will be committed to reading. After all, tomorrow morning I am in yoga class again. The teacher may ask questions.

It is easy finding the book Aleni recommended. The aisle is inundated with pictures of fit men and women in all sorts of poses. I wonder if they dated. I remove the book from the second shelf and walk back to my table. Placing it down, I realize the woman I tripped over is sitting behind me with a pile of books on her right. I make a point to have my back facing her back.

The activity of the afternoon makes me think of the brownies in my freezer. My blood sugar needs a boost. It is time for a refill and a brownie purchase. Then I'll settle in and review the yoga book before heading home. The first bite is a wonderful surprise: dark chocolate, smooth, and not too sweet.

While reveling in the sensuous taste, I look to my left. Is that Lamar and Vito sitting over there by the door? Are they following me?

* * *

Oh no. She can't believe it. She doesn't know whether to be curious or frightened. As soon as she, Ms. Crosby Jones, sits down with her collection of information, she notices a tall thin dark-haired man approaching her. He resembles the look of one of the drug crowd she is following. The hair is different, but he is familiar. She changed her appearance and name for protection. Why can't he at least change his bad dye job? She can't hide the books. He is bound to be suspicious of her. He must have been following her so his group could question her. Is she being paranoid? Time to think fast and hope her acting ability is as good as her disguise.

"All the tables are taken, do you mind if I sit here?"

Their eye contact is like a laser, keeping their heads in place. Catherine quickly turns her head to the right, avoiding his penetrating stare. Noticing the odd couple sitting by the door, their presence starts to register with her.

"Fine."

She quickly opens a text on capsule manufacturing and buries her head in it. He still is looking at her. She can feel his eyes on her and has a feeling he is reading her pages, upside down. The grouping of books next to her is now receiving his gaze.

"I do some work in the pharmaceutical field." She keeps reading, or trying to. "Actually, I am a consultant to the manufacturing groups around the country." He tries making conversation.

"Really, that's interesting." She does her best to sound uninterested.

She opens the door. After it opens, she realizes it is a mistake. He sips his huge coffee and smells the essence. He likes sitting where he is.

"Was the granola bar good?" Sam asks.

It is time to close the door. "Frankly, I have work to do, please give me my space."

Catherine crosses her legs and leans to the right, trying to close off and distance herself from him. She can't take all the books and leave; she'll just take notes. She has at least a good hour left. He closes his lips, and his chin moves toward his neck. His stare is empty. After three minutes, he leaves his coffee, quickly stands up, and walks to the magazine section. He selects a *Car and Driver* and walks back to his still-steaming brew and the chilly lady.

* * *

As soon as she sat down with her granola treat, he knew he had to sit next to her. Her plain looks attract him. After spending all his dating life with flashy women, he wants the experience of a nondescript, intellectual one. The plain looks and pile of books seem to meet the criteria. She probably teaches geophysics at Harvard.

Once he sits down, his sixth sense alerts him that he is seeing what she really is. Just a sense, nothing for sure. The subject matter of the books confirms that he has to find out about her. This may be a great contact, in every respect. The conversation isn't exactly warm and cuddly; that turns him on. Nothing like being turned on by a negative, wormy-looking intellectual in a crowded bookstore. The thought is exciting, peeling off her layers of inhibition.

Like a splash of cold water, he feels a chill go down his spinal cord when he spots Adam approaching the table. Sam picks up his magazine and buries his face in it. Adam sits at the adjacent table, not positioned to look at them. Sam is figuring out his exit strategy when he notices the two detectives seated by the doorway. Is the bookworm across from him an undercover cop? Is this a setup? There is only one way to find out.

* * *

Vito has to admit, the coffee is good. Just like the fancy coffeemaker in the conference room back at the station house. All his wife would make him was instant coffee in the morning. Another reason to be suspicious of her.

Lamar appears deep in thought. "It was worth the wait. Great stuff. I like good French roast with a touch of mocha java thrown in." Lamar has to analyze everything.

"Just what I was thinking." Actually, he once arrested a hooker from the other side of town whose name was Mocha Java. Vito analyzes on a different wavelength.

"How can you be looking through a book about dog breeds when we have serious issues to consider?" Lamar never lets it go.

Vito wonders if Lamar has a life outside of the force. Looking through the history of corgis, Vito feels good that Bentley has lost weight under Adam's guidance. If only he could do the same for himself. Looking around the room, he sees the professorial lady seated by a pile of books. She isn't alone as a male companion is reading a magazine at her table. And there is Adam at the next table. Boston really is a small town. He has to go over and see how his new roommate is doing. He helps himself to the open seat at Adam's table.

"Hey, what a surprise, how are doing?"

"Fine. Is this how you and Lamar work hard on the weekends? Are you guys on the hot trail for a good spy novel?"

"Naw, you know Lamar and his coffee fetish." Vito looks down at the book on the table.

"You like looking at the women in these positions?"

"Only in real life."

"What is that you are reading?"

Adam tells him about his yoga adventure. All Vito can think about is that there's no way he is ever going to do that. He notices the woman at the next table with the pile of books with the man reading the magazine. They are a quiet couple. The books are all on the same subject, pharmaceuticals. Hey, maybe he has found his expert. He stands up, pushes his chair back, and walks over to the next table.

* * *

Catherine is buried in the sequence of outsourcing compounds to manufacture tablets. She actually finds it interesting. Her new tablemate is buried in a magazine devoted to Corvettes and is ignoring her. Occasionally she glances at him, but very briefly. His angular face, slicked-back dark hair, and lean body intrigue her. He has a presence that is difficult to ignore. A huge shadow suddenly blocks the light. She looks up, and a wide, large darkly-dressed man is standing over her. The dark presence looks at both of them.

Vito stares at her and smiles. "Hi, my name is Vito Castellano, detective with the Boston PD."

The end of the sentence elicits a slight jerk of the head and a reflexive twitch in her table companion. She looks up without expression on her face. Behind the blankness is a blanket of protection. If needed, a very large blanket.

"Yes, what I can help you with?" Her tablemate is staring at an article on comparative brake linings, like he cared.

"I couldn't help notice that you are reading about pharmaceuticals. May I ask why?" Her first thought is that it is none of his business. But logic dictates; he may be an ally in her quest. She has to think quickly and do so in the framework of her new persona. Putting herself together to present a package of ultimate professionalism, she responds, "I am gathering information for a paper on drug manufacturing and possible problems that may occur with processing."

"Do you know anything about people selling drugs that are tainted or stolen and the fake drugs finding their way to patients?" Vito always gets to the point.

Sam's upper body is rigid; his feet are moving as if his calves are contracting. He can't just abruptly stand up and leave. He is convinced that this is a setup. They all are out to get him. He places his right hand over his eyebrows.

"Excuse me, I need to get a refill and look at some new paperbacks. Feel free to use my chair."

Within two seconds, Sam is on-line for a refill. It takes more than two seconds for Vito to sit down and share the table. The woman called Fern that they were all looking for is in arm's length from them. None of them realizes that. Except her, the now Ms. Crosby Jones. How can Catherine use this to her advantage?

* * *

Lamar is in his own observation tower. After reveling in the French roast blend in his cup, he reaffirms why he is there. It is developing into more than the coffee. It is good to see Adam feeling better and relaxing. He realizes how wired Adam had been in the station house.

The tall thin fellow at the table that Vito is standing over could fit the description of the man with the Lopez lady who swept through Adam's place. This guy's body language seems out of place for what is occurring. Lamar would like to question him. Sam stands, leaving his jacket at the table, and walks over to the counter to refill his French roast. Lamar wants to size up the fellow. He wonders about Vito's style, but not his results. He has his own way to uncover information, but then again, don't we all?

* * *

"Hey, Adam, move your chair back, I need some room."

I am trying to understand the diagram of "The Eight Limb Path of Yoga" from my new book when my Buddha-like friend moves in like a defensive lineman from the New England Patriots.

"Sure, give me a second, OK?"

Vito actually looks at his watch. The scary part is I don't know if he is serious about the timing. I move the book back and slide the chair in the opposite direction. Standing up, I survey the room. I notice Lamar is not seated at his table; he is walking to the counter with his mug, looking at the tall guy that Vito dispossessed. So there is Vito elbowing me to sit down with the bookworm I had tripped over and Lamar walking, looking at the bookworm's tablemate. All I need to see is the bright vest of the Lopez lady walking through the door. I wonder if they serve margaritas here. I figure I will find out next week in our Monday morning meeting at the station house.

"You have enough room?"

"Thanks."

I notice the librarian-looking woman across from Vito eyeing me during this whole transaction. She must be wondering how I am so familiar with the big guy. Wow, I'm thinking too much. Let's get back on one of the yoga limbs. I have to read some of this stuff; I have a class tomorrow morning. But I can't leave yet; I have to watch my partners in action.

* * *

Catherine is in fear of being discovered. She needs more information about the illegal drug transactions before meeting with the police. Yet there she is, sitting with the detective that is trying to locate Fern and trying to figure her place in this confusing picture. She is convinced she is on track with one scam. Drug companies sell a large volume of drugs at a wholesale price to locations outside of the continental United States. Puerto Rico is one such a place. Cargo planes with discounted drugs turn around and land in Florida, and their contents are resold at a higher price to middlemen who turn around and resell them for another increased price to pharmacies and other middlemen. If the patients are lucky, these medications are kept under proper temperature and humidity conditions to maintain their potency. That usually is not the case. Ms. Crosby Jones looks at the bulk sitting across from her. His hands are on the table, and both move to an open-palm position as if to say, "Talk to me." She does.

"I've heard about the counterfeit drug problem. I feel sorry for the patients." Vito drops the smile and somberly stares at her. "It can kill people."

"Obviously. What do you want from me?"

"Maybe you can help us."

"How?"

"We have some general information about the scams and what's happening in the bogus drug trade. It's all standard computer stuff. We need someone with an insight to this to work with us and, maybe, be part of the team."

"Do I get paid as a consultant?"

"We have a few dollars set aside for this sort of thing."

"Give me your card and I'll get back to you."

"Fine, when will we hear from you?"

She breathes deeply and thinks how fascinating this is becoming, a chance to get on the inside while keeping a foot on the outside. "I'll call Monday, one way or the other. Now please, let me get back to my work."

Vito stands up slowly and places his card on the table. "Looking forward to talking with you."

He has his chubby hand out. Ms. Crosby Jones stands up and briefly shakes his paw. With a noncommittal look on her face, she limps to the ladies' room. She hopes they will all be gone when she comes back to the table. Seeing Adam again isn't easy.If she were Fern and they were in the park or a trendy bar, it would be different. That's how confident she is about who she is or was. She would have liked to spend some time with him. The mystery of his past and who he is interests her. Is it emotion or just another challenge?

* * *

Sam is starting to feel squeezed. He just can't walk out; it will be obvious to the cop that he is running from something. He has to try to blend in with the crowd. He refills his cup with decaf so he won't be bouncing off the walls.

"It's half price for a second round, but espresso shots are extra." The skinny spiked-hair tattoo lady was replaced by short well-spoken black lady. No tattoos on display.

"How about house decaf?"

"Room for milk or crème?"

"Yeah."

Strange, he has a feeling that someone is watching him, and it is not his tablemate. He slides the money across the counter, and his cold hands grab the burning cup. His hands are still cold.

"Excuse me; do you like the house blend?"

He hears that from behind him, but not knowing it is directed his way, he walks back toward the magazine section. Delaying a decision on his next move is easy when staring at the *Sports Illustrated* cover girl edition. It is like a *Playboy* cover with the challenge of needing to use your imagination. Just a little.

"I never thought *Sports Illustrated* would be publishing this stuff."

It is the same voice he heard at the coffee counter. Turning around, he realizes it is the tall black man who was the cop's partner. Obviously, he must be part of the detective duo looking for him. They fit the description of the information he got from the inside cop, the Redpath lady. It is time to be a pro. He turns and faces the tall cop.

Smiling he says, "I guess they're checking if these babes are on steroids."

The black fellow picks up his own copy. He slowly turns the pages. "I'm sure there were some visits to the plastic surgeon."

"Hey, we're both pretty cynical. Maybe they're just gorgeous and work out a lot."

"Sure. You know, you look familiar to me."

Sam's hands are getting even colder as his body is becoming more rigid. He squeezes the paper cup a bit too hard. He doesn't react to the small amount of hot coffee burning him. This isn't what he planned on for a quiet escape to the bookstore.

"You get this magazine regularly?"

Lamar keeps the same noncommittal stare during this whole conversation. His eyes are not moving, but he surveys this fellow's reactions to all the stimuli. Nothing he learned at the academy, just an ability he has. That is one reason he reached detective at the age of thirty two.

"Why, do you sell subscriptions?"

Sam forces a smile. His coffee drinking gives his teeth a tan tinge. Back in Miami he sees his dentist for bleaching once every two weeks. No charge, just an envelope of white powder slipped into his doc's coat.

"No, but my picture was in there a few years ago."

Lamar finally changes his expression. This is becoming interesting. "That must be it, but I forgot. What was it for?"

"I ran track for Miami and just missed making the Olympic team by 0.08 of a second."

"That's where I saw you. I was at the same trials."

Sam doesn't know what to make of all this. He never felt comfortable with the word *trials*.

"What event were you running?"

Lamar will never forget that day. He trained for years only to have his right foot hit the last hurdle and slow him down enough to be out of the picture. He remembers being alone in the locker room and crying.

"Two-hundred-meter hurdles. I had some bad luck and missed out also. I know the disappointment."

All of a sudden the two men on opposite sides of the law have something in common. "You look like you stay in shape, still running?"

Lamar can't help but like it when someone recognizes his athleticism. "Yeah, you?"

"I jog, about five miles every other day."

"Well, it sounds like we ought to share a run one day, talk about the old days in training."

Sam has no choice but to say, "Sure. Look, I have to get some stuff done; maybe I'll see you out there one day."

The cop in Lamar sees an opportunity. "Hey, let's exchange numbers and touch base. A run goes quicker with a buddy." He says this as he places the magazine back on the shelf. He looks up, and his new track mate is suspiciously nowhere to be seen.

* * *

Lamar and Vito are both staring without seeing anything. Vito is staring in the direction of the ladies' room, waiting for the lady he left his card with to return to her table. Lamar is staring at the outside window and wondering how he screwed up. The guy he spoke with had to be the suspect they were looking for. Why else would he disappear? Vito is lamenting his basic error. He can't believe he never got the name and number of the women he spoke with. What if she doesn't come out of the bathroom? He's seen everything happen in his career. He remembers her limping with her back to him. Oh well, he'll just sit and wait. He gets paid to do that. He wonders what Lamar's quiet deal is. Those things just didn't happen to Lamar. Lamar's gut is feeling like he hit the last hurdle again. It is not a good feeling, one he never shares with anybody in the department.

Vito breaks the ice. "Hey, what's going on? What are you thinking about?"

"First tell me about that lady you were talking to."

Vito has to sugarcoat it. "Great news. We may have found the drug expert we're looking for to add to the team."

Lamar just stares at him with a little smile. "Oh, I thought you were looking for a date."

"Not my type. She was pretty tough, wouldn't give me her name. But she said she'll call me Monday to say whether she'll work with us or not."

"Tell me more about her."

Realizing he has nothing else to tell him, Vito thinks fast. "She said if she's interested in working with us, she'll call for an interview. This way I didn't have to give too much away about us and how much we don't know."

"Good work. We'll see how it shakes out Monday."

Vito is happy with himself. If only he could figure out his wife as easily. "What have you been thinking about?"

Lamar looks down at his cup for two seconds, looks outside, then at his partner. He inhales through his nose three times without moving. Vito feels like he is sitting at a poker game.

"I think I may have talked to one of our suspects in this murder case. He fits the profile, and he just vanished when I looked away for a second." They both recognize that behavior. If you are not sticking around, there's a reason.

"Get anything on him."

Lamar takes a magazine out of a green plastic bag announcing the name of the bookstore.

"Hey, I gotta check this out."

Lamar has never seen Vito move this fast. His hand is quicker than his partner's. He grabs Vito's wrist firmly. "I'm looking for his prints, not yours." He puts the *Sports Illustrated* back in the bag and smiles. "Sorry, you'll have to buy your own copy of the enhanced girls."

Vito sits back and smiles. Even when both of them could have done better, they bring back some goodies to promote their cause. He leans back on the chair and hears a creaky sound. Then his visual sense kicks in. He notices his potential expert limp back to her table. Vito looks at the plastic bag and the table where he questioned the limping intellect.

"After you're done with your second round of java, let's pay our respects to Adam and head back."

"Sounds good."

* * *

"Do not take counsel of your fears."

I am randomly turning pages of the book I am about to buy. This quote on page 78 by General Barry McCaffrey stares at me. I cannot turn to the next page. I didn't think I had any fears before I met Fern. I was in a nice little cocoon, just keeping things simple. Then I met her, someone who was in and out of my life in one evening and spun it out of control. An occasional thought entered my mind about her, but I have to let it go. Then a windfall of events opened chapters in a new book that makes me think about myself in new ways. Some good, some unknown.

"See you later at the condo."

I wonder, is this book good for me? I look up and see my two detective buddies, which removes me from my introspective mode. "Sure. I'll take the crew out for a walk after I eat dinner. If you're back before ten o'clock, it's your turn."

"No problem. I should be back around nine."

"See you then."

Looking at Lamar, I say, "What time do you want me in station house on Monday?"

"We have an early meeting. We'll get together in the conference room at 10:00 a.m."

"See you then."

Before leaving, Vito makes it a point to introduce Lamar to the possible pharmaceutical expert at the next table. Vito smiles as he walks out. She now has a name. I turn to her and smile. She doesn't return my smile.

"Ms. Jones, I'm sorry about tripping over you. May I buy you another coffee or something to eat?"

She runs her left hand quickly through her very short black hair. Without expression she replies, "No."

I watch her as she turns her gaze back onto the book she is reading. Her high cheekbones and full lips hold my gaze. They remind me of someone; I just cannot pinpoint who or when. As far as she is concerned, it is as if I don't exist. Seeing the subject of the pile of books on her table and her focus, I assume she is a PhD candidate at some college. Whatever. Taking a deep breath and staring at the contemporary bright painting on the wall makes me realize how everything we do is just interpreting circumstances. Wow, I'm getting deep again. I need to go home and chill out. A long walk with my four-legged buddies will help ground me.

Walking through the marvelous wood doors at home with my purchase in hand, I sense another chapter opening. I just have to remember, *Do not take counsel of your fears.*

* * *

Settling into the Ford and strapping on the seat belt for the boring ride to the station house, it hits Vito. There is something strange going on. Something was not right with that woman who introduced herself as Ms. Crosby Jones. It is bouncing back and forth in his gut. With Lamar behind the wheel, they sit forever in front of every stoplight in Boston. Or it just seems so. Lamar is quiet. He is looking forward to clearing his mind out with dinner at his girlfriend's apartment. He isn't thinking about the case now and feels relieved.

"She was limping!"

Vito is yelling. Lamar looks at him as if he lost his mind. "I know. I saw that earlier. No big deal."

"Maybe a miracle occurred in the ladies' room."

"What the hell are you talking about?"

"On the way in she limped on her right side. On the way out she limped on her left side."

Lamar looks with an open mouth at Vito. The light is green, and he doesn't hear the car horns blasting.

Chapter 24

Sam feels pressure. He has a feeling that the game is over. The world that he and the Lopez lady created is being invaded. He can't believe that this cop at the coffeehouse was really interested in his athletic history. The odds are small that his tablemate was just an academic information gatherer in the world of pharmaceuticals. Like, who really cares about that stuff? That's why they were so successful; it was easy to fly under the radar.

The deals they made may have harmed some people, but they never made page one. As soon as he sees the black cop turn back to the magazine section, Sam bolts out of the store. No one gives him a second look. Many people in Boston take off in a rush to make their train or bus. He is lucky; a woman just opened the large wood door from the outside for him. Before she lets go of the large brass handle, he slides out without saying a word or making any eye contact. Not running, but at a brisk pace, he moves in the opposite direction of where his apartment is. Reaching the Italian section of Boston, he is among the Saturday-afternoon tourists. He'll stop at a bar and nurse a beer for an hour. That will give him time to think about the recent events and decide what his next move will be.

* * *

Before I knew it, Ms. Jones and I were the only players left in our little group at the coffee shop. Our goodbye was one-sided, and I just wanted to get the hell out of there. I'm not thinking about the case even though my police friends never seem to leave me. Monday morning is close enough. I need space from all this. Enough has happened in too short a time.

Once out of the bookstore, the Saturday-afternoon crowd brings me back to reality. It feels good to breathe the outside air. Never say fresh air in the city. Any city. My mind isn't clear. I feel out of sorts. The city air and the usual sites on my walk home are like reciting the alphabet. I decide to turn around and walk through the Italian section. The canine crew has the ability to wait another hour or so. I am in the tourist crowd;

I hate crowds. What the hell am I doing? I see a cozy-looking little bar across the street. Why not treat myself to a beer. I need a counter to all the afternoon caffeine.

Standing on the street corner, I wait for the light to change to a friendly green. The green hand lights up, and I am off to the cute little watering hole. The green and red awning and old metallic doors give the place a unique look. There is a brass railing on the outside of the large dark window that invites me to lean on it and peek into the bar. The place is packed, which immediately tells me to go home. On my second look, I think I see a familiar face. This is becoming ridiculous. I have to stop seeing people I think I know all the time. Besides, I realize a beer the day before my next yoga session in the hot room is not a good idea. I am such a good boy. I will go home.

The walk home goes quickly.

Opening the familiar doors, the members of the canine gang greet me in their own special ways. Fern goes to the umbrella stand and plucks her blue leash out and walks down to the landing. Bentley runs around in a circle until I manage to grab his black collar and clip on his black leather leash. He always runs in one or two more circles just to show who is in charge. Bowser, well, he sits down and watches the show. As a well-bred bulldog, he measures his energy expense. His eyes look at his fellow roommates, then at me, as if to say, "OK, I'll join the gang." He waddles up to me, and with a red cloth leash in hand, I attach it to his red cloth collar. With Bowser and Bentley in hand, I slowly manage the stairs to the bottom landing where Fern is waiting with her leash in mouth. I hook her up, and off I go to the park with my crew.

A number of times, strangers have walked up to me for my card; they assume I am the local professional dog walker. Just such an event occurs after ten minutes in the park. A young couple approaches me.

"Excuse us, are you the local canine helper?" Their accents are distinctly British.

"No, they're all mine." My accent is distinctly American.

"Sorry, how do you manage with three?"

"Actually, quite well."

Just the type of mindless conversation that feels good. They nod and walk away. Oh well, time to feed the trio and myself.

Chapter 25

She knows her partner in crime has returned by the smell that just entered the room. Not turning her head as the door closes, she mutters, "I hope you didn't do anything stupid." The smell of beer makes her open the window. She has just cleaned herself up and applied the cheapest perfume she can tolerate. Blending in with the neighborhood is an insult to her.

Sam looks at the Lopez lady in her ill-fitting outfit and just shakes his head. "I didn't have time to, I was surrounded by cops."

"What the hell?"

"Yeah, I don't know if they were trying to trap me or what."

"What do you mean?"

"The shrink was there with the two cops that we've been watching. There was also a lady that had to be with them, but I'm not sure."

"What do you mean not sure?"

"She didn't seem to be with them, they didn't seem to know her. But you know, it could be part of a set-up."

"Did that Adam guy know her?"

"He was talking to her. They even talked in one of the aisles."

"What else?"

"She was a wormy chick, but the books she was reading caught my eye."

"What books?"

"Books about making pills. Who reads that stuff? She has to have some link in this. I just can't figure what."

With her bejeweled left hand on her upper lip, Isabella looks at her companion in crime. He turns to the fridge and grabs a can of Bud, pops it open, and takes a long chug. He barely finishes swallowing when he feels a sharp sting across his left cheek. Trying to figure it out before the second slap is impossible.

"You fucking idiot!" Sam lifts his hand and puts it down when he sees the expression on her face. He'll get even later.

"You fucking idiot!" He moved away toward the door.

"You're not going anywhere. Sit your skinny ass down and let's figure this out."

He has two choices: Bolt out the door and let her cool down. The second choice makes more sense: let her think she is in charge and sit down like a good soldier. Placing the cool can against his cheek, he pulls up a chair from the table. Flipping it backward, he sits with his arms over the back.

Running her hands through her hair, Isabella stares at him with wide eyes. "OK, tell me everything." She continues to pace around the room.

He tells her all about his afternoon at the bookstore. He then remembered the last scary fact. "Shit, I put the magazine back on the stand." They both know what that could mean.

"We have to get out of Boston."

Sam looks directly at Isabella. There is a heat emanating from her presence. She looks like one angry babe. His mind is racing. Hey, he had two years of college and sold more drugs than he used. His mind is still an asset. Time to take charge. "I agree, we have to get out of here. But the deal is sweet, we can't lose control. Let's find a place that's not too far away and where our profile can be low."

She looks at him and nods. "We have to go somewhere where our local contact can meet us for the payoff without us sticking out too much."

The transfer of the pills is happening as they speak. He will monitor it and order a change in route. This could work.

"We have to leave here without anybody noticing us."

She is beginning to look rational, though not quite there yet. "Easy, we go food shopping with the rental car, just head out from there."

"Yeah, the rent we paid in advance covers us for this dump."

"Yeah."

"Where are we going?" Sam smiles and finishes his beer.

Standing up he moves his chair to the side. His left hand puts the beer can down on the table. The back of his right arm moves across his mouth. Walking over to where Isabella stands, the force of the back of his hand across her face propels her against the wall. With his palms on each side of her head and his body pressed against hers, she welcomes his lips.

Chapter 26

I like my eggs well-done. It's nice to know salmonella bacteria won't be joining me for dinner. Eggs and an apple for dessert. Just getting ready for the yoga crowd. The class Sunday morning is at eight thirty, so I start to plan my routine. I set up the same outfit I wore for my first class. The table is set for my morning meal, the coffee machine is loaded with beans and water, and a note is on the table for Vito to not disturb anything.

My canine troopers are settled on their own places, and I find my spot in the leather chair. I don't turn on the television. The new book is on my lap, and I stare at it. I think about seeing Aleni as my morning teacher. I am being in the moment. I am proud of myself. The soft cover feels smooth to my hands. The picture on the front is nice to look at.

I randomly open the book. I am looking at page 39. My eyes settle in the middle of the page. "If we knew who we really were, there would be no need for practices like yoga." I take the book into the bedroom. I read that sentence over and over.

* * *

I beat the alarm this morning. What an accomplishment. Hitting the round old clock before its noise hits me makes me feel like I'm in charge. It's amazing how I rationalize neurotic insomnia to a win-loss situation. I should be happy a nocturnal seizure didn't occur. I have often read that meditation is one step to control seizures. Now I have a bona fide therapeutic reason to enter a hot room with half-naked, glistening women. Women don't sweat; they glisten. Or glow. I'm getting too fixated on this issue, time to start the coffee, shower, and take my friends out. Either I am exhausted or Vito is learning to be quieter around the place. I didn't hear his entry into the condo last evening. I must have been out of it.

The different color bowls all line up for feeding time, and the gang plunges in to munch. Of course, they go to different bowls each time. I can never figure why they don't care where their food is placed. With respect to my oncoming self-induced dehydration, I limit myself to one cup of coffee.

Listening to the chomping in the background, I mindlessly stare out the bay window. It is quiet. A typical Charlestown Sunday morning. I will leave it to Vito to sort out the Sunday newspaper groupings in the stairwell.

Picking up my gym bag with a change of clothes in it, I head out for my yoga class. At least I have some idea what to expect this time. Then again, my teacher is different and knows me. I hope I meet her expectations. It is overcast and windy. The kind of weather that makes you ask yourself, "Why am I out of bed this morning?"

* * *

Aleni loves her Sunday-morning class. She stopped going to church a long time ago, much to her parents' chagrin. It wasn't as much the religious thing; they thought it was her best chance of meeting a nice Greek boy.

She is a perpetual questioner of everything about life. Her study of yoga grounds her. It slows her down and gives her the chance to look at everything in new ways. She ended her relationship with a lawyer from New York about six months ago. He had an answer for everything. At least he thought he did. It was not the traveling to see him that became annoying; it was him.

She hardly knows Adam yet finds him interesting. He has a mixture of maturity and vulnerability that she finds attractive. The age difference doesn't enter into the equation. Maybe it does, in ways she is not quite sure of. Hopefully, he will be in class. She decides that if he is part of the group, the focus will be on fundamentals.

The early hour is so quiet. It is wonderful. She never takes notice of the weather. She has learned not to think about things she cannot control. Nodding to the crowd in the corner Dunkin' Donuts reassures her of her self-control. It reminds her of the days she lived on butternut crunch donuts and black coffee. Now it is yoga, granola, and green tea.

Being the first one to open the building, she turns off the alarm and takes the elevator to the dark gym. Arriving two hours before class gives her time for her own practice. Seeking inner peace. A constant search. Turning on the lights and walking to the studio, the patter of her feet echoes off the old brick walls. Entering the studio, she leaves the windows covered and the lights off. Once again, the image of Adam is in her mind. She senses his life is in a floating transitional mode. He appears strong yet floundering. She will hold his hand and guide him through his confusing journey. Time to clear her mind for her own practice.

Chapter 27

The newly minted, limping Ms. C. Jones is finishing her fact gathering. The store is ordering *Dangerous Doses* by Katherine Eban for her. It will take five days. That book is the best reference to real-life events about the counterfeit drug trade.

Looking around, she is the last of the dynamic, strange gang that was thrown together in the last hour. The hardest part was pretending she didn't recognize Adam. She was tempted to ask about Fern and what beer was in the fridge. But that would have ended her cover and the chance of staying a step ahead of the drug baddies. Besides, being someone else is a buzz. The idea of working with the cops was something she had never thought of before. Why not? She didn't have to tell them everything she knew. The information they have will be at her fingertips. Sounds like a good deal. If things get tough or a little scary, she can always call on her cop friends to bail her out. She thinks about the guy who shared her table. Scary, interesting, and he bolted out without a goodbye. He is so much like part of the couple she is tracking who were part of turnaround deal with the stolen AIDS drug Seriatim. One of the facts she gathered was about this Miami couple who organized a system that buys Medicaid patients' medications from them. They don't pay much for the drugs, the patients just want cash. Using fake invoices, they re-label and repack the drugs to look like new. They then sell these "new" medications back to the drugstores or to a wholesale house for a higher price. But their price is lower than the name brand competitor. It's amazing how many Medicaid patients would rather have cash than their meds. If they end up in an emergency clinic, the treatment is free. These guys are so smooth that the buyers never look twice at the newly minted, forged invoice.

This dude at her table was like the tall thin partner of the Hispanic lady. She can't pinpoint what the difference is. Anyway, she feels comfortable that nobody recognized her. She looks forward to phoning the detective she met and negotiating a deal to be part of his team. She doesn't need the money; it's just part of who Ms. Jones is all about.

Holding her notes, she leaves the bookstore with a feeling of accomplishment. On her walk back to the Marriott Residence Inn, her mind is racing about what to do next. She doesn't notice the uneven curb as she steps to cross the street. Her right ankle twists slightly, forcing her to limp back to the hotel.

Chapter 28

Vito is enjoying his Sunday morning. Adam has left, the dogs are walked, and the coffee is fresh. Better yet, the *Boston Globe* sports section is at his fingertips. His wife never permitted newspapers on the table. Instant coffee and no newspapers, why the hell did he marry her? Vito is settling into this new life. He isn't stupid; he knows his welcome will wear out.

He grabs his second bagel to toast and glances at Bentley staring out the front window. Before, Bentley couldn't jump up to the window perch. The Adam diet has him fit and active. He stares at his corgi. *I can do that.* The bagel goes back into the freezer. He grabs an apple. A new goal. On his second bite he thinks about that bookish broad with the fake limp. It is obvious she is hiding something. He'll touch base with Lamar early on Monday for a strategy of dealing with her.

First, they have to make sure she is clean. Then again, if she isn't, they could use her as a plant without her knowing it. He likes working with Lamar even though he never offers any information about his private life. The guy is smart and probably alone. Too bad, not his problem. He closes the paper and turns to the phone on the pass through to the kitchen. It is white and always clean. He knows to wipe it down before Adam returns.

The only time he hears his wife is on his office voice mail. It hurts, but he dials the number. The high-pitched voice is familiar. "I got your department paycheck; your portion is in the mail to that address you left. I'm going to look for a job. I need more money." That was it. Not even a question about the corgi. He feels empty. He needs someone to fill the emptiness. It is coming to the time when he will schedule a meeting with her. He'll ask the guys how to get a good divorce lawyer. Erasing her voice is starting to be something he looks forward to.

A second message is beeping to be heard. He hits the right buttons.

"Detective Castellano, this is Ms. Crosby Jones. You introduced yourself to me at the bookstore yesterday. I have considered your proposal and have concluded that we meet at your office. I have to evaluate your work environment and goals as you, equally, must vet me. Therefore, what day and time do you suggest?"

Vito stares at the phone and says to himself, "This broad is whacked out of her head." Taking a breath, he returns, "I will talk with my colleagues and get back to you Monday." He smiles. If the guys he worked with heard him calling them "colleagues," he'd be buying the beer for a month.

No more messages. It was time to check the Celtics schedule.

Chapter 29

It looks like a scene from an old French movie. Clothes are all over the apartment. The blanket in the bedroom is on the floor. The couple languidly looks up at the ceiling. They are both staring, but not at each other. They share a feeling of satisfaction.

The look on Isabella's face is not revealing her thoughts. Her hair going in every direction, clutching the sheet up to her neck, she wonders how it is so good with someone she doesn't like, much less love. The air is heavy with humidity from the open windows. It isn't warm, just humid. She moves sideways to be in position to retrieve the quilt on the floor. Her partner in bed interprets her movement differently.

Chapter 30

I read a few chapters of the new book in bed. Some of the ideas are bouncing in my mind. I am actually looking forward to the hot room. I can't help wonder, if all this wisdom originated in India, why do they have such a poverty-stricken stratified society?

Here I go again, thinking too much. The foyer in the building that houses the gym has maintained its original look. It's amazing how old brick with modern lighting can look warm. Not cozy, just warm. I enter the elevator to the gym. At least I know where the yoga room is. Taking my shoes off and leaving my coat on the hook, I carry my mat, towel, and water bottle into the room.

The heat is welcome, and I place my mat down behind the first good-looking woman I see, near the corner. Placing my towel over the top of the mat, I take a drink of water. The room is half full, and class is scheduled to start in fifteen minutes. Aleni is in the corner with her back to the students. She is wearing black tights with a low-cut black top. How am I going not to look? It appears as if she is adjusting the sound system. I observe the class, mostly women on their backs or practicing poses. I sit, legs crossed, eyes open, and pretend I am thinking something ethereal. The room fills quickly, and Aleni stands facing the class.

She smiles. "It is a beautiful day, as all days are."

Was this going to be a '60s rerun? I look around again. Well, love, drugs, and sex—I can pass on the drugs. Before I know it, we are all intoning "ohm."

Aleni speaks, "Today I will concentrate on the fundamentals of yoga. Breathing and posture are so important."

I can stand up straight and breathe, so I should be all right.

A half hour into the program I am soaked and struggling with the poses. My neck muscles are tight, and my jaw is clenched shut. When I am in trouble, I try to remember that the book kept stressing it is a process. I figure I was at the ground floor of the yoga process. Aleni then leads us into the standing postures. That is, for everyone but me. I develop my technique for falling postures. Funny, I can stand on one leg with hockey skates and full gear in all game conditions on ice but not half naked in bare feet on a little blue mat.

Jaw clenched, standing on two legs, a new sensation envelops me. The warmth of Aleni's body is pressed against me from my right side. Her right hand gently moved down my neck to my tight trapezium muscle.

She whispers into my right ear, "This is not a competition."

It isn't just the heat in the room that radiates through me. I melt. Closing my eyes, with her body against my side, I lift my right leg. I breathe slowly. I breathe slowly and deliberately. Her warmth slowly leaves me. I open my eyes and focus on the grain in the wood floor. I smile. I am sweetly lost in the moment. My first understanding of the yoga experience.

I am the last to leave the yoga room. Aleni and I make eye contact, and she smiles. I am buzzed, relaxed, and confused. My whole life has been a competition. My brain is trying to find a place to register this morning's events. There is no such place.

* * *

"You didn't leave a note, where were you? I was getting worried."

"What are you, my Italian mother?"

"You got some of that right, I am Italian."

"I'll tell you after I shower."

"It looks like you just had a shower."

"I did."

The shower is on, and I let the water wash the salty sweat off me. I am breathing in a slow sequence. I am imaging the total morning experience. I remember the moment Aleni guided me in the standing sequence. I replay the words she said to me. Over and over. I sit down on the tile floor, breathing slowly. It was nice, I had my own spa. It was all in the mind.

Old jeans and a historic-frayed sweatshirt are just right for this Sunday afternoon. Vito is sitting at the dining table. The sections of the *Boston Globe* are everywhere. He is wearing dark blue Adidas sweats bought on sale. The stripes running down the side don't enhance his profile.

"I thought you were drowning."

In a way, I was. "No, just enjoying the warm water on my sore muscles."

"You said you were going to the gym and doing a yoga class. You get sore doing that stuff?"

"Yeah."

"Maybe I should try it. You never know I might meet some babe."

It's time to change the subject. "Do I need to do anything to prepare for tomorrow's meeting?"

"No. Just think about what you know about this drug stuff. Oh, don't forget about the characters we're looking for. I have to call that woman I met at the bookstore and set up a meeting. I need to speak to Lamar and see what the deal is."

"OK, I'll just chill this afternoon. Maybe you and I will take the pooches out for long walk later."

"Sure."

With the word *walk* in the air, Fern jumps down from the couch and runs for her leash. Her two friends glance at her and go back to sleep. I look at Fern sternly and say, "No." With her mouth on her blue leash, she walks to the door. I follow.

Chapter 31

Sam has never been in love. He just likes sex. The variety of women keeps him interested. Another challenge. His present challenge can't stand him. That's why he enjoys her so much.

Lying in bed on a lazy Sunday morning, his mind is racing. They have to have a plan. They have to execute it. The bacon and eggs smell good. Over breakfast he'll run a few ideas by his reluctant but satisfied partner.

"I can't eat this, it's not cooked enough."

Isabella has bathed and smells like the flowered scent on sale at CVS. Her hair is tied back, and she is wearing black sweatpants with a tight purple top. She doesn't look bad. She looks at Sam and smiles. "Cook your own breakfast."

He doesn't answer her as he walks into the bathroom. Fifteen minutes later he remerges with his hair still wet and dressed to go out. Old jeans, yesterday's shirt, and black shoes.

She is glad when the door closes, and he is on the other side. Sam can't wait to get to the corner diner. He always thinks things out best alone. Writing on those little paper napkins gives him a sense of security. They are so easy to tear up and dump into the trash cans as he walks back to the apartment.

The chubby waitress with the yellow smile places his order on the table. He has a booth to himself. The well-done, over easy eggs and home fries are done just right. He knows it is foolish, but they will help him regain his feeling of control; he wants to leave in forty-eight hours. He will rent a car with a false identification card and destroy the card at their destination. He draws a circle within a two-hour drive from where they are. He'll check out the towns on the computer when he returns to the apartment. He has a pretty good idea of what they should do. He leaves cash for the meal, and the three cups of coffee have him moving quickly back to the apartment.

He finds Isabella doing her nails, watching some stupid television show. She goes to light up a cigarette, and he rips it from her hand. "Listen to me, I have a plan."

"Fine, I'm all ears."

"Look, in about a week we need to meet the drug buyers for a payoff. It can't be here, the cops are smelling us out."

Isabella changes her expression from total boredom to serious attention. "I know, we agreed to leave this dump. But where are we going?"

"I need the computer; I have to scope out what's around a two-hour drive from here." Fifteen minutes later he smiles. "It's better than I thought."

"You talking about last night?"

He ignores her; he is in a different zone. "I have a place that is perfect for us to use as a base."

"Go ahead."

"It's about a two-hour drive from here and about an hour and a half from an airport. The security won't be as tight as at Logan."

"Yeah."

"It's a town with a college right next to it, so all types of people are there. We won't stick out."

"OK."

"We can rent a small house not in a neighborhood so nobody will watch us."

She just stares at him.

"It's got artsy people, so the restaurants are good and cheap. Plus there is shopping at all the towns near them."

She smiles, "It sounds like I may want to stay."

"You won't."

"Why?"

"You'll freeze your nice ass off in the winter."

"OK, where is this paradise?"

"Hanover, New Hampshire."

Chapter 32

The five of us are quite a sight. The three pooches leading the odd couple. Vito holds all three leashes, and I trail behind with the plastic bags of the *NY Times* and the *Boston Globe*. I have quite a handful and am looking for the nearest garbage can. Walking in the dog park is always a great social event. When the five of us materialize from underneath the bridge, all eyes are upon us. We are like Wyatt Earp and his brothers arising from the mist. Well, maybe not that dramatic.

My mind is still on rewind from the morning yoga experience. Vito lets the gang off leash, and the free-for-all begins. Fern struts to all four corners of the park to let the world know it is her turf. Bentley is trying to herd anything that moves into the center of the grass. Bowser sits in the sun and takes it all in. At first he sits and rotates his bulky head to view the crowd. Now satisfied, he is on his belly with a knowing look.

Vito sits on the bench facing the park and a view of the water. He looks content. I dispose of my duty as a good pet owner and sit next to him. The sounds of the cars on the bridge above us are a familiar sound of Boston. Seeing the tourists discover the Freedom Trail is a reassuring sight. Americans know we have a history. Good. What a wonderful Sunday afternoon. I feel good. My mind is open. Please make it last. At least until dinner.

The rest of the gang joins Bowser and us at the bench. It is as if we all breathe together. In sync. It is probably one of those moments that will never happen again.

"You want to go out or bring in for dinner?" No surprise, Vito is thinking about food.

"Bring in."

"Sushi?"

"Sushi."

"My choice?"

"Your choice." Neither one of us moves during this deep and meaningful conversation.

"It's going to get dark soon."
"Yeah, it will get dark." He looks at me as I stare into the park.
"Has yoga sucked out your brains?"
"If it has, I can't wait to go back."
"OK, let's get the group rolling." Vito ends the conversation.

Our Wild West version of herding in Boston moves out. The gang moves with a unique gait under the trestle with the dog-walking park at our back. The Marriott Residence Inn is on our right as we leave the shadows. Before we make the left turn up the hill toward our place, Vito and I stop in our tracks. Standing in front of the Marriott we face an office building with the bay as its view. There is a railed walkway with a view of the USS *Constitution*.

We both look at each other with the same expression. The smartly dressed, attractive woman limping toward us from across the way looks very familiar. He and I don't have to say a word. We walk directly to her. The wind is at our faces. Fern stops, nose angled up in the air. Before we realize it, she takes off. I let go, and with the leash in her mouth she's running towards the woman.

* * *

The woman stops cold. Fern is running full speed with a flying blue leash. We are about twenty yards from catching up with this interesting duo. Before we know it, Fern is jumping up and licking the face of the limping woman. The woman is bending down, leaning to the left. It is obvious her right ankle is not taking much weight. By the time we arrive, she is sitting on a park bench facing the bay. Fern is at her feet, leaning into her. Setting up for a belly rub. Fern only does this with people she knows and likes. There aren't many who fit in that category. My mind is racing faster than my feet. I know it is the person whom Vito met in the bookstore. The same one whom I tripped over in the aisle.

About ten yards from collecting Fern and confronting this woman, I turn to Vito. "What do you think?"

"It's the woman from the bookstore. I'll get more info now."

The closer we get, the less frumpy she looks. She is rubbing Fern's belly. I am jealous.

Five yards from contact, Vito speaks, "Let me do the talking."
"I can't say hello?"
"Only to your dog."

I just look at him. I see a serious expression in his eyes. Showtime. As we approach, Fern sits up to greet her canine roommates. From the outside looking in, it appears like a meeting of old friends.

Vito stands in front of the person we know as Ms. Crosby Jones. "It seems as if you two are old friends. She's only that friendly with people she knows. Where did you meet before?"

She isn't looking at Vito. She looks at me. I have the desire to take her hand and go someplace private. Why? How can this stranger have this affect on me?

Vito sits down next to her. He smiles. "What's with the fake limp?"

"Are you always this charming?"

"I'm a cop, remember?"

She smiles and looks directly at me. What's going on? I am glad Vito is the one talking. "Yes, I left a message for you. Do you have the information for me? Tell me what the structure of the work arrangement will be."

"Stop the bullshit. Answer the question."

"For your information, the limp is real. What do you care?"

"I saw you limp on two different legs. I know what I saw."

She is expressionless as she rolls up her jeans from her right ankle. She undoes the bandage that wraps the swelling on her right ankle. It is swollen and black and blue. "Does this look fake to you? I don't know what you are talking about. You probably need a good night's sleep."

When saying the last three words she again looks at me. Fern licks her swollen ankle. I have never seen Vito speechless. He just looks at her right ankle and back at her face. She is making eye contact with me.

"OK, you have a swollen ankle. Now tell what you are really about. Wouldn't you rather talk to me here than in the station house?"

She smiles. "We'll be there this week, after we settle what you are paying me."

It's a good thing Vito said he would do the talking. "I'll call you tomorrow morning and will make the arrangements."

"I look forward to hearing from you."

During this whole conversation, Fern is getting her belly gently rubbed by this Ms. Crosby Jones. I make a decision. "Vito, why don't you gather the gang and take them to our place? I'll meet you there."

"What about the sushi?"

"Go ahead and order what you like. I'll have whatever you don't want. I'm easy with sushi."

Ms. Jones's gaze is fixed across the bay. In a matter of moments it is the woman and me. It starts to rain. The rain is light and cold. I don't feel it. We both sit on the bench overlooking the bay with a view of the bridge to our right. We are about two feet apart and staring at the same view. As the rain increases, there are fewer and fewer people outside.

I break the silence. "Who are you?" There is no response. No change of expression. "Fern would only act like she did if she knew you. I don't take her to book stores."

I turn to stare at her. The hair and eyes are different, but those are things easily changed. The bone structure, voice, and general demeanor are the same. It is her. The rain picks up and is beyond the refreshing stage. It is soaking. Neither of us moves. Her blouse is soaked, and her breasts are outlined. I feel like I am in some black-and-white European movie.

She stands up, looks at me, and speaks, "Let's get dry. I have a suite at the Marriott. Follow me."

We are quickly in the elevator and out on the sixth floor. Entering room 615, our clothes are off, and fresh towels in our hands. As we dry each other off, I know for sure.

* * *

We dry each other off a second time. This time after a warm shower. She puts on dry sweats, and I put on the one available robe. I didn't bring a change of clothes, obviously.

"I'll take your clothes to the dryer down the hall, do you have any quarters?"

"No."

"I'll put it on your tab."

"I'll pay for room service, will that make us even?"

"Maybe. Be back in a minute."

The door to her suite closes, and total silence is broken only by the rain against the windows. Drying each other off, losing ourselves in each other, and sharing the shower—it is as if we rediscovered each other. It is obvious we have.

"Your clothes will be dry in forty-five minutes. Enjoy the robe."

"Let's order dinner, I'm hungry."

"Don't you think we need to talk?"

She is being the aggressive one, wanting to find out what I'm about. I look at her, without the thick glasses and frumpy clothes; she is my friend, my partner of one night, Fern. Sure, the hair and eye color are different, but women do that all the time. I think. It is a Marriott, so the menu will be simple. She orders the fish; I order the chicken.

"Why should I tell you what I'm about? There's not much to tell. You are the one who got me involved in this, whatever it is. You came in to my life unannounced."

She stares at me and nods. "You're right."

I gather the white robe around my ankles, sit back on the couch, and place my bare feet on the coffee table. I'm not going to talk until she tells me what she is all about. I can wait and stare and stay the night. What concerns me is that it will probably be fine with her.

"You're going to pay for the food in cash?"

I shake my head no.

"Then I'll take care of it. I can't have you with a paper trail to this place."

I nod my head yes.

She tells me her history. The woman I know as Fern is Catherine who calls herself Crosby. I get the story, or I think I do. Dinner arrives, and we eat without speaking.

"How much are you telling the police?"

"That is what I am going to decide tonight. Our reunion makes me think about this a bit differently."

"Look, we're not the enemy. We all want to get these people. Let's meet tomorrow at the station house and figure out what's up." Catherine, Fern, and Crosby—they all look at me at the same time.

"You're right. Let me get your dry clothes. I'll be right back."

I stand up and look out the window. The cloudy sky, wet sidewalks, and dreary view of the covered boats make me really want to stay the night and share her warmth. On returning with my dry, warm clothes I modestly go into the bathroom to get dressed. She is sitting by the desk against the wall working at her computer when I return.

I can't help but ask, "Do you think we can have a real date now?"

She turns and has a radiant smile. You can see familiarity is entering the equation. "Frankly, no. Not if we are going to be working together. I'll see you tomorrow at the police station. Stay dry on your walk home."

I spent my entire career studying human behavior, and I still get surprised. I don't say a word as I turn and walk home.

Chapter 33

They don't have much to pack. They are pros after all. Isabella spends more time on her makeup kit than her suitcase. Sam never travels with more than a small suitcase and an attaché case. He never lets the documents of the deal stray far from his sight. They head out to the local supermarket, looking like a couple shopping for a weekend getaway. They buy all the basics they need at the local IPA and fill the trunk of the rented green Toyota Corolla.

Isabella is impressed with his organizational skills. She knows when to take a seat and let him take charge. By giving him the feeling of control, she feels that she is controlling him. It is easy to find a place to rent. The nice-weather owners are leaving and renting to the winter people. He rents a small one-bedroom cape just off Route 10, between Hanover and Lyme. It is set off the main road by a winding dirt road, and evergreens keep it private. They can come and go without worrying about others watching. Besides, New Englanders keep their distance.

The place is furnished, and the owner stops asking about references when he is paid for the three months in cash.

Their focus is on their first deal. It is the anti-anemia drug, Epogen. It comes from the company Amgen. They actually aren't dealing with the real drug. They have a counterfeit deal working. The patent is still protecting the original which is super high in price. They have a twist to this deal. Veterinarians have no source for a generic knock off of this drug.

It is a high expense to the chemotherapy regimen needed to keep the animal making red blood cells when bone marrow issues are present. Usually, they need three injections, then two, and finally a single. The vet charges about $100 per injection. There are many owners that will try anything to save their pets. The facts show that an increasing number of dogs are succumbing to aggressive cancers.

There is a market for this drug. In a warehouse in Fall River, Massachusetts, an expert is labeling phony vials of saline marked Epogen. He pays the counterfeiter in cash, sells them to a New England distributor, and makes a lot of money. He has no conscience; he figures he saves pet owners some money and long-protracted grief. He wonders if vets will know the difference. By the time they figure out the drug is phony; he will be long gone to his southern home. The sunny sky is getting darker as they drive toward their rented home between Lyme and Hanover, New Hampshire.

Chapter 34

I thought weekends were supposed to be relaxing. I did have my moment of yoga. I was looking to read more of the book Aleni had me buy. My thoughts are on trying to figure out what this Catherine woman is all about. It is obvious we will be spending more time together.

"I saved some sushi for you. I know you like spicy tuna rolls."

Those are the first words I hear on reentering my place. "I ate dinner."

"You going to tell me about this woman?"

"As much as she told me."

I relay the story. Vito sits on the couch with his feet splayed across the cushions. He looks at me and doesn't say a word. Our canine friends show no interest in our conversation.

"What am I going to do with this sushi? I can't save it."

"Call the older couple upstairs. They always take what I can't eat." The Wilson's are a couple in their seventies who are vigorous and always willing to engage in conversation. He is a former ice hockey referee, pretty tough.

Vito puts the phone down and is walking the food upstairs when the phone rings. I pick it up and listen to the familiar voice. "I'll be in New York this week for a deal. I'm free Wednesday night. I'll be at the Plaza." I am staring at the phone when Vito comes back in to the place.

"It won't work. Maybe I'll call. Take care."

"Who is that, some babe you just met?"

"No. The woman I spent most of my life with."

* * *

What's happening? Why is not even in the equation. My simple existence is becoming a myriad of complex relationships. What was once an appreciative adopted dog and I is now an existence that I need a score card to figure out. Who is who and who is where? The excitement is fading and the energy level following. Sure, I made some new friends and rejuvenated my sex life. I'd be happier with the rejuvenated sex life without the mystery.

Chapter 35

Isabella has never been in a house like this. Wood ceiling beams are something she has only seen in architectural magazines in doctor's offices. It is small with one bedroom, a kitchen which shared a dining room. In the damp basement are the laundry room and a lot of open space. There is a study upstairs in the corner. The catty-cornered windows give a good view of the dirt road that approaches the house.

Sam is setting up the computer in this room. For all its appearance of a classic log cabin, it has all the modern electronic connections. The owner is a computer nut. The large flat-screen television in the main room will keep Sam and Isabella from succumbing boredom. They have found shopping only ten minutes down the road. The crowd is a lot different than the people they deal with in the Boston projects. They never lock anything here, not even their home. The owner tells them it isn't necessary. They are afraid if they do, it will arouse suspicion. Not having to look over their shoulders is a new experience for Isabella and Sam.

"I'm about all set up. I'll contact the guy in Fall River late tonight. He knows what the code words are."

Isabella looks at Sam and lets the words register. She is hungry. "OK. Do we need to buy any cops off here?"

"I don't think so. Let's keep our profile real low."

"No noise in bed?"

He smiles and looks in the yellow pages for a pizza shop. "Let's go to the Brick & Brew on Main Street. They got pizza, and we can check out the local color in town."

"Fine. I need a few minutes. How about a half hour?"

"I'll be reviewing the deal and asking you the questions. You better know the answers."

She knows it will be after dinner; they can't talk in public about this stuff. "When haven't I known the answers?"

He turns back to the computer as she heads for the one bathroom.

Chapter 36

Vito is taking care of all the chores tonight. He is smart enough to see I am drained. He knows that without letting my mind and body rest, I am subject to a seizure. He is right. I head for the bedroom and say good night to the in-house gang. Halfway down the hall I turn to go back to the dining room table where I left my new book about yoga. I stop to view the picture of Vito standing and leafing through my book. He has a serious look as if he is seeing something for the first time.

"Interesting stuff, it makes you think in a different world."

He closes the book and hands it over to me. Looking at me and then turning and looking nowhere in particular, he says, "See you tomorrow. Good night."

Seeing his expression, I simply say, "Good night."

I remove my clothes and, in my boxers, slip under the covers. I bunch the pillows behind my neck so I can read. I pick up the book, hold it without opening a page, and think about the weekend. Practicing yoga breathing, I randomly open to page 72. The beginning of the paragraph says,

"Aparigraha embodies the idea of good things to come."

I'll sign up for that tomorrow.

I guess I'll go to Aleni's five-thirty-evening class tomorrow. I think of her and I feel good. That hasn't happened in a long time. I close the book and my eyes.

* * *

It is my turn for the early-morning walk. My favorite one. I force myself to arise at five-thirty and make the coffee and set the table, then I gather the gang. It never enters into my mind that one day this wonderful dynamic will change. Dogs only live so long, and we take their loyalty for granted. Good companions are so hard to find.

The outside darkness is giving way to the slowly rising sun. The quiet of the city and Charlestown is part of my yoga breathing. It is nice to learn how to enjoy my senses. My neighborhood dog walker nods as we pass by the monument and rows of bare trees. The starting of the green MGB parked on the corner takes me out of my internal zone. The unique sound of the engine and shifting gears make me smile. Standing with a big smile on my face at the corner near my condo with three dogs, I have the distinct feeling I am becoming a neighborhood institution.

As I return to the condo, the smell of my French roast and Vito's aftershave change my mood. "The group did its bit. Remember, only one bagel." I love giving a veteran cop orders.

"I only listen to you because we're getting results. I need new clothes."

"The saggy look is in. Don't worry, you look cool."

"Not in the station house."

The words *station house* puts me back in the past events. "I remember that Lamar had said he wants me there around ten."

"I'll check and call you when I get in."

"You calling the mystery lady?"

"She's not much of a mystery to you."

I look at Vito. I'm not happy with that remark. As he leaves, his parting words are "Make sure you do your homework before you show up. We want to get this investigation rolling."

The Y chromosomes fighting for turf. It never stops.

Chapter 37

Finding the right person to work both sides of the fence for Sam and Isabella is a big challenge. Using their past favors and payoffs always is the answer. Everyone has a hook. Jamie Axelrod always blends into the background. Somehow he managed to attend the best schools, finishing in the middle third of his class. Since the schools were so prestigious, getting a good job was never a problem. A PhD in biochemistry from the University of Michigan attracted the pharmaceutical firms on the East Coast. Manufacturing drugs from scratch has always turned him on.

He enjoys making new drugs especially in his private lab at home. The experiment doesn't end there. He likes to take them too. His nonconforming behavior in the lab and conferences never has him at one job for more three years. His talent is recognized; that keeps him hired at one company or another. He never ages; he looked forty at twenty. At thirty-five, he looks forty. Spending all his time indoors leaves a pale pallor to his skin. He's had grey, thinning hair since he was twenty years old. His small, thin bone structure always is covered by a white button-down shirt and rumpled khaki pants. His black wing tip shoes have never seen fresh polish.

Every so often he will remember to wear the one belt he owns. It is light brown and an inch too small. He never stays long enough at any company to rise beyond an entry-level pay scale. His contact with women is through the Internet. He only knows the softness of the keyboard.

When the attractive Spanish lady approached him at the bookstore he didn't know what to do. He remembers that day well. Very well. He was in a bookstore in Boston near Harvard that specializes in scientific journals. Jamie enjoys staying current on all the new techniques of putting chemicals together to affect behavior. He especially likes figuring out new ways to create drugs to make him feel better.

The companies just want him to make sure the manufacturing process is up to standards. They never listen to any novel ideas from him. Besides, even if they did, the patent would be theirs.

"Could you help me find the way to the pharmaceutical section?" He did not even notice the missing tooth in her smile. He was overcome that a woman this attractive was asking him a question.

"This is the biochemistry section; the pharmaceutical section is three rows down, and make a left turn."

"Show me." It was an order he couldn't refuse.

"Sure, follow me."

"Let me take your hand, I don't want to get lost."

Her warm soft left hand slid into his cold clammy right hand. She did not change her expression even when glancing at the tall thin man sitting at the magazine section. Jamie was confused and excited. Nothing like this had ever happened to him before.

They arrived at the area she asked for only to have her turn to him and say, "I need your help."

"What is it?"

"Do you work for a drug company?"

He shook his head yes. "My friends told me you were very good at the manufacturing process."

"That's what I do."

She and Sam heard about this guy from some of their contacts. He was supposed to be good, unhappy with authority, and in need of money. Sam stalked him for two weeks. He looked like the right one to counterfeit this drug for them.

"Let's go back to my hotel and talk about this." His head was spinning. The hotel was only a few blocks from where they were. It was always busy with students, parents, faculty, and other visitors. They weren't noticed as they crossed the dark lobby and entered the elevator. She smiled and hit the number 9 button. The elevator was slow, and Jamie was starting to feel scared. He had never been in a situation like this before. Once inside the room, she showed him the documents about making drugs that she wanted him to read.

Sitting at the desk against the wall, he felt her breasts against his right shoulder as she leaned over him. "Is this a hard drug to make?"

"Yeah, it's not easy, that's why it costs so much."

"My friend and I need your help."

"What kind of help?"

She stepped away from him and turned her back. He was engrossed in the documents she has him to read. He didn't notice that all she was wearing were dark slacks. Nothing else. She tapped him on the neck. "I have something I want you see."

He turned and opened his mouth in astonishment. He did not say a word. She took him to the bedroom.

*   *   *

Sam planned the whole scene. She agreed; the bottom line was what they were there for. Just another experience, her body part of the trade.

The warehouse in Fall River is easy to rent. Vacancies are all over and accept cash as a blessing. He finds a small one on a side road with decent lighting. He arranges for the purchase of the vials in Canada. Nobody is interested in the delivery of empty vials to Massachusetts. Now they need someone to make a liquid and labels that have the authentic appearance.

It looks like they have found the right person. This will give Jamie the opportunity to get back at authority and have a woman at the same time. Throw in a few bucks, and he is hooked. The added bonus is that Jamie can't stand animals, except in zoos. He'd be happy to fake this drug for the vet practices.

The next step is sitting down with this guy and working out the details. He hopes he is as good as his sources said he was. If not, his sources pay. Not just with money.

Chapter 38

After Vito leaves, I know I will need to review my notes on what has happened over the last few weeks. I really don't have much to look at. They want somebody with a *Dr.* in front of their name to give them the security of knowing they are touching all the right buttons. The mystery lady actually knows more than all of us. I clean the morning breakfast's mess and shower. I always find comfort in routine.

With the water flowing over me, I think of the evening yoga class. It is nice to have something to look forward to at the end of the day. I'll keep that in mind no matter what I deal with this morning. I'll try to, at least.

There are two phone messages.

"Are you going to call me? We do need to discuss the finances for the next six months."

My ex-wife always knows how to get my attention. The erase button feels good. The last one is Lamar telling me to be at the station house at 10:30 a.m. I thought they wanted me at 10:00 a.m. He must have his reasons. I sit down in the dark leather armchair to read what information I have. Fern gives me a look like I am usurping her turf. I am, but soon I'll be gone, and it will be hers again.

I'm looking forward to the station house meeting. What the newly minted Ms. Jones has to say hopefully will start making sense of this whole situation. I look at the three remaining roommates, and they all stare at me. All eyes large, innocent, and expecting nothing but the 11:00 a.m. dog walker.

* * *

"I think we can complement each other, but we have to be careful." She talks like it was the old days and she was Catherine, Queen of the Law. Lamar is not happy with a stranger trying to take over his turf. She is there two minutes and is already offering the morning's agenda. If their research was thorough, they should have known this would happen.

Who ran the show in her Florida law office? She wears a marked-down, on-sale business suit. It is violet and not shrinking. Vito just sits and says very little. He lets Lamar run the show.

Making eye contact with Lamar and barely nodding, he says, "We know there are some fake drugs around. We don't know the pattern. Who is making them, who is fencing, and who is buying?"

She took turns, looking through her blue contacts at her tablemates. Neither one shrinks from her stare. The good-smelling hot mugs sit untouched. "I can help you. What do I get out of it?"

Vito tilts his head slightly to the right. He squares his shoulders in her direction. "You get to be a good girl."

She smiles and stands up unevenly, her swollen right ankle worse than yesterday. "Good luck."

Lamar jumps in, "Hey, cool down. Vito needs to drink some coffee. His roommate doesn't let him eat enough."

He gives Vito a blank expression, "Hey, buddy, this is not an interrogation."

There isn't anything that's not an interrogation in this building. She is happy to sit down; the two Advil haven't kicked in yet. That is the only painkiller that works for her, thanks to that guy, Cooper, who did the studies in Georgetown. She heard he was a dentist that didn't go the practice route. Maybe she'll meet him some day and thank him.

"Talking about your buddy, is he showing up this morning?"

"You should know, you're a lot closer to him than us." Lamar hopes Vito knows what he is doing.

She looks at Vito and smiles. "You're a real fuck-face, aren't you?"

Vito flinches.

Lamar smiles. It is time for him to get this under control. "He'll be here at ten thirty. He's on an assignment for us."

A three-sided chess match. She places her sore leg on the empty chair next to her. The door opens; Adam, in a blue blazer, tie, khakis, and smile, says, "How's it going?"

She looks straight at him and smiles. "How'd your assignment go?"

"What assignment?"

She looks over at the two professional detectives and says, "My price just went up 25 percent." The money isn't the issue; it is power.

Vito's stomach is flipping. Less food and more stress. Not good. "I'm gonna get some donuts."

Knowing the players, Adam figures out what is going on. "Hey, guys, I didn't know I was allowed to talk about the morning's assignment in front of her. I mean, is it OK?"

Lamar answers quickly, "No problem, keep it brief."

Vito nods and says, "Yeah, brief." With Adam on the scene, he passes on the donuts.

They keep their professional cool. No one knows what is going to be said next, including Adam. "I checked all the computer info I got from the yoga lady on the deals the Greek guys are making. All food deals, no drugs. No international drug company contacts. They should be clean."

She looks at Adam with a quizzical expression. "Clean olive oil? Can I see the report?"

Vito has had it. "Lady, let's see what you got for us. I don't like playing games and wasting time."

Lamar calmly takes the mugs and dumps the contents in the sink. Returning freshly filled mugs to their owners and taking a deep breath, he says, "We can offer you the standard consultant fee for your time, a hundred dollars an hour. You in?"

Pursing her lips, scanning the room, and taking a tentative sip of coffee, she says, "In."

Vito smiles. "What do ya got?

Adam makes eye contact with Lamar. A tiny nod makes him finally feel part of the team.

She isn't worried about the honor of their word, but business is business. "What do I sign and when?"

Lamar says, "The paperwork will be ready for tomorrow's meeting."

"Fine, that's when I talk."

She slowly stands, using her good left leg for support. "What time tomorrow?"

"Eight in the morning, right here." Lamar is quick with a change of inflection in his voice. No anger or annoyance is evident.

"Good, see you then." She limps out, and that is that.

"Fuck, she's a pain in the ass." Vito gets to the point.

I know exactly what she is doing. I know she's dealt with cops before. The alpha female taking charge. Or trying to. It will be interesting watching this group work together. I'm part of the group, not observing. I had a career of observing; now I'm in the middle. I must act on the issues, not study them.

* * *

Catherine, a.k.a. Fern, Crosby, etc., is exhausted back in her room at the Marriott. It isn't the ankle; it was the meeting. She did what she had to do. She couldn't just walk in, sit down, smile, and spill the info she had. That isn't her style. She also wanted to see how the three men dealt with her. If they're any good, she could recruit them for her consulting company. The company is not there yet, but it is in her mind. It will be the best pharm/legal/investigatory firm in the world. And she will be in charge. It is time for more practical issues. Like her low blood sugar.

Calling room service for a Greek salad and tea for an early lunch will help get her grounded. Her plan is to rest, organize, and research for tomorrow. No different than when she was a student. Some patterns of behavior never change. Thinking of Adam is a nice diversion. They are beginning to lose themselves in each other. Both are old enough not to have any inhibitions. What is involved? There are no rules in or out of the bedroom. Just like she likes it.

The phone rings. "Ms. Jones?"

"Yes."

"When do you want your rental car?"

"Two hours."

"It will be waiting for you in the outside lot on your left. The keys will be at the front desk."

"Fine."

She selects the Earl Grey tea from the container. She knows her body. The two sugars and the caffeine will help her get through the next event.

Chapter 39

Sam and his lady friend can't stand living in a New England college town. It is the opposite of any world they have ever inhabited. The pizza is good, and the location works for hiding out, but it is weird. They have this feeling everybody is smarter than they are. Sam feels a certain awe walking on Dartmouth's campus. A new feeling for him. Every so often he thinks of his last moments with Gord. Gord knew it was over that night.

Talking to that woman from Florida about his deals killed him. She gave him two grand for the information. He still had the cash in his pockets when his life ended. Sam had no desire to touch the cash. He wished it didn't end that way, but he couldn't trust Gord. He lost his value, plus he was working the other side. Gord's job was to take the fake vials of Epogen from the Massachusetts warehouse and put on his best suit and represent Premier Veterinary Company. A company they just created as a privately owned business. From there he would drive to as many veterinary practices as possible to sell the tainted product. It is always a "discount price." An easy sell, no one asks any questions. The practices all thought they were such smart business people. Professionals in all the health fields are usually naïve when it comes to business. Getting the nicely packaged containers is always an event. It is no problem taking over Gord's route. As long as you look professional, nobody looks twice.

Sam never noticed the woman following him on some of his calls. He was a blonde then, and so was she. Fern was newly created; she no longer was Catherine. Looking up an old college friend in Boston who went on to veterinary school, she heard the familiar story. She leaned over a Cobb salad and white wine and heard how loved animals were dying sooner than they should be. At that point she decided it had to be easier than in the large medical field to find the crooks doing this. Probably the same sleazes in the vet game were in the human game.

* * *

Ms. Crosby Jones always enjoys cars. In that respect, she is like a guy. She'd rather read *Car and Driver* magazine than *Town and Country*. After a year of research, a decision was finally made as to what she would buy for herself. It was a Mercedes C Series wagon with all-wheel drive. Then she became ill. Going to the dealer after her recovery, she found out the model was discontinued. She only wanted a new one. It was like turning on the FM and the mellow voice telling you the fifty-minute set is now over. Timing is everything.

It's all timing. We think we have some control, but we don't. Renting cars is fun. It gives her a chance to play with all the brands and not care. Just like all the people she becomes and the relationships that happen. Wearing an all black outfit of pants, a low-cut sweater, and a jacket, she presents herself at the front desk at the Marriott.

The young man behind the desk recognizes her. "We have your keys to the rental car for you."

"Thanks."

A simple smile and she walks to the lot and finds the black Chevy Malibu. Heading to Fall River, she is surprised at the competent power the car has. Maybe the American manufacturers are finally getting it right.

Chapter 40

"OK, let's review what we got."

I just look lamely at my two law enforcement teammates not knowing what to expect. We spent ninety minutes talking about everything we knew already. It is obvious we need Ms. Crosby Jones to tell us what is up. We all have the feeling she knows enough information to get this case going. There has to be a tie between Gord's killing and what we are doing. I feel that is why these two detectives are involved. I can't imagine either one caring about counterfeit drugs.

Vito leans back on his chair. "Gord couldn't be living so nice without getting money from other dealings. I can't imagine a legit business in the picture. He thought aliens placed computers on Earth."

Lamar turns his body toward me. "Really, when you spent those nights with him, what did you talk about?"

"The Red Sox." My response is barely audible.

"Who paid for the seats at the games?"

Good question by Vito. Two points. "We split them. We paid our own way."

"Where did you sit?"

"Wherever was available."

"This doesn't give us shit." Understatement wasn't one of Vito's strengths.

"Sorry, that's just the truth."

"Truth, what a novel term."

Lamar says the magic words, "Let's break for lunch. See you back here in two hours."

Lamar goes back to his computer; I follow Vito outside. We stop on the concrete steps; we breathe in unison; sharing a yoga moment without knowing it.

"How are you feeling?" Vito moves his head in a circle as he speaks. He looks like a living bobble-head doll.

"Doing well, no problem." I don't tell him about my evening yoga class. The thought of it kept me going while sitting in the claustrophobic room.

"You taking your medications?"

"Yeah."

"You have enough of them?"

"Two days ago I put in the phone order; I'm covered for another three months."

"Good. Make sure this stuff doesn't get to you. Get enough sleep."

"No problem."

I think he thinks I am his little brother. That's OK, sometimes. "Coffee shop for a wrap and a soda?"

"Sounds good to me."

The camaraderie is good. Too many years in the same room in practice made me forget the simple pleasure of working with someone you like.

* * *

The drive to Fall River is an easy one. It is a chance for Crosby to think. Her goal is to buy some boxes of the fake Epogen from the guy doing the dirty work. She also hopes to get a video of the guy fencing the stuff going into the warehouse. She had tracked Gord to this location and was able to meet with him and strike a deal. The deal that killed him. She has no remorse. He was bad and needed to be punished. There was no trial so she figures the taxpayers saved money.

It is not difficult to enter the warehouse and buy some of the stuff from the weirdo making it. She has an instinct about men. This one will do what she wants for a peek at her cleavage. Pathetic. She uses that to her advantage and buys a box of the contraband. She gives him more money than Sam and Isabella had contracted for. He promises not to tell anybody. She believes him. A big mistake.

The ride is uneventful, and she stops three blocks from the warehouse. With plenty of street parking available, the Chevy is parked at the end of a street facing in the direction of the highway. Another black American car blending into the street.

She wants to set up a steady business relationship with the guy making the stuff. Then there will be a steady pipeline of evidence and information. It only follows that the others involved will be identified. Walking to the nondescript old grey building, there were butterflies in her tight stomach. She didn't know how this dork was going to react this time. If he gets physical she has her cell phone preprogrammed for

911. That's about it, no weapons, no self-defense training. The hours at the gym are to lose weight and maintain her body; that's it.

Arriving at the grey door, looking over her shoulder right and left, she knocks firmly twice. No answer. She knocks again. No answer. She is getting pissed. She spoke with this Axelrod guy two days ago to arrange a second pickup of the product. It was agreed that late Monday afternoon works for him. She is here; where the hell is he? The door flings open, and a smiling Jamie presents himself. He looks the same as he did at their last meeting. She wonders if his clothes are ever clean.

"Hello, how are you?" This guy is such a dork. Stepping inside the entrance room is like going to the doctor's office. A Medicaid office. Old furniture, threadbare carpet, and flat beige-painted walls.

He looks directly at her cleavage and says, "Sit, and let's talk."

"No. I want to see the lab and the material you're selling me. I have another appointment in Boston this evening. Let's make it quick."

The look on his face shows that is not what he wants to hear. "Follow me."

The next door opens to another world. In direct contrast to the entrance room, it is bright, well ventilated, and clean. Tables and labeled machines are organized in a professional manner. She feels like she has entered a manufacturing facility of a major pharmaceutical company. The reality is the opposite. She entered an illegal lab that makes fake drugs for sale. For sale as the real thing. The real thing is killing innocent animals. People may be next.

"Let's see the process, I need a review. You know I was with the FDA a few years ago." Actually, as an attorney she prosecuted for the FDA early in her career.

He is excited. "Let's go on the tour."

This is the first time she sees positive animation from him. The tour takes twenty minutes. She pretends to understand the scientific stuff. "OK, I want to see what I'm buying today." She follows him, dragging her right foot, to the end of the room. Opening the large stainless steel door of the fridge, he smiles and says, "You buying two cartons?"

"No, three."

"Take what you want."

She pulls out the closest three boxes from the bottom shelf. Why fake drugs are refrigerated beats her. "Why do you keep these boxes in the fridge?"

He looks very serious. "I do things the right way."

She is getting a headache from being around this guy. Her ankle is hurting like hell. It is time for two Advil. "Where's the bathroom?"

"Second door to the right."

"Any paper cups?"

"Why?"

What a dumb question. "Time for some Advil, have a problem?"

"There are two sterile beakers on the shelf to your left, take one. Sterile water is in the jug to your right."

She believes him about the sterile issues. Taking what she needs, she limps into the bathroom. It is clean in a hospital kind of way. As she closes the heavy institutional door, she doesn't hear the outside door opening.

Sam enters the lab. "Jamie, what are the three boxes doing outside the fridge?"

Chapter 41

I don't know what it is about turkey and cheese wraps. Another addiction. I could live on strong coffee and these wraps. Whole-wheat wraps, of course. Are these wraps or roll-ups? I guess it depends what part of the country you are in. Vito is just happy to be eating. The place is simple. Slick's has been in business for just two years and is always busy. The lines waiting to place their order reassure me that everything is fresh. I hate waiting in-line. I don't, I find the table, Vito waits in-line. We each have our role.

"Diet coke?" His voice booms from across the room.

I nod. Bringing the goodies to the table, he places the tray down and is a happy camper. I had grabbed the paper napkins and set the table. We have the finest plastic table setting.

"So what do you think about this morning's meeting?" Vito asks as I sit.

"A waste of time. An ego trip for Ms. Jones." I offer my response as an ex-shrink.

Vito is working on an oversized bite and chewing while his mind is bouncing the response. He takes his time chewing and swallowing. You can see he was raised not to talk with his mouth full. After a slow swallow, he looks away from the white plastic plate and says, "You missed the point." He takes another bite. A smaller one.

I mull over his statement, and then realize something important. They used Dijon mustard. I wanted deli mustard. I will speak to Vito later about this. The sunlight disappears; it is pouring. "What do you mean?"

"The lady is a smart cookie. She has stuff she knows is of value to us, and she wants to make sure we know that. She isn't going to spill her guts, smile, and leave."

"So she's for real."

"I think so. We're not dealing with some amateur. Tomorrow morning will be a meaty meeting."

Meaty meeting. It must be cop talk. "Great. Now what's on the agenda for this afternoon?"

"A strategy session about tomorrow, it will be brief. We'll have some paperwork to play with from the dispatch lady."

I forget about her. The rain stops; the sun comes out. Walking back to the station house on the wet street, I think about tonight's yoga session. It is good to know that this afternoon's session is going to be brief. No problem making the five-thirty class.

Chapter 42

Isabella feels out of place at the coffee shop on the corner of Main Street. She doesn't wear the Gap outfits of the younger crowd or have the meaningful, serious look of the people over thirty. She keeps going there for one reason: the best French she's ever had. Not only does it taste good, it has the caffeine to juice her up. Sam isn't with her; he took the car to check on the manufacturing of their product. They agree that this guy is doing a good job, but they can't tell him that. His insecurity is a tool to use. She meets him at different hotels as infrequently as possible. She has to admit; there is one area he is getting confident in. That is her body. It isn't all that bad. She does make him shower first; she told him a warmer body turns her on.

The coffee shop is crowded and noisy. The wailing folk music is barely audible. "Do you mind if I sit down?"

She is startled by the request but, thinking quickly, answers in heavily accented English, "Sorry, I am waiting for a friend."

The tall thin young man looks disappointed. His wispy dark beard and flat dark brown hair touching his shoulders give him the appearance that he is lost from the sixties. There isn't much turnover in seating. It is the kind of place that that you linger over that one cup of brew. If you add a baguette to the formula, you could be there forever. She orders a baguette with peanut butter and slides her half-full mug in front of the empty chair opposite her.

"Your friend drinks from your mug?" The long-haired young man is watching her from across the room. He sits down opposite her mug. "Don't worry, I have my own coffee."

She doesn't say a word. Words aren't going to happen. Abruptly standing, she leaves the baguette and coffee. She finds herself in the bookstore down the street buying the NY *Daily News*. At least this is something she understands. She has another one and half hours before Sam picks her up in front of the Hanover Inn. Holding the paper close to her body she walks across the street to the Inn. Settling in to one of the wood rocking chairs on the long porch, Isabella is tempted to light a cigarette. She doesn't; attention isn't what she is looking for. The nicotine urge can wait. She looks directly in front of her. The open green lawn surrounded by ivy-covered buildings is a natural relaxant. She wonders what is on the minds of the young people moving at different speeds on this peaceful setting.

Her ringing cell phone quickly takes her from the laconic to the urgent. It is Sam. "What's up?" His voice is barely audible.

"Nothing, just getting bored sitting on the porch of the Inn."

"I have a surprise."

"What?"

"You'll see when I pick you up." The phone went dead.

Chapter 43

The sound of Springsteen is blasting in the room. "Countin' on a Miracle" is bouncing off the four walls. Vito seems as if it is business as usual. Lamar is sitting, holding his mug with two hands and nodding his head up and down. He is facing the wall, his back to the door. Vito walks in and sits down at his regular seat. I just stand at the door of the conference room watching this surreal scene. Vito reviews papers, Lamar zones in on Bruce, and I close the door feeling a desire to ask someone to dance. There is nobody that is my type in the room. The music stops.

Lamar whips his chair 180 degrees to face me and looks me square in the eyes. "Energy, inspiration."

I nod. Frankly I am clueless.

Vito is the first to speak about the morning session. "She's credible. She is pulling our balls to see if they will hurt."

Lamar's turn. "Tomorrow morning we find out the skinny."

They both look at me. I nod. I don't know how to deal with skinny balls that hurt. Must be cop talk.

Lamar takes a drink and says, "Vito, stay for a bit. We have some paperwork to sort through."

"Sure."

My turn. "You can check out. Remember, tomorrow morning we're here at eight."

"See you in the morning." It feels good walking out.

* * *

I didn't feel or smell the mustiness of a just-rained-on city on my walk to the yoga class. I walk with a new confidence knowing I am not going to the unknown. The thought of seeing Aleni is exciting.

"You fucking dork head!"

I immediately enter the moment. But not in the preferred yoga style. The light is red, and I am walking straight into a Ford pickup truck.

Well, almost into the truck. I still have my reflexes. I have to admit, I am looking down the street trying to see who the dork was. Picking up the pace to the studio is easy after realizing I was the one being called a dork.

It is a relief going through the outer door and up the elevator to the fitness center. Placing my mat down in the barely lit yoga studio creates an instant feeling of peace. Yoga is working; the visceral dork-head feeling is left at the door. The other students are either unrolling their mats or finding a place for their own little territory. Nobody speaks or looks at anyone. The room is filling up. I look around and notice I am the only male in the room. I look around a few more times.

The average age appears to be about thirty. I am the oldest and least-experienced person in the room. I sit and cross my legs, lean forward, and breathe slowly. Sitting up, moving one vertebra at a time, I open my eyes. The woman in front and to the left is practicing down dog. Her well-shaped butt and pendulous breasts make it difficult to concentrate on my warm-up. I am sitting in a crossed-leg position and leaning forward. That's when I noticed the sight that is going to challenge my concentration. The same woman of luscious proportions has hairy armpits. OK, I can deal with it but will not fall in love.

Aleni softly enters the room and shuts the windows. Turning to face us, she smiles and quietly, softly says, "Welcome. Today is beautiful, focus on the moment. Enjoy the process that only you can feel with your body and soul. Let us stand up with feet and big toes touching. Close your eyes and breathe. Think of your intention and breathe."

Closing my eyes, my intention is to not be obsessed with the hairy armpits in front of me. The session is flowing from one pose to another. I am lost in my practice. Knowing moments of discomfort are just that, moments. I have learned to deal with the present feeling and know I will benefit from ignoring the uncomfortable times. I am amazed how, when I relax, certain poses just happened. I smile during the one-legged double-eagle pose. I am happy in my moment. The conclusion of the practice feels good. I know I am building something here.

As I am rolling up my mat, a female voice is near and directed toward me. A distinct French accent draws my immediate attention. "I have never seen you here before." The hairy armpits have a voice.

"My first evening session."

"A good instructor, eh?" French Canadian. The only country in the world to say "eh" after every sentence.

"Yes, very good." I wasn't going to match her "eh."

She turns and walks toward the door. Interesting. Putting the blocks away and picking up my rolled mat, I walk over to Aleni.

"Maybe we can find time to talk outside the studio after practice one night."

"That would be good. How about Thursday night?"

"Great. After the practice we'll decide what and where."

"Deal."

Walking back to my place, I am feeling good on all emotional fronts.

* * *

"Do you notice anything different about Fern?" Vito's back is to me, and he is sliding the veggie pizza into the oven. I am still in my floating yoga mode and don't want reality to intrude.

"What?"

"I mean, she's drinking and peeing twice the amount of Bowser and Bentley."

I switch gears and become the doctor doing a differential diagnosis. I wish it didn't happen. My gut is constricted and loses the yoga peace. "How's the rest of her behavior, anything different?"

"Not that I see. We should check with the dog walker."

"Let's observe her a bit more before we run to the vet."

"OK."

I never took pet insurance. No reason, just never did. I look at Fern. I don't have far to look; she is lying down on my bare feet. She looks OK to me. Big round dark eyes. Let's take one day at a time.

Vito brings the pizza over to where I am sitting. The coffee table is big enough for a large pie, veggies, and all. "How'd the afternoon meeting go with Lamar?"

"No surprises, nothing to bore you with now."

"OK." I have the feeling that I am being put on the bench for part of this operation.

We finish our slices: two for me, three for Vito, and the rest in the freezer. We both are sipping our beer from the dark bottles when he asks me a question, "Meet anyone interesting in yoga?" How the hell does he know everything?

"Yeah, a gorgeous French Canadian woman with hairy armpits."

He looks at me and walks to his room with a restrained smile on his face. It is my turn to walk the dogs. Going down the musty hallway and the two stories of carpeted steps, I am working on my yoga breathing. The feeling of the class disappeared when Vito asked his first question.

Chapter 44

Ms. Crosby Jones's Advil doesn't prepare her for the pain waiting for her on the other side of the door. It happens too fast; the moment is an overwhelming shock that extends from her head running down her spine. She doesn't know she is being held in Sam's arms. He doesn't want to kill her, just knock her out. Questions have to be asked; he has to know what she knows. He is pissed at Axelrod for letting her in and buying the stuff. What an idiot. He'll deal with him after figuring out what to do with this knocked-out lady in his arms.

He looks at Axelrod. "Get your coat and put it down on the floor."

Axelrod is not happy taking orders, but one look at who is barking them makes him hurry to the closet. Placing the beige raincoat on the bare floor, he helps slide Ms. Jones gently down.

Sam leans over her face and makes sure she is breathing. Her breath is steady and quiet. He then looks at Axelrod. Jamie is terrified. Sam looks at the lady on the floor and then at his employee in crime.

"That would be you if I didn't need you. I wouldn't be checking your breathing. Sit down at the table."

He does as he is told.

Sam has the floor. "OK, we discuss your fuckup later. But I tell you one thing; I'm cutting ten percent off our original deal."

Jamie nods. He isn't going to speak and say the wrong thing and lose another ten percent.

"Watch her. I'm moving the car to the front door. Find something to tie her hands and legs with."

Jamie quickly grabs two rolls of brown packing tape and places them down next to the lady. Before going to the car, Sam wraps her wrists together. He does the same with her ankles, taking special care with the swelling on her right ankle. The two of them carry her to the open door of the backseat of the car. Sam checks her taped legs and arms and makes sure she will be relatively comfortable. After getting instructions from Sam, Jamie heads back to the warehouse at a brisk pace with his head down.

Sam settles into the driver's seat, takes a look back at the woman lying on the backseat, and says to no one, "Shit, I found you, now what the hell am I going to do with you?" He aims the car north and blends in with the traffic.

Chapter 45

I didn't know why, but I let Fern sleep on the bed with me. Maybe I did know why but didn't want to think about it. I was thinking about the morning meeting with the whole team together. Rubbing Fern's soft belly helps slow down my thoughts of the real world. I need an empty head in order to get a good night's sleep. Not easy, I'm still looking for that switch.

An hour before the alarm, I am awakened by Fern's whining. She never did that before. Ignoring her canine roommates, we quickly find our way out to the cold, dark park where she pees more than her usual volume. I'm going to have to find the time to get her to the vet. Maybe she's just getting old. With my routine off, I am going to be tired all day. I knew it; it happens every time.

"You got up early, what's up?" Vito needs to know everything. I like the guy, but I'm starting to see his wife's point of view.

"Fern had to go out, she peed a lot. I'll make a appointment with our vet."

I'm not sure how old she is. The rescue group was just happy I adopted her. I really didn't care at the time, but it would be good to know her age now.

"She'll be all right, I've seen dogs go through stages of problems, they usually get better." I think Vito was trying to be understanding.

I have to change the subject. "What's the plan for this morning's meeting?"

Vito looks at me as if it is a stupid question. "Just follow our lead. Lamar is the quarterback. We've had plenty of experience dealing with the experts of the world."

I knew it is a turf issue with him. It bothers him to have too many outsiders enter their world. It is even tougher when you really needed them. Paying them was the ultimate insult. I have to get this on the table. "It really is a problem for you having this woman on the team."

He is tying his shoes, the left one first, and the right lace breaks as I ask the question. "Shit, I hate when this happens." He connects the separated lace, and the left shoe has two knots. "See you at the station house."

He never answers the question. I am left with the dishes, Bowser, Bentley, and Fern. I attend to the dishes, clean myself up, and dress in grey pants, white shirt, and a charcoal grey tweed sport coat. I look like the professional shrink I used to be as I walk my three little friends through the park. Fern is keeping up with her friends and looks fine. They are the Three Dogateers off to conquer the world. At the very least, their neighborhood.

I am looking forward to this morning's meeting. I want to know more than facts about false medications. I want to know why she has three identities. I need to find out who the hell she is. I don't like being used. I need to know if I am in the mix in her world. I am getting tired of being an interesting add-on.

I take public transportation to the morning meeting. I let Vito go ahead. I liked being alone in a crowd of strangers, all heading to different places. No eye contact, no connection, just caring about their own destination. It is a clean feeling.

I have specific questions to ask her about her interest in bad drugs. Hopefully, that will open the door to her past. I know enough to let Lamar and Vito run the show, but I am there for a reason. I haven't quite figured out that reason.

I arrive ten minutes late, no one comments. The administrative woman gives me a folder without saying a word. By the time I look up at her, she is gone. A quick look-through reveals an outline of the present level of information and possible avenues to follow. There is even a breakdown of her three identities. Gord has his own section. It is still hard to accept that he was playing both sides of the legal fence. Didn't he care that people were being hurt by fake drugs? What if my epilepsy pills were fake? I could not believe how wrong I read a good friend. I'll never again trust the bond of beer.

Sitting down, I receive cold stares. Two cold stares.

"She's not here. If she keeps playing games, we're going to tell her that the deal is off." Lamar is not a happy camper.

All I can offer is, "She may have trouble getting a cab."

Vito frowns and says, "I didn't expect this."

My turn: "And you're pretty good at figuring things out."

More cold stares, the last statement doesn't win me any points. Nobody talks for fifteen minutes. Reading about her background, her connection with this case is starting to come together. She has a legal background, understands the need for drugs, and has the energy of someone given a second shot at life. Somehow there is this Florida connection. The two bogus cops and my one-night stand. My own version of *Miami Vice*. Two more cups of coffee, a trip to the bathroom, and no more conversation.

Lamar breaks the silence. "Either she got cold feet or her attention is somewhere else."

Vito nods. Looking serious, he pushes his chair back, stands up, stretches, and adjusts his black belt. He is in all black. So is Lamar. I look like an Ivy Leaguer with two bouncers.

"What if the people she was trailing got wise to her?" Vito directs the question to Lamar as he looks at the ceiling.

"You mean they have her or worse?"

Lamar answers staring at the same ceiling.

"Yeah."

I can't imagine any of this was really happening. I am out of my league. For twenty-five years I listened to problems of others, offered perspective, and, hopefully, helped. I don't know how to help here.

Lamar is in charge again. He closes his eyes, clenches his jaw and he purses his lips into one line. "We know where she was staying, let's trace her every move and all her calls."

"Let's go." Vito is on his way out the door.

The two of them are out the door without even looking at me. When I am at the door of the station house, their car is gone. Talk about not being in the mix. Not exactly how I thought the morning was going to play. Taking the bus back, I share the empty stare of my fellow passengers. I have lost that mental clean slate. Walking the two blocks back to my place, I feel like a total idiot. What was I doing with this group? Maybe I should check out too.

A block away, I spot the dog walker with her contingent of six dogs. Three of whom belong in my place. She is tall with short blonde hair with tight blue jeans and a formfitting pink turtleneck, letting the world notice her bare belly, then her four-legged troops. Fern seems to be keeping pace with her colleagues. The only one who looks out of place is the one with jeans and the turtleneck. I have spoken briefly with her in the past few months; she is a part-time student at Boston University. We met in front of the steps of my building.

"Hi, how's everyone doing?"

She smiles, a bright, natural smile, and hands the three leashes to me. "They're fine, occasionally Fern would just stop and sit, but I think that's OK."

I am starting to worry. "Thanks, I pay you on Friday, right?"

"Right."

"I'll leave the check on the kitchen table."

"Thanks." She turns with the remaining gang, two boxers and a beagle, and heads across the street.

I look at the four of them walking; actually the human has my attention. The six dark canine eyes all look at me in unison. "All right, time to go home." I follow up the steps.

Chapter 46

"What's happening?"
"You'll tell me that."

Catherine can't remember who she is supposed to be. Her head hurts, her ankle hurt, and she is more frightened than she has ever been. She only sees the back of the head driving the car. She is able to change her position to sit up in the seat. Her hands are taped at her wrists, her feet angled to her right and wrapped at her ankles. After overcoming the initial fear, her first thought is that the guy making the drugs is kidnapping her. She needs the facts so negotiation can follow.

"Nobody is going to pay money for me except my boyfriend." She doesn't have a boyfriend. She thinks of the name of a veteran FBI agent she knows in Florida. If they called that guy, he would know what to do.

Sam thought that they should have taped her mouth shut. He is pissed at himself for forgetting to do that. He decides not to talk to her. He needs time to think of how to deal with her. It is obvious she knows what they are doing. He has to find out how and who she has talked to. The more he ignores her, the more vulnerable she will feel. Another forty-five minutes and he will be in Hanover. He realizes he has to think of something so she won't be screaming when they are in Hanover. It doesn't exactly look like a fraternity initiation prank. He smiles at the thought of that idea; oh, those were the days.

Chapter 47

I open the door to my place to the sound of the telephone ringing. Dropping the leash collection, I lunge to the ringing phone. Do I make it in time?

"Hello."

"Adam, were you running, or what?"

I am breathing fast. Hearing the phone from the second floor switched me into running mode. A simple reflex. My lungs try to keep pace with the rest of my body. "Yeah, I was opening the door when I heard the phone, isn't that the way it always is?" I recognize the voice of my old college roommate, Jeff Tindale. My only remaining contact from the innocent days.

"How are you? Is life interesting enough for you now?"

Jeff always asks the same question. He was into computers and had a head for business. He put it all together at the right time. A wealthy man, he has all the toys but never someone to share them with. I have the impression that's the way he wanted it. I see him about once a year in New York. He gained some weight on his football player's frame but still carries it well. The full head of reddish brown hair is his trademark.

Thinking over his question, the answer is obvious. "Interesting? That's a given. I've been in a bit of whirlwind, still trying to figure things out."

"Maybe I can help you."

"All ears." Actually, while on the phone, all ears.

"I'll be in San Francisco for four months, so my place in New Hampshire is yours if you want it."

I don't have an immediate response. I have been there once before. It is fifteen miles outside of Hanover and is on four acres. It is a warm house, all wood and high-beamed ceilings. Of course, all the latest wiring and electronic toys are there. I few winters ago I met him for a week of skiing and drinking. In that order.

"Why are you so quiet, are you there?"

I look at the phone and don't say anything.

"Look, if you can't use it, tell me. I will make some other calls. I'd feel better with someone living there when I'm away. The cold weather is kicking in; I don't want to deal with frozen pipes and all that."

"Great, I'll use it."

"Good, the keys will be mailed tomorrow. Enjoy. I'll call from the coast."

"Thanks, I'll take good care."

He hangs up. Once again, out of nowhere things happen in life. This is good. I need a change that is not a radical one. Just a two-hour drive to transport to a new world.

Looking at my canine roommates, I say, "Well, I'll be up north soon. Vito will take good care of you. I hope you don't all get fat."

Looking out the window at the grey sky and the oncoming season of dullness and less sunlight, I think of how I ache for the feeling of my yoga practice. Is it the yoga or the instructor I ached for?

* * *

Things just don't happen like this. Maybe it's the older-man syndrome. Whatever that is. It is so soon, so spontaneous, a whirlwind of joy and truly losing myself in another person. I am afraid to speak. I do anyway.

"Weren't we supposed to go out to dinner first?"

Aleni rolls over and smiles. A soft, welcoming smile. Lips that had said yes. "You hungry?"

"Absolutely famished."

"Order the shrimp pizza; they deliver."

She tells me the number, and I do as told. I need to clear something up. "Isn't this a bit soon in the relationship for us to be like this?"

"What have I taught in yoga? Live the moment. This is a moment I didn't want to lose. It is so much better when it just happens."

I look away. "Does this happen often?"

"I don't sleep around. I just wanted you. The dating ritual will be for someone I marry."

There it is again, a mature sex object. Better late than never. On the other hand, I am hurt. "No marrying for me? What's the defect?"

"You're not Greek."

"You are kidding, right?"

"No."

I didn't think this was happening. But it happened, and a reality hits me. I can't convert to Greekism. "Hard-and-fast rule?"

"Yes."

We don't say much until the pizza arrives. It doesn't last long. The pizza that is. There is a second round before I go home. As I leave, I have to ask, "What are the rules for a non-Greek?"

"I take each day for what it is. Enjoy the moment."

"Ohm."

Chapter 48

Back at the station house, Lamar and Vito are also dealing with the moment. It is late, but they don't notice the time. They both agree that if Internal Affairs becomes involved in the death of Gord, it will just be more administrative bull to deal with. It is always painful to find out about a cop who betrayed his values. It happens more often than they would like to admit. Seeing the high life of the crooks sometimes just gets into the soul of someone who really wants more. It is as simple as that or as simple as needing the money for your kids, wife, or girlfriend. Not in that order.

The puzzle is coming together. They hope the lady will tell them where the fake drugs are being made. The manufacturer and the sales middleman have to be identified. They are convinced she is trailing the leaders of this ring and can fill in the gaps.

"We know she has a few IDs, and she's from the south. Well, coming up north is not always for the lobster." Vito has a way bringing food into the mix.

Lamar knows without a source from the outside they are going nowhere. He looks at the ceiling and makes a pyramid with his fingers under his chin. "We need to use our resources to locate her. Now."

"OK. How are you going to do that?"

"Let's see what the computer boys picked up from her hotel."

They both are quiet in the elevator to the third floor. The meeting with the tech crew is short. A rental car, a few calls to a town in Massachusetts. Like an old marriage, they don't need to communicate by speaking all the time. With the notes from the meeting with the tech boys in his hands, Lamar leads the way to the car. Vito is in step behind Lamar's walk of purpose and authority. They both have the buzz of going into the unknown. Being the crime busters, it still turns them on.

With the snap of his seat belt, Vito is facing his partner when he says, "Going with the obvious is the first choice."

Looking straight ahead at the traffic light, Lamar offers his wisdom. "It better make sense, the captain is being a pain about using our gas allotment this month."

"You got to be kidding; the Arabs are telling us how to do our job now."

Lamar ignores Vito's remarks; he is lost in the possibilities of what they may find.

Chapter 49

"Where are you taking me?" She is shifting in the large backseat, angling herself to see his face in the rearview mirror. Finally her contortions reveal him. She isn't totally surprised. It just confirms her investigation. However, this wasn't the confirmation venue she was hoping for.

Sam realizes that she is looking at him through the mirror. Nothing he can do about it. He has to use fear to keep her under control. It is time to kick in the plan he just thought of. "You know who I am. You have an idea what we are doing. But, lady, I found you before you found me. You know what that means? You play by my rules or you lose more than the game."

All she sees out of the back windows are the outline of mountains and the headlights of the cars bouncing off the irregular granite walls. Obviously, they are going north. There are lots of secluded places a body could be dumped. She has no choice but to be compliant. "What are the rules?"

"We're coming into a town in about twenty minutes, and I'll be picking up my partner. You'll just be quiet. If not, I tape your mouth real tight. Any more trouble and I tape your nose too."

"OK. I'm quiet. Where are you taking me?"

"Where I want to."

She knows now isn't the time for negotiation. Sam flicks the right blinker and slows down as he cruises into the right lane. The next exit on the road is Hanover/Norwich. It comes up quicker than he remembers, and he turns and angles right on the bridge over the Connecticut River. The speed limit is thirty mph, and he stays under that by a few ticks of the speedometer. The cops up here don't have much to do, so they watch the speed limit closely. The last thing he needs is to be pulled over and have to explain a taped-up lady in the backseat. He doesn't think they would believe him if he said it was his wife and she was into bondage.

Picking up the cell phone, he dials Isabella. "Walk down to the first large tree on the road. I'm going to stop and you have to get in the front passenger door real quick."

"I'll be waiting. I'm walking down the hill now."

He knows if he stops by the big tree, there isn't an overhead light there. He looks up at the rearview mirror. "You're about to officially meet my partner."

Chapter 50

Expectation. Is it a form of wasted energy? I look back at my day and think about the previous day's expectations. The long-awaited meeting with the full investigatory team just didn't happen.

The yoga class is smooth, challenging, and emotionally cleansing. To a point. The follow-up with my yoga teacher was unexpected, exciting, and disappointing. I feel that I have experienced all the colors of the rainbow in one day.

Now I am at the end of the day ready to enter my place, and somehow I know that there is no pot of gold at the end of this rainbow.

"OK, gang, I'm back. What's up, Vito?" The only sounds are assorted barks.

"Give me a minute to walk myself, and then it's your turn."

Closing the bathroom door, I notice there is no Vito. I'm not worried; he is a cop. In and out with the gang and back into the bathroom for the second shower of the day. As I wash Aleni off my exhausted body, I wonder when and if I will see her again. Does she do everything by "living the moment"? Is there no value in planning and anticipation that is satisfying? I am in no condition to even consider answering these questions.

Looking at the gang as I slide onto the couch for a beer, I notice Fern's eyes do not have their usual sparkle. I make a note to myself to call the vet in the morning for an appointment. As the cold liquid cleanses my dry mouth, I start thinking how going up north will cleanse my body and soul. Help clear out the city dust from my brain. As much as I love the energy of the city, I know a change will be good.

I just don't know what a drastic change awaits me.

Chapter 51

Most hospitals buy their drugs from big-name houses. Literally, they cannot afford to have a bad drug make a patient sicker, or worse, kill them. Usually pharmacy managers' at large hospitals receive flyers every day pushing cut-rate prices for drugs. Large wholesalers and well-established buying groups are the standard for doing business. Large well-named firms have thousands of people on staff for marketing and research. The security departments are an afterthought. After all, they are so pure; how can the public think it needs any security?

It is amazing how many smart people can be so stupid. Sam and Isabella picked up on this. They also know how, even with a huge market, one mistake on the hospital scene can make the evening news. In this isolated, electronic, busy world, people are turning to their pets for comfort. This leads to more visits to the vet. Pet insurance is still a developing deal, so the high-tech treatments are big bucks. Sam and Isabella notice how people are willing to pay for the love of an animal.

It is so much easier to penetrate the vet market than the human one. If vets who have to make all the decisions of a hospital and run a business at the same time can get what they perceive to be a deal, they jump at it. Sam and his partner found a profitable niche with little control or agencies over their shoulder. A very profitable niche.

The business plan they follow is to divide the country in sections. They will see what drug for the vets in the area is a big seller and set up a team. All they need is a manufacturing source to copy the drug, package it exactly like the original, and sell it to the vet practices. Reorders will be only by computer, "for efficiency." Of course, their version of a drug is a cheap fake. Just like the cheap handbags on streets of New York City. Except fake handbags don't kill people. No one will look twice. The placebo effect will keep enough of the sick animals alive for a time.

Somehow, Sam is tailed by this lady from his state of Florida. He has her now. The dilemma is how to quiet her. A second murder will have the cops swarming over them. His plan is to threaten her and also offer her a large sum of money. If he can frighten her enough to accept dirty dollars, then he wins.

The inn is on his right; the traffic is light and slow. Isabella is waiting under the large old oak tree on the right. There is nothing unusual about the scene.

"Welcome back to the boring North." Isabella has a way with words.

"Just close the damn door and look in the backseat."

The car takes off toward Route 10. Isabella doesn't bother putting her seat belt on. It is easier to turn without it. Twisting to her left, she stares at the eyes of their captive. "So we got her. That's my surprise? I was hoping it was jewelry."

Sam briefly glances at her and restrains from saying what he wants to.

She looks at him and says, "Nice. Now what do we do with her?"

"She goes back to our place and she talks."

Catherine is being talked about as she if she has a choice in the matter. She knows she doesn't.

Chapter 52

Lamar and Vito love the hunt. The trip into the unknown. That's what keeps them going. It isn't the money or the shiny badge. It is the buzz. Emotion is always the drive before logic.

"You think we'll find her now?"

Lamar just looks forward and listens to the jazz station on the radio.

"Not talking anymore, or is it me?" Vito remembers conversations like this with his wife.

Lamar, staring straight ahead, says, "Either we find her talking to the people we are looking for or we find worse."

"Yeah, I've been thinking the same thing."

Lamar has that serious pursed-lip look that makes him look like an indecisive professor. "She could be hurt; she's in over her head."

"Let's hope we find her sitting in an empty room looking at invoices."

"That would work for me."

He keeps up with traffic, no heroic driving tonight. The jazz that fills their car is mellower than the feeling in their guts. Looking at the papers from the tech team, they find themselves in front of a nondescript warehouse in Fall River. Not a surprise. Her rental car is nearby. They close the doors to their car softly; attention is not what they are looking for now. Lamar leads the way to the front door. Showtime.

Lamar bangs hard on the metal front door. "Police, open up."

Vito has his right hand on his holstered gun. Lamar has one hand hitting the door and the other holding his badge. There is no response.

"Police. Open the door now."

No response. They wonder if this is the right place. They walk around the dismal building and try to look through the windows. All the windows are blocked. They can't find any sign of life in the area. This isn't the first time they have had to deal with scenes like this. Nowadays, they need a court order to break in and search a place. They both miss the old days when they just did what they had to. All that happened then was they caught more criminals with less hassle. Now, you have to go to law school to say hello to a stranger. They know that they need the papers to get in the place.

With a shrug Vito looks at Lamar and says, "I hate when this happens, it sucks."

"We have no choice." Lamar, the logical one.

"Well, we have a drive back to Boston, and I'm starved."

This is not a surprise to Lamar. "Let's head back. I'll call a friend of mine who might be able to help us find a place to grab a decent meal on the way back."

All Vito can think of is that this part of the job sucked.

Chapter 53

I don't mind packing. I am old enough and experienced in traveling. I only take the basics. Besides, the town of Hanover has some pretty nice stores. I pack what I think of as comfort clothes: old jeans, khakis, gym clothes, and a few turtlenecks. That's it. One suitcase does it all. It is reflex when it comes to my shower needs. I always travel with my own antibacterial soap and shampoo.

With all that done, it is time for the most important part of the packing deal. Counting the pills. This is a cold reminder of my epilepsy. I make sure that I have more than enough. I double-check in my wallet for the emergency prescription in case I lose any of the meds. The date is valid for another five months.

I look at my four-legged roommates sitting around my suitcase. They all know something is changing. The wait-and-see attitude is a collective strategy for the gang. I made arrangements with Avis to rent a Chevy SUV. I need the comfort of size on the highway. The weather up north is also an issue. You never know what the next front will bring.

I leave a message for Vito telling him where I will be with a phone number. I have my computer with me. E-mail always works. I reason that if it is an absolute necessity, I can head back to Boston. The way the deal is breaking, that seems remote to me.

I don't know why, but I am excited with anticipation waiting for a rental car. Probably a Y chromosome thing. I am not disappointed. A bright red Chevy Equinox with grey leather seats is waiting for me. It looks brand-new. Cool.

Dressed in old khakis, grey tee shirt, and crewneck black wool sweater, I am set to go. I throw my bag in the backseat and head up north feeling free. It isn't until the last exit on Route 91 that I realize I forgot two things. Very important things. I never made an appointment at the vet for Fern, and I left my pills on the bathroom sink.

Chapter 54

"Where are we going to put her?"

Sam thinks that is a good question that deserves an answer. The only problem is that he doesn't have one. Every *i* is not dotted and every *t* not yet crossed now. Open-ended issues scare him. Once you are a control freak, it is hard to let things happen without a plan.

They undo the tape on her ankles, and her first step is a wobbly one. It is obvious she isn't going to take off once out of the car. She crashes on the maroon-felt couch, butt first. Breathing deeply and quickly, the first sounds come out of her since arriving in Hanover.

"Where the hell are we?"

Sam and Isabella look briefly at each other. It is understood that this is Sam's show. "You're in a nice town in New Hampshire. Think of it as a vacation. We provide the food, lodging, and entertainment. All you have to do is answer some questions and be a good girl."

"This good girl needs to use the bathroom. I also need some Advil. My head hurts like hell. I wonder why? You always hit women when they are not looking?"

Sam smiles. "Only tough bitches like you. My partner will walk you to the bathroom and give you the pills."

"Are they real or counterfeit?"

So she knows their business. They have to find out how much she knows. "Take them and find out."

Isabella walks her to the main-floor bathroom and gives her two Advil. She has her own supply, the original formula. Removing the tape on her hands, she waits outside the door. The window is small, not an escape route.

"Don't lock the door."

Catherine closes the door and runs the water. She needs to figure out the deal here. It is all one big unknown. Somehow, fear isn't in the picture. Just another challenge. Her CV will look even more impressive after this closes out. She has to think this way, there is no choice.

Chapter 55

Finding the right station on the FM car radio is a simple pleasure. The simple pleasures are what I live for. The jazz is smooth and finds just the right place in my soul. Charles Brown singing "Set 'Em Up Joe" takes me back to a basement jazz club when smoking was something we all did. It is in Greenwich Village—who knows when. It was so easy to feel grounded in those days. We all had the illusion of self-knowledge.

Whatever woman I was with always seemed to be interesting and eager for discovery. Those moments in the past seemed simpler. What an illusion. It is nice to remember what you want. Selective memory. The idea of a long-term marriage wasn't even in the thought process then. And here we are now with the question put forward to Robin Williams, in a movie, playing the President of the United States: The reporter asks "What is your view of same-sex marriage?" His response: "You mean people married longer than twenty years?"

It must be nice to say what you want and have people laugh.

I am driving at seventy-five miles an hour on a highway heading north, thinking of a woman I hardly have said a word to. I can't get her great body in all those positions in yoga class out of my mind. I just have to get past the hairy armpits. Of course it is "so European." So is a history of the great horrors of mankind.

Chapter 56

"So what do you think of this place?"

Lamar looks at Vito with one of his patented cynical looks and says, "I'll tell you when the food comes. This place will look as good as the food is."

Vito nods. It makes sense to him. A one-room café on the first floor of a fancy three-story dress shop. The rooms are all small, except for the café. The food is simple, and that appeals to both of them. They both order the same thing off the menu: a turkey, cheese, and sliced tomato panini. In the old days it was called a grilled cheese with turkey sandwich. It is also five times the price of the old days. Vito can't even pronounce the name of the cheese.

"We need to find her. I think she's in trouble." Lamar has repeated this a few times in the car. Not a pleasant thought.

"We should talk to Adam. For all we know she's with him."

Lamar nods at Vito's idea. "Go ahead."

"I'll check in with the phone in Boston." Vito does what he always has done, check on Adam with the message machine. This time the look on his face is confused. "He left us a message. He's going to New Hampshire to stay at a friend's house for a few weeks. If we need him bad enough, he'll come back. Otherwise keep in touch with his contact points."

"Independent fellow, isn't he?"

"Yeah, I didn't have a clue, and I'm living with him. That's makes me responsible for three dogs and my own meals." He doesn't mention the cleaning.

"It's kind of odd to have him just leave without consulting us." Lamar has this fantasy of being in charge of everything, including other people's lives. Maybe that's why he never married.

"He left a number. I'll call him tomorrow. I want to make sure there are no other surprises back at the place." Vito knew this was the first step to living on his own. Not that Adam had that in mind.

Their plates empty quickly. The place looks real good to both of them. Back in the car on the final leg to Boston, the conversation is on the rebuilding of the Bruins. They know the new season brings changes to the team, but then again, new seasons always bring changes, don't they?

Chapter 57

I love the sound of gravel when driving up the winding road to my buddy's place. The woods with their mix of evergreens and maples are simply wonderful. The smell, the sight, the feel of the cool New Hampshire air just does it for me. Does what? Places me on this earth with a feeling I belong. Why is it I am always seeking the simple peace of belonging?

Maybe I am lucky that the sound and feel of gravel under my wheels and the smell of the woods do it for me. I am taught in yoga to truly live the moment. My teacher is an expert. I have to let it go. Let it go.

The open contemporary shape of the house is offset by the warmth of all the wood used in its construction, inside and out. The quiet has me thinking of Fern, Bowser, and Bentley. I'll call Vito and ask him to call the vet for Fern. I am done and washing up in the bathroom when I remind myself to get a supply of carbitrol. I need my meds.

I'm glad I carry an emergency prescription.

My nighttime seizures are under control with that drug. I am in trouble without it. I set up all my little different-shape bottles of pills on the shiny dark graphite countertop in the bathroom in my bedroom. Vitamins, aspirin, and extra vitamin C are all in attendance. No carbitrol. I run to the SUV where I left my wallet in the center console. I remember I had checked for the emergency prescription, but I was not a tower of security at that moment.

The damn doors are locked in the car. My blood pressure is cooking, and my temperature is frying, emulating every study of anxiety I have ever read. Back and forth from the house to the car once again, this time with a key that has a Chevy symbol on it. Clicking the unlock symbol, I grab the door and dive into the front seat. Flinging open the black center armrest, there, resting peacefully is my well-worn wallet. The Rx is in place; my temperature and blood pressure go down. Logic takes over. Once again, the New England air is appreciated, and I slowly walk to the house.

The yellow pages confirm the CVS on Main Street in Hanover is open all night. My plan is to relax for thirty minutes and go into town. A visit to CVS to get the prescription filled and a visit to Molly's for a beer and dinner.

It always works out. I used to say that to others; maybe it's true.

*   *   *

Isabella's job is to bring in the burritos. They have plenty to drink in the fridge. Waiting in-line at the basement burrito joint, she realizes she is the oldest person in the shop. She makes eye contact with a Hispanic-looking young male. He has a dark complexion with a small scar on his left cheek. His hair is black and worn in a ponytail. He is in front of her with three young white women separating them. She needs to speak Spanish. In her native language, she asks him what is good to order. He looks at her as she is from Mars. He then turns, so all she can see is the ponytail. She struck out on that one.

The car smells of the spices of three large chicken burritos. The odor of home. She feels good; the food has her thinking of the warm South with its palm trees and breezes. The hills and cold of New Hampshire make her feel bitter and icy. Inside and out. Her soul is not made for this part of the world. It is worth it for a short time. The money will be good. It better be what he promised.

Damn, she missed the turn to the house. All these damn little roads are the same. She looks for a place to make a U-turn. She is worried that the food will be cold and soggy when she gets to the house. Driving up a quarter of mile, she puts her left blinker on. To her it is just another gravel road going up to a home. She makes the left and eases up a bit on the road, noticing the lights of an SUV moving down the road. It is going pretty fast for such a narrow private road. She stops, hits reverse, and backs out. It happens just before the two are nose to nose. Neither driver notices the other.

Both drivers have their missions and are engrossed in their own thoughts. Just as well. If they had made eye contact, it would be a miracle if their vehicles didn't also connect. It would have been interesting.

*   *   *

"No problem, in an hour you can pick it up."

The small grey-haired man with a stoop has a perpetual smile. I wonder if this pharmacist is taking, or selling, what is behind the counter.

"Thanks, I'll be back around nine o'clock."

"No problem, in an hour you can pick it up."

With a forced smile, I escape the asylum. Since I have no quarters, it is nice to know that parking in town is free after five o'clock. I hate carrying change. It's bulky and noisy. And dirty.

I am able to park about two blocks from the restaurant. The walk is good for me. The energy on the street reflects the young crowd. A few older people filter through them in an effortless stream. The blend works for me. At least tonight it does. Molly's seems to have been around forever. All it does is serve good food.

I find my way to the bar and order a Smutty Nose Old Brown Dog Ale and a hamburger. Of course, the Sports Channel is on, and a review of all the hockey teams is in progress. College hockey. I didn't even know the season has started. But then again, I don't know what is going on in a lot of places. I am halfway through the ale when the hamburger arrives. I don't care how well-done it is cooked; I am hungry.

I needed to get away from Boston. I felt out of place at the station house. An amateur hanging out with the pros. The way I was used by the woman with many personalities has me concerned about my own validity to this whole investigation. After my last French fry and halfway through the second ale, I have a scary thought. I sip the brew, and each time I place the mug down, I think of waking up next to the various women I have been with over the last month. The chill doesn't leave the mug. I was spending the last third of my life as a sex object. It doesn't get me excited.

Chapter 58

Vito loves being a cop. He's always been a cop. His father was a cop. He didn't know his grandfather. Politics always affect how to be a cop. Lamar is a hard-driven intellect. He likes to work his part in the puzzle. For Vito, this is all he knows.

Being in the condo by himself doesn't make Vito feel comfortable. Somehow, the presence of his loose cannon roommate gives him comfort. Working with him is good for both of them; they get the view from each other's world.

The only sounds that Vito is greeted with are of two hungry dogs. Fern is quiet in a corner by herself. This is not like her, and Vito knows it. Picking up the phone, his friend's message is loud and clear: get Fern a vet appointment. Looking at her, he dials the vet. He sets it up for tomorrow morning. He'll drop her off for tests and observation. He'd call Adam and keep him updated.

The case is a sloppy one. Neither he nor Lamar has a time line or feeling about it. There is no rhythm to it. No precedent. It is hard to investigate a murder and a drug counterfeit ring at the same time. He knows that they both are on the same playing field. He needs a score card. Finding a link would be nice. You need the people to question. The only people he and Lamar have now are each other. Of course, Adam is in the picture as well. The kind of picture called modern art.

He feels bad for Bowser. They go to the same old park where he'd walk with Gord. You can see him looking over at the apartment that is all roped off. That was his home. Not anymore. Maybe there s a way they can get information from Bowser. He has to know the contacts Gord made. Those dark eyes and piggy ears have to have a wealth of info. Maybe he'll start taking Bowser and Bentley on his investigations. It might be worth seeing how Bowser reacts to certain people. Dogs can do better than talk; they sense who is good and who is bad.

Tomorrow he'll call Adam and update him on the investigation and Fern's condition. Hopefully, the vet will find Fern with just a minor issue.

Tomorrow morning Lamar will pick him up with the paperwork to open the door to the warehouse. He is hoping that there is someone in the shop. He is looking forward to seizing material and questioning a person. If they can get their hands on someone making fake drugs, they could convince them to turn state's evidence. That would open the doors to the next stage of the investigation. But he learned a long time ago: don't get ahead of yourself.

He realizes that Fern won't be with them tomorrow.

The next morning Vito makes his own coffee. He is good and keeps the breakfast carbs at a minimum.

The weather is clear, clearer than Vito's mind. His three companions guide him through the routine.

Vito turns to his right to notice the Canadian neighbors with their dalmatian, Spot. They aren't the creative types.

They like to talk.

"Where's Adam? We haven't seen him?"

Vito's jaw muscles tighten. It's none of their damn business where Adam is. He needs to change the subject.

Time for him to take charge.

"In and out, project he's with buried him in the folders. How are your Hab's this year?"

"New coach, they should be flying. Can't wait for Wednesday's game on TV. Hockey night in Canada, eh?"

He has to get out of this, now. "Have fun, I'm into the Celtics." As he is walking away he can't resist. "Are your five-dollar bills still blue? Very pretty." The color alone makes them worth less than the U.S. dollar. Vito can't imagine it any other way. His back doesn't notice the look on their faces or their answers as he is a quarter mile away. He is not waiting for a response.

Chapter 59

The microwave saves the night. Saving the evening means keeping Sam fed with plenty of beer. Isabella arrives back at the place with lukewarm burritos and her partner looking at his watch. The captured woman is going to be treated nicely, at first. They will be good: feed her, give her what she wants to drink, and make her comfortable. If she talks and works with them, good. If not, then Sam shows his mean streak.

Anyway, a few seconds in the microwave oven and the burritos are as good as new. Hot, meaty, and spicy. For a few minutes they eat, looking like old friends getting together. They are together; like a horrific blind date Sam takes the lead. No surprise. "Good, aren't they? You didn't think up north they could make these this good."

"Yeah, what a surprise." Catherine isn't stupid. She knows a show is being put on for her. They untie her and feed her. They sit closely on either side, she knows she isn't going anywhere on her own choice. She slowly drinks the Bud from the bottle. She needs a plan. She slowly eats from the plastic spoon that is provided. They are taking no chances. Catherine decides that time is not on her side. It is now or never. "What do you want from me?"

Sam and Isabella glance at each other. Neither one responds. Sam takes his time eating. Isabella is done eating, just taking her time with the bottle of water.

"Do you want coffee or tea?" Isabella is so civilized; that is plan 1.

Catherine immediately thinks: a steaming, hot cup of liquid would make a great weapon. "Thanks, tea would be good, no sugar or milk. A big mug, please." A quick flick of her wrist in Sam's face and the gamble she can outrun the woman—a simple plan. While they untied her before dinner, she overdid the limp. It is now just Sam and her at the table. The water is being boiled and the tea bag placed in the mug.

"Thanks for the tea; I need to warm up some more."

"No problem, I understand how we Southerners can't stand the cold."

Sam smiles and makes eye contact, "I know you've been tracking us from the South. Who are you?"

It is time to buy some time. It really doesn't matter what they know. Isabella disappears. She needs her near Sam. "It doesn't matter who I am, I know who you are."

Sam wants to slap her. He wants to beat her and tie her to a tree outside to spend the night. Let her freeze. The front door opens, and Isabella comes in with three cut logs. They are dumped in the pile with the others by the fireplace. They both watch Isabella as she removes her layers of clothing and mittens.

She throws the blue crew sweater and the black ski jacket in the corner. "It's cold out there."

Sam stares at Catherine and repeats, "Cold out there."

Catherine isn't going to let this be her last meal. "Who am I?"

"Don't push my patience, you do the talking. What do you know about us and who is working with you?"

The kettle starts its annoying whistle. Catherine has never been so happy to hear water boiling. "OK, I was an attorney in Florida on both sides of the aisle."

"How do you like your tea?"

"Strong, thanks."

Sam stares at her. He needs to find out everything. They can't screw this deal in Boston. Isabella removes the tea bag from the mug and walks it over to the table. She sits down on Catherine's left and places the large green ceramic mug with the logo of the Dartmouth ski slope painted in white on the sides. Sam and Isabella flank Catherine shoulder to shoulder. They are controlling bookends to the wounded woman. Sam doesn't move his upper body as Isabella sits down and places the steaming mug in front of Catherine.

The mug sits in front of Catherine. It sits for ten seconds. In one motion she grabs the mug and flings the steaming contents directly into Sam's face. Her left hand, holding the handle, smashes the hot mug into the center of Isabella's throat. She can hear them screaming as she bolts through the front door. She moves as fast as she can to the main road. Adrenaline will only keep her alive so long without a coat.

Chapter 60

Peace of mind is a nice feeling. A beautiful emptiness between my ears as I walk to the pharmacy. The pharmacist is smiling as we do the deal; I know why I am smiling, but not a clue as to what is going on in his mind. A good meal, good beer, a good parking spot, and a fresh supply of anti-seizure meds. What else is there? Well, I wouldn't mind finding an interesting woman on the road back to the place. Fantasy has entered into my reality.

The cold air on the way to the car starts to get clarity into my thought processes. I need to talk to Vito about what was up with Fern. I am wondering if the last few weeks were just treading water in my life. I wasn't unhappy floating day to day with little purpose except walking the dog and reading the sports section. What's wrong with that after all those years dealing with other people's problems and my own? You meet others and help carry their baggage. Some people's baggage never gets checked. Mine's heavy enough.

Meanwhile, I totally forget the color of the Chevy I rented. There are two parked next to each other, and fortunately, I press the right button, and the lights go on. Starting it up and feeling the hot air blast on my feet, I pull out of the spot and look forward to a quiet evening by myself in my friend's home. I drive slower than usual on Route 10. I am always cautious when I have had a few beers. Also, up here, you can never tell what animal will emerge from the side of the road. I figure my usual twenty-minute drive will be twenty-five minutes tonight.

Listening to the oldies on FM, I never expect to see this life-form. It looks like an underdressed woman jumping and waving on the side bike path. It's probably some drunken freshman student or a sorority pledge. I decide to drive by, no need to get involved in some undergraduate prank. Then again, it's not a busy road, and it is cold. What the hell, I'll be doing some parent a favor. Years down the road, I'll be a story to reminisce about her college years. I pull over into someone's drive and back out in a U-turn. She probably won't even be there on the way back.

The radio has the Rolling Stones singing "You Can't Always Get What You Want." I can't add too much to that. There she is, kind of running toward town. Not a run, not a walk, just a quick ambling in distress. In a few moments I'll be showing up to the rescue. I just hope she's not some wacko. As I drive up behind her, a steady, light rain announces itself on the windshield.

Pulling up behind her, I say, "Do need you a ride somewhere? You look cold." I only see her wet hair and shivering arms.

Chapter 61

"I see the merit in the idea. It's not as out of left field as you think. It could hook us up with some kind of connection to Gord's world."

Vito knows that Lamar will see this his way. The only downside is looking ridiculous traveling to a crime scene with a bulldog and a corgi. But he makes the arrangements for Lamar to pick him and the crew up in Charlestown. The gang at the station house misses the chance to offer their encouragement. Vito keeps hearing Lamar's words, "I see the merit in the idea."

Lamar seems so formal, their styles so different. That's why they work so well together. It is now seven thirty in the morning, and Lamar will be out front of the condo in thirty minutes. A busy day: a visit to the crime scene, a call to the vet about Fern, a call to his wife about their next step, and a call to Adam. Looks like a roller-coaster ride. The trick is not falling off. The sedan pulls up, Vito opens the back door, and the two canines jump in as if they'd been on the force for years.

"Our new partners seem pretty comfortable."

Lamar hardly looks at them, accepting they are part of the team. Vito knows he has two new allies. "Open the back windows a bit. Our partners like the air." Lamar needs to be told the new rules.

"I am going to stop by the corner place to pick up some coffee and the papers." Lamar never stops the Ford. In a minute they are on the curb opposite the coffee shop.

"I'll get the two large coffees, four waters, and the *Globe* and the *Times*." Vito thinks of everything, including hydrating the dogs.

This is the best part of the day, the drive down to the warehouse. Nothing to do but drink coffee and talk. Nerves are a thing of the past. They have done this enough to make this just another part day.

"It would be great if the whole group were in the warehouse with the fake goods."

"A dream."

"Yeah, I'd be happy with Gord's murderer and the fake drugs."

Vito thinks about that. He knows that isn't going to happen. He doesn't know why, just knows it. "I'd be happy with prints and fake goods. So let's settle for finding a bit of anything."

Lamar is driving with one hand, the other holding the steaming coffee. He looks, as always, straight ahead. Once on the highway the windows are all closed. Bowser and Bentley are in separate corners, curled up and sound asleep. Vito admires them; he wishes he could do the same. Lamar doesn't have a clue that there are dogs in the backseat.

An hour and a half later, they pull up a block from the warehouse. The dogs are let out to take some water in and let some out. They are on short leashes. The four of them marching to the front door does not give the appearance of detectives with police dogs on official business.

Jamie Axelrod, in his entire rumpled splendor, casually glances out the side window next to his computer desk. This is his one window to the outside world. His view is of an empty industrial street. That's why he is surprised to see two middle-aged men with two dogs walking toward his office. He figures they are people involved in the veterinary world. They probably want to check the drugs on the dogs before buying them. Make sure they like the taste. If they don't take it, why buy it?

He figures he can be a big help in selling the stuff. If he increases sales, maybe Sam will give him back his cut. This is all about the money. The knock on the metal door is expected. He waits a minute and walks over to open the door.

"One minute, be right over."

Lamar and Vito keep their badges in their pockets. Bentley and Bowser keep their tails down. Axelrod opens the door. He doesn't wonder why they didn't call first.

"Hello, what can I do for you?"

Lamar and Vito make quick eye contact. It is understood that Vito will lead. "We'd like to come in and ask some questions about what you're doing."

"All four asking questions?" Jamie thinks he has a sense of humor.

"Yup."

Vito knows he has a sense of humor. Lamar is absorbing the sights in the room. They need to get through the next door, into the lab. Vito lets go of the leashes, and the dogs are in front of the door to the lab, wagging their tails.

Jamie looks at them and says, "I see they want to ask questions in the other room."

"Yup."

"No problem, we need their opinion." Lamar is fighting back a big smile. This guy is an idiot. If they play him right, they will finally start to put it together. The door opens to the lab, and Bowser leads the way.

"Give me a minute and I'll show you what we have in inventory."

"Sure."

The door to the lab closes. The five of them are standing in the center of the room; Jamie has his back to his new acquaintances.

"What exactly do you have for us?"

"The Epogen is what we're doing now. The acceptance has been good. Our price is a good one."

Lamar looks at Vito. Lamar's turn to take the lead. They had a "no knock" clause; they didn't need it.

Jamie likes to talk to strangers. "Our price is real good. The more volume you buy, the cheaper it is."

Vito is thinking of course it's cheap. It is expected to have treatment value; it doesn't. The boxes of Epogen and the vials look authentic to the generic eyes.

Lamar takes over and says, "You make this product here."

"Yes, I have complete control. I have been in the business many years."

"You made everything you want to sell to us."

"I'm proud to say yes."

"Turn around and put your hands behind your back. Vito, read him his rights."

The look on Jamie's face is a combination of surprise and fear. The cold real world has smacked him head on. Bowser barks and Bentley is lying on his stomach, observing the entertainment. Soon Bowser joins Bentley and is lying on his stomach, sharing the view.

With their badges showing on their belts, they spin him around and sit him down firmly on the metal desk chair. They just stare at him without saying a word. Three men and two dogs, all seated and four of the five staring at the geek in handcuffs.

"I didn't mean to do any harm, just make some extra money."

The two cops just look at him blankly. Bowser and Bentley both yawn and roll over. The snort from the bulldog breaks the silence.

"What do you want?" The words came out a high pitch from Jamie.

Vito stands up slowly and goes to the bathroom. The flushing toilet is the only sound in the room. He closes the bathroom door and puts his chair in reverse and moves it in front of Jamie. Lamar stands up and walks across the room in direct view of Jamie.

Vito speaks, "Do you want some water?"

Shaking his head up and down vigorously Jamie quietly says, "Please."

Lamar walks over to the fridge and takes out three bottles of Poland Spring water. "Is this the real stuff?"

"Yes, I bought it from the supermarket in town yesterday."

"Fine, you drink it first." Un-cuffing him and re-cuffing his left wrist to the back of the chair, Lamar gives him the freshly opened plastic bottle. He quickly drinks three gulps of the water.

Vito takes over. "Tell us who you are and who you are working with. The more you tell us, the easier things will be for you." Vito is in his professional zone. He feels like a defensive lineman nailing the quarterback. He is a lucky man, happy in his job and not thinking about his retirement. When the divorce battle begins, then the test will come.

"If I tell you who they are, they'll kill me."

"We'll protect you."

"How can I be sure?"

Lamar joins the session with his flat, firm, monotone voice. "You have no choice."

No one speaks. Vito sips his own bottled water and is eye to eye with Jamie.

Jamie's shoulders are slouched over, and his head starts to droop. He oozes defeat. "I'll help if I get protection and a deal. I need a lawyer." The dirty six-letter word finally comes out.

"Time to walk the dogs and take you down to the station house."

Lamar abruptly re-cuffs him and holds him by his left arm. Vito walks the dogs around the lab to see if any smells get their attention. Nothing deserves a return sniff.

The rear seat is shared by the two dogs and Jamie. As they head back to Boston with Lamar at the steering wheel, Vito turns to face the three occupants in the backseat.

Speaking to the one in cuffs, he says, "You better not move quickly, those two can be pretty mean."

Bowser's snorts come just on cue. Jamie scrunches toward the window in his side of the backseat. Every so often Vito turns and stares at the crew in the back. Jamie's fear has Bowser and Bentley staring at him for the whole ride to the city. They all are excited. Different types of excitement, for different reasons.

Chapter 62

I never liked stopping on the side of a main road. At nighttime in the rain, I enjoy it even less. Picking up a stranger isn't something that is in my repertoire of experience. The apprehension that I feel is like living on the wild side. Going into the unknown for a good reason, I am still going into the unknown. The yoga part of me is saying to just live the moment, take it for what it is. The pragmatic part of me is saying that I am out of my fucking mind. The yin and yang. Momentum doesn't give me the luxury of philosophizing any more.

I stop the car and put the window down and ask the person, "You need a ride?"

Seeing the back of her head all that is visible is wet dark hair and damp clothes. Not enough clothes to keep her warm. Her arms are crossed and held close to her body, and she starts to turn toward me.

When our eyes meet, we both yell at the same time, "What the hell?"

She may have been chilled, but I am totally frozen. My mind is moving faster than my mouth. Nothing comes out. Not the same for her.

"Let me in." It is said softly, no energy, so out of character.

The front passenger-side door opens; she slides in. Taking off my coat and covering her shivering body, I know I am not destined for quiet moments alone in the mountains. I raise the thermostat and hit the button that starts heating her seat.

"Get us out of here, now."

I look both ways across the road and head toward my rented house. "Should I drive past my place in case anyone is following us?"

"Yes."

I drive past the town of Lyme and head toward Orford where I know a few back roads. Going past the four historic mansions on the right, I turn up a narrow dirt road and continue up a steep hill. Looking in the rearview mirror I see only blackness. I stop on the dirt incline with my blinkers on. It is my turn to talk. My brain and body are starting to recognize each other.

"What's going on?"

"I found where the fake vet drugs were being made. At the warehouse the guy I was following showed up and knocked me out. He and the woman from Florida have a place up here where I was held. I escaped, and what are you doing up here?"

I guess if this was thirty years ago, other hormonal thoughts would be controlling the scene. What a difference time makes. "Getting away from the whole investigation. Guess I'm not doing such a great job."

She just looks at me, still shivering.

"Let's get back to my place and get you in a hot shower."

One way or another I go out and come back with a woman taking a shower in my place. The unbelievable is my believable. The whole story is told to me on the way back. I feel secure that no one is following us as I pull up the driveway to my place.

Her wet clothes make a trail to the shower in the bedroom. With a shot of twelve-year-old scotch in her hand, she closes the shower door. I open a can of chicken soup and put on the stove to heat up. She needs more than tea.

I sit on the couch with my own glass of scotch and try to make sense of this. All I know is that I miss Fern in my lap. Scotch and Fern have a way of giving me instant perspective of any situation. It hits me: Vito should know what's going on. I need to know what the deal is with Fern. I let the Balmoral roll on my tongue and slowly slide into my body. Two deep breaths, I hear the water stop.

I pick up the phone. It rings four times, no answer. A familiar voice, my own, tells me to leave a message. I hate talking to myself. "Vito, call me up here. The number is on the pad by the kitchen phone. It's very important."

Yellow bubbles are making noises from the black pot on the stove. The yellow bubbles look like they are going to explode from their confines. I jump up and take the pot off the burner as she enters into the kitchen. She has on the heavy blue sweats that I left on the doorknob. I don't know why, but I also left her a pair of my red boxers with little blue doggies on them.

"Do you want a mug or a bowl?"

"Trust me with a mug?"

I look at her and wonder how far this experience has affected her judgment. "Sure."

I pour the soup into a large black mug and set it down on the breakfast bar. I go back to sit on the couch. I'm not taking any chances. Sitting down and sipping the soup you'd never think that she was held captive by two criminals. It looks like a guy and his girlfriend settling in on a cold night in the mountains.

Another beginning. Can you have another beginning with the same person three times? Who knows what she calls herself now. They all seem to share the experience of the shower in her or my place. Do a bunch of short-term relationships with the same woman equal one long-term relationship? Of course, we have to factor in the other adventures I had with the other women. Does my energy thinking of the possibility of the hairy armpit woman count?

"This is getting insane and a bit scary."

Is she reading my thoughts?

* * *

Isabella is on her knees. She uses both hands to grab the nearest chair to pull her up. Sam is on the floor, bent over, and screaming in pain. He somehow knows enough not to touch his face with his hands.

The shock of the force on her throat is wearing off. Sam is getting worse with time. Isabella needs to get him to a hospital. She can't believe they were that stupid. They actually gave a scalding weapon to someone they had captured.

"Get me to a hospital." Sam keeps saying that over and over.

She knows that had to be done; she also knows that they need a story to tell the doctor. The only thing she can think of is that he was holding a pot of hot water, and he slipped and fell face first into the kettle. It is worth a try.

"My lips, my lips hurt."

"Look, there's that big medical school hospital not from here. Let's go."

The cold air feels good to him as he is guided to the car.

"Leave all the windows open."

She understands how the cold, damp air lets him tolerate the pain. The Dartmouth Medical School and the Mary Hitchcock Hospital complex are ten minutes away.

They know they are not in the big city by how clean the place is. The immediate attention and courtesy of the emergency staff is something they are not used to. The tall heavy, big-boned intern looks more like a lineman for the New England Patriots than a doctor. Looking at the two of them as he enters the cubicle he knows something is not right. The Hispanic woman with a quickly darkening bruise on her throat and a pale-skinned male with a bright red face are not discussed in any textbook. He picks up his cell phone and signals his resident that he will need her help.

"I'm Dr. Chuck Lees, the emergency room intern. The resident, Dr. Cam Wong, will be here in a moment. What happened?"

He is reading their paperwork and waiting for a response. The medical histories are negative. He gives a shot of morphine to Sam. They both just sit there, with Sam going into a mild narcotic daze. Chuck looks at both of them again and decides the man deserves his attention first.

"I'm going to call the burn specialist, but it looks first degree, you should be all right. We just have to manage the dead tissue and keep the area from infection. We'll inject an antibiotic and use cold compresses. You're lucky that the burn stopped at the bridge of your nose."

Turning to Isabella, he examines her throat inside and out. It is just a bruise.

"Miss, place this cold pack on the bruise. I'll get the ear, nose, and throat specialist to check you out."

Now comes the interesting part, getting the history. He has to present this to his resident. He needs to score some points with Dr. Wong. She is bright and beautiful.

Isabella tells him her story. He writes it down and doesn't believe a word of it.

Chapter 63

The drive to the station house is a bit tricky. Not the drive itself, but just being careful in what they say. The discussion has to be pretty general and not let Jamie know how in the dark they are.

Getting back to the station house, the crew makes an interesting presence. Three males of assorted sizes and moods, accompanied by two dogs of assorted sizes and moods. Amazingly, they are ignored by the regulars as they walk in. They have seen it all.

Jamie is booked and put in a detention cell to wait for his assigned lawyer. It is an opportunity for Lamar and Vito to walk the dogs and to talk.

Vito has the floor, or the street. "This dork should open up for us."

Lamar has a small smile. "I agree. Let's find out who he works for and where they are. Then we go after them."

"He may be the opening that we've waited for."

"Yeah, but we have to be careful in trying to tie him into Gord's murder."

"We still haven't figured what Gord was doing to get killed."

"He had to be tied in to some drug deal, who else kills?"

"Husbands who find out where their wives are on Tuesday afternoons."

"Why just Tuesday afternoons?" They both look at each other and shake their respective heads.

"You ever done it on a weekday afternoon?" Vito is exploring.

Lamar ignores him and watches Bowser claim a fire hydrant as his own.

Back at the office, they see Jamie talking with his attorney. She is a six-foot woman with bright red hair. Patty Quinn takes all the cases thrown at her. She wins the ones where the judge is hypnotized by her bright red hair at such an altitude. They are usually the petty cases. This isn't petty. She is unpredictable. So we have someone pretty, used to handling the petty, representing the dorky. OK.

The two detectives sit down in the main room. Their desks face each other. One a total mess, the other a picture of neatness. You can tell who sits where. As they finish the reports of the morning drive, they both look up. Look really high up. The muscles in the backs of their necks are crunched. Ms. Quinn has the attention of more than the two detectives.

"We're ready to talk." Vito stands and brings over a chair.

Lamar smiles and speaks, "I'm getting some water, anybody want anything?"

"Water for me, thanks." The attorney was thirsty.

Vito just shakes his head no.

She turns to Vito. "These your dogs?"

"Yup."

"You take them to work all the time?"

Vito utters the magic word, "Woof."

Lamar joins them, sits down, passes her a bottle of water and says, "What do you have for us?"

"What are your charges?"

Lamar looks down and smoothes his solid dark blue tie. His dark eyes are as cold as his expression. "Time for the DA's office to join us. Let's schedule the next meeting."

The high cheekbones and minimal nose makes you wonder if she lived with a plastic surgeon. Actually, it is the real thing. So is everything else she has.

"Tomorrow afternoon."

"Tomorrow afternoon." She is out the door before the men stand up.

Vito and Lamar finish the paperwork and head out. Vito is on his cell phone as he walks the dogs to his car. He is calling the vet to check on Fern. The news is pretty good. She is regaining her energy, and the lab work all was normal. Maybe she just misses Adam. He tells the vet's office he'll swing by on his way home to pick her up.

He sits in his car after placing the two canine buddies in the backseat. Before he knows it, Bentley is in the front passenger seat. He can never figure out how he jumps so well with his little corgi legs. Probably a rare genetic trait. Very valuable. He starts the car and sits, looking out the window. The collection of dead bugs and city pollution give the windshield character. Actually, it's just a filthy car.

He delays the next call as long as he can. Dialing his wife's number creates more anxiety than going to arrest a serial killer. At least he has an idea how a murderer will act. The phone rings. The ringing keeps going on until the high-pitched voice of the woman he once found attractive answers.

"Leave a message; I want to know who called." So charming.

"I need the name of your lawyer so a meeting can be set up." To the point.

He'll wait to call Adam when he gets back to the condo. He needs to settle in with a beer or two or three and a big bowl of linguine. He hopes the Celtics are playing; watching them takes him to a place he'd much rather be.

Chapter 64

Catherine looks warm and snuggly on the sofa. The soup is finished and traveling where it is needed inside her. The boxers and sweats seem as if she's owned them for ten years. Comfy and cuddly. With all that was going down, this is a sweet moment.

I just look at her and imagine when I met her that night in Charlestown. I woke up without her warmth next to me, just emptiness and beer bottles in the dishwasher. Now it is the quiet of the New Hampshire woods and just the two of us absorbing the heat of the fire.

She turns her head and puts down the mug on the side table. "You have anything for dinner?"

"I ate in town, but I can make you some eggs with some rye toast."

"Well-done?"

"Well-done."

Everything I do is well-done. I find the right pan hanging from the ceiling and crack the eggs and throw the bread in the toaster, of course I had just the right amount of butter, when the phone rings. Catherine goes to pick up the phone.

I yell, "No!"

She jumps back as if she walked into a glass door.

"Watch the food, I get the phone."

It is Vito. "I got Fern, she's OK. The vet seems to think it's some kind of separation anxiety from you. Maybe I can get her up there over the weekend. I need to get the hell out of the city."

I just look at the phone and hope Vito has eaten dinner. "I'm in the middle of cooking something; can I call you after I'm done?"

"Sure."

I knew he would understand. Will he understand what I would tell him when I call? I check to see how many bedrooms this place has. When I return from my tour, Catherine is finishing her eggs.

"It was well-done, I mean really good."

"Thanks, but you cooked them."

"Who called?"

I look at her and decide it is good that she is here and Vito is coming up. Fern's presence will be a bonus. I guess Bentley and Bowser are part of the picture as well. It's getting to be one big family. All we need are the bad guys to convert, and we can all sit in one big circle and chant, "Ohm."

* * *

She is used to second looks. Her presence is that of the famous actress that she almost was. It was Broadway or medical school. The artistic part of her brain was put on hold, and Duke University School of Medicine was lucky to have her grace their halls. Camilla Wong knows she has it all. Dr. Chuck Lees does not have a chance. He thinks he does as he presents the case of the first-degree facial burn and throat trauma.

Sam has calmed down; he finally understands his pain was temporary. He starts to think of finding Catherine and teaching her what burns can do. Isabella just wants to get the hell out of the hospital with the meds needed. She wants to go down to the factory and see how the sales are going. If the numbers are good, take the money and run.

Dr. Wong reads the report and looks at Dr. Lees and shakes her head. "I don't believe what they said to you." It's amazing how a few words can deflate such a big fellow. She continues, "I'm going in with you to examine and question them. I want you in the room, taking notes and not talking. Understood?"

"Yes." He feels like the intern he is.

Dr. Wong is running the show. She opens the curtain to the cubicle where Isabella and Sam are seated. What she sees are two people with immediate trauma that are not life-threatening issues. This will be a teaching session for her intern. He has to learn to get straight histories from patients. If drugs were involved, they have to know what, where, why, and when. Any bullshit will delay diagnosis will lessen chances of resolution. She stares at both of the patients and rereads the story that Dr. Lees wrote. She reads it three times.

"I don't believe a word you told the intern. I need the truth to really get the right diagnosis to give you the right medications." It is her turn to expand reality a bit.

Isabella turns to Sam. "Sam, I have to tell her the truth." In her mind she feels there is no harm in a tale of domestic dispute. The quicker they get their meds, the quicker they get out of there.

Sam moves his sore lips surrounded by the red skin and says, "OK, but, Doc, you have to understand, this never happened before and will never happen again."

Dr. Wong knew they'd be straight with her. She pulls a chair over to use and motions for Dr. Lees to bring one in for himself. "Tell me what really happened."

Isabella hunches her shoulders and looks at the floor as she speaks. "We have been living together for three years, and we're not getting along. We decided a week in New Hampshire would be good for us. It didn't work. After dinner we had a big fight, I threw my tea in his face after he punched me in the throat."

She continues to look down at the floor. Sam looks at the back wall. They both know eye contact is not their friend. Dr. Wong and Dr. Lees are writing this all down.

Dr. Wong stands up and says to her intern, "Let's talk outside, then I will examine the patients alone."

Once outside the cubicle, Dr. Lees is losing his meager supply of cool. "Why can't I watch the exam? Isn't this a teaching hospital?"

"Because you're calling the police. This is domestic abuse, violence, or whatever you want to call it. I won't tolerate this kind of behavior. Call the cops, I'll take my time in the exam room and stall."

* * *

There's no TV in the place. I haven't been living anywhere without a TV since I was in utero. Sure, all sorts of computer hookups and technology are available, but no TV.

"There's no TV."

Catherine's eyes are half closed, lying on the couch. "So."

"What am I going to do?"

"Did you ever read a book?"

"I'll go into Hanover tomorrow and find out where I can buy a widescreen TV and hook it up here."

"I don't want to be left alone."

"Come with me, we'll decide what we do with all this info and with the police over breakfast."

Catherine's eyes close, and she is resting on the couch. I decide to leave her and call Vito. He picks up the phone on the first ring.

"Hey, how was your dinner?" He should be a chef on TV.

"Great and the company I have is amazing." I wish I could see his face now.

"Don't keep me suspense, remember I am a detective."

"Our friend Ms. Jones, or whatever she calls herself today, is sleeping on my couch."

"Get out!"

"No. Real deal."

"How the hell did that happen?"

I tell him the story, being a little more dramatic about the conditions on the highway. There is silence on the other end of the phone.

"Hello, you there?" I can hear his thinking all the way up north.

"I'm going to call Lamar and have him go to the DA's meeting alone tomorrow. I'll be up there before noon tomorrow."

"Fine. How's Fern?"

"She looks a little less energetic, but OK. You want to say hi?"

"I'll see her tomorrow, make sure she eats."

"Yeah."

I wake up Catherine and aim her toward the bedroom with the canopied blue bed. The beamed ceilings and classic, antique New England furniture make me think this is where she belongs. I tuck her in the down white comforter and place a bottle of water on the nightstand.

I find my way to the bedroom across the hall. Decorated in simple wood furniture, the same color as the wood paneling on the walls. Its charm is in its simplicity. Throwing my clothes in the corner I lie down on the bed. Instantly, I am fighting entering the twilight zone. The beige comforter is over the three pillows. It is an effort to slide off the bed, slide down the comforter, and rearrange the pillows. Task complete, I decide to rest a bit and let the day play out in my mind before I get up again and get my meds in the bathroom.

The meds stay in the bathroom.

I lay down. I am exhausted. My mind is blank by the time I am visualizing the drive in the rain. There is a sense of quiet with all my nerves and muscles on vacation.

I feel noise and movement, vacation over.

Looking at the clock on the night table, it is one thirty in the morning. Turning to my left and regaining some conscience, I recognize Catherine. She is leaning over me in my loose sweatshirt and boxers. She stares at my face with her right hand pointing finger on her lips.

"Shhh."

She pulls back the blanket and slides on top of me. Her sweatshirt and doggie boxers join intimately with my pile of clothing in the corner.

Chapter 65

Lamar hates meeting with the DA's department. It makes him feel that he didn't reach his potential. He knows he is just as smart as them, just never had the money for all those years in school. He needs the money now. He gives the world the impression of being in total control. That wasn't the way it was in his younger days. Gambling ate away whatever income he saved. Gambling was his only serious relationship. He was a good, hardworking cop that marched up the ladder to detective. He'll never know what it was, but one day he just stared his bad habit in the eye and said no. It made him feel clean. The money stayed in his pocket. The devil still bounces in his mind but is locked away. For now.

Knocking on the door of the assistant DA's office he hears the usual hoarse voice. "Come on in."

Alan Cohen never has to be concerned about money. His family owns all the General Motors dealerships in NYC. Four years at Penn and three more at Penn Law cocooned him from the real world. After six months working in the DA's office in Boston, he proved to be a natural. He presents as a short, thin guy, with a bad haircut and a grey pin striped suit. All he does is win cases. He wants to protect the people.

"Alan, have you looked over the Axelrod case?"

"Yes, straightforward. You guys did a good job in nabbing him with the goods."

"We need him to help find us the other two who are behind this. I think the murder of the ex-cop will tie into this also."

Alan pushes his chair back and swivels to look out the window. The Charles River is in his view. "I'll max out the charge and work down. The meeting with Quinn is at three this afternoon. See you then."

"My partner is following a lead in New Hampshire, it will just be me."

"Fine." Alan has always felt that Lamar was a good detective but that he always seems to try too damn hard.

Lamar stands up and, before leaving, has to add, "These guys are real bastards."

Alan looks at Lamar, runs his hand through his unkempt brown hair, and mutters, "They usually are."

Chapter 66

She is holding my hand and rubbing my arm. I am totally disorientated. The flashing lights and oxygen mask make it a bad dream. But it isn't a dream. The stranger sitting on my right is taking my pulse. Lying on a gurney in an ambulance is ridiculous. I realize I have had a seizure. Evidently, it was a bit much for Catherine to deal with. So here we are being driven to the local hospital emergency room for a team of doctors to tell me what I already know: I didn't take my medications before going to sleep. At least I didn't wet my pants.

"I tripped over you going to the bathroom early this morning. You were on the floor, not yourself. I didn't know if you had a stroke." Logical. "I was scared, I called an ambulance."

"I understand. I had a seizure, I'll be all right."

"I'm sorry; I didn't know what to do."

I was tired, very tired.

"Can you take this oxygen mask off me?"

The tech is a crew cut middle-aged man who isn't going to let me take charge. "No. Wait until the doctor looks at you in the hospital. We're just about there."

My next step is giving a neurological seminar to an intern. I feel bad for Catherine; she looks exhausted and stressed. Usually it was stress and sleep deprivation that initiated my seizures. Tonight it was sex and no medications. If I had to let my brain have its way; this was the way to do it. I just lean back and try to enjoy the ride.

The ambulance door opens and I am on the gurney being slid into the emergency room. I do my best not to sit up and direct traffic. Lying down, I am wheeled into a room next to a whining couple. The man is asking for more pain meds, and the woman wants to know when they can leave. The woman has a Spanish accent. It takes me back to my intern days. I try to tune them out and concentrate on getting Catherine settled.

"Don't worry, I'll review it all with the medical team, and they will let us out of here with a lecture on taking medication."

I have never seen Catherine, in all her characters, be so down. I didn't think vulnerability was part of her makeup.

The intern comes in, all 240 pounds of him. "Hi. I'm Dr. Lees and . . ."

"I'm fine. I have a diagnosis of idiopathic, nonspecific, nocturnal seizure syndrome. I was worked up at Penn. Here's my neurologist's phone number for confirmation."

"Then why are you here?" He asks the right question.

"My girlfriend and I had sex. I forgot to take my five hundred mg of carbatrol before I fell asleep. I had a seizure; she didn't know what to do. Call your resident to sign the chart and we'll take a cab home."

"Let me get the resident."

Dr. Wong presents the opposite of Dr. Lees. As soon as she walks in the room, Dr. Lees goes next door to attend the whining couple. She looks at us and rereads the notes left her. Looking at me directly she says, "How was it—"

"It was great." I don't let her finish the sentence.

"That you could forget to take the meds."

I just look at her and then look at Catherine.

She smiles and quickly says, "Let me call this number at Penn for confirmation and get you out of here."

She is gone, and Catherine's first smile of the evening is shared.

I overhear Dr. Lees say to Dr. Wong, "The police will be here in fifteen minutes."

I bet there never before was this much excitement in Hanover in one night. I hope the school newspaper doesn't send in a reporter. Wait a second, the police aren't for me. Who knows what went on in the minds of young doctors? I sit up, take a few deep breaths, and have Catherine help me out of the gurney. Once I get my bearings, I seek out the resident. She is at the nurse's station writing up the chart.

"I spoke with the people at Penn; you'll be discharged in a few minutes."

"Fine. Who are the police for?" I switch gears, with what strength I have, to be very authoritative.

"Not for you."

She was a cool cucumber. It legally is none of my business. As long as it isn't for me, who cares? Catherine calls a cab on her cell phone, and we wait back in the treatment room.

"You OK?" She regained her color and confidence and is starting to look like her old self. Whoever that may be

"Fine. I just learned that those black and green capsules are part of your foreplay."

"Only at night."

"I'll remember that."

Chapter 67

Patty Quinn knows she doesn't have much of a case. This isn't *Boston Legal*; she doesn't have any cute angles she can present to have her client walk. She wishes the meeting were in Lamar's office; his good coffee is legendary. Here she is in a generic office drinking generic coffee with a frightened dorky client. The DA is also dorky but not frightened.

"We're waiting for Lamar to join us. He will be here in about ten minutes." The DA speaks without looking up at her.

Patty hasn't sat down yet, she just holds her paper cup of coffee with two hands.

"I'm surprised; it's not like him to be late."

"Traffic."

"It is Boston."

Jamie is in the room sitting in the leather chair in the corner facing the DA's desk.

"Sorry, I'm late, traffic." Lamar speaks as he enters the room.

They all look at Jamie, not Lamar. Alan comes from behind his desk to lean on it; the remaining participants arrange the chairs in a semicircle facing him. The DA has the floor.

Alan looks directly at Jamie as he speaks, "You are facing serious charges. The more you cooperate with us the better chance we will consider a deal."

Patty says, "I need to speak with my client privately."

Alan and Lamar stand up, "I'll give you a few minutes." Alan has a feeling they will get what they want from this guy.

Five minutes have passed when the tall redhead and the dorky scientist return. "I recommended that my client fully cooperate."

Alan and Lamar look at each and know they shared a first. Never before had Patty Quinn been this easy. Ever. She must want something beyond this case.

Jamie has never been in a situation like this; tears are backing up in his eye ducts. "I'll tell you everything from the beginning."

Alan turns on the tape recorder, and they all listen.

Chapter 68

I reassure the staff that I will take my meds as soon as I return to the house. The place is only twenty minutes down the road. The taxi arrives as the police enter the hospital. The head nurse directs them toward Dr. Wong. I overhear "assault with trauma," "domestic violence," and "do you want to speak to each one separately?"

Catherine goes ahead of me to talk to the taxi driver. I linger as close to the treatment area as I can. I don't know why I am so interested in what is going on; maybe it is the Spanish accent I heard. That is not usually heard in this neck of the woods. Dr. Wong directs the police officers to the treatment room where the couple was placed. The two police officers look the same, and both are named Anderson. One has blonde hair, the other brown. Must be inbreeding in New England. They return from the room and walk up to Dr. Wong.

"Doctor, there is no one in the room. Is that the right room?"

She whips by them and flies into the room. It is empty. "They were here five minutes ago." Turning to the staff, she asks, "Anyone see the patients in room 6?" All she gets are blank stares.

I feel a tug on my left arm; it is Catherine.

"The meter is running."

"Wait, I have to speak to Dr. Wong and the police."

"What?"

"I have to find something out. Just hang in there."

"The meter is running," She says it a bit firmer this time.

I ignore her and go to the two policemen and Dr. Wong. "I have to ask a question." They just turn to me with blank expressions.

I knew this is totally ridiculous; I wouldn't even put it in a book if I were writing one. Could these two be the ones we're all looking for? With Vito not coming up until tomorrow, I have to be the investigator now. I describe the two whom the Boston police are looking for and that I am on the team. I tell them about the fake drugs they are pushing for veterinary use and that human use isn't far behind. The descriptions match Sam and Isabella. This is unbelievable. I set up a meeting tomorrow afternoon with the police and doctors in town. I finally find my way to the cab.

Catherine looks at me in a way I haven't seen before. "Fifteen dollars."

"What?"

"That's what your socializing costs you."

"It wasn't a social event." I then tell her the story.

With her arm resting on my shoulder, we sit in silence during the ride back to the house.

* * *

"I wrote a fake address on the forms. Don't worry." Isabella is driving in the opposite direction of the house they rented for a good fifteen minutes. She is sure they are not being followed as she does the U-turn back to their place. They have to lie low for a while, at least until Sam's face doesn't look so red. Maybe they can go back to Florida where he can say he fell asleep on the porch. Too much sun, not uncommon.

"What the fuck." Sam has a way of being direct. He has his cell phone and is madly dialing numbers. He is getting no response. He clamps it closed and turns to Isabella. "No one is answering any of my calls."

Isabella is making a U-turn in the direction of their place. "You sure you got the right numbers, you know you're a bit hyper."

"Fuck you. I know what I'm doing."

She is glad she is driving. That gives her some protection and control.

"I've called Axelrod at every number he gave us, and I am getting nothing. Where the hell is he?"

"I don't think he's on a date. I'm the only woman he's ever had."

"This is bad."

Neither one speaks for about five minutes. Finally Sam breaks the silence.

"He either got cold feet or took off, or he's selling on his own. Or maybe the cops got him. If the cops got him, he'll talk."

Isabella never trusted that guy but has kept it to herself. They are five minutes from their place. Sam was back to being the alpha.

"Look, this is what we do: We go back and clean up the place. It's gotta be cleaner than a hospital. Then we head back to get a place around Boston and check out the warehouse where the drugs are being made."

"Yeah, but the cops will be keeping an eye on the building."

"That's one way to find out how much that jerk told them."

The idea of cleaning the place makes Isabella's stomach twist. It reminds her of the days when she was cleaning hotel rooms.

* * *

Fern's image is dominating my mind. I know Vito said she seemed all right, but I have to see for myself. That's what I'll be doing in a few hours. As soon as I open the door to the place, I wobble over to the bathroom to get my meds.

"Here they are, I'm popping them now and going to bed. I need to be alone."

I am delivering the message that post seizure sex is not in my playbook. Catherine is relieved to be back and that her worst expectations are not reality. She looks at me and walks over and presses herself against me.

She whispers in my ear, "See you in the morning."

That is it. Nothing profound. I keep the bottle of water and find my way to my bed. My body is there, but my mind is thinking about tomorrow. I am looking forward to seeing Vito and the canine gang. I am sure that Bowser, Bentley, and Fern will love the property. Although none of them have long legs, they have to enjoy exploring the open fields. Vito will enjoy the modern kitchen. I found it hard to explain, but I am looking forward to playing at being a cop again.

Shifting position, I am flat on my belly. My head is resting on the mattress totally on my chin. I lift my outstretched legs and keep my arm's palm down under my chest. I am in cobra pose. My yoga breathing is steady, my lower back feeling tight. I drop my head to the right and let the big toes in each foot touch each other and my hands go down on either side of me, palms down. I am out cold in three minutes.

Chapter 69

The private meeting with the DA and Patty Quinn starts as soon as Lamar leaves the federal building. This was set up as soon as Alan looked at the small yellow post-up paper crunched in his hand. It was delivered during his handshake with Ms. Quinn. They met in the hallway outside the men's room, and she followed him back to his office.

"Close the door."

She doesn't like taking orders, but she agrees with him. The sound is slightly less than a slam. He looks at her and motions to sit.

"What do you have for me and what do you want?"

"I have some info about the dead cop."

Alan leans back in his chair, and before his feet hit the ground on the return, he says, "I'm the one to determine if the info is worth anything. You still want to go ahead?"

"Yes."

"Go ahead."

"My client heard the two people who hired him talk about how they murdered the cop."

"Did they identify the victim by name?"

"Yes."

"Did they pinpoint the time and place?"

"Yes."

"Do you think your client is telling the truth?"

"Yes."

"How did he come by to hear all this, and who the hell are these people?"

"You interested."

Alan nods.

"What do we get in return?"

"If this proves to be true and I get a conviction, your client gets a minimum sentence. Of course, he has to testify."

"OK, let's set up a meeting where he can tell you the information."

"Fine, as soon as possible, and I will have one of my assistant DAs present."

"How about tomorrow? We are supposed to meet anyway."

"OK, I call the chief of detectives to send Lamar on assignment for the afternoon."

Patty flashes her white smile at him and, as she walks out, says, "Good, see you tomorrow."

Alan watches her butt walk out of his office with only one thought. This is too easy; what did she really want?

Chapter 70

The smell of pancakes hits my nostrils as soon as I wake up. Waking up to comfort food in the mountains, what could be better? Actually, I could think of a few things, but this isn't bad. Catherine must have a persona that I haven't yet seen. Somehow, domestication is not easy to imagine. I wonder what she calls herself in this role. Did she go into the woods and look for fresh berries? At this point, anything is possible.

I feel stronger than yesterday, which is not a surprise. My upper body recovered quicker than my legs. I don't plan to go to the gym today. On my way out of the bathroom, into the hallway, I peek into Catherine's room. Did she make her bed? The blankets are scrunched up in a ball in the center of the bed. The surprise is that she is underneath them. She is out cold, in a fetal position.

I turn toward the kitchen, not knowing what to expect. As soon as I enter the hallway, I am overwhelmed by three leaping dogs. Fern is the first up and looking no worse for wear. The gang settles down and follows me to the smell of breakfast.

"You always sleep this late?" There is Vito, wearing a red apron and flipping the pancakes. They form a tantalizing pile under a heating light on his right.

"What the hell are you doing here so early? How did you get in?"

"I got up early; I want a full day in the mountains. The gang slept in the backseat; they got their rest."

"How did you get in?"

Vito just smiles as he turns off the stove. "I'm a cop. These locks are pretty basic. Nice dishes, I like the off-white motif."

I'm not ready for this, especially Vito using the word *motif*. Maybe he said *motive*, and I am just still fuzzy. I need a strong cup of French roast coffee. I smell that too. The table is set for three, the dogs have eaten, and the shower is running. Catherine is in for her surprise soon.

I sit down on the high stool by the breakfast bar and say, "Why didn't you pour the orange juice?"

He looks at me seriously, "Everyone may like it at different temperatures."

I'm definitely not ready for this. All I need to hear is Vivaldi's *Four Seasons* and see Catherine sitting naked and crying in the shower. The Big Chill redefining itself. Actually, I wouldn't mind seeing Catherine naked in the shower.

Not noticing the temperature, I drink my orange juice and head over to her shower. Pancakes can only stay warm and fresh for so long. The shower is off, and she is in the hallway, engulfed by towels from head to toe. The towels are a tasteful shade of vanilla. My favorite.

She looks at me and says, "What's the latest surprise? You hire a chef too?"

"No, Vito is here with the dogs."

She looks at me, turns, and goes back to her room.

"Where's the lady?"

"Getting dressed. Pour me some coffee; I'm going to walk the dogs."

This time I just open the door and watch all three enjoy the freedom of some land. No concrete, just greenery and trees. They bound and sniff with tails wagging. They are a happy pack. Fern is looking fine; I'll still have the local vet check her out. I wonder if they miss the city fire hydrants. I'll take them in town later so they don't lose their roots. I watch them in their freedom and admire what they are feeling in the brief time they are here. I wonder if I will ever get there. I open the door, and they instinctively know to join me back inside.

Catherine is seated at the breakfast table with her juice, coffee, and pancakes all in the process of disappearing. She's wearing my old khakis with the legs rolled up. A belt is holds them up, hidden by a grey tee shirt and blue sweat shirt, looking like the latest style. On me they are old clothes with a history. I join them and watch our four-legged pack find their niches. We talk about Vito's drive and the dogs. I have lined up all my morning pills on the table next to my mug. The vitamins join my juice, the carbitrol follows the pancakes. My daily ritual that keeps me out of trouble.

Catherine observes what I am doing, and her expression seems to say, "Don't forget the meds!"

I volunteer to do the dishes, delaying updating Vito about the recent events. The dishwasher closed, I lean against the dark granite tabletop and say, "Vito, if you want to get away for a few days, it's not going to happen."

"What do you mean? I'm here."

"That's what I mean."

Catherine gets up and pours more coffee for Vito and me. I then tell him the whole story. You can see the gears switching in his expressions as he listens to the unfurling of events.

Sipping his second round of caffeine, he says, "What time is the meeting with the local cops and docs?"

"Three thirty this afternoon."

Catherine enters into the conversation. "I need to get into town first to buy some clothes."

"OK."

I have no idea what type of shops there are in Hanover, but people have to dress.

Vito motions for a third cup of coffee. "Let's go over this again, we need to be prepared."

We all know that this afternoon will be more valuable for shopping than police work. The sense is that the two we need to find are nowhere near us. We just don't know where. Vito picks up his cell to call Lamar.

* * *

"You want me where?"

"I need you to review some of the cold cases." The head of detectives does not like repeating himself.

All Lamar has to do is to look at the pile of folders on his desk to see what the deal was. "You know I have a meeting this afternoon with the DA on the fake drug/murder case that Vito and I have been on. We're getting close to finding out who these people are."

"We need you to push these other cases."

Liam Smith, with his twenty-five years experience on the force, knows his orders are part of a bigger political picture. Lamar is good, but just a player. Liam is balding with the creases on his face reflecting what he's seen from his years in Boston. His roots are so deep in Boston that he'd vacation in the Pocono Mountains and think he was in another country.

Lamar is biting his lower lip, and his mind is racing past the speed limit. He knew something was going on; he's been around long enough. He looks at Liam and, with no expression, says, "I'll open the cases, but you have to explain why you don't want me at the meeting this afternoon."

Liam looks at him and turns to walk to his office. He stops as if to speak to Lamar, thinks again, and continues on to his office. Lamar is pissed; he didn't like being treated like a cop just out of the academy. Sitting down at his desk, he looks at the pile of records with their computer codes. It will take him a week to sort through this mess. Once Detective Smith is out of earshot, he picks up his cell.

"Vito, call back when you can. I was taken off the case. Something is going on."

His second call is to Adam. "Adam, call back on my cell. I have some questions."

He needs to speak with the guys on his team. He hopes they still are on his team. He hasn't felt like this in a long time. He is fighting the battle to go to the gambling table. After two hours of boring computer information, detailing on a kidnapping and murder from forty years ago, he has had enough. He gets up and walks out to his car. Maybe it isn't such a big deal. It could be that the DA wants to speak with Axelrod and his attorney without any cops there. Or maybe the case is broader than he thought, and the Feds are involved. As he walks the two blocks to his car, his mind bounces from logic to paranoia. It would be safer to get the calls in his car.

The cell phone rings. "Where are you going?" It's Liam.

Damn, he was either being followed or simply being treated with no respect. "I'm going to the neighborhood where the Wilson kidnapping took place. I need to see a few things."

"What Wilson kidnapping?"

"The one you put on my desk." The silence is deafening.

Finally, "Yeah, sure, just touch base with me later. I need to send a report to my superiors."

"Sure."

Lamar sees an open spot to park the car and slides into it. It is part of a bus stop, but his city cop ID keeps him out of trouble. Walking into the bookstore that he visited with Vito a while ago, he searches out the section on compulsive gambling. He isn't going to let events drop him down the well.

Chapter 71

"Do you have any idea where you want me to drive to?"

Driving down the highway toward Boston, Isabella knows that she doesn't have a clue what is going to happen next. Sam's mind is on overdrive, planning on the run. He hates doing that; he is more comfortable knowing the whole picture.

"We'll stay at a Holiday Inn outside of town. We'll use one of our fake IDs."

He knows he needs a night to think this through. As they drive toward Boston, there is a sense that the deal is over. They are going to score or be shut out. Sam doesn't like to have a partner. If they score, he feels secure that she won't open up to anyone. Why would she? There is too much to lose. But if they are shut out and on the run, she is a liability. Then there is only one thing to do. It will be easy, she won't be missed.

They find a Holiday Inn just inside Boston city limits and check in. The room has two separate beds which takes the pressure off. Her perfume makes him nauseous. After settling in, they drive to a McDonald's for a hamburger and fries. Trans fats are the least of their worries.

She looks at him as they sit in the front seat of the rented Ford Escape and, with half a fry in place of her missing bicuspid, says, "Any ideas?"

"Yeah. I need a drink. After we eat this stuff, I'm going to find a bar. I need a few beers."

"I'll go with you."

Sam has no answer; he just looks out the windshield.

* * *

"What do you think?"

"It's fine." I don't know what else to say. I haven't been shopping with a woman in about a hundred years. It is usually something I avoid at all costs. But I can't let Catherine go into town by herself. Besides, she is scared. Who knows, maybe the bad guys are still around.

We are on Main Street, around the corner from the Hanover Inn at the Gap. Catherine is finished redecorating herself, and we have our choices for lunch. I flip my cell open and call Vito. "What's up?"

"You want to meet us in town for lunch?"

"Maybe."

"What do you mean maybe?"

"I just got a call from Lamar. Did he call you?" Looking at the cell I see there is a message.

"Maybe."

"What do you mean maybe?"

"I have to check it."

"Check it and call me back."

The message is from Lamar. He wants me to call him on his cell. I do it immediately.

"Adam?"

"What's up?"

He tells me the story with the DA, Patty Quinn, and Axelrod. Then he tells me about his temporary reassignment.

All I can think of is the obvious. "Don't overreact. I'm going to meet with Vito, and then we talk with the doctors at the hospital who treated the two suspects. The local police will be there too. We'll keep you in the loop."

"Call on my cell."

"Done. Hang in there. Hey, don't drink too much of that good coffee."

As Catherine is paying with my Visa card, I call Vito. He picks up on the first ring. We both had the same conversation with Lamar. I pick up the lead. "Meet us in town at Molly's. Bring the dogs; after we eat we can work off the calories with a walk on the Green."

Dartmouth has a gorgeous large area called the Green surrounded by vintage buildings and benches. We would look like visiting parents walking the family pets. "See you at one."

Catherine comes over holding two large bags advertising her purchases at the Gap.

"See you at one."

Catherine has morphed into clothes that fit her. Somewhere buried in one of the bags are my friendly clothes with a scent that will reluctantly disappear in the washing machine.

"Vito is meeting us at Molly's at one. Anything else you need to buy?"

Stupid question. Two things are fortunate; I have an excellent credit rating and I've rented an SUV. We load up the back of the Chevy, and I slide the privacy cover over the back.

"Anywhere else?"

"Let's head to the CVS, I need shampoo and stuff."

It's like we've been married twenty years. I follow orders on the shopping tour of duty. I am exhausted when I sit in the booth at Molly's. We have a view of Main Street and observe the traffic as we drink coffee. Vito should join us in about ten minutes. I tell her about my chats with Vito and Lamar and how we need to have a meaningful session at three thirty. We have to find the perps, and the longer we wait, the bigger their advantage becomes.

"Vito is going to ask you questions about what happened with those two. You up for that?"

"I'm not one of your wimpy patients; I want to get these two bastards."

It is going to be an interesting lunch. We tell the waitress to come back when our third party shows up. I feel like I am on vacation.

The mountain air, the surprise company, and the great mix of young and old in Hanover have me in a mellow mood.

"It looks like you had fun shopping."

She takes one sip of her coffee. "I did."

"It's kind of neat being here." She looks me eyeball to eyeball and says, "I don't recommend the mode of transportation and the first place I stayed at."

I don't need to say anything.

Thankfully, Vito slides into the booth. "I'm hungry, must be the mountain air."

In Boston it must be the city air. We all order some form of salad. We could have shared two of them.

"The dogs are in the car, they seem happy."

"Vito, we need to speak with Lamar as soon as this afternoon's meeting is over." There isn't much to say; the meal is finished in silence

* * *

The bar is smoky even though there is a no-smoking ordinance. The place has been around forty years; no one is going to tell them how to operate. The name is Smokes. No surprise.

"We have to track Axelrod. It won't be easy. I don't think he has the balls to go out on his own."

Isabella agrees. She nods. They sit at a corner table in the dimly lit room. She lights a cigarette and inhales deeply. She turns her head to exhale. She is happy that Sam let her smoke.

He nurses a cheap scotch and stares into his glass. The place doesn't ooze cleanliness. The next step is easy. Holding his glass with two hands, he says, "I'll call our contact at the station house. Simple. We find out if they have our guy."

He continues,

"It's time to have our contact work for us. We know she's good, she helped us nail the double-sided cop."

"You can set up the usual meeting."

"Yeah, sounds good. I'll call from the parking lot in at the hotel."

It is time, again, to use the woman who hated everybody where she worked. It is that simple. Feed the hate, get the information. It isn't even that expensive. Her mother worked there, was never promoted. Her brother was a good Boston cop that was killed on the job. A representative from the department came over and told them a junior officer would represent the force at the funeral. She was told she had a job there forever. Well, her brother is lost forever. She enjoys hurting the force that insulted her. In her car at the end of a day full of sitting at the front desk and running errands for Lamar, she hears her cell phone ring. Her car starts as she adjusts her seat belt and opens the phone.

"It's time. This time for double the dollars."

She licked her lips. "Yes."

"I need info on Jamie Axelrod. Who has him, what he's said, and who they want. I need it soon. Real soon, like now."

"Yes."

"Call me at the following number tomorrow."

"Yes."

* * *

"We agree."

It is not a surprise from the policemen named Anderson. Even weighing the same, they are not related. Technically. Thank goodness for blonde and brown hair.

At exactly three thirty, they all meet at the Hanover station house on Main Street. Dr. Wong is presenting a case to the attending for tomorrow's surgery. She'll be a bit late. I can't wait for her pragmatism; she doesn't look bad either. The agreement is to start the meeting at three thirty and not wait for Dr. Wong. Vito, Catherine, and I sit on one side of the long table. The Anderson cops sit on the other side with the chubby intern. I want it to end quickly; Vito and I have work to do. We are looking forward to questioning Catherine and funneling an avenue of info from that. We don't need the Hanover police involved. The blonde Anderson cop is the lead.

"So they were pretty beat up, and you think it's domestic violence?"

The intern looks down and says, "Could be."

"Do you have descriptions for us?"

"Yeah."

"Let's hear them."

It sure sounds like the two that first came to my apartment. Vito and I don't even try eye contact. We're such pros. At least he is. We can't wait to question Catherine. Especially since she is kicking my shin a dark blue. In the car on the way back we'll unload and confirm who these people are.

"We'll circulate descriptions of those two through town. Now, why are you guys here?"

Vito gives me a subtle nod, which means shut up. It is my turn to give Catherine kicks in the shin; she better shut up. Vito stands up and looks the cops straight in the eyes.

"You guys have been an awesome help. You're part of the team. This gang lives and works in Boston and is probably heading back there. But if anything is stashed, including them, we need you." He reaches into his right pants pocket and passes around his card. "OK, guys, we'll stay in touch." We're heading out to leave, and the door opens. Out of breath, here's Dr. Wong. Vito stays in charge. "We have another meeting; the boys here will update you. If you need us, here's my card." He leaves two cards and a swirl of dust as the three of us bolt out.

On the street, Catherine grabs my sleeve. "You know, that's the two." I looked at her.

"Not a surprise, not many couples come in to emergency for facial burns and traumatized throats in one evening."

We walk with Vito and take the dogs out of his car to run on campus. Catherine stays with them and holds court on the Green. Vito and I are seated on a bench looking over this wonderful, innocent scene.

To no one in particular, or to everybody, he says, "If we just find out where they are going, we can find them and wrap this up."

I stare at the dogs running freely and the students smiling. I think; I need to go back to the beginning. I don't need all this complexity. I'm leaving behind complex stuff, not seeking it. Does it just seek me out? I miss my apartment in Charlestown with Fern. Exercise when I want it without deep, meaningful moments. Ignoring phone calls from my ex-wife. Although, there is one new challenge that I enjoy. Yoga seems to be offering a different window to look out of. Or is it the instructor that is the challenge?

Vito looks at me. "You know what I mean?"

I look at him and through him and say, "Yeah."

Chapter 72

Lamar is running two projects. One, he couldn't care less about; the other is urgent. He couldn't care less what happened forty years ago. He tries to stay focused on the case he is working on with Vito. From speaking with the boys up north, it seems like the woman was abducted by the two they are looking for. We always are a step behind them. Somehow, he feels like we are catching up. He doesn't have all the papers on Axelrod; he doesn't know what is going on between the DA and the perps' attorney.

His phone rings. His boss, "The DA wants to speak to you now."
"What line?"
"Not the phone, his office."

Lamar hangs up without a goodbye. He knows that to see the DA on short notice is either really good or really bad. Getting in his car, he is debating whether or not to call Vito. No point, it's better to call with the results of the meeting. He has no idea what to expect. His hands are cold when he parks in staff parking in the public building where the DA's office is. Standing in the elevator, he realizes he doesn't have a clue what number to press. Since he was the fifth and last person in the elevator, he goes for the full ride. Feeling like an idiot, he reenters the entrance and asks the officer at the information desk where he has to go. For someone who presented with confidence, he feels like he is a freshman.

His second elevator trip is a lonely one. Alan Cohen, rumpled grey suit in place, is holding court with young law students in the hallway in front of his office. Lamar is hardly out of the elevator before the students disappear, and Alan is at his side.

He still has the floor. "Glad you came over immediately."
"Sure."

They are in his office—Alan leaning on his desk, Lamar standing after closing the private office door. Alan closes his mouth and looks up at the ceiling.

He leads the talking, "I'm sorry. We needed to make it look like you are a suspect. There's a leak that needs plugging."
"I don't understand."

"We're losing information on certain cases. We have to make it look like you are being investigated. You have such a good rep that by taking you off a case, it takes heat off the suspects."

Lamar sits down in the same leather chair that Jamie used.

"What's going on?"

"How do you like your coffee?" Alan wants Lamar to settle down; he sees the gears switch behind his eyes.

"I'm fine, what's going on?"

Alan finds his way to his own chair, sits, leans back, and puts his hands behind his head. "There's someone in-house who is feeding info to the drug players. I not only want the players but the rat too."

Lamar finally realizes what is going down. They are using him as a decoy to have the in-house rat think that Lamar is under the gun. Abruptly giving him cold cases and removing him from the hot one, it seems obvious he is under suspicion. Lamar looks at Alan and says, "What do you want me to do?"

"I need to ask you to volunteer to help."

Lamar looked out the window and said, "I'll take my coffee now."

"Good. I have to give you some information. Remember Gord?"

"Sure, he's part of our investigation."

"He was double, but he still had a badge. He worked for us."

Lamar doesn't know what to say.

"I need you to take his place. Everything is all set up. If everything goes according to plan, we nail Gord's killers. We believe they're the drug makers you are tailing."

Lamar starts to feel alive again.

"Remember, your role will change, you have to find the one who's working for them and convince them that you can do a better job. It's dangerous, we need a volunteer."

"I take my coffee black."

Chapter 73

"I'll buy the fish; you buy the coffee and vegetables."

I have my assignment; I look at Vito. So does Catherine.

"You buy the dog food and desserts."

It is obvious who is in charge as soon as we cross the threshold of the food co-op. The dogs are content in our cars, resting from their jaunt on campus. The three of us have a false sense of domesticity. It is as if nothing has happened and nothing was going on. Miraculously, we all met at the same counter. The tall fellow with a ponytail behind the counter somehow knows to ask me for payment. Do I look like their parents? No, they just point at me at the crucial time.

Everything is stuffed into our two vehicles: paper bags, beer, wine, food, and bottled water. With an assortment of dogs added to the mix, we blend in with the crowd. It looks like we're in for the winter. We aren't.

Catherine still has a slight limp, but she isn't complaining. I assume it's getting better. "Leg's improved?"

"No."

"You're not limping as much."

"I'm tough."

In the kitchen we store all the provisions. Catherine organizes her bedroom and bathroom. Vito makes sure the couch folds out in the living room. We all know we are staying in for dinner tonight. There is a lot of catching up to do.

As Vito is taking the big bag of dog food to one of the closets, he says, "I left a few messages for Lamar. Any of you get a call from him?"

"No."

"Not like him not to return a call."

"Try again."

Vito sits down on the couch, legs up, Bentley on his belly, and dials. "Hey, where are you?" Vito nods to us.

"Working on all these cases. They need me in-house now."

"Why?"

"I'll get back to you in a day or two; I have to get ready for an early meeting tomorrow."

"Sure."

Vito just looks at the phone. He doesn't say anything. Catherine is grilling the swordfish; I have finished making the salad and am opening the chardonnay. Vito looks at this scene. "Enjoy this. Tomorrow morning we get back to work. Something is not right with Lamar."

* * *

It is like those Jean le Carre's spy thrillers; meeting in the park on a bench while the sun sets. Part of her is excited, the other part petrified. She was told to meet the Spanish lady at 5:15 p.m. on the bench under the biggest tree. The Spanish lady would be wearing a red striped scarf. She is to wear a black scarf. They've met before; she wonders what this scarf ID stuff is all about. Standing in the center of the park, she looks around at all the benches. Looking at the trees, she has to select which is the largest. Two on either end look the same size.

She figures it best to walk around the block just to see where the red-scarfed Spanish lady sits. It is five fifteen, and no one is sitting on either bench. She starts walking to the closest bench.

"Sit down on the second bench to your left."

She recognizes the voice; it makes her decision easier. Following the directions, she sits where she is told. A hooded woman with a red striped scarf sits next to her. She recognizes the strange smile.

"What do you have for me?"

"I can update you on the investigations and who is working them. When do I get paid? You said it is for twice the usual amount."

"I know what we said. Start talking. We only have fifteen minutes."

"The team that is investigating Gord's death is the same that is following the fake vet drugs. They think there is a link between them. The cops are the Vito and Lamar team. They have a shrink consulting with them. They were going to meet with that lady from Florida; they think she could help them. They don't know where she is. She didn't show up at a meeting."

"We know this; I may not pay you at all." The Spanish lady looks like she was ready to leave.

"I have more."

The Spanish lady looks at a young mother watching her little daughter as she says, "You better."

"They took a veteran cop off the case and buried him in cold cases to watch him. This cop also has a gambling problem. He's tight as a drum and needs money."

"Can he be flipped for a buck?"

"I think so."

"Here's half your money. Find out if this cop can be flipped. If he can, you get triple what we first said we'd pay you. If not, the double is the deal."

"OK."

"Who is this cop?"

"The black cop, his name is Lamar."

Isabella is churning. Wait until Sam hears this about Lamar. They knew he was breathing down their necks. If they can work him and finish selling their supply, well, they got it all. But first they have to figure out how to work this cop. The last one they thought was flipped wound up working with the force. They have to put him away, or they're cooked. Sam likes to be one step ahead.

Isabella looks at their snitch and quietly says, "We'll call you tonight with the next step."

Before there is a reply, Isabella is lost in the darkness.

* * *

have I been blind
have I been lost
have I been wrong
have I been wise
have I been strong
have I been
hypnotized
mesmerized
by what my eyes have found.

Looking at the fire with Natalie Merchant's words filling my head, I see the dogs resting with Vito, and Catherine staring at her wineglass. The only sound is the beauty of Merchant's voice and Fern's sighing. What a wonderful place to be.

I am so afraid. Whenever anything has felt this good, there was something hard ready to hit me around the corner. No one speaks. The

Tigerlily CD has each of us together in our own place. Look at our three lives. We all need each other at this time, but we all know the future is better on our own trails.

Our closeness is good, but not warm. Not like a thick comforter you come home to every night. More like a special run down a great ski trail. With conditions just right, great while it lasts. But you know time melts what you have to a memory.

Chapter 74

"Let's see if we can buy that son of a bitch." Sam is getting his buzz back.

He figures if they turn him for a few bucks, they make a killing with their drug deals. They just let Axelrod stew where he is, occupied with the DA's office. He could feed him a few bits of information about what they have done. By the time they verify that stuff, they will be done with the plan. If this Lamar guy is as good as they think he is, they keep him on their payroll. You never know when they can use him again.

Isabella feels like they are back in the game. She has to ask Sam this stupid question, "What's with this colored-scarf ID deal?"

Sam smiles; it is just another way to let her know who's in charge. "It gets dark; I need her to ID you. That's all."

"Whatever. She still is hungry to work with us, I can tell."

"Good."

"I call her at midnight, wake her up. She has to find out if this detective is really in the hole from gambling. If so, how much? Then, if the info sounds good, we set up a meeting."

"A meeting with her or the cop?"

Sam actually likes listening to Isabella's ideas. She has started to become attractive again. "Let's meet with her first. The more we know about this Lamar guy, the better to figure out how to deal with him."

"OK. Call her tonight. Set up a meeting, quick. We have to close this as quickly as we can."

Isabella walks over to the cheap desk in the hotel room. She picks up the hotel stationery and starts to outline her game plan. The least amount of questions and the less the snitch has to do, the less chance of a screw-up. Sam looks at her working at the desk and walks over and put his hands on her shoulders. In five minutes he is licking the makeup off her bruised neck.

* * *

I always wondered why Gord wore black all the time. Sometimes I thought it looked cool. Other times I thought he should be in the West Village in New York, not in Boston. We were in his old 4Runner with the dogs in the backseat. The windshield wipers were going; it was a quick rainstorm. The radio was on; always the AM sports talk show. As usual, everyone in Beantown was bitching about the Bruins and the Celtics. The Patriots walk on water or turf. I learned to ignore the radio.

We were headed out to one of our favorite delis near the suburbs. I figured the aspirin I took would counteract the fat in the corned beef. I knew he once was a cop. I never gave much thought to what he did every day. He never asked me any shrink questions. We always paid for our meals in cash. I just never thought much about it.

One day he kept looking in the distance, no eye contact. We were at the local bar, having a few beers, and chatting like old buddies. That is the beauty of the friendship. It was like I was back in undergrad, without the loans. That's why I never asked much about his past or present; it was a way to be young again and not care. Sort of.

"Want to get Bruins tickets this year?"

"I may be busy."

That's the first time he ever indicated he had any responsibility. I didn't make any eye contact and waited for the bill.

* * *

Lamar is a bit taken aback by her smile. The last time he had anything to do with her was when she dropped off administrative papers for him to sign. Her expression is usually miserable or blank. He forgets her name.

She remembers his as she says, "Must be tough doing two jobs at once, Lamar."

It is his turn to keep a blank expression and talk. "What do you mean?"

"Hey, I know what's happening. You get the cold cases, and they expect you to concentrate on them. What happens to all your effort with Vito?"

"You're right; this is a bitch, not fair."

She looks around, there is nobody paying any attention to them. She says, "You've been on the force a while. You shouldn't be treated like this."

Lamar just stares at her. For the first time he recognizes she isn't bad looking. Looking at his watch he says, "Maybe you can make my job easier."

"That's why I am here."
"Let's meet after work."
"Here's my cell, call after five thirty."
Lamar nods and wonders what trail he is traveling on now.

* * *

The bullet wound made him think about who he really was. Lying in the hospital bed forced Gord to think about his life. Before the lead tore through his left shoulder, he just took one day at a time. Worked and had fun. He never had much purpose or goal. Now he knew he was mortal. Bowser would be taken care of by his friends; his place would be maintained by his cleaning service.

Money was never an issue; both his parents were prominent corporate attorneys who left him a large amount in their wills. They were older; he was adopted when they were in their fifties. He was in his last year at BU when they died four months apart. It wasn't difficult for him; he had minimal contact with them. As soon as possible, he was at boarding schools, expensive, caring, and demanding ones.

After graduation, he worked in Europe in whatever job he could find. He enjoyed women but never stayed with one beyond six months. He kept that pattern back in the States. Police work was something he always wanted to do. He liked having authority and climbing up the ladder. Simply, it gave him a buzz, a legal one.

After recovery he approached his captain. "What if the guys on the force think I retired on early pension and I work the other side for you? Game?" After being sent for specialty training, he came back to Boston and took his time finding his niche. He enjoyed his friendship with his buddy, Adam. It made it look like he had a normal life. Unfortunately, it didn't end in a normal way.

* * *

"I want you to arrange a meeting with him and me."
That is what she hears when she picks up her phone at midnight. Her mind isn't clear; the fog from three glasses of wine is present. Looking at the white phone she says, "Who the hell are you?"
"I guess the deal is off." The hint of a Spanish accent brings her to her senses.

"No, I'm sorry. I spoke with him today. I think he's ready to work with us."

"Why?"

"He's not happy the way he's being treated. He hinted that he needs more money, and he may look for more work."

"Arrange a meeting at the same park where we met last. You meet with him at the same bench. When I show up, you leave. This is going to happen tomorrow."

"When do I get my next payment?"

"We'll see how this meeting goes."

"What . . . ?" The only sound is the dial tone.

Isabella turns to Sam, and he shakes his head in approval. "Good work. Let's rip up your outline sheet, we don't need it anymore."

She stands up and tears the page into many pieces. She is wearing grey sweatpants and a Miami Dolphin tee shirt. It is midnight, but they are all business. Sam is looking in the mirror at his healing face. "We have plenty of cash. We can make this cop feel sweet with us. Once we are in his head, we can get moving again."

"We can't kill this one too. The Boston force won't give us any room to breathe if we do."

She wants to say "you" not "we" but knows that will press a hot button in Sam.

"Hey, we turn him and get this deal done; you and I go our separate ways not to be found."

Sam has no intention of letting Isabella know where and when he is going. He had no choice with Gord. It was a good deal for a while. Gord kept the cops away from their setup of drug manufacturing and selling. He didn't need much money from them, just a grand a month. He also gave them names of vets to work with and what patrols were working what parts of the city. It was easy dealing with fake vet drugs. The feds were not exactly channeling their resources on that avenue.

But something started to seem funny to Sam the more he tracked Gord spending time with that guy Adam. When Adam was seen having dinner and spending the night with that woman from Florida, he knew it was time to do something. That woman had a history of working with law enforcement; and she was showing up, in one form or another, wherever they were. He stopped trusting Gord. He figured that guy Adam was working Gord for info and feeding it to the lady. That lady was connected to law enforcement, and if not here, it was going to happen. He was able to track her to the DA's office in Miami. Gord couldn't be trusted. He couldn't just stop paying him and let him go; they weren't in that kind of world. There was only one way for him to disappear. He set up the meeting for the two of them to meet at night at the construction site under the bridge. Gord figured it was payoff time. It was.

Chapter 75

I wonder if I am to be alone all night. I'm not sure about Fern or Catherine. Fern has settled in the leather chair in the living room; Catherine has her own bedroom and bathroom. Both of them seem quite content on their own turf. Vito is sleeping in sight of the kitchen. He must be in heaven. Cleaning up after dinner was taken over by Catherine. Vito just held on to his phone as if expecting an important call.

I open the front door and call out to the dogs to have their evening walk. "Let's go, come on out, follow me."

One by one, they follow me. Leashes aren't in the equation out here. The air is so clear; I just stop and hold my hands up and breathe. Yoga breathing outdoors. I wonder if this is where it was intended for in the first place. The sight of the half-moon was hypnotizing. Clear air, pure breathing, the crystal moon, they add up to a reenergizing of my senses. I smile to no one but myself when I think of the possibility of company tonight. Not knowing where the canine gang is, I call out to them. Their collective barking is calling for me on the front porch. I wonder if they had the same experience I had.

"Vito, are you going to sleep with the phone under your pillow?"

"What?" He looks at me after he answered.

"Never mind. You said tomorrow we have a lot to review. What's the schedule?"

"Yeah. Let's have breakfast at seven thirty, and I'll go over my thoughts on the case. I need to sleep on it. I don't want to clog your minds now."

I turn to Vito and say quietly, "See you for morning coffee."

As he unfolds the couch, he mumbles, "Good night."

Catherine is in her bathroom. Quietly, she leaves the talking to Vito and me. I slip a note under her bedroom door about the seven-thirty breakfast time. The dogs all curl up together in the corner of the living room, not too far from Vito. Sitting on the edge of my bed, I pop my two anti-seizure meds. If I don't have them with bottled water before bedtime, my brain sends out all kinds of wrong messages. I never know where I might wake up. Aware the special chemical cocktail is floating around in my bloodstream controlling the electrical circuits in my brain gives me, literally, peace of mind.

The mellow mountain ambiance starts to fade as I slide under the covers, not feeling tired at all. I think about what I saw in Vito's eyes. It was a different look than I had seen before. It has to do with his call from Lamar. They were such a smooth duo; there had to be something wrong. I have no idea what it is. I hear a door close. Is it Catherine? No question I want her. Why don't I ask, why wait for it to be her call? Hearing footsteps in the hallway, I decide to take charge. With all the lights out, I open my bedroom door and explore the hallway. My hand touches another hand.

"What the hell?" I am shoved against the wall with both my hands forced against my back. Vito lets go and smiles; turning the light on, he whispers, "I'm a cop, it's a reflex; when touched in the dark, I react to protect myself. You OK?"

"I guess you keep the lights on when you're with a woman."

"Hey, I'm going to the bathroom in the hallway, what the hell are you doing?"

I look at Vito. "Oh, sorry I have a Y chromosome."

The door opens to Catherine's bedroom. Wearing a long green tee shirt, she yells out, "What's going on out there?"

Vito smiles and says, "Nothing, just catching up on the fantasy football results."

She looks at both of us like we are nuts. Shaking her head, she mumbles, "That better be the only fantasy you are discussing."

Her door closes.

* * *

Lamar stays in the clothes he wore all day. He doesn't have much time for dinner, so he goes to the local diner. Sitting at the counter with a tuna salad sandwich and a diet coke, he feels pretty good. He did have some concern for Vito, but he figures Vito will get his signals, and they will be on the same page sooner or later. In this case it better be sooner.

He knows the park where this lady wants to meet him; it is safe and busy. He isn't wired; the risk of blowing the whole deal isn't worth it. He knows the game he needs to play, and the whole package could be wrapped up if he does this right. This could get him a niche to climb up the ladder. Or get him killed. He parks three blocks away from the park.

He doesn't need to be seen leaving an unmarked cop car for a meeting with the other side. Closing the door, he feels alone. The evening chill will have to be ignored. He wishes he had brought his wool scarf.

"It gets cold when the sun goes away in the winter." It sounds like a CIA code, but it's just the woman from his office.

"I was just thinking that myself."

Someone else might think those were the recognition code words. He just doesn't know what else to say. He follows her to a bench.

She speaks again. "Let's sit down. There is someone who wants to meet you. When they arrive, I will leave. I'll see you in the office tomorrow."

"Sure. Who wants to meet me?"

"Someone who may be able to help you."

"Help me do what?" Lamar was in uncharted territory.

"Here she is, just stay here. See you at the office."

Lamar turns to see a short dark lady approach him. The black hood is up on her sweatshirt. Her long coat is also black. He instinctively feels for the handle of his gun. She walks as if she's been down this road before. He keeps looking at her, totally forgetting the other woman who set up the meeting. This isn't the type of scenario that he had classes for at the police academy. She slows her walk and finally sits down next to him. She looks straight ahead; he can only see the side of the black hood.

Without moving, she says, "Thanks for meeting with me. I need you to confirm some facts for me."

Lamar wants to stand up and face her and take her in for interrogation. He can't do that now. He stays cool and stares straight ahead. "Sure, but I need to know who you are and what this is all about."

"Our friend tells me you aren't very happy at your job. All of a sudden you're not the shining light of the force. They have you holed up in the cold-case file, not by your request. Right?"

"So what's it to you?"

"You a good cop?"

Lamar's stomach is churning. "Always have been."

"See where it has gotten you?"

"What do you want?"

"You like Vegas and Atlantic City. I know that. It's no secret."

"So we all have our escapes."

"You're still paying for yours."

Lamar is becoming scared. His debts are still being whittled down, but they are still there. Who is this lady? "Nothing I can't handle."

"I can make them disappear."

Lamar has one thought: don't screw this up. "Then what do I owe you?"

"Just some information. You won't be asked to do anything actively on the wrong side of the fence."

"You can make all the debts disappear?"

Isabella knows she has him. So does Sam; he is sitting in the car outside the park. She has the wire and earpiece in. So far no comment from Sam. She must be doing well.

"All of it."

"Who are you?"

"You'll find out if you want your debt to be history."

"I have to think about it." He starts to stand up; she places her hand on his right forearm.

Without turning to face him, she says, "Our friend will tell you how to contact me tomorrow. If you don't, the deal's off."

Before Lamar can answer, she is gone.

* * *

It looks like a bunch of old friends having breakfast before skiing. The truth is that they are new friends having breakfast, and they are going nowhere near a ski slope. The only mountain they'll deal with will be the unknown.

The dogs are settled; they've been outside, so happy in this environment. You wonder if dogs should be allowed in cities, for their own good. As they find their indoor comfort, the humans are waiting for their own comfort zone to disappear.

Vito stands up and points a finger at Catherine and Adam and says, "Lamar is doing something that is dangerous and will help crack this case."

The tone of his voice is no different than in the interrogation room in Boston. They might as well have been there.

Catherine looks stern as she says, "OK, what's he doing and how do we help?"

"First, you and I have to review what happened to you. Adam, you can sit in on this meeting. After we get all our facts straight, we decide on a plan of action. Let's start now."

Catherine clears the table and Adam brings paper and pens for his roommates.

All three sit around the dining room table as Catherine relives her adventure. It seems like a memoirs class. No emotion during discussion, just a discussion of the facts.

Then Vito, the professor, takes over. "It's obvious these two are the ones we are looking for. The guy we got back in Boston is a link to help us. He's new at this game, so it shouldn't be hard to play him."

Adam asks, "How does Lamar's new role help us?"

"I need to contact him and figure that out. I also need to contact the DA."

Catherine is exhausted after reliving her kidnapping. She is human. You sense that she is wondering if this is all worth it.

A phone rings; it is Vito's cell. "Yeah." He looks over at his two housemates and says one word, "Lamar." Vito speaks next, "Can you run it down?"

Lamar is driving to the office using a disposable cell. Being stuck in traffic makes it easier to talk. He looks through the windshield as he says "I can talk; I'm on a disposable cell. We were wrong about Gord. He was working both sides and he was on the line for us. He was with the DA. They were getting close to setting up a sting with the two that we are following. The two weren't convinced he was with them, and one of them put him away. He was doing a good job keeping the secret. He was close to ending the final deal."

Vito doesn't seem surprised. He's been a cop long enough; the facts are the facts.

Lamar continues, "The female administrator assigned to us is the snitch. She set me up with the Spanish lady to have her turn me. They're using my gambling debts as a lure for me to work with them. They'll pay off the debt, probably give me monthly cash to keep them informed and our guys misinformed. I'm going to keep the ball rolling to let her know I'll do it. Oh, the DA asked me to volunteer."

Vito knows no matter what happens he is losing a partner. Vito turns to his team and relays the information. He then speaks to Lamar, "I can't tell you to back out, can I?"

"Not a chance."

"You keep us in the loop."

"Sure."

Vito hangs up. The Charles River swallows Lamar's cell. Vito tells the story to Catherine and Adam. Neither one knows what to say.

"OK. Here is what we are going to do."

Chapter 76

Kim Wilson never thought she could share so much with the male sleeping on the couch. They shared the morning exercise and breakfast together. But sharing their fight against cancer and ingesting the same drugs were beyond her imagination. Especially since the male was a Doberman pinscher named Blackford. He was known around the neighborhood as Blackie.

They both had undergone surgery and chemo. They both had the same post-op drugs. Thankfully, they both were doing well. That is, until last week. The Epogen weekly injection at the clinic was always painful, but a blessing. It renewed the red blood cells and gave them both the energy to live. Blackie's injections were following the same pattern as hers. They have been able to continue their one-mile walks together in the cool New England woods. But she knew it was a short-term solution for him.

But lately Blackie has become listless, and the vet's blood tests show a decrease in red blood cells. This was not expected so soon. Kim is always amazed that her vet bills were never as high as she anticipated. She never thought to get vet insurance. You usually think about insurance when it is too late.

Her vet is a single practitioner with two young vets as part-time associates. He prides himself on his frugality. In fact, Dr. More always prides himself on getting things for less. He loves telling everybody that and playing off his name. More for less. Well, he was so proud when he found how he could get specialty vet drugs at the manufacturing source at a great discount. His office lab fridge is full of Epogen. Only now, patients are returning with serious problems in direct proportion to his frugality.

While waiting in the vet's office as the doctors are deciding what to do, Kim picks up her cell phone. She has only dated the guy twice but really likes him. They met at a group treatment for gambling addiction. She hasn't yet told her Irish parents that she is dating an African American. They've had enough issues dealing with her gambling. He had given her his card; she never thought she would dial his work number. She has to talk to someone, so she dials. On the second ring he picks up. She speaks with a bit of fear and insecurity.

He says, "Hello. I never really expected you to call me at work at this hour, or any hour. I have a meeting in fifteen minutes, what's up?"

"Lamar, I need to talk. I'm sorry."

"It's OK, you have fourteen minutes." She flies through her experiences with Blackie and his drugs and where things are now. She is shocked by the change in his voice.

"I need to speak with your vet. Now. This may help us, and we may be able to help your dog."

She drives to the vet's office, a quick drive with no traffic. Odd for Boston.

Before she knows what is happening, Dr. More is on the phone with Lamar. Dr. More tells his office manager to have Kim come inside to speak with him.

"I'm getting new bottles of meds immediately. We'll keep Blackie here; as soon as the drugs come, he gets treated. Hopefully, this will help."

Dr. More knows there is a possible autoimmune issue with dogs and Epogen. But Blackie is at the point of needing this drug. He wishes all human drugs were easily transferable from species to species. Unfortunately, it doesn't always work like that.

Kim looks at him with a combination of gratefulness and confusion.

He continues, "What number can we use? I'll keep you up to date."

She gives him her number and leaves the vet's office and drives to her office in the real estate agency. As she leaves, Dr. More tells his office manager, "Get all the drugs we bought from that wholesale house in Fall River and put them in a box in the fridge. The police are coming by to pick them up."

* * *

"Get the gang together; we're heading out to Fall River."

I know that the mountain mellowness is going to be a quick memory. I never really unpacked, so repacking is not an issue. That is, until Catherine shows up in my room.

Wearing one of her new outfits, she asked, "You have room for my stuff?"

"For some of it."

"All right, I'll just use the bags that I kept from the stores."

She gives the term *bag lady* a whole new definition. Vito has all his stuff in his car with Bentley hanging out on the porch. Fern and Bowser complete the trio. I have forgotten about Fern's history of a medical issue.

She is looking and acting fine. I put that thought on hold. Hopefully, it was just a separation anxiety event.

Catherine and I stand in the hallway like campers going on an away trip as I say to Vito, "Why are we going to Fall River?"

"It has to do with a call I just got from Lamar. We're going to a vet office that bought some bad drugs from the place where that guy Axelrod was making fake stuff."

I feel that we are finally going to get a handle on this deal although it's unsettled. Once again, I feel like I am going for a ride on some experience that has jumped into my life. It isn't fun. I don't know what it is. Catherine is happy and talking intensely with Vito. She announces that she will ride with him.

I get Fern and Bowser. At least after we've heard the truth about Gord, sharing Bowser's loss is easier. If only Bowser could understand that Gord was a really good guy. Damn it, I really want to live the small-town New England life. I already called about joining the gym at Dartmouth. The energy of the young people doesn't permit me to get tired. I'm not concerned about the weather; I adapt. Besides, I am looking forward to reading by the fireplace on a cold night. Standing on the porch and staring at the pile of logs only convinces me that I should stay.

"Are you daydreaming or coming up with the ultimate psychological answer to this case?" Vito's booming voice slaps me back to the present.

"No, just waiting to see if the dogs need any more time to roam."

I know that isn't the truth. I'm the one who needs more time to roam. Vito walks over to me as Catherine is loading her bags in the backseat of his car. From looking at his car, she knows she doesn't want to go near the trunk. Vito puts his pudgy hand on my shoulder and looks at me. He has the friendly look of concern.

"Are you all right?"

I have to tell the truth; he is a cop. "Well, it would have been nice to spend some time up here. I have to call a real estate person to get someone up here to check the water pipes and that stuff." I don't know how long the house will be empty.

Vito's arm is now around my shoulders. It isn't a hug, just a caring grab. "When this is all over, you'll come back."

Catherine's voice bellows out of the front passenger seat, "Are you guys in love, or is separation anxiety too much for you two?"

We both walk to our separate cars. The plan is for me to follow him. The challenge is to follow him. He drives as if he has a squad car with the flashers and siren going. What he is in fact driving is a dirty generic American sedan with eight cylinders, and he has his badge in his pocket. I drive a Chevy SUV with two dogs and a suitcase. All I have for authority recognition is my driver's license and a gym pass. I just hope Vito remembers that I'm behind him. I have his cell phone number. I'll call when he starts to go airborne.

Going down the highway at seventy is smooth. Every so often, Catherine turns and waves. I wonder why. Well, once we get to the vet's office where the bad stuff is located, we then will question the veterinarian. This is Vito and Catherine's show. I'm sure they won't mind if I see an angle in this and throw in my two cents. I have Vivaldi's *Four Seasons* floating through the SUV.

It starts to rain lightly, and that brings me back to my encounter with Catherine, or whoever she was, at the Warren Tavern. I always spouted in my lectures that the most important events in life are those that you never planned. It is how you react to these events that makes the difference in your future. If I stayed home that night, I wouldn't be driving in the here and now. But you can't live in the past. If you do, you just die in the past.

But still, it is difficult not to think of that evening in Boston. She is someone special. Special enough to make it an effort to try to erase my time spent with her. That will never happen. Vito has his blinker on; an exit is coming up in about a mile. This must be the town near Fall River that has the building needing to be investigated.

This will be interesting.

Chapter 77

Paris. I don't remember how many years ago. My wife was in Paris for an interview with a prominent international law firm. They had been chasing her for half a year. I was in Lyon as a guest lecturer at their medical school. We decided to meet in Paris for the weekend. Isn't that the way it is done in movies for romance?

I think the gradual signals of our relationship's decline were crystallized in the City of Lights. After minimal conversation over drinks and dinner in the hotel bar, we both came to the same conclusion in the morning. We both woke up at sunrise. The taste and texture of the fresh croissants were more interesting than the taste and texture of each other. Satisfaction comes in different degrees. We went through the motions of a marriage for rest of our stay.

She was confident in how the interview went. I am sure she was interviewing the firm to see if it was up to her standard. When she looked at me, I wondered if she was evaluating if I was up to her standard. We said our goodbye after lunch on Sunday.

"I think they will need me in this firm. I am the missing link in their corporate puzzle."

I looked at her bending over her suitcase looking at her clothing as she spoke. I wasn't sure if she was talking to me or her clothes.

I was already packed, so I said to her, "I'm sure you'll get what you want."

"I usually do, don't I?"

She was now talking to the closing zipper of her suitcase. Her question was one that I didn't answer. She continued talking. To the suitcase.

"They will notify me in a week about the position. If the numbers and benefits are in order, I will be moving to London. Of course, they put me up in a corporate flat. I heard it was quite spectacular."

"I am sure it is. I'll be leaving Lyon for home in two days. I don't plan on moving to England."

"That doesn't surprise me."

The legal papers kept our conversation quite civil after that.

Chapter 78

"It's called state's evidence."

Axelrod looks at his tall, female, red-haired attorney and doesn't know what to think. He has seen this stuff on TV. Maybe they should give him a script from *Law and Order* so he will know what to say. The prison jumpsuit is surprisingly comfortable. Other than the fact that he is scared shitless, he is getting a strange sense of empowerment. For the first time in his life he is the one who is being listened to.

Patty Quinn looks at him and sees concentration in his eyes. She can't quite figure it out. That doesn't make her a happy camper; she prides herself on understanding her clients. She has to admit, her client doesn't look bad in his orange outfit. They are sitting across from each other in the room used for this type of thing. The prison guard is staring at her and letting his imagination run amuck. When she throws him a smile, his short pudgy body is in heaven. It also buys her twenty minutes of overtime with her client. She is convinced a deal can be made with the DA, and she will get her client off. Legally speaking, of course.

Axelrod looks at her and quietly says, "What do I have to do?"

She feels that keeping things simple will work for everyone. "Just be honest with me and the DA. Tell us who you worked with, why you did it, and answer all his questions."

"What do I get?"

"A lesser sentence or you might even walk."

"You mean no-prison time?"

"It's up to the DA. It depends on how good your information is."

"What makes the information good?"

"That's easy; info that gets the murder of the undercover cop solved and they nail the ones who did it. If it also helps get this counterfeit drug ring nailed, you're a star."

"If I do this, won't the friends of those I rat out want to kill me?"

Neither one of them knows that Isabella and Sam have no friends. Patty knows that at this moment Axelrod has the stuff to make everybody happy. It is up to her to get it out of him. With the right info, the DA is easy to handle. She isn't sure if the Boston system has the resources to protect Axelrod. She'll get the info and then work on the DA to see if he can keep his side of the deal. She does feel obligated to protect her client; it's her job. After all, how else can she find out about this Vito guy?

She is not a stalker. She is realizing that aging is not going to stop, even for her. Of course, when needed, there always is the plastic surgeon. That is just a temporary confidence builder. It is common knowledge that Vito is in the middle of a divorce. She is three inches taller than him and three inches thinner. So what? Whenever they have to work together, she always feels good at the end of the day. She can't think of anyone else that she has had that experience with: feeling good after leaving their presence. She needs to spend some quiet time with him to see if this is for real. Her client is linked to the case Vito is working on. She is motivated on all fronts.

* * *

I hadn't even parked yet, and Catherine and Vito are already in the vet's office. Vito leaves Bentley in the car. There aren't too many corgis in police work. If I take Bowser in, maybe some of his tough look will transfer to me. Not likely. By the time I enter the vet office, Vito and Catherine are on their way out.

"Let's go."

I look at him opening his car door and, with a degree of exasperation, ask, "Where?"

"To the Fall River warehouse where the Axelrod guy was."

"What did you do in there?"

As Vito starts the engine, the window shoots down, and he says, "Catherine will ride with you and tell you. Just follow me."

Catherine is next to me, and I didn't know it. She gently punches my right arm as she whispers, "Don't worry, I know where he's going. I've been there."

By the time I realize Catherine is on my right, Vito is nowhere to be seen. Catherine raises her voice a bit; "We're moving now. Let's go."

It seems like everyone is in the flow except me. The dogs even have their collective ears up. It is silent until I hit the first red light. Then I hear her take on what is happening. In the vet office they seized the bad drugs and have them wrapped in a cooler in the trunk of Vito's car. They received by fax the legal papers to do what they needed to do in the warehouse. Axelrod starts to turn state's evidence, and they have the preliminary information they need. We are on our way. Picking up speed on the highway, I hit the button that fills the cabin with the violins of Vivaldi.

Catherine's hand finds the off button. "I can't stand that stuff."

I realize then, in the pit of my stomach, there is no future for Catherine and me. But did I ever really imagine that? Yes, I did. You think I would have learned from my yoga classes. Besides sore hamstrings, it was drilled to live in the moment. It's all in the process, not the result.

As soon as the word *yoga* enters my mind, Aleni's lean body and sweet face flood my internal senses. At some point, I have to call her. I am missing not only her but the sweet movement of body and mind in the quiet company of myself.

"Are you always this quiet when you drive?" Catherine is looking straight ahead. I look over at her sitting without her seat belt hooked up and blasting music of the '60s from an oldies station.

I lean a bit to my right and hit the off button. My turn. I can't stand oldies. She shoots me a cold glance. I have to say, "I can't stand that stuff."

"I can't stand the silence; we have to find some sound we can agree on."

I look over with a little smile.

She returns the smile. "We can't do that that in a moving car."

"Especially when I am driving." Eric Clapton is playing in the background. We finally are agreed on a safe sound.

Catherine's expression abruptly changes as we approach the warehouse. It is serious time. We let the dogs out to meet Bentley on the street where they behave like they miss the countryside. Looking for trees and fields, they all give up and perform their functions illegally on the street. They must know Vito has the badge. I escort them back to their respective cars.

Vito opens the doors and waits for us to enter. With a quick slam, we are all locked inside. Without being asked, Catherine relives her trauma at the hands of Sam. I can't help think, what was the other guy doing while this was happening? He better have a good story for the police to let him off easy.

We are all given our assignments in the building. I am to photograph everything, and Catherine is to show Vito what she saw of the operation. According to Vito, there is plenty of physical evidence to indict Sam. Lamar should have enough to indict Isabella.

As soon as Vito mentions Lamar's name, we all freeze and look at each other. No one has a clue where he is or what he is doing. We don't talk about it, but uneasiness is the mood whenever Lamar's name is mentioned. Time flies by. We all do our jobs and feel a case is building if the guy back in Boston has good info.

I feel like part of the team again. I am in the present. The gift of a day. The present.

* * *

"Hey, don't worry; we can't go down for murder."

Over morning coffee, Sam is trying to reassure Isabella. She starts to pout about having to deal with a cop. It scares her. She looks into her third cup of black coffee while Sam is quietly talking.

"These drugs may kill dogs and cats; we're not doing people pills." He conveniently forgets about his termination of Gord. In his skewed mind, Gord's murder was a sideshow.

She talks to him about cashing out. She doesn't care if Sam has more than her. She knows how much she needs to keep her house, Cadillac Escalade, and street deals going. She figures she'll do what Sam wants to get this cop in the hole with them and then check out. The heat of living with Sam plus the cold of Boston is setting up an explosion inside her head. What she doesn't know is that Sam has that all figured out. He isn't about to let her go. They'll get this cop to feed them the info to keep them protected and ahead of the detectives for as long as they need him. Then he will disappear. It is Sam's show.

The eggs reflect the grimy café they are in. Slimy, with too much salt. Isabella doesn't care. Sam needs to get his body moving again. A three-mile run is a good start. Maybe he'll go for a run with Lamar. He'll get a buzz on all fronts, the high of endorphins and the adrenaline rush of his power over the police.

"I want you not to think so much. Leave that to me."

"I thought you needed me when we met for this deal."

"I do. You're doing a great job. Just keep doing it and everything will be all right."

The fat waitress walks up to them and offers more coffee.

Sam, without looking at her mumbles, "Just the check."

Walking outside in the light snow, he outlines his plan to Isabella. She just walks with her arms across her chest, trying to keep the heat in. Whatever clothes she has on are never warm enough.

The sound of her cell phone scares the shit out of her. Who the hell is calling? Hey, maybe her old boyfriend from Puerto Rico. She starts to get real warm thinking of him. Her cold hands dig out the cell from the recesses of her purse.

"Hello."

"Lamar here. I've been thinking."

She shoots a glance at Sam and mouths the word *Lamar*. Sam takes the phone and hits the speaker button. "I said we would get in touch. This better be important."

"I need to meet with your partner."

"How do you know that I have a partner?"

"The same way you know I used to drink and gamble. I do my homework."

Sam shook his head up and down.

"OK. I'll get back to you. I'll call in"—Sam holds up two fingers—"two hours."

* * *

She hits the off button. Lamar hits the off button. He has gotten what he wanted. He wanted to move this quickly, not wait for them to run him at their convenience. The DA has told him what he needs, and Gord deserved his best effort. Lamar is focused on playing the double game. This is one gamble he enjoys. After all, he is being paid for this bet. The only difference is his life is on the line.

It is time to let Vito know what is up. Hitting the buttons of the new cell phone, he wonders how Vito is doing with the woman and Adam. He thinks she is a loose cannon and Adam is nice baggage.

"Hey, what's happening?" Vito's voice is like a shot of good scotch.

"It's good. I have a meeting scheduled with the guy who is behind the whole deal. It's being set up. I have my hand on the stick shift, and the gears are all mine. I may need you, don't go too far away."

"Don't worry; I'm heading back to Boston. I have a bunch of evidence, forensic stuff, and the rest of the gang is with me. How much more can you tell me?"

"Just that the DA is on our side and that the attorney for the creep making the fake drugs has her client crying on her shoulder."

"I remember her, the tall redhead?"

"Yeah."

"I'd like to cry on her shoulder."

"How's the divorce coming?"

"We're throwing paper at each other. I want it to end."
"I hear you."
"Hey, keep your eye on the road. We'll talk."
"Yeah."

Neither Lamar nor Vito say a word to anyone after folding their phones.

Chapter 79

There is a committee for everything in government. To regulate anything you need a committee to regulate the committee that regulates the original issue. Not exactly a model of efficiency. It is no surprise that counterfeit drugs in the veterinary world are flying around everywhere. All sorts of people are raking in lots of money. With the computer sleazes that are available, a world-class team of bad guys is easier to put together than a few good guys.

It is also happening in the human drug world. That's how Catherine got in this game. It just happened that the animal world stumbled across her path. Harm to any living creature, human or otherwise, upsets her. But if a pet of a major politician was put in trouble by a fake or a drug not cared for, then something would be done. Hopefully, not by committee. These are some of the thoughts that Catherine has while sitting in the Chevy SUV on the way back to Boston. Adam is quiet, and the radio is off. She looks in the backseat to see the sweetness of the dogs sleeping. It could be nice, Adam and her in a cabin surrounded by the winter of New Hampshire. It isn't going to happen. He is a nice guy. But she can never stay with nice guys for very long.

It looks like this case is taking shape. They'll get the two she was following and put them away. Then there is Florida and her turf. She will set up the consulting company she dreamed about. She will play at any identity she wants to. She treats herself to a little smile. She reaches over and buckles her seat belt. The click of the buckle has Adam take a quick glance at her.

"You lost confidence in my driving?"

"No, I just gained confidence in the case we have."

Adam is wearing his perpetual black cotton turtleneck and jeans. Fern's blondish hair can be seen on his chest. Remnants of resting in New Hampshire. Adam speaks quietly to her.

"Do you think we will have a meeting with Lamar at the station house in Boston?"

Looking straight ahead and realizing she hasn't a clue what is happening next, she turns and says, "That's up to Vito and Lamar. I don't know what Lamar is up to."

It dawns on her that they are going back to Boston, and she never closed her account at the Marriott. Well, at least she has a place to stay without having to deal with the temptation of Adam. Well, maybe.

She wonders if the clothes she is wearing are knockoffs made in Karachi. Knockoff paranoia is invading her full blast. She forgets that she has Gap outfits, not Gucci. Everybody is into things. The real deal. They care more about the effort put into the jewelry they never wear than the pills they need to stay alive. Her thoughts are getting heavy; she needs to talk about nothing over a drink at a bar. Maybe tonight.

Adam's cell tweets its stupid sound. He plucks it out of the drink well in the console.

"Vito, what's up?"

"Let's all meet at this bar I know in town tonight. I have to update you guys." Vito isn't going to give any information over the airways.

"Sure, where and when?"

"The name of the place is 'Knockoff's.' It's on Craig Street. How about nine?"

"Fine. I'll tell Catherine. They got food?"

"Would I take you to a place that didn't have good food?"

"See you there."

The skyline of Boston is in view. Before he can say anything, Catherine looks at him, all business. "Drop me off at the Marriott in Charlestown. Thanks."

"Sure. Then we're meeting Vito at nine at this bar called 'Knockoff's.' You in?"

Catherine shakes her head up and down. Knockoff's? You got to be kidding. Actually it is a misspelling of the owner's Russian name. She would never believe that. "Why not. I need a drink. Or two."

As he pulls up to the Marriott and Catherine has her window down, the dogs have their noses up. It is obvious they are back in the city. Bowser and Fern stretch in the backseat, and Adam knows it is time to walk them.

The doorman helps Catherine with her Gap bags, and she doesn't say a word as she disappears into the lobby. Driving in the familiar streets and waiting for red lights to flip to green made Adam feel at home. Not a bad feeling. Interesting, a week ago waiting at a traffic light was stressful;

tonight it's part of the charm of Boston. I guess we're programmed for when it's time for a change. Finding a parking spot around the corner from his condo and walking the dogs in the park are hitting the memory replay button. Fern and Bowser know the familiar scents. Why is it you have to go away to enjoy what you have?

Chapter 80

Sam never told Isabella that he had two other operations in the fire. The Fall River deal is the small one. The other two are in New Jersey, not far from where the big pharmaceutical companies have their manufacturing plants.

Being near New York City makes it easy to find the right people to do what he needs. For money, a person is always there no matter what has to be done. He set up an organization that buys real drugs from the geriatric crowd that prefers cash to staying alive. He has a crew that wholesales the newly purchased drugs to vet offices. He also found the right characters to bribe the truckers taking the drugs from the manufacturers to somehow lose a portion of the delivery to his crew.

There are all sorts of ways to get his hands on the items he needs. Selling them is always easy. Nobody ever looks to see if the pills, capsules, chewables, and liquids have to be at certain temperatures. Some need to be light free. They don't care; they all look good at sale time.

He also has a team making copies of different drugs in a warehouse in North Jersey. The product looks real and is packaged like the real thing. Occasionally, a small difference happens in the packaging, but only an FDA pro can notice it. A vet in a busy practice is concentrating on care, not authenticity of drugs. They have enough to deal with besides playing the role of a government agency.

A professional-looking salesperson presenting to the practice meets the office manager, offers a huge discount on a large package of drugs, and it's a done deal. The Massachusetts deal is a trial to see what he can do up north. There are plenty of vet practices in New England, and he likes keeping his business in separate parcels. These Northeastern people treat their pets like family. They spend the money to keep them healthy.

The different operations are unknown to each other, and he gets all the profits. The Spanish lady just makes his latest deal a little easier, an experiment in cop control and a bit of spice at night. His take-in is massive. He has deposits in all the right places. Whenever Sam looks at *Forbes* magazine, he wonders why he was not written up as a young success story. It must be the lack of a college degree. He doesn't realize what a sick motherfucker he is. It isn't the money alone; it is controlling people and getting the rush when he wants it.

Hearing that Axelrod is in custody rocks his boat a bit. He has to figure out how that can work to his advantage. Not an easy task. In fifteen minutes it will be time to call that cop Lamar. It looks like he is smart and experienced. He'll figure him out and have him by his balls by the second mile of their run.

* * *

Lamar is sitting at his dungeon on the computer. The lady who connected him to the other side stands next to him and leans faintly on his right shoulder.

"Everything going well? Need anything?"

Lamar looks up with his perpetually bemused, staid look and stares at her right breast. It is for his imagination since it was covered by three layers of clothing. He looks up as he realizes he must be socially acceptable and smiles. "I'm fine; I need to go out in about five minutes. You need anything?"

"A Dunkin' Donut's latté."

He regrets asking; he doesn't drink the mixed coffee stuff. "Sorry, I won't be anywhere near one. Another time."

By the time he says the word *time*, he is alone in his cubicle. He knows how to say the right thing to get his way. This is one of those times. Not forgetting his Dunhill scarf, he puts his layers of clothing on and walks outside checking to make sure his cell phone is charged.

There is a decent café two blocks south of where he is stationed. He isn't hungry, but they make a decent cup of espresso. He likes to order a double in a mug. Those little cups are for the pretty boy crowd. The chilly walk gives him a bit of hunger by the time he arrives at Chino's. It is long and narrow, great because no one can sit next to you. It is pretty full when the warm air and smell of cooking hit him full force on the other side of the entrance.

"Usual seat, Detective?"

The older woman at the front knows him; he never got her name. That is her way of asking if he is alone. She prides herself on knowing the patrons. A slight nod and he is in a little booth halfway between the door and the kitchen. Facing the door, he never has his back to the entrance; he doesn't see the waiter approach him.

"Your preference today?" The place has its own charm.

"Two egg omelet, no cheese, just peppers. No fries, a double espresso. Thanks." Lamar has his own charm.

He wasn't hungry twenty minutes ago. With the walk over in the chill and the smell of the kitchen, who wouldn't be hungry? The short thin young waiter slides over his mug half full with the thick dark liquid. This guarantees that he will stay awake for another five hours. He sips and enjoys the aroma and bitterness of the hot drink. Without warning, there is an acute vibration over the area of his left chest. His cell phone is alive. It joins him.

"Yeah."

"I'm Sam. You know who I am, so let's not play the good-guy-bad-guy game."

"We're both bad guys in this game."

Sam looks at his phone, not expecting that response. "Whatever. Let's meet and move this along."

Lamar is trying to prolong the conversation so he can get the location with his tech guys under the DA. "That may be a problem. I have meetings the next few days and nights."

"Then, I guess this is not going to work. I tell you what; I'll call you in twenty minutes and see if your schedule has changed. It will be from a different place."

Lamar hears nothing. He knows he's dealing with a pro. His eggs arrive as soon as he closes his cell. This guy must be in the restaurant; he's giving him time to eat. Cold eggs would have been a deal breaker.

His table is being cleared, and the waiter is bringing the check as his cell is once again giving him the signal. Lamar stands up, leaving cash on the check, and flips open the cell.

He just hears "BC running track tomorrow at noon. Wear running shoes. A no show and your DA's office get a copy of the tape of the meeting with my lady friend."

A smile crosses Lamar's face while leaving the café. It looks like the other side is buying into him. He also knows it is becoming more dangerous. The next call is to the DA on his private line.

It is half a ring, and he hears, "Yeah, make it fast."

"Noon, tomorrow at the BC track. I'm jogging with the man. Have some student-jogger types for backup if I need them."

"Done."

* * *

I almost cancel my meeting with Catherine and Vito at Knockoff's. Once home, it will be tough to get off the couch. Add the blanket of dog warmth on my knees and chest and it will be a challenge to move at all. Bowser finds a niche curled on my ankles, and Fern is in her own circle on my chest. The phone rests on its charger an arm's length away, so I am not totally cut off from the outside world.

The housekeeper has done her job; my clean clothes that were in the dryer are folded neatly on my bed. I return home to order. I really don't want to go out with my new colleagues. The reason is simple. I want my old life back.

I learned a lot about myself in these last few weeks. Important real-world stuff is a buzz for a short while. Then, when real work kicks in, I'd rather be home or doing something else. The gym, yoga, a good book. A mindless relationship with an intelligent, beautiful woman would do. I am sinking into a nice never-never land. The space that I have spent a few dollars at a yoga session to achieve. My yoga instructor would be proud of me; my breathing is orchestrated in a rhythmic motion that emanates a sense of peace. Actually, I am following Fern's breathing so I'm not inhaling doggie vapors. Her nose is facing my chin. I wonder when was the last time my two buddies had a bath and their teeth cleaned. I know the sweater I am wearing is going to the cleaner.

The phone rings. Goodbye breathing zone and peace. Hello to my ex-wife.

"Don't you return calls?"

I am not going to review the last weeks of my life. I also haven't checked the messages. "No."

"I'm dating the president of a major British pharmaceutical firm. I doubt if I will be chatting with you soon."

"Is he married?"

"I'm working on that."

"Good luck."

"Goodbye."

How do I respond to that? I don't. Placing the phone back in its stand I notice it is five o'clock. I must walk the dogs and feed them soon. They aren't moving, so neither will I. Thinking about the last few weeks, I feel lucky that neither Bowser nor Fern are on any meds. This reminds me: I still have to make an appointment with the vet for Fern's exam.

The phone rings.

"Hello, Adam?" It is Catherine.

"Nobody else lives here."
"Funny. What time are you picking me up?"
"Eight thirty."
"OK." End of conversation.

It is nice having a car again. Maybe I'll buy this rental. I'm not due to return it for a while. Bowser has his eyes half closed. Fern is out cold. I close my eyes. The phone rings.

"What?" It is Vito.
"Pick me up at eight thirty. Deal?"
"Deal."

I hang up and realize I told Catherine the same pickup time. Good. Somebody will be pissed at me. My choice. I close my eyes. It is six forty. The phone rings.

"Yes."
"Hi. Are you OK? I haven't seen you in yoga class."

It is Aleni. Wow, I feel good with this call. Amazing the difference the sound of a voice makes. "Good to hear from you. I'm fine, just away on business."

"I'm teaching tomorrow's early class. Try to make it."
"I'll try. What time is it?"
"Six thirty."

Not a chance. "See you then."
"Bye."
"Bye."

Am I a liar or what? In a few hours I will be at a bar for dinner and whatever with Vito and Catherine until who knows when. I'll have to get up at five thirty to make her class. How will I explain the alarm going off at such a terrible hour to my two sleeping companions? I close my eyes.

There are a series of loud knocks on the door. All three of us, two-footer and four-footers, perk our heads up in the same direction. A new sound. The dogs jump off and bark toward the new sound. I unwind myself and get up and look through the eyehole in the door. I see the grey face of my downstairs cigar-smoking neighbor. Non-threatening. I open the door, and there he stands with a bunch of newspapers in his hands.

"Hi. I've been saving your *Globes*. You want them?"

Damn, I forgot to cancel the papers when I took off for New Hampshire. "Thanks. Sorry for the inconvenience, but you can chuck them."

"No problem. I'll use them for kindling."

I close the doors and quietly thank the quirky downstairs fellow for waking me up. The boys and I go outside for a walk. I agree with the present Queen Elizabeth, nothing like a walk outside to clear the mind.

"It's nice that you're taking care of Bowser." A female voice on the steps of the park is directed at me.

I turn to see who it is. One of the bulldog fraternities is looking at me with her American bulldog pulling the leash toward Bowser and Fern. She is wearing faded jeans and a dark green ski jacket. The color of her hair is hidden by the dark wool ski cap pulled down over her ears. She does look familiar, like the entire dog-walking group.

"He's been good company for Fern and me. It's tough what happened to Gord."

"Yeah, I heard about that. Is this neighborhood safe?"

"I don't worry about it."

The leash switched hands, and she puts her black-leather-gloved right hand out.

"My name is Leigh; I've seen you here for a while."

Our gloves clasped. "I'm Adam."

She smiles and says, "Nice meeting you, Adam, have to move on, Lane has his needs."

Don't we all. Looking at her elegant walk and Lane's waddle is an interesting sight. My immediate concern is handling the plastic bags with good form so as to keep my mucking technique efficient. Leigh and Lane, not too difficult to remember.

By the time I returned to the condo, the stale cigar smoke of the foyer is no longer stale. My paper policeman is burning his tobacco and a fire. So what? It doesn't bother me. Just another smell of the big city.

I miss smoking my pipe. The whole culture of pipe smoking seems so harmless. The esthetics of the grain of the wood pipe, the various tobacco blends, and the specialty shops I spent hours in. There isn't anything you can do for pleasure without a price. If I make it to eighty years old, I'll smoke my pipe again. Why not? I am about to place a Joni Mitchell CD on the sound system, but it is seven forty-five. I need to get myself together for an evening of real-world stuff and food and drink.

I can't tell Vito and Catherine I don't care anymore; just let them take off and fill me in when it's a done deal. I used to call that avoidance behavior. OK. Cold water on my face and warm coat on. The Chevy is waiting to be turned on.

Who do I pick up first, and who do I piss off?

Faking It

* * *

Lamar doesn't know that the DA and Axelrod's attorney are meeting as he is lacing up his Nikes. A deal is being made, a pretty simple one. Axelrod will tell them everything he knows, and they will relocate him to New Mexico. He will have a new identity and be given enough money to live on for a year. That is, of course, if his information is true and they accomplish their goals. It is possible. Jamie is looking at this whole scene as an investment.

A chance for a new life. That is what Jamie has been trying for all his life. He's found himself circling over the same scenes forever; now a window opens for him. He doesn't realize that the drop from this window could break a few bones. His.

Patty Quinn is in uniform. That is, lawyer dark business suit with no intra-boob view. The buttons are there for a purpose, now. Meeting in the conference room next to the DA's office is getting to be a second office for her. Her client is relaxing as if testifying and going to the Southwest in a new identity were going to Disney World. He is so damn smart and so damn stupid. Not unlike her recent boyfriend.

"You do understand that if the case is not won, you go back to prison?"

He shakes his head up and down. "No problem. You'll win."

"We better."

The DA opens the door a crack. He motions with his right hand for Patty to step out.

She turns to her client. "Don't go anywhere." She walks out and closes the door. She knows the windows are locked, and they are on a high floor. She doesn't think Axelrod will jump.

The DA speaks in a hushed voice. They are eyeball-to-eyeball. "Lamar contacted me. He's meeting with that Sam guy on the BC track in an hour. We don't have a wire on him. The best we can do is have three of our people running on the track when he's there."

She focuses on him. She's never seen him this intense. "If I can make a suggestion?" He just stares without expression. "Make sure your people arrive at staggered times."

The DA looks at her and looks down the empty hallway as he mutters, "We're not paying you for your consultative wisdom, just rep your client. For us this is routine. I'm informing you so you see how quickly we are moving. We expect the same from you."

She's usually able to figure the pace of whatever activity she's in. Not this time. Showing that she is on his team, she crisply says, "Not a problem. I'm right with you."

"Better be, or there is no deal. My people in Santa Fe aren't holding their breath for this guy."

She opens the door, and gives the DA a view of the back of her head, the word *understood* is heard by those on both sides of the door.

WWhile all of this is happening, Lamar is going to the track. He wears black sweatpants and a hooded grey sweatshirt. They have no insignia, school, or brand name on them. He dug up his generic gym gear for this occasion. The heat is turned up in the car so his legs have a chance at a quick warm-up. He keeps in shape; his running is on the treadmill in the downstairs gym of his apartment building. He is actually looking forward to running outdoors. He can't imagine any guy who is spending time making and dealing fake drugs could outrun him.

He is closer to the track, and his instinct has him park three blocks away. He doesn't want anyone to know what car he is driving. Being a cop is ingrained in him.

Another gloomy day in Boston. The type of weather that makes you crave a hot bowl of New England clam chowder. Lamar isn't hungry now; his stomach is too tight for food. He knows what this guy looks like from the composites they have. Acting like it is a first meeting will take no effort; he has confidence that he can pull this off.

The three-block walk is good for his legs. It is good because it always takes him forever to loosen his hamstrings. About a block from the track he stretches using a ten-year-old black Honda Civic as support.

"Hey, that's my car. Get your damn hands off." The voice is coming from a tall solid-looking guy wearing a dark green Dartmouth-hooded sweatshirt and grey sweatpants. He walks up to Lamar and stands an inch from his back.

Lamar moves his hands off the car and turns to face the guy. "Sorry, man. Hey, no harm, no foul. OK?" The dark green hood contrasts the white face as he moves even closer to Lamar. Lamar stands up tall and freezes. He realizes he doesn't have his authorized piece. He stares at the blue eyes in front of him.

Blue eyes move closer so he is now an inch from Lamar's face and whispers slowly, "I got your back. There's a female cop in a red Adidas tracksuit practicing sprints and stretching on the turf inside the oval. Just push me away and say something."

Lamar reacts quickly, pushing him away, turning his back, and moving as he says, "Fuck off."

The cop in green smiles inwardly and yells, "Fuck you, jerk."

The man walks away and plans to enter the opposite entrance that Lamar used. While this melodrama is being played, Sam is completing his mile warm-up. He has layers of light track clothes, the outer being cheap grey sweats. No logo, K-Mart specials. He knows what Lamar looks like; his lady accomplice is good at these details. He breaks into a light sweat when he sees the hooded black man stretching on the goalpost. There are a few others running on the track; he expected that. You can't go anywhere in Boston without runners around you.

He isn't sure if this is the guy he is meeting. He walks over to the goalpost and figures out what he is going to say. He already knows what he is going to do. With his tall slim body looking taller and slimmer with his shoulders straight back, he approaches Lamar. Lamar notices a female in a red tracksuit winding down a sprint about twenty yards away. The athletic dark green-hooded guy is just entering the outer circle of the track.

"You work out here before? You look new."

Lamar stares at Sam's cold eyes and knows this is his man. "There ain't nothing new about me."

"You Lamar?"

"Why you asking?"

"This is my new office; I'm meeting Lamar for a business discussion."

"Let's talk business."

They don't shake hands.

* * *

I decide to pick up Catherine first. Stupid decision. I drive up to the Marriott, and she is nowhere to be seen. I call Vito.

"What's up?"

"I'm going to be late."

"They're not closing the place down. Don't be too late. You know how I get when I'm hungry."

"Hey, I'm waiting for the lady."

"Tell her what I'm like when I'm hungry. She'll move her ass."

I have different thoughts of her than what Vito intends.

I close the cell. As soon as I close the phone, Catherine slides into the Chevy front passenger seat. She has to slide; she is wearing a tight skirt with an open-neck wool sweater. It is all the same dark color. I don't notice what the hue of whatever color it is, just that the open neck is very open. I turn the car on and dial Vito.

Catherine just looks at me and says, "You calling the fashion police?"

Vito answers on the first ring. "What?"

"Five minutes." I close the cell and look at the road.

"I've evolved from the Gap picture girl. Can you handle it?"

Obviously she has a closet full of clothes in her suite. Actually, I've been there and seen it. Yes, I've seen her, so why am I thinking about everything all covered so nicely? Reassuring that my id is still in full expression, still trying to dominate the Freudian impulses. Oh, oh, I'm thinking too much.

I am saved by Vito standing on the curb waiting to be picked up. "Just ten minutes off schedule, not too bad."

Vito just shrugs. "You guys will like this place."

The two of us in the front seats echo in tandem, "Why?"

"This bar is unique. It is shaped like a babe with big boobs." Vito leans forward and puts his meaty hand gently on Catherine's left shoulder. "Sorry, I didn't mean to sound—"

"Shut up. I get the picture."

"So do I." I pipe up.

"Such an understanding team. That's why we'll have a good time tonight and solve this crime." Sometimes Vito has a way of oversimplifying things.

Following Vito's directions, I stop in front of a tattered old green awning. The windows on either side of the front door have "Knockoff's" in faded green. I think it is green. They leave me to find a parking spot, and they disappear on the other side of the entrance. What if I left them here and keep driving to the airport? Take a plane to Paris and find a little hotel on the Left Bank? Hook up with forty-three-year-old blonde female artist whose specialty is reclaiming wandering over-fifty-year-old American ex-professionals?

The red Mercedes pulling out of its spot on the right wakes me up to the present. I park the Chevy, and a weighty issue confronts me. Yoga says live the moment. My French fantasy of the moment isn't a reality, but it certainly is more in contact with my soul than the immediate need to park my vehicle. I hope Aleni has the answer at 6:30 a.m. tomorrow morning. I am getting motivated to find inner peace on the mat. First I have to find a seat with my two friends at the shapely bar.

As soon as I enter Knockoffs, I hear my name called out. It isn't a familiar voice. I do recognize the face. This time it has hair and a body. Actually, it is hard to hear anything with CCR blasting "Proud Mary" from all corners. I have the feeling that I am a guest at a friend's fraternity party. She comes up to me, and I receive a quick full-body press.

She turns to her girlfriend who has dark hair down to her shoulders and says, "This is the guy I was telling you about. He rescued Bowser."

Oh, this must be Leigh who owns the bulldog named Lane. She won't let go of my hand. "Join us for a drink."

Before I have a chance to speak, Catherine grabs my other arm and says, "Sorry, gals, he's mine for tonight. You have to take a number." I'll remember this moment the next night or two when I'm alone.

Sitting at the curvy bar facing Vito with Catherine between us, I still haven't said a word. My legs and head are bouncing to "I Heard It Through the Grapevine." Yes, I am about to lose my mind.

Vito leans over and says over the music, "The first round is coming, and I ordered the special that we all share for dinner."

The Smutty Nose Old Brown Dog Ales are set on the bar before he finishes his last sentence. I don't ask what the special dinner is. Halfway through the beer, Vito tells us what Lamar was doing earlier today and that he has confidence that between the confession of Axelrod and the forensics of the warehouse that the case will be sealed in a few weeks. He says that Lamar going undercover is a good career move for him and that his back is being watched. He says he knows that Lamar is going to nail this Sam and Isabella to the wall for counterfeit drugs and murder.

A second round of beer arrives. The special is nowhere in sight. Catherine is surprisingly quiet. The special arrives on one very large platter. It is placed in front of Vito for all of us to share. He has a huge smile. Sushi pizza. That's right, sushi pizza.

Now I know why Catherine is so quiet. CCR is singing "someone said there is the calm before the storm."

* * *

Very light sprinklings of tiny snowflakes make the run seem like communing with nature. Not so, Lamar is communing with evil. Not a word is said for five minutes. It is a game of chicken for big stakes.

Sam decides it is time he takes the lead. He picks up the pace and is two yards ahead of Lamar. He picks it up and is four yards in front of Lamar. He is going to show this cop who is in charge. The light snow stops, and the track dries quickly. They both pass the slow-moving tall fellow in the green sweatshirt. It is obvious that Sam is showing he is the alpha male.

Lamar is smart enough to let him play his game. Sooner or later they have to stop and talk. He'll just let Sam stay ahead. Give him a false sense of being the man. The first mile goes quickly. The second mile is going even quicker. Sam's breathing is light and smooth. Lamar is starting to feel the effort to keep up the pace. Lamar is a five yards behind Sam. He doesn't think of his backups in green and red. The third mile is even faster. It has Sam feeling like his old track days at Miami. Of course, it had to be an away event, no snow in Miami.

It is obvious that Lamar is losing form as the third mile kicks in. He is starting to wonder if he should slow down and let Sam come back to him. At three and half miles Sam accelerates. Lamar feels he should pass him. Enough of this crap. The competitive mode kicks in to Lamar's stride. His jaw tightens. Ignoring anything around him, Lamar pushes to get even with Sam. Sam is gliding at this fast pace and is in the middle lane. Lamar sees the opening in the inside lane and takes off to pass. He pulls up next to Sam's left. The two cops are watching the event from the turf in the center of the field.

Sam is hearing the breathing from his left ear. Just as he planned. He cuts in front of Lamar, stepping on his right foot and crunching his rib cage with his left elbow. Lamar feels like he was hit by a city bus. His right hamstring is extended beyond its limits. The slow strain evolving into a tear is a terrible feeling. His right rib cage lets him know that damage is done. Trauma to the ribs is excruciating. Every breath is horrible. He collapses on the track.

The cops watching this scene start to run to Lamar. Sam just stands two feet away from Lamar and watches him in his agony. He bends down to give the appearance of concern, but he is actually doing a security check to see if Lamar has a gun. The two undercover cops are getting closer.

Sam whispers into Lamar's ear, "You will tell them you're all right. I'll help you up, and we're going to a place where we can talk."

"You bastard."

"I'm not convinced you can be trusted. I'm going to find out within the next two hours. If I am convinced, we can work together; your pain will be richly rewarded. If I'm not convinced, you won't have to worry about pain. You will never feel anything ever again."

"You guys all right?" The woman in the red outfit arrives before her companion.

"Yeah, we collided. My buddy got the worst of it, but we'll handle it."

She tries to establish eye contact with Lamar, but Sam stands between them.

"You need any help?" The guy in green tried to get into the act.

"Thanks, everything's under control."

The lady sees the angle of Lamar's leg on the track. "You need medical attention?"

"Yep, and that's not an issue. I'm Dr. Samuels, and my friend is on call at the hospital ER. I'm taking him there now."

Sam lifts Lamar and supports him totally, making his way to a car near the track. Isabella is sitting in the driver's seat.

The red Toyota has dirt smeared over the numbers of the license plate. Sam and Lamar are in the backseat. They are around the corner before the backups can see what is happening. They call the station house and feel like idiots.

* * *

"We played two ends of the process." Jamie Axelrod is talking, all his words are recorded by the tape machine sitting on the table.

His attorney leans back in her chair and consults her notes. The DA, in his perpetual grey Brooks Brother's suit, looks back and forth at the eyes of both of them. He is fascinated with the case. This was why he ran for DA, to clean up the city of bad guys doing bad things. He tries not to appear too smug.

Patty Quinn has her elbows on the table. Her black wool turtleneck covers her neck and flops down to her dark grey skirt. Her only jewelry is the silver Rolex on her left wrist. Its dials are precisely at three o'clock.

"Alan, you're looking pretty smug. You still have to prove what my client has said is true."

"Isn't that your job?"

"It's both our jobs."

Axelrod suddenly is the spectator. Both ends of the process are manufacturing and delivery. He would manufacture what Sam wanted him to copy. The delivery end finds truckers looking for extra cash. Sam's men offer these guys the cash for the good drugs and replace them with the counterfeit ones. They also have their own supply of fake drugs. They then sold the inventory for less than market price to whoever would buy. If a trucker said no thanks, they would ask about the health of his family.

Alan Cohen finally has a hook on the situation. What he needs is hard evidence and to locate the perps. He is confident the team he has in place is going to take care of that issue. He wonders how Lamar's meeting is going. He doesn't expect to hear from him for a few days.

Alan looks at Axelrod and asks the obvious question. "How are you so good at what you do?"

"For over ten years I've been the chemist making prototype drugs for three major pharmaceutical firms in the Northeast. It's what I did every day."

"I don't think you need a new Mercedes every year, why did you do it?"

Actually, Jamie has done his research, and he is a big Toyota fan. Not only the product's reliability, but how in the manufacturing process all team members have a say in what is occurring. Nobody listens to him in the process of making new drugs. He is paid to put the chemicals together like he is told. That's it.

Alan remembers that Adam told him his thoughts on Axelrod. Just a self-image thing. Getting even and showing the world he has some control is part of the equation.

"No, I don't even like Mercedes. I finally did something I wanted to do."

"How did you get involved with these people? Tell me specifically who they are."

"They came to me and asked me to work for them. The money was good. They found me."

He then describes Isabella and Sam. With the description comes the names. He doesn't include his affair with Isabella. Ms. Quinn and Mr. Cohen have the same thought at the same time: it's amazing how smart people can make such stupid choices in their lives.

The afternoon just plows along with questions and answers. Nothing surprises anyone. During the breaks, Patty and the DA go their separate ways. Alan is thinking of Lamar and wondering how he is doing. He is concerned about his safety. He hasn't heard from the two cops he put on the case to protect Lamar. He assumes that is a good sign. Patty's thoughts are of Vito. She wonders if she could get him to lose another twenty pounds.

* * *

I have no comment on the pizza. Actually, I do. This is a perfect example of putting two wonderful, independent items together, and it simply not working.

The same could be said about people.

"Any questions, guys?"

Vito ate half the pie, Catherine and I ate the remaining quarters. The sashimi slices were quite unique.

"Yes, I do."

"Shoot."

I hate that expression.

"It's for Catherine, not you."

Vito nods and orders his third beer. Catherine and I stop at two. She angles her head to look at me directly. The look is one I can't quite read.

"What are you doing in this deal now?"

"Want to nail the bastards that kidnapped me. But I have the same reasons Vito does. You know I was in law enforcement. Remember?"

I don't respond. Looking at her, she suddenly seems unattractive to me. I can't explain why.

She puts her hands on her forehead and, looking through her fingers, says to me, "You asked a question, I'm waiting for you to talk."

Vito is nursing his third and last beer of the night. He is taking this all in.

Looking directly at her fingers, it is my turn to talk. "You're right, for a moment I forgot your background. Sorry." That seemed to satisfy her curiosity.

"So what do you guys think of this place?"

"Different." It was a chorus from Catherine and me.

"Yeah, that's why I like it. Sometimes you need a change."

Neither one of us responds.

"See you in the park." It was Leigh and her long-haired friend.

It's amazing; from a total secluded life, I am now meeting all these people from everywhere. It would be nice to chat with her over drinks. I am going to ask her out the next time we meet with the dogs. Once again, three names, this time Fern, Bowser, and Lane, sound like a prestigious law firm. Maybe their representation of the canine world is fodder for a good TV special.

"Adam, Adam, are you all right?"

"What do you mean?" Vito is shaking my right shoulder like a piece of gym equipment, and Catherine is standing in front of me.

She is doing the talking. "Was that some type of seizure?"

My doggie daydream had me in a kind of meditative state. I don't think I can tell my fellow crime fighters that I am just buzzing out on a beautiful woman and a law firm composed of two bulldogs and a mutt.

"I'm fine, just thinking about what's next for us. We really need to tie Lamar's work and the DA's deal into one piece. We need to understand the whole picture and get this done."

Vito understands the reality of getting things done. He pipes up. "Adam's right. We need to meet tomorrow for lunch and tie in what all of us found out in the morning. We work the angles and tie them together."

It makes sense.

Vito looks at his watch, and we know the party is over. "Bentley's on overtime, get me home."

Vito looks up at the bartender and pays the bill. Catherine doesn't care, and I wonder what his tax return looks like. On the drive back, all we hear is a rendition of the time line of getting a sushi chef and a pizza chef together. Vito feels strongly that if this is done, there could be world peace.

Bentley's needs take priority; Vito is dropped off first. Catherine doesn't say much on the ride back to the Marriott. I am wondering if I should invite her to my place so she needn't be alone.

I drive to Catherine's hotel with the only sound from the cabin the all-news station. Without a doubt, neither one of us is listening to it. She opens her passenger door and steps out and stands looking at me.

"I think it's best if I'm alone tonight."

"Me too."

I notice the wool sweater is buttoned up to her neck. It did get colder.

Only the outside temperature stayed the same.

* * *

The backseat of the Toyota is filthy. Old gum wrappers and remnants of past meals on the run are scattered on the seat and floor. Lamar is not used to being on this end of a relationship. He isn't cuffed or otherwise physically restrained. He doesn't have to be, between the pain and Sam leaning on him. He will just have to see how it plays out.

The bags of ice on his legs and ribs keep his hands occupied. He had not thought of using them as weapons, not just yet. Lamar knows he's dealing with professionals.

Sam feels pretty good. So far it is pretty easy. He has this cop under control and scared. Isabella knows this is Sam's show. She has done her job. They have checked out of the dump they first stayed in, and she is driving to the hotel she booked for two weeks. The location gives them access to the city and the highways. Tourists and business types stay there, and there is a constant ebb and flow in the lobby. Plus it is all suites with kitchens. She had done the food shopping after checking in. The Marriott Residence Inn in Charlestown seems like the right fit for them now.

Isabella and Sam look like they are helping a medically compromised old friend through the lobby.

"Can I offer a hand?" A tall blonde fellow in a dark suit walks over to them. He looks like he is part of a Harvard crew reunion.

Sam smiles and gives his best imitation of concern as he says, "Thanks, we're OK. My old college buddy thought he was twenty-one again on the basketball court."

The fellow nods knowingly and moves out to grab a taxi.

Sam approves of the location of the hotel. They realize that Adam lives in walking distance from where they are sleeping. They'll be able to keep an eye on Adam. Lamar has to answer questions about Adam and what his deal is with the cops. They have no idea where Catherine is sleeping.

Next door.

Chapter 81

Blackie is responding to treatment. Sometimes it is luck, sometimes just tincture of time, sometimes all of the above. The Doberman is running and eating the good food and depositing the waste in good form and on time.

Kim Wilson is a happy camper. That special feeling when a sick member of the family turns the corner for the best is one of the moments to be treasured. Kim is all warm inside especially when Blackie comes over for a belly rub. She will never know if the medication Blackie took was the real stuff or not. So what? He is well. The vet's blood tests confirm it.

She wants to share her joy with Lamar. Even though they only spent a few times together, she has an affinity for him. She doesn't care if her parents have a race issue. It is her life. She feels uncomfortable leaving all these messages on his cell; he usually returns her calls within the hour, if not sooner. She has the afternoon off, leaving at two o'clock and picking up Blackie at three-thirty. It is now five o'clock, and she hasn't heard from Lamar.

Kim is wearing her favorite jeans and white cotton J.Crew turtleneck that shows all of Blackie's hair. It is nice to have them freshly deposited on her clothing.

The mellow happiness is leaving her core. It disappears after the third call is not returned. She thinks *where the hell is he?* She is worried; it is time to break a rule and call his home number. No response.

He often talked about how he enjoyed working with this guy who used to be a shrink. He said this guy lives near the Bunker Hill Monument. She isn't going to call the station house; Lamar would be pissed at her. The comforting feel of Blackie's head nuzzling is competing with the bottle of Bombay Gin in her kitchen cabinet. Walking to the kitchen, there is only one thought in her mind. She needs answers. Opening the gin bottle is easy. Holding it with two hands, the next step is critical. The clear liquid goes down easy. Very easy.

She rationalizes that it is a good antibacterial for the kitchen sink. Hot water soon follows what was poured down the drain. The bottle slides into the recycling bin. That feels good. Oh, it was not enough to share with a bunch of strangers on a Thursday night. Damn, where the hell is Lamar? She dials information and says Adam's full name. It was a start.

* * *

Maybe I should call Catherine. Maybe I shouldn't call Catherine. It doesn't even rhyme, yet I keep saying that to myself all the time I am walking the dogs. As soon as I return, lock the door and give my companions their treats, the phone rings. Maybe my rhyme is answered.

"Hello, Adam? You don't know me; I am a friend of Lamar's. A special friend."

I guess that ends my adventure into poetry. "Yes, who are you?"

"My name is Kim Wilson. Has Lamar spoken of me?"

"We never crossed the personal line. How did you get my number, and why are you calling?" My guard is up. The mention of Lamar's name quickly has my attention.

"You're listed in the phone book, and Lamar once spoke of where you lived. He knows where everyone lives that he deals with." She is speaking quickly with a level of anxiety.

My antenna is up as a reflex from my days in practice. Thirty years of routine doesn't go away by stopping your practice and changing your location. I wish it did. "I've worked with Lamar. Who are you?"

"I am dating Lamar. We met at an AA meeting a month or so ago."

Somehow that doesn't surprise me about him. He is so wound up with perfection in appearance and performance. The pressure valve has a need to explode somewhere. Alcohol and gambling are not as uncommon in this personality type as most people would like to think. Even with her connection to Lamar, I still am uncomfortable revealing anything about Lamar and the rest or our group of law enforcement team to a complete stranger on the phone. I need more from her, yet it still is a voice on the phone. It could be anybody; I remember the first two who investigated me in my place.

She continues talking; her voice is becoming firmer, with less of a high pitch. "I am really worried about Lamar. I care about him; he's always been there for me. Can you help me?"

"Can you meet me in fifteen minutes at a bar in Charlestown?" Boston isn't that large of a city.

"Give me the name, I'll leave now."

I give her the name of the Greek restaurant that is five blocks from me.

Her voice is in high gear as she says, "I'm on the way." She hangs up.

I hit the dial tone and call Vito. He answers on the first ring. He always answers on the first ring.

"What's up?"

He always knows I have something to report when he answers like that. I fill him in.

He is hanging up as he mumbles, "I'll stop by your place first to pick you up. What does this girl look like?"

"I never asked her."

He doesn't respond.

Walking the dogs in the cold evening air, I am hoping it will not be a social event. When Vito shows up, I am gone. Fern and Bowser sense my electrical waves; they do their elimination quickly and pull me back to my condo. I owe them one. As they wait for their treats, the horn sounds from the street. It is Vito's. I know it. As they munch on the biscuits, I head through the door. It's amazing, however fast I check out, I always stop to lock the sequence of locks. City life has a way of imprinting in me. I don't lock the door to Vito's car. It is so filthy and generic; I cannot imagine anyone breaking into it.

Vito speaks to me while driving the five blocks to meet her. His attention is scanning the road like I didn't exist. "Did she tell you what she was wearing or anything to help recognize her?"

"No."

"Did you tell her anything to recognize you or that you'll be with another guy?"

"No."

"You're a fucking idiot."

I guess he isn't impressed by all my degrees. They don't help me too much now. We pull up to the curb about a half block from the bar. Half the car is on the curb in a no-parking zone.

"Let's go, I've had a few there. Good Greek food."

Why am I not surprised?

He keeps talking. "You know, every woman who walks into the place you can ask if they called you. I hope you find her before they kick you out."

I have no answer for this. I really screwed up. How do you place a voice with an unknown face?

Sitting at the bar to my right, Vito is sipping a local beer. I order the same. And I keep twisting to look at the door. All I see are guys or couples, both genders. I am halfway through the beer when I am about to give up. Maybe it is just Lamar testing us out. The chair next to me moves, and I feel a strong tap on the left shoulder.

"You looking for somebody?"

It is a preppy-looking blonde with tied-back hair and jeans and a light sweater. Somehow I know this isn't a line to open up my life with her.

"Why?"

"Are you Adam?"

"Did you call me?"

"Yes."

"Then let's do us both us a favor and exchange IDs."

She dives into her purse, and I slide into my jacket. Vito stares at his beer. Happy with who we each are, smiles are shared. It's like we forgot why this is happening.

Before we know it, a badge is reflecting light in front of us and saying, "Let's move to a booth. Do you want anything, lady?"

Wasting time is not in his CV. Kim sits opposite both of us, staring at neither of us. She is looking at the table and turning a shade of red.

"I feel like such a fool doing this. I hardly really know the guy; we did share some time."

"It's OK; we're here because we care about Lamar. And you, of course." I am so empathic.

Vito's leg quickly jams sideways as he kicks my shin. His turn, his show.

"I agree with Adam and you. Tell me what you told Adam."

Kim relays the story and tries to squeeze every memory for Vito to appreciate.

"Lamar hasn't been working with us, he's with another department. Every so often we get a call from him."

"Where is he?"

"We'll find out."

"When you do, tell him Blackie is OK. Oh, and that I tossed out a bottle of gin."

Vito doesn't change his expression, no matter what he hears. That's when I knew he was all business. "Sure, we're right on it. What number do we call?"

She writes down all her numbers.

"Sure you don't want something?"

She gets up and leaves. Vito turns to me and is nodding subconsciously. He only does that when things are serious. "We have to find Lamar, I don't like this setup. We need to cover, whether he wants it or not."

I offer, "I can contact the DA's office and get an update. Update them too. I'll pretend that's why I'm calling."

"Yeah."

* * *

Lamar is trapped by his fresh ice bags. He is sitting in a chair and footrest with his right leg over one ice bag and his right hand holding another on his ribs. Moving himself or one of the bags hurts like hell.

They know what they are doing with him. "Nice place, huh?"

Lamar looks at Sam walking in circles in the living room. It seems like Isabella is playing a secondary role. He can see and smell dinner cooking. He has no assumption that any food will be for him. "It's as only as nice as the view."

Sam walks over to the windows and opens the curtains. "The harbor, what could be better!"

Between grimaces, Lamar sputters out, "That's not the view I was talking about."

Sam drags over a kitchen-table chair, spins it around, and sits down facing Lamar. "I know what you meant."

Isabella disappears into the bedroom. Sam leans into the back of the chair; his long legs keep him from falling facedown. It's time to find out what this Lamar guy is all about. A cop has to go a long way to prove he's turned for Sam. This one doesn't feel right from the beginning. Lamar is no fool. He is on the line. Now.

"I can give you something for the pain. I'm in the pharmaceutical business."

"I'll stick with the ice." Lamar is not taking anything into his body that this guy would give him.

"I need to know why you're in this."

"Money."

Sam know that more often than not, money is enough to keep a source. People never have enough money. But a single guy in the police force all the years this guy has put in; it has to be more than money. His drinking is under control; and his gambling debt is manageable. It just doesn't sit right. He needs some passion from this guy, not just about money.

"What are you going to do with this new money?" He can't see him in a new Porsche tooling around Boston.

"Save it."

Isabella pops her head out the bedroom door. The chili is stewing. She mouths, "Save it?"

Lamar doesn't see her, and it is just as well. He doesn't know what to say. Sam stays in place and forms the next question. There are all sorts of interviews in life. This one simply determines if Lamar has a future.

"I need a better reason for believing you than money. Look, your injuries are painful but can be managed. If it works, we can do a lot together. You can be a big player in my Northeast territory. I need someone to run my operation here when I go back South." He lies. Once this deal is done, he is out of the drug business in this area. But if this cop is bad, it couldn't hurt to cultivate a future reference up North. You never know.

Lamar thinks it is now or never to play his card. He hates to play this card, but he knows he has a chance with this mentality.

By now Isabella is boiling the rice. She has said the salad is in the fridge. Lamar shifts a bit and gives his hamstring and rib a rest from the ice. Isabella walks over and takes the cold, damp bags from him.

"I'll freshen these up."

"Sure."

Sam stares at Lamar.

"I'm black; I am as far as I can go in the force. It's not like I have developed a gang of close buddies. I'm a loner; people respect my work and listen to me. Sure, money helps; I want to retire down South without having to do security patrols on a warehouse at two in the morning."

"Keep going."

"I've been there long enough that I can go anywhere and access all sorts of information."

Sam stands up from the chair and takes the ice bags from Isabella and hands them to Lamar. Lamar is long past saying thanks.

"How do I know you're not a double, setting me up?"

"You don't."

Sam knows he is right. At some point it is always a leap of faith. Interesting, needing a leap of faith in believing in the criminal intent. If he is a double, Sam can toy with using him. He almost did with Gord; it just got too complicated. It was easier to kill him. Isabella is setting the table for three. Lamar knows that can change.

"If you're on our payroll, you answer to me. If I need you to do something and you have no sleep, I don't want to hear about it."

"Look, I'm trying to set up my independence from being in law enforcement when I retire," Lamar speaks with about as much passion as the ice bag on his leg.

Sam walks into the kitchen and touches Isabella on the shoulder. If you just walked in, you'd think they were a married couple tending to an injured friend. The only accurate part is the injury.

Isabella is all done with her preparations when Sam says, "Let's eat." He has made his decision.

* * *

"Ms. Quinn, are you still with us?" The DA gets to the point.

She hasn't been with them; she is thinking about how much she needs to get away from this life. No, not forever, just a break. Now is not the time to be thinking about a break. All the guns are pointed at her; she has to come through for everybody. Avoiding the pressure cases has always been her quiet way to keep a low profile. It is time to grow out of that mode; she now has the case to do it. Patty knows that she looks flashy; she just doesn't yet have that flashy legal reputation.

She looks at the DA and, putting her most serious face on, whispers, "I never left."

"What, I don't hear you."

"I guess you don't pay attention very well, do you?" She speaks in a quiet monotone.

Alan Cohen feels his gut tighten a bit. So she is going to be a tough lady. Why can't the other side just work with him for a change? Is it him? He went to all the right schools.

"It's amazing how much they don't teach you in school about the real world," she says this a bit louder. The DA doesn't respond. Patty knew his background and likes to remind him that they were equals in court.

The loose ends of Lamar's work are working on Alan Cohen. There is concern here, having a team player in the enemy's camp. He is a seasoned veteran, but there is never enough training for undercover work. He can only imagine how his old partner, Vito, feels.

He doesn't have to imagine too much longer about Vito's thoughts. The phone is ringing, the private line.

The DA walks over to his desk and picks up the phone. "Yes."

"I need to meet with you. Now," Vito speaks as if he is talking to a rookie cop.

Alan ignores Patty, looking as if she is a third wheel. At this point she is. "Why now? I'm busy."

"We need to talk about Lamar." That hits a cord that resounds in Alan.

"Come over to the office now."

"On the way."

What makes it sad is that each side expects something important from the other. They are both fishing for information to build on. They expect the other to be the closer in this deal. The same team, the same goal, and no official communication with each other.

"Something I need to know?" Patty is not going to be left out of the loop. It isn't too hard to read Alan's face.

He turns back to her. "That was Vito. He wants to talk about our undercover man on this operation. He's on the way over now. That is, Vito is."

For all the unprofessional reasons, Patty feels a charge of energy. "OK if I stay, I'd like to ask a few questions?"

"You are kidding, right? You can question him in court."

She tried. Alan sits down at his desk and turns to her with his serious look. He saves the furrows on his brow for special occasions. "If you want to stay and continue our chat, OK. It's also OK if you want to chat with the police, off-the-record. I'll have to clear it with Vito first."

"Sounds good. I'll stay."

The phone rings again. Alan picks it up and quickly responds, "Come on up, you're clear with security."

Turning back to Patty, he realizes she really wanted to stay. Tough. This is not school; she is not getting inside. He'll let her play a bit for a few minutes. Let her feel like she can relax with them. This way he has a better chance in court. He also wonders what the story is with this Adam fellow. He never checked if they contracted him for this case. He wasn't on their roster. He wonders what he is offering to their department. If no checks have been cut for him, how can this guy care about all this?

Vito is wondering if Adam is happier being on the outside. He never felt that his soul was into helping the force. He is a good guy; he gives a helping hand, but he's not someone who understands the heart of the badge.

He will never forget that he was there when he and Bentley needed a place to live.

Catherine is another story. Vito thinks she is a loose cannon. That appeals to him. He knows she likes getting down and dirty and is one tough lady.

He sends both of his outside teammates to their quarters so he can be efficient with the DA. He owed Lamar. "Thanks for seeing me." Vito is talking before he is totally in the DA's door.

"Where's Lamar, and what's he doing?" He said as he helps himself to a seat in the private office. Introductions and handshakes aren't going to happen.

"I know that you have been his partner for a while. Sorry to split you guys up, I hear you were a pretty good team."

Vito sits up and doesn't appear to hear what Alan Cohen has said. If he did, he doesn't care. "Where's Lamar? Is he in trouble?"

Alan opens his top right desk draw and pulls out some papers. He slides them over to Vito. "I really wanted to keep this as efficient as possible, minimal people involved. Neither one of us has heard from Lamar, my uniforms have lost him, sign these, and we talk."

Vito has seen these before, standard confidentiality papers. He quickly scrawls his name on the bottom and dates it. He wants it documented when he was on this case. The DA tells him about the meeting on the park bench and the track.

"Your people are real fuckups. How can they let one of our people be injured and carted off in front of them? Why were they there?"

The DA just looks at Vito. He knows Vito is right.

"OK, they must have Lamar. The two we're talking about are the same two who are running the fake vet drug deal. They killed Gord, didn't they?"

"Most likely."

"Why won't they kill Lamar? We're closing in on them, and how is he going to give them info to make them feel clear?"

"If he gets inside, we can get definitive evidence against them, and we nail them."

"Do you have a clue how badly he's hurt?"

"No."

"Do you have a clue where he is?"

"No."

Vito holds his mouth. He wants to say what a loser this guy is, but it could screw his career. He remembers the lady attorney for the chemist sitting in the reception room.

He gets an idea. "Let's bring her in here."

"Why?"

"We make like she's a team member and open her brain up. Maybe her client may have heard where they have Lamar now."

Alan looks out at the Charles River and half closes his eyes. Patty Quinn was right; they didn't teach much about street smarts in law school.

* * *

Well, Vito likes my idea. It is obvious that he feels I am not up to the task. I have no problem with it. My ego took off a long time ago. It is important that we find out what Lamar is up to. It is not important that I be the one who finds out what's happening. Catherine doesn't seem to care; she is tired and just wants to get back to the Marriott. The three of us go our separate ways.

It is good to be back in my nest with my canine buddies. I'll never forget Gord as long as Bowser is Fern's roommate. I feel that the three of us are about to go on our own paths. Humans, that is. Oh, we'll get this case finished, but that will not tie us together. These last few days have shown how different we are. Walking my two buddies at night gives me a sense of quiet. I can't tell you why; it just does.

Even though I only own one floor of the building, it is mine. The shared entrance has my character imprinted on the two locks as does the entrance door to my condo. Three locks, different sizes, give me my own identity into the cocoon I call home. I slept well last night. Unfortunately, I set the alarm for 5:30 a.m. the next day. My draw to yoga, or was it just to the instructor, forced me to adjust the alarm dial.

The next morning my sound sleep is hammered awake by the buzz on my nightstand. I am careful to minimize the amount of coffee I drink; hydration is always an issue with the heat in the yoga studio. My canine roommates take the morning walk and time change in stride. They know they are going back to sleep when I leave. I have the feeling that as soon as the last door lock is closed, Bowser and Fern make eye contact and amble off to their own turf to sleep.

It is a nice walk to the gym in the early morning. When I enter the building and take the elevator to the fitness center, all of a sudden I have a bit of anxiety. I haven't been to a yoga class in a while; will I remember what to do?

Aleni's back is to me in the yoga studio. She is meditating, planning the lesson, or perhaps none of the above. The room is filling up. I have totally forgotten the uniqueness of this class. One thing that strikes me immediately is the higher amount of men present today. It must be the early-before-work-hour crew. I kind of miss being the only guy.

Unrolling my mat between two young ladies, I have my system, and the room quickly fills up. It is quiet. No talking, no music. Just breathing. Systemic, rhythmic breathing. I am on my back and join my two canine companions in spirit.

"Another wonderful morning to celebrate. Let us stand with our feet together on the top of our mat."

I am surprised how my practice flows. Aleni does not acknowledge my presence, never talking to or adjusting me. Being lost in my poses, my focus is on myself and nothing else. I do miss the woman with hairy armpits. Some things never leave you.

During my shoulder stand, I wonder if Aleni is going to come over to me. She does.

She whispers in my upside-down ear, "Let's talk after class."

I can't figure out how to nod yes upside down, so I smile.

In a crossed-leg sitting position, the class ends with one "ohm" said in unison. The room has emptied out, and I roll up my mat in slow motion.

"Good to see you."

"I thought the session would be tough, it wasn't."

"You've been OK?"

I'm not going to do a total review of the last few days. She is my escape. "Yeah, you?"

"I have news." She smiles and flicks her left hand.

An engagement ring glitters in my eyes. She wasn't wearing it during class. I can't say I am happy, but I say, "I'm happy for you."

"Thanks."

What do I do now; ask her for dates until she's married? My sense of peace slides into the conflict of my emotions. I like her. Simple as that. Now she belongs to somebody else. No fair. I don't know what to say; I turn to leave the room.

"We're friends, right?" Actually, that is what we are. To her.

To me she was a lover. Note the word *was*. "Sure. You've been seeing this fellow for a while?" Why the hell did I ask that?

"Two years."

I turn and look at her.

She must have read my mind. "I needed to be with you, a need had to be met."

I don't know how to respond to this.

"He is an old friend from the past. He is part of a big family business and the Greek community."

"I guess I didn't pass the paperwork." I am hurt, it shows.

She looks down and then at me. "I'm sorry. I don't want to say goodbye."

I say one clear word as I leave the studio, "Goodbye."

The walk back doesn't carry the spirit that I hoped for. I am getting that empty feeling. I am an observer again. Before, at least, I was paid for it. Maybe I should associate with a hospital practice where I will become part of the professional world all over again. Get into that title "Dr."

No. The thought slips through my system like liquid. A needed process that does not linger. With all the excitement and new people in my life, the last few weeks I sensed my bruised feelings evaporating quickly. Maybe I am overreacting in a teenage way. I don't remember being hurt by a woman since I was seventeen years old. What if after her marriage settles down, she wants to be with me occasionally? I certainly have a need for her. Could I handle that type of a "friendship"?

I am standing on the outside of my place, deep in thought. Isn't that what yoga's goal is? Perhaps my canine companionship will take me where yoga was supposed to.

I open the door.

"What the hell?"

Vito is sipping coffee and holding court with the gang.

"They are walked, all departments accounted for."

"What are you doing here?"

"You don't say thanks for brewing the coffee? I made fresh."

"Thanks. Now why are you here?"

"I met with the DA and the attorney for the Axelrod guy."

I pour myself a mug of black coffee. It does smell good. With two hands on the warm mug, I don't say anything; I know better. I just nod.

"We don't have any concrete facts as to where Lamar is. But we are pretty convinced that he is with the two we have been following. The Spanish lady and the tall thin guy are the same that first questioned you. Axelrod has been with them, they set him up in the warehouse to make the fake drugs and package them like the real thing. He was there when Catherine investigated and got hammered. They took her up to New Hampshire, and you know the rest from there."

I am halfway through the mug. I nod again. I just realize locks mean nothing to Vito. He goes wherever he wants. His world has no boundaries. He gives me the Lamar update. The tone of his voice isn't as professional as usual. He is concerned. So am I.

Vito continues, "From what we put together, they probably are in Boston. After all, they met Lamar at the BU track and nailed him there. The cops checked the ERs of the hospitals, no luck."

"How badly is Lamar hurt?"

"It sounds like a quick trip and pounding. Probably in pain with decreased mobility, but nothing permanent."

"If they hurt him, they must be on to him."

"We figure they're testing him now. I have a feeling we'll know one way or the other pretty soon."

"So you want to pull him out."

"Yes."

"How do we do it, where do we go?"

"Nowhere."

"What?"

"The DA says wait."

I am shocked. Logically it looks like if these two are arrested, there is enough to put them in jail for at least pharmaceutical fraud. Can't the DA see Lamar's life is in danger?

Vito slowly walks to the bathroom, the three cups of coffee caught up to him. It is quiet; the three, Bowser, Fern and Bentley, all stare at me. Direct eye-to-eye contact. Do they know what is happening? At moments like this I wish I had their ability to curl up on a chair and close my eyes. Following the flush, Vito returns and slouches on the high chair by the breakfast bar. He doesn't sit for long as he walks over to the window facing the park. The silence is awful.

I used to love the silence in my place. It's amazing how one person sitting in an empty chair at a restaurant can change your life. That seems so long ago. I stand up and look out the adjacent window to Vito.

Turning to him, I speak, "What's Catherine's read on all this?"

"I don't know. She took off to her hotel last night without saying much."

"Let me give her a call. Maybe we should meet at her place. They let dogs in there."

"Sure."

* * *

Catherine slept in. She was awake at six but didn't find it difficult to keep her eyes closed until eight. Her plans for the day are not to have any. She needs time to recharge. That's what they say nowadays, recharge. Listen to your body. Being alone is therapy, having space from all the new people in her life. When she was a DA in Florida, she would tell those working a case with her that she was in research when she needed time alone. Well, she's telling herself she's in research.

Her plans are breakfast and doing the laundry. It is time to wash her Gap wardrobe. Before she knows it, midmorning has arrived. She appreciates the fact that her neighbors are quiet. Except for hearing the door open and close last evening, for all she knows, she has no neighbors. She is concentrating on the facts for the meeting with the Boston DA. It is a connection that won't be tough to make. She'll call after her "recharging" time is over.

The phone is ringing. She knows recharging is officially over.

"Hello." It is Vito's charming voice. "We're on our way over. The whole gang is visiting; we'll walk them by the water first."

She's not interested where the dogs exercised. "Fine."

"We'll bring stuff to eat." The guys know a good local take-out place. No surprise.

Removing the robe that's been on since her quick shower, Catherine selects a pretty generic outfit in case they wind up in some official's office. You can never tell; a handwritten schedule isn't given to her every morning. Unless, of course, she wrote it. She sits down and slides the hotel notepad over to her.

A list has to be made so there is order when Adam and Vito walk in to her place. If all five come in at once, there will be chaos. Interesting, if it was family and a holiday, there would be camaraderie. This is not family, and it's no holiday.

The blank notepad stays blank for ten minutes. Catherine gets up and makes fresh strong coffee. She needs that brewing smell to get her in the thinking mode. The paper stays blank. For the first time in years she needs help. Murder, her abduction, bad drugs, vets involved, her time with Adam, the Boston detectives, and Lamar disappearing—it is a mix that has no handle.

Catherine is sitting at the kitchen table in her grey suit with pen and paper. She sits staring at the poster of the Boston skyline on the opposite wall, not hearing the knocking on the door.

"Hey, are you alive?" Vito's voice has a way of bringing you back to earth.

Standing up with the same blank look, she says as she opens the door, "Didn't you check in with the desk?"

Vito just gives her a quizzical look and shows her his badge on his belt, not too far from his gun.

"I forgot you're the tough guy."

As Vito walks in, the entourage of Adam and the dogs comes through with their distinctive pace. The dogs immediately investigate the smells of all corners in the suite. Adam wonders if his scent is still there. If so, it is their secret. Catherine stands by as the guys organize bagels and cheese on the kitchen counter.

"You have plates and cups in this place? Also, a big bowl of water?" Organizing the food is Adam's role.

As she shows them where everything is, she hands a big bowel to Adam. "You thirsty?"

Adam doesn't answer. He walks around, looks in the bedroom, and says, "Nice place."

She looks at him, shakes her head and pours coffee in her cup. They know that Vito isn't going to talk until after his second bagel. The dogs are still in discovery; only Fern finds her spot on the chair in the bedroom.

The second bagel disappears. "The DA thinks Lamar can handle himself and get info that will be some big stuff. Not only nail the two we're following but a larger gang."

Nobody says anything. What can you say, he's right or wrong. It's a guessing game. It is weird, and there is silence. All of a sudden, Fern is out of the bedroom and smelling at the door to the hallway. She is moving right to left at the door and smelling at the floor opening. A door is heard opening and closing out in the hall near them. It is a Marriott; doors do open and close. They ignore Fern; dogs always smell something.

"While you crime fighters figure out what to do next, I'm going downstairs to get a paper at the front desk. You want anything?"

She receives silent shaking of the heads.

Walking into the corridor, the scent of a familiar aftershave comes to her attention. Oh well, these public places are not like being in your own home. She shares the elevator with a young couple with foreign accents and a tall older businessman. She assumes every man in a dark suit and attaché case is a businessman. She works her way to the back of the elevator and wonders if the *Wall Street Journal* is available today. She knows the *Boston Globe* is there.

The door opens to the lobby, and the three companions walk out. Catherine waits her turn, and the elevator door starts to close when she is six inches from it. As she places her hand in the path of the closing door, another hand beats her to it from the outside. It is a large thin-boned male hand. The door stops, and moves back to open. The tall man moves into the elevator quickly.

He places his right hand firmly on her left shoulder, and his left hand shoots out to hit the number of his floor. He does not let her go.

She can't move, including her frightened unblinking eyes.

A smile breaks out across his face as he says, "What a surprise."

Chapter 82

Alan Cohen is not secure. Oh, he is secure in his political position, in his term in office, in his personal life. No threats there. He is not secure in how to handle the undercover detective. Maybe he detects that Lamar is not the right person for this job. It is too late to do anything about that now.

He feels that Vito wants to abort the deal immediately. That is a decision tainted by emotion, not logic. Logic always prevails in Alan's life. Well, it is time to meet with the lawyers working with him and see what the day has to bring. He has to appear confident just as if he were going on an interview. Nothing ever changes.

He makes a note to call Vito after his morning meeting with his group. He stands up and walks to the door when his secretary tells him that Patty Quinn is on the phone. What the hell does she want? They spent a half day going over everything.

"Alan Cohen here."

"This is Patty Quinn; I need some more of your time."

"You have two minutes now."

"I just got a call you would be very interested in."

"Tell me about it in one minute."

"I can't. It's from one of the people you want to convict."

Alan puts his hand over the mouthpiece and says to his secretary, "Cancel my morning meetings."

Back to Patty he says, "Where do you want to talk?"

"My office in a half hour."

"Where the hell is your office?"

When Patty remembers she shared it with three other lawyers, she changes the venue. "Forget that, how about a Starbucks downtown?"

"Thirty minutes."

They both hang up with nerves attacking their guts for different reasons. If he didn't have all this anxiety, he would be looking forward to a good cup of coffee. He grabs a taxi out front of his building and is wondering what and which one of the two had called Patty. Didn't they have their own connection on the force with these people? It's obvious the Axelrod connection is getting to have a greater value than he first thought.

He is early and blends in with the morning crowd at Starbucks. He sits at the last little table for two at a window. He wonders if Patty will be afraid of the window. The bad guys could shoot her. He'll have to stop watching *Law and Order*. He leaves his raincoat on the chair and is second in-line for his large coffee. Thirty minutes and one half mug of coffee have passed without sight of Ms. Quinn. Is this a setup? No, too much TV. The concern and caffeine have him bouncing off the chair. He'll give her five more minutes, and after that, no credibility.

He looks at his shoes and notices they needed polishing. OK, at least he'll accomplish that today. He'll stop off on the way back to work to get them cleaned up. He is embarrassed with his image. Time to go, get the coat on, and don't give second-level lawyers the same time as the Ivy grads.

"I can't help it that the cab was stuck behind a fire truck." There she is, red hair, looking as if the fire truck was chasing her.

"Sit down, what kind of coffee do you want me to get you?"

"Anything that's foamy and decaf."

He is thinking that she made a good choice for her condition. He erases the thought about the second-level legal crew. She sits down and Alan returns with the foamy decaf. She immediately bolts for the ladies' room. She returns all Ms. Professional and sits down. His turn, he goes to the men's room, not to do his hair.

Finally, they both occupy the table. He leads off. "It better be good."

"It's delicious, thanks."

"I'm happy for you. I was referring to the information. Remember, you called me about a phone call you received."

She sips the concoction and looks out the window. From the outside looking in, they look like a couple meeting from a computer dating service. You'd never know they were about to determine if certain people will live or die.

"The woman called me about an hour ago."

"What woman?"

"The Spanish lady from the duo you're chasing."

"And?"

"I could hardly hear her; she was on her cell whispering in the bathroom. She had water running in the sink the whole time she spoke."

Alan's interest suddenly has him forget all the previous bullshit. His stare is directly at her. He knows he has to listen.

"She told me where they have Lamar. She's concerned what her partner will do him."

"What does she want?"

"If she tells us everything and Lamar is saved, she wants immunity."

"Pretty soon we'll have everybody, and they all will walk."

"I heard a door slam, and she hung up."

"What's the next step?"

"I don't know she hung up quickly."

This is just the type of information that makes you crazy. Not the type of crazy that a shrink can straighten out. Which reminds me, maybe the ex-shrink on the case should know about this. He sees Patty take out a writing pad from the Holiday Inn. Her pen is from a local bank.

"What are you writing?"

"I think it's best I write where they are keeping Lamar."

"Good idea."

Quickly the Charlestown location is on paper and passed to Alan. He looks and shows no expression. He knows if he tells Vito everything, he will be over by the evening.

Once again Alan looks directly at Patty but touches her arm for affect as he needs to know, "Did you tell her that this will be passed to me?"

"She hung up right after she said the name of the place."

"Why don't you go back to your office and act as if nothing happened. I don't think telling your client about this will help his case. Of course, I never said that."

Regaining her sense of presence, she lets Alan know she heard him. "Thanks for the coffee; I have a load of paperwork to do this afternoon. Goodbye."

Alan leans back to watch her leave Starbucks. In a minute, she blends in with the city crowd.

There is a lot to chew on here. The best part is he knows where Lamar is being held. The lady didn't speak to him, so no promises were made about immunity at trial. Maybe he'll have the place staked out and be sure Vito doesn't get this information. Vito would play the cowboy and get his friend Lamar without regard to the big picture. This needs a bit of finesse. He'll need to find some cops who have more to gain by being loyal to him than their old buddies. Being an elected official always makes you the outsider. Picking up his cell, he dials the private number of Gord's best friend. He is a retired officer with his own security company.

Sometimes you have to think out of the box.

Chapter 83

"Where the hell is she? Did she go to New York to pick up the *Times*?"

It doesn't make any sense that it's twenty minutes later and Catherine isn't back. I'm not used to hearing any level of anxiety in Vito's voice. I hear it now. I turn to Vito. "Do you want me to check the front desk?"

"Sure, you'll look for the *Montreal Gazette*, and I'll see you after the hockey season." Rationality was leaving my friend.

"Why don't I call the desk to see if she showed up there or is having something at the coffee shop?"

"Good idea."

I call. The woman at the desk remembers who she is and has not seen her in the past hour. This really does not make any sense. I can't think of any reason why she would take off on us. None.

Vito is walking in circles. I stand in front of him to stop him. "Why would she want to take off on us? Am I missing something?" I'm not a cop, maybe I am missing something.

Vito sits down; Bentley waddles over and sits next to him. He knows something is wrong. Fern and Bowser change their expressions; heads are down, with eyes looking up.

"They got her."

"Who is 'they'?"

"The two bastards in this deal."

"What do we do?"

"I don't know."

I stand as cold waves travel from my skull to my feet. Vito is not supposed to say that. He sits with his hand on his mouth. I stand looking at my feet. We are not a picture of optimism. There are no more bagels, so I can't fuel my friend. Maybe it's something about me; it seems that every woman I sleep with winds up somewhere else.

The phone rings. We both fly like the Patriots' defensive line after the quarterback. We collide, and our friends are running around and barking like crazy. I win; the phone is in my hand. "Yes."

"Housekeeping will be one hour late today, sorry." I hang up.

"And?"

"Housekeeping will be late."

Sitting on the floor with our dogs now quiet and looking at us, I feel like a total idiot. Again.

The phone rings. It is still in my hand.

"I needed space." It is Catherine's voice, but it sounds as if she is a recording of herself.

"Where the hell are you?"

"I'm fine, I just need some room. I'll be in touch." Nothing but a dial tone.

I say to Vito whose eyes are on fire, "Something's not right."

"No, shit. This isn't normal."

"Can we trace the call?"

"Not on long enough, but I'll try."

We both stand up at the same time. Neither of us is thinking about counterfeit drugs. The dogs are dancing; they need to be taken out. We all need the walk. Vito is moving in slow motion, and that is really slow. He leashes up Bentley and Bowser while I hook the familiar blue cloth leash on Fern.

I follow Vito and his two companions out the door to the elevator, a right turn from Catherine's suite. I am behind Fern and she abruptly stops in front of the door of the suite next to us.

She sniffs at the base of the door.

She plants herself at the base of that door.

* * *

"You all right?" This may be the first time Sam ever asked that question to another human.

Isabella is leaving the bathroom, holding her huge purse. "Sure, sometimes mother nature has her own schedule."

Sam knows enough not to pursue the topic any further. Besides, he has enough on his plate. Lamar and Catherine, a duo he never expected to have to deal with at the same time. When he brought Catherine in, he couldn't help notice the quick eye contact between the two of them. It doesn't take long for Sam to make a decision. Lamar's fate is sealed. Lamar's facial expression is stoic, but Sam did see the quick communication between them.

"Here we are again, this time you stay with your hands tied. Enjoy your chair."

He talks to both his captives. Sam ties Lamar up without any regard for his injuries; Catherine's arms are laced behind the chair she is sitting on. Sam looks at her. "Neither one of us forgot what you did to us."

Isabella is trying to figure out how to get out of this scene.

Catherine isn't going to stay quiet. "You're not going to get away with this."

Sam isn't letting go of his smile. "With what?"

Catherine stays quiet; this isn't an interview for a debating society. Sam has to get his money out of the northeast operation. He knows Lamar has to go, and the lady needs a lesson. He's had enough of this whole operation. He turns to Isabella.

"I need your help."

"Sure."

"Untie the woman and tie her up in the bedroom. Let's separate these two."

It makes sense to Isabella. Actually, she likes the idea. If she were alone with her, she could call the right people again and be the hero in the eyes of the police. She already sent cash she had taken from her cut to her post office box in Florida. She likes her future.

"No problem, maybe we could give her private time in the bathroom in there. Some water wouldn't hurt her."

Sam thinks she is playing the old good-guy-bad-guy routine. What the hell, he'll go along. "Go."

She unties Catherine and grabs her two arms with hers. She lets one of her arms go to get her purse.

Sam grabs her purse and says, "You need both your arms to control her. I'll follow you with your bag."

Isabella does as she is told. Catherine figures that Isabella will call her room again, and this will come to an end. She gives Isabella no resistance.

Lamar watches this whole scene unfold like a surrealistic melodrama. It is as if he is in a bad movie. The ladies are in the bedroom, and Sam follows with Isabella's purse. He stops at the door and closes it from the outside. He places a chair under the door handle, which will keep the women from escaping.

Quickly he disconnects the phone service to the room. He reaches in to the purse and grabs the cell phone. He tosses it in the trash compacter with the remnants of their last meal. He hits the switch to turn it on and it all becomes one unknown compacted blob.

Lamar moves his limbs to try and loosen the tape on his wrists and ankles. Sam quietly, slowly walks behind him.

He slips a plastic laundry bag over his head.

Chapter 84

Andrew Dodge has always found the DA a world-class bore. On a good day, he thinks he's a jerk. Driving his Dodge pickup is part of Andrew's image. There are actually some who think that he is part of the car family. There are so many idiots in the world; he stopped counting. Seeing the DA's name on his phone while driving to a client is interesting. He gets a call from this guy about twice a year, always for a favor in a hurry.

"Yeah, what's new?"

Alan takes it for granted there is no socializing. "I need a stake out that my people won't know about."

"Remember, just because I was once a cop, it's not for free. I'm a businessman now."

"Why should this be different than any other time?"

"How urgent is this?" Andrew needs to adjust his schedule. In other words, whoever pays the quickest gets his attention.

"I need you now. Usual deal?"

"You need me now; the state can afford another fifty bucks an hour."

"Bastard."

"I guess that means deal."

"Deal. Bastard." Andrew ignores the description and is pleased with his business success.

"We meet now. My office."

"I'm on the way over."

Alan is in a cab about three blocks from Dodge's office during this conversation. He pays the cabbie and starts walking over. He still has the caffeine buzz. He walks in the door to his office on the fifth floor of a nondescript building in an area of Boston that may one day undergo urban renewal. Andrew Dodge is right behind him, all two hundred pounds of muscle. The weight room is his second home.

"Coffee, water?" It's Andrew's turf, he makes the offer.

"Water, thanks."

Andrew hands Alan the bottle and offers a chair as he leans against the desk.

"What do you need?"

The DA tells the whole story. After a few minutes of silence, he then asks Andrew for his read on the deal. Andrew learned years ago not to give his opinions to his clients no matter who they were. He just focuses on his job.

"I have the right person for you. He'll be there in twenty minutes. No problem."

"Good. How do get in touch with him?"

"Easy. His code word is Superman. You're looking at him."

"You're cell phone number?"

Andrew walks around to the side of the grey metal desk with the drawers facing him. He opens the right one and takes out a sheet of paper. "Sign this, all the numbers are on this. I'll contact you, you don't call me."

Alan quietly follows his new agent outside, and they part ways. The DA knows he made the right decision. Andrew Dodge is very good at what he does. He isn't surprised he calls himself Superman.

Well, back to the office and wait for the calls. In the meantime, he'll finally have that meeting with his staff and pretend to be interested in their cases.

Dodge has only one thought as he drives his Dodge to the Marriott in Charleston: this is such an easy way to make a buck. He knows all the people who work at that hotel; that's where he puts his out-of-town clients.

He nods at the front entrance attendant as he drives down the ramp to indoor guest parking. He doesn't need his big black Dodge getting dirty; besides, the receipt is tax deductible. His accountant is also a client, but that's another story.

The friendliness of the front desk people looks normal. "Hello, Mr. Dodge, can we help you?"

Wendy, the short skinny blondish front desk girl, is an old girlfriend from his days as a cop. He seems to know everybody in this city. It's no surprise he and Vito didn't have much to say to each other. "Yeah, how you doing?"

"Great, what do you need?"

He hands her his parking ticket to be stamped for a discount. On sliding the ticket across the desk, he gets to why he is there.

"You want to go out again?"

"I know what you need, why are you here now?" An older couple is behind him, waiting to check in.

"When can we chat over there?" He points to the grouping of leather chairs around the gas fireplace in the lounge.

"I have coverage in ten minutes."

Andrew walks over to a small couch angled near the fireplace and takes his leather coat off. He opens his weathered light brown attaché case and withdraws a set of pictures and a yellow legal pad. He studies the photos and makes notes on the yellow paper. Then he takes out a manila envelope with sheets of white paper with words printed on them. He matches the pictures with the white papers. He continues to make notes on the legal pad.

"Doing homework?"

Looking up, he sees Wendy standing in front of him with two mugs of coffee in off-white Marriott mugs. Her work outfit does nothing for her figure.

"Thanks, take a seat. I have some questions." He turns the photos toward her. "Recognize any of these people?"

She doesn't need much time to answer. "They're all here, even the dogs."

He ignores the comment about the dogs. "All of them."

"Yep, in rooms 516 and 515." He stares at her.

"Anyone leave?"

"Not as far as I know." She then looks at Sam's picture and points to it. "He came down to the lobby this morning but went back upstairs."

This was too easy. Andrew knows what was next. "I need a cart with towels. It's time for room service to freshen things up."

"You going to tell me what this is all about?"

He stands up, bends over, and whispers into her ear, "No. But how about a drink tonight?"

"I'll get the cart for you; touch base with me before I leave this afternoon."

"Sure."

He never could tell if her smile is the real thing. Whatever, he has a job to do. As promised, the towel cart is in the back hall by the elevator on the main floor. Sharing the ride up with two twelve-year-olds, he hits the number 5 on the panel.

* * *

Fern is a stubborn friend. It isn't the first time she has had to get her way. But why the hell is she not moving from the room next door? I remember this happening once before in my condo building. The guy downstairs is cooking chili, and she is addicted to the smell of the spices of that dish. That is the one meal I am good at cooking. She will sit on the kitchen floor the whole time it was stewing. The wonderful smell of meat and spices has a way of throwing a blanket over the cigar smell from the floor below. Anyway, a dog biscuit always gets her attention. But I am dealing with something very different now.

There are no cooking odors coming from the next-door suite. Fern is sniffing at the opening at the base of the door and looking up at me. I wish I could read her mind.

There are no dog biscuits handy, so I stand there waiting for Vito to notice I'm not behind him. Fern isn't listening to any of my commands. I guess her performance at obedience school was only for the final exam.

Not smelling anything, I put my ear to the door. Not a sound. Finally, Vito shows up with his contingent. "Who's in charge here?" A typical Vito comment.

"She is." I could say that about a number of my relationships with females.

"That's obvious. Give her a yank and let's get moving."

I just look at him. That last command just doesn't sit right with me. "Something must be going on in this room or she wouldn't be acting like this." This is one of those situations where I have to throw the obvious in his face.

Vito looks at me as if I am nuts. Bowser waddles over to Fern, looks at her, and then looks at the door. Bentley sits down on the other side of Fern and starts sniffing the same place as Fern.

"Maybe someone is making dope in there." Vito is the perpetual cop.

"These four-legged detectives aren't trained to smell anything that I know of." I am analyzing again.

"Yeah." Vito starts to walk toward the door and is about to open it with his universal computer card.

"I wouldn't do that if I were you."

Turning, I see this tall athletic-looking man pushing a towel cart down the hall in our direction.

Vito quickly turns and says, "OK."

Now I know I am in the twilight zone.

The tall man walks over to Vito, totally ignoring me. As he walks by, I notice a gun strapped to his right ankle. The two of them stand face-to-face.

"It's my show," towel man speaks with authority.

It certainly is a show. I feel like the audience. "What's going on?" My question is totally ignored.

Vito takes a step toward him.

"They're all in there." Towel man speaks again.

"Who are they?" Vito doesn't blink as he talks.

"Everybody you've been looking for and the woman who was working with you. Oh, your old partner, too."

Vito and I just look at this guy. I have to ask, "Who the hell are you?"

Without change of expression, he glances over at Vito and quietly whispers to me, "Ask him."

"Long story." That's all Vito was saying.

"I'm going in. I was hired to watch this crew, but I don't like it with the good guys and the bad guys in the same room. Didn't you know what was going on next door to you?"

I never imagined Vito taking a backseat to anyone other than his first wife. I was wrong. The dog brigade just watches this play out. Somehow they know not to bark at the stranger giving us orders. Too bad the older couple opening their door across the hall can't stop their two white West Highland terriers from barking like they are defending the city. I am afraid this new guy on our scene might shoot them.

"Shut those yappers up. Now," towel man spoke.

The couple takes off with their little defenders to the elevator.

"No choice now."

"Understood, Andrew, go."

So Vito and this guy know each other. Before I have a chance to think about their possible history, the door is open, and I see a sight I will never forget for the rest of my life.

Chapter 85

Patty Quinn is feeling pretty good about herself. She is mixing with the DA, and he is listening to what she has to say. If nothing else, she knows she has to get into the head of her clients. And now she is finally learning how to get into the heads of those in power. There isn't much difference dealing with either one. Her other clients aren't getting the amount of attention they deserve. True, they have minor infractions of the law and don't pay her very much, but she still should give them equal attention, and she isn't. That bothers her. She went to law school so she could help people. Now she is sliding into the scene of the big guns-big money.

Wait a second; she is helping an awful lot of people by being in this case. It's easy to get caught up in the personalities and lose sight of the big picture. The thought of bad drugs frightens her. What if her birth control pills were made in someone's garage in China? She wouldn't know the difference until she had to decide whether to have an abortion.

"How's it going?" One of her office mates pops in to chat.

"An abortion is a big decision." It just popped out. The two women looked at each other, and Patty turns the color of her hair. "It's not my decision, never mind."

"That big case snowballing you?" Her office mate, Ms. Jacobs, changes the subject.

Patty smiles. "Yeah."

"Don't forget that tonight the gang meets at Skewer's for drinks."

"How can I forget, the first round is on me."

Once alone again, she realizes how she is becoming overwhelmed by the whole package. There are days that she feels she is just not in the right job. This was one of those days. She is having trouble staying on the right track. Screw it; she grabs a few charts and walks to her rent mates' desks. She hands out the charts at random.

"You guys want these cases? They're yours."

She doesn't give any thought to the fact that the two guys and one woman in the office are all tax attorneys. Patty's mind is on overdrive, all thoughts overlapping each other. She flies out the door and takes off to where she always goes when she feels insecure. He will listen, and that gives her the perspective that she needs. Losing herself and having her pulse pound away is all part of letting go. Feeling good is a simple by-product of the process.

Alonzo greets her with his smooth smile. She escapes to a private place to slip into something that is more revealing. She moves rhythmically, and the world's problems melt away. Her heartbeat increases as she looks at him. He doesn't move at all.

He speaks softly, "Don't say anything yet."

"I need to." This is their usual routine. He moves to touch the place that creates even more intensity. She is totally lost in the moment.

"Five more minutes." He presses the speed increase button on the elliptical machine.

She doesn't know if she can last that long. He turns and goes to get her water. Having a gay trainer at the gym is the best thing she ever did. Patty hates the elliptical machine that he forces her to use. She burns the calories that she ate for breakfast. Without specifics or breaking confidence, she can always use him as a sounding board. It clears the muck from her brain.

Upon stepping off the machine, Alonzo hands her the cold plastic bottle of water. She follows him to the treadmill where she walks uphill for two miles and chats, "My head is all over the place."

"Again?"

"Yep."

"That's why you're in such good shape."

She doesn't tell him about the drinking she is planning to do that night. Patty rambles on about the complexities of her career. He maintains that permanently implanted empathic expression. An occasional nod shows he is still paying attention. Two miles are two minutes away, he hits the pace button to increase her speed.

Patty looked like a regular gym rat with her black tights and grey sweatshirt that has "Red Sox" on her rounded chest. Her hair tied back tightly reveals the glistening on her brow. Horses sweat, men perspire, and ladies merely glisten. Whatever. She and Alonzo walk around the gym as part of the cool down. She turns to him when they stop. It is time to get his perspective. This is why she always comes back here when her mind is a mess.

"What do you think?"

"You have to do what is right for you. If you don't, everything after that will be like climbing a wall of ice. That ice doesn't ever melt. Do what is right and you never have to see that wall. Your climb will be a sweet effort up a wooded mountain trail in the spring."

He has a way of saying the right thing at the right time. She often wonders if she could turn him away from the gay world. Better leave what works alone. Climbing up the wooded mountain in the spring sounds great. Then she remembers about her pollen allergies.

Chapter 86

Lamar knows the end is near. A sense of peace, not fear, is enveloping him. He knows trying to fight is a waste of time, so he just goes limp. His whole life was a fight; why should the end be a battle? He would smile, but there isn't much room inside the plastic bag. He hears strange sounds around him. So this is what death is like.

* * *

I've never seen anyone move so quickly. It isn't Vito. Andrew, the towel man, is almost off the ground. What he is going towards is a sight I've never seen before. It looks like someone is either dead or dying. I only saw dead people in my medical-training days, and we always found a logical reason for the event. The logical reason for this event scares the shit out of me.

As if by planning, Vito moves toward Lamar while Andrew goes directly toward Sam. I pick up the leashes that Vito dropped and hold all three with one hand. I don't know what else to do. Before I have a grip, mentally and physically, the three dogs are chewing on Sam's legs. They growl and make sounds I can only imagine coming from a horde of angry wild canines.

As Sam bends over, Andrew draws his fist back and, in one short movement, punches Sam in the chin. Sam goes down and rolls on his stomach. The dogs still have their jaws on his legs, and continue their attack. Andrew looks at the three dogs and firmly says, "No." They back off and sit down about two feet from the prone body of Sam. It is as if they were in training with this guy for years.

I don't know what to do. So I just stand in the middle of the room. As Andrew does his bit with Sam, Vito rips open the plastic bag over Lamar's head. He rips from the front so an immediate airway is possible. Lamar is tied to the chair and not moving. His head is slumped down toward his chest.

I yell to Vito, "Untie him, and get him on the floor . . . quick!"

Lamar is on the ground and not breathing. I tilt his head back and put my ear to his mouth. Nothing. I open and breathe into his mouth. Vito starts pressing on his chest. I don't feel a pulse. Vito keeps pounding.

I feel sick as I say to Vito, "We may have lost him."

It is as if Lamar heard me and has to correct me. He gasps and rapid breathing returns. His pulse is weak, but it is there. Andrew has dialed 911, and the Boston Rescue Squad is on its way. The canine division are all sitting and rotating their heads in unison, taking this all in.

I don't have time to celebrate Lamar's return to life; I am thinking about his possible brain damage. I don't even consider the emotional deals that come with this package. My adrenaline is fueling me, and I am ready for the next event. Sam is cuffed with his hands behind his back. Vito adds his signature by taking Sam's belt off and tying his legs at the ankle. With Andrew and Vito in the room, I have the feeling when this guy wakes up; he is going to wish he were still out. My two law enforcement teammates are attending to Sam; they want to hear his first words when he returns to consciousness.

Scanning the room, I notice the chair under the door handle of the bedroom. There are female voices yelling and trying to get our attention. I slide the chair from the doorknob and open the door. Catherine is tied to one of the bed posters and looks as pale as a milk carton.

She looks at me and screams, "I'm OK, don't let her escape!"

Isabella is running out the door as soon as I open it. I reflexively stick my leg out, and she trips and goes flying into the coffee table in the living room. Her head hits the wood, and the sound reminds me of the puck hitting the goalpost. She is out cold. Vito cuffs her closest hand to the table leg. Nobody checks if she is breathing.

I finally feel part of this law enforcement team. It took tripping a woman to do it. What a scene: one guy out cold and cuffed and tied with a detective and ex-cop standing over him, and a knocked-out lady cuffed to a table with an ex-shrink looking at her.

At least it is under control, but it is too quiet. Where is the canine patrol? Feeling that I am no longer needed in the living room, I walk into the bedroom to untie Catherine. She is peacefully lying on the bed with Bowser and Bentley on their bellies at her feet. Fern is resting with her head on Catherine's belly. The big brown eyes just stare at me. That is, all sets.

"I won't even comment on you being tied up in bed."

She doesn't answer me. Her glare says it all.

I untie her and climb up to lie down with the crew. I slide over to Catherine; silence is the word. We both need each other's warmth.

Chapter 87

"I'll walk the dog. Don't forget to take your pills." You'd think we were married for twenty years by the tone of her voice.

It convinces me we are never going down that path. "No problem. It's that obvious how beat I am?"

"It's that obvious."

After the longest shower in my life, I collapse on a blanket. Wearing old red boxers with little hearts on them and a grey Philadelphia Flyers ice hockey tee shirt, I look like a college student recovering from a long night at the frat house. I lean over to the nightstand where my trusty carbitrol is sitting. One dark one, one light one and hopefully no evening seizure.

It is hard not to notice Catherine next to me. It isn't the borrowed orange Philly Flyers tee shirt and black sweats that do it. It is simply that she is here. I hear the door open and close, open and close. Fern's needs were met. Our needs would be met soon. It is simply a good night's sleep. Like I said, it is as if we were married for over twenty years.

She couldn't stay at her place at the Marriott since it is a crime scene. Vito is home with Bowser and Bentley. His now—ex-wife has moved to Florida and ceded their old place to him. His old home is his new home.

Lamar is in the hospital, and tubes and a respirator are keeping him alive. We'll check on him tomorrow. Andrew, towel man, rescue man, or whoever the hell he is, is somewhere. Sam and Isabella are in a holding cell. Maybe getting reacquainted with Axelrod.

The vanilla smell of Catherine wakens me, and her warmth lulls me back to sleep. It isn't for long.

The phone rings. "You never got back to us." It is the Anderson cops from Hanover, New Hampshire.

How the hell did they get my number? I look at the phone. "You're right." I hung up the phone.

"Who was that?" I barely can hear her whisper.

"Wrong number."

We both roll over and try to sleep. *Try to sleep* is a ridiculous statement. Either you sleep or you don't.

The phone rings. "You were sleeping?" As usual, Vito gets to the point.

"Yeah, I talk in my sleep."

"I can't sleep."

"Welcome to my world."

Catherine moves and mumbles, "Tell me you speak to wrong numbers."

"No, this is a right number."

I sense Vito doesn't want to be alone. Maybe the scent of his first wife is still there. I open the door. "You can use the couch in the living room. Fern won't mind the company."

"Me or the dogs?"

"What do you think?"

"I'll be right over."

I turn to my bed partner and say, "He's coming over to spend the night."

Not a sound from Catherine, only steady breathing, bordering on snoring. She must be so well adjusted and trusting. Or just damn tired. I am just damn tired and have to stay up for Vito. I know it won't be long before he shows up. When he spoke, he was on his cell, probably already on his way out.

I get out of bed and walk to the fridge, checking the beer inventory. It isn't fresh, but five bottles stare back at me. I crack one open and nurse it while waiting for him. I don't wait long. I look up, and he is walking toward the fridge with his tail-wagging followers.

He never gave me back the keys. Not that he needs them.

He takes three gulps of his beer and, without looking at me, says, "Do you think Lamar is all right?"

"I'll know more tomorrow when I see him in the hospital."

"You know, I don't know of any family to call for him."

I nod. Lamar only gives away what he wants to. His private life is just that, private.

"Catherine OK?"

"She's a tough little lady. She's sleeping."

"You OK?"

"Yeah."

No, I'm not OK. I am insecure, upset, sleep deprived; and a host of other issues are bouncing around my brain. Sometimes knowledge is a liability especially when it affects you. We both finish our beer in silence.

Heading back to bed, I turn to Vito. "See you in the morning. You walk the dogs."

"You make the coffee."

Talk about old married couples.

Chapter 88

It was a great day skiing. Utah has the best snow on the planet. I feel like I skied every trail on the mountain. The soreness in my legs confirms that. My wife is drinking a scotch by the fireplace and reading the local paper. The only sound I hear is crackling of the aged wood burning. I walk to the bedroom, my quads and calves keeping me in first gear. I can't help but to take a minute to rest before dinner. I move the three pillows on the bed to prop me up as my legs stretch out as a reward for working the mountain. Picking up the paperback mystery I bought at the airport, it isn't long before my eyes close, and I slide into my own quiet place.

I don't know why I am on the floor, on all fours, and feeling totally disorientated. I can't make any sense of the outside voice through the mist my thought processes are in. I fight through the haze of that familiar territory I despise. Not again. A seizure. Most likely it was brought on by exhaustion, low oxygen at a high altitude, and sleeping without taking my medication. It's happened before. The only way to deal with it is to let it run its course.

Luckily the condo floor is carpeted; it cushions my fall. No head bruises this time. There is no long-term damage to me physically; I can't say the same emotionally. Her voice is banging off my brain, and I continue to ignore it. I refuse to move. I suddenly sit up. I feel strong and stable. Nothing had changed before I closed my eyes. I am in Boston. It is getting harder and harder to let go. I look at my two bottles of capsules that are my window to normalcy and deny my dependence on them. It's hard to admit how thankful I am for their existence.

Mr. Independence needs little organized products of organic chemistry to live a normal life. The grateful part of me is fighting with the denial team. Grateful always wins. When am I going to just accept it?

"You woke me up," my bedmate says with one eye open.

"Sorry. I'm having flashbacks. It won't happen again."

She rolls over and goes back to sleep. At least she doesn't move. She doesn't care or doesn't understand. I cannot sleep. I try yoga breathing and position myself on my back in a resting pose. It worked better at the studio.

I don't have to wait for the six-thirty alarm to go off; I am up at six. Showered, dressed, and headed to the kitchen where I make coffee. Fern looks at me, jumps off the couch, and waits by the door. Her two roommates follow. Being outside early is always energizing for me. No matter how tired I am, walking through Monument Park with just my little buddies, I feel Boston is all mine. No matter what is going on in my life the night before, the morning is always a fresh start. The dogs do their business and I follow up with my responsibility. I am such a good citizen.

Is that why I am involved in all this cops-and-robbers stuff? I could have walked away early in the game. Was I the good citizen or just bored at the moment?

It doesn't appear as if the sun is going to make an appearance today. Walking back to my condo, only the kitchen light is on. My human roommates are listening to their bodies and resting. Coffee will get me through the day, or I will crash at three. It's happened before.

The keys, the dogs, the climbing up the steps—returning to my routine. I'm kidding myself; routine will only happen when I am living alone. Of course, Fern is in the equation. Entering my condo I notice the bathroom lights are on, and I hear the flowing of the shower. I feed the canine gang and take care of myself too. We take turns watching each other eat. I wonder if I returned too soon for Catherine. I flash back to her leaving my place with everything she touched placed in the dishwasher or gone. She disappeared before I had wakened. It isn't easy forgetting our first night together.

Looking away from the window, I see my old faded red McGill sweatshirt with its black companion sweatpants. They are moving.

"Good morning." Catherine appears in my old sweats that were from my bottom left drawer. She remembered.

"Good morning."

Vito, in his white Holiday Inn bathrobe, lumbers into the kitchen, taking two frozen bagels out of the freezer. The large orange juice is poured. The big white mug is set up with the dark fuel of the day. He doesn't bother to look for anything to smear on the bagels. He remembered.

"The dogs are walked and fed. So am I. I'm going to the hospital to check on Lamar." There is no point in calling. I'd rather see him and touch base with the team treating him. I still have the "Dr." in front of my name.

"We'll meet you there," they speak in tandem.

"No, let's not make this a circus. Vito, check on the updates of the cop things. Catherine, why don't you check in with the DA and check the status of the legal case?"

They both have the same look; who is this guy giving us orders? They never were offered the chance to ask; I am in a cab halfway to the hospital, and I am sure Vito is toasting his second bagel.

* * *

I have no idea what to expect when I see Lamar. My mind is still in a blank state, that is, until I enter the hospital. I reflexively feel I am onstage again. I walk to the coffee shop and buy a *Globe*. The paper is always good company if I have to wait. The front page is running an article on tainted pet food. It is killing cats and dogs. Is this ever going to stop?

"Doc, good to see you."

I turn toward the voice and look directly at a young resident standing two feet in front of me. I have no idea who she is.

"I was at your lecture at Penn. The one on the interaction of mind and disease."

That was six years ago; it might as well have been a hundred years ago. She keeps talking. An energetic short thin and animated woman. Probably an Olympic medalist in floor exercise in gymnastics. I can still fantasize. For all the long hours, her brown hair has light streaks in it. Very stylish. She takes care of herself. Wait a minute; I'm starting to think like a cop.

"I'm the senior resident in pulmonary." Her name tag reads Dr. D. Taylor.

"Of course. You still happy in the profession?"

She rolls her eyes and her lips create one thin firm line together, telling me that is a stupid question.

"Absolutely."

It is said with a touch of arrogance. No one "absolutely" is happy about anything. At least I wasn't. "Great. A dear friend was admitted yesterday, can you help me catch up on his status?"

"No problem."

Within five minutes I am outside of Lamar's room reviewing his chart. He shares the room with a young lung cancer patient. Lamar is going to make it, his roommate isn't. I walk into his room.

"You look a lot better than the last time I saw you."

"Thanks."

I have an immediate sense of relief. He is going to recover, at least, physically. "Vito and Catherine will be here later. I'll call them with the good news."

Strangely, there is no change of expression on Lamar's face. His roommate is getting an MRI this morning. That insures privacy for us.

"Anything you want to talk about?" I am back in the office.

"Yes. I want to speak to Alan Cohen. I need to give him my testimony as soon as possible. I'll speak to Vito and Catherine to make sure they are all right."

Interesting, he still is all business. But there is a different look in his eyes. They are as vacant as a movie parking lot at seven in the morning.

He looks at the tubes going in and out of him and says, "I need you to contact someone for me."

"Sure."

"Her name is Kim Wilson. I'll write down her cell number. Just tell her where I am and that I'm fine."

"No problem."

I know when not to ask questions. I sit down and look at him. He is fighting the transition from being officer in charge to the passive patient. My feeling is that as soon as he is unhooked from the IVs, he is out of there. He will be shocked at how weak he is. He is inert on his raised pillows, not saying a word, just staring at the blank wall in front of him. I need to get out of here. I am having trouble figuring out my exit strategy. He does me a favor.

"Why don't you contact the DA and our two buddies and get the ball rolling. Only one of us needs to stay here."

I am the one following orders now. But I have the feeling he knows what I need. I make my calls, and my evening roommates sound upbeat. I leave a message with the DA's office. The call to Kim Wilson is a bit different. After identifying myself and, without giving away what really happened, I pass on that Lamar is in the hospital and doing fine. There is total silence. I can't even hear breathing. I leave her the phone number and the room number. She just hangs up. I am sitting in the lobby making the calls from my cell. I fold the phone and look at the *Globe* again. My next call is to the vet.

* * *

I am still on hold as I am leaving the cab at my place. I imagine every pet owner in Boston is calling their vets now. My place is empty, and the silence is what I need. The dog walker has the gang for at least another twenty minutes. The dryer is on, and the dishwasher competes with it for loudness. I run to the dishwasher to see if any beer bottles were put there. None. The toothpaste is still in my bathroom. Just checking. I don't have it in me if there is going to be a second round of mystery woman.

Catherine is past using me to hide from Sam and Isabella. She followed them until they caught her. Her work was the glue that held this investigation together. Now it was up to the DA and his group of legal wizards. I am hoping the papers will be part of this deal. What do I mean? Unless it is pushed in our faces, we never will question if the drugs we are taking are the real thing. Unfortunately, the pets have to suffer first before we move our asses. I know the FDA is undermanned. A girl I met in college used to work for them and was swamped with enough work for five agents. She disappeared from my life, hopefully to have her own. They all disappear from my life.

I hope Gord's killer is caught. We all know it's Sam. I have a feeling Vito and his fellow cops are going to make it a tough wait for trial for this guy. Being alone in my apartment is the way this all started. But I can't continue to think about the past. I have to live the present. Yoga thinking. I move to the computer and check the yoga schedule at the gym. There is a class at nine in the morning. If I don't have any police work to do, I'll be at that class. I have to get back to working out. Time to do something for me.

The door opens. It is the dog walker, a man in his forties wearing a ski vest, flannel shirt, jeans, and a smile. I'll never figure out the spell he weaves over his four-legged clients. They all act as if they have known him since they were puppies.

"Don't worry, I checked; your dog is fine."

What the hell is he talking about? Fine for what?

He looks at me and sees I haven't a clue. "You feed her dry dog food. The bad stuff is the wet stuff."

"Thanks. Oh, how do you know?"

As he walks out he says, "Your vet is my brother-in-law. I checked for my clients."

This guy is worth the money.

He continues, "I own the agency. I like to meet the clients too."

I guess he searched our places to check what we were feeding our pets. Probably an ex-FBI agent. Paranoia, welcome aboard. Fern is busy doing down dog, and her dog walker is gone. Up dog is next. I wonder where she learned how important it is to stretch after exercise. I'll have to ask. Slowly, I was returning to my former irrational self. Good.

The three of them gather by the door where the bag of dog food is stored, and six big round eyes penetrate my soul. It is early, but they deserve to eat. After all, if it wasn't for Fern, we never would have found Catherine and the bad guys.

The phone rings, I pick it up on the second ring. "He's going to be OK. He made it." As usual Vito gets to the point.

"Yeah. Good news." I already knew that.

"You know, he does have a spacey look."

"Wouldn't you if you were tied up and a plastic bag was on your head?"

"Here's Catherine."

"I think we lost Lamar." She knows where my thoughts were when I saw him.

"Let's see how it plays out. Time has a way of healing."

"We're going to the DA's office. You're not needed until tomorrow afternoon."

"Where are you staying tonight?"

"Am I still welcome?"

"Sure. Vito?"

"Why don't you ask him?" She gives the phone to Vito.

"Where you staying tonight?"

"I'm going to my place. I can handle it. Besides, Bentley and Bowser are my buddies."

"Dinner?"

"I don't know how long I'll be at the DA's. I have reports to file back at the precinct too."

"OK." I don't know when I'm going to see Vito again. That is, to hang out with. Things are changing.

Catherine has the phone. "Be back around seven."

"I'll order in."

"Sushi?"

"Sushi."

* * *

I stay away from the soy sauce. Too much salt. We both fight over the stingy supply of ginger. The nice part of sushi is that cleaning up after dinner is as neat as the spicy tuna rolls.

"Still hungry?"

"You always order less than we need. Why?"

"Easy, sushi the morning after doesn't look so good."

"I guess that's what a night in the fridge will do to you."

"I have some oatmeal cookies or how about an apple?"

"Red or green?"

"Both."

"You go both ways?"

"Only with apples."

Catherine smiles, opens the fridge, and takes out one red and one green. Looking at me, she places both apples on the table on either side of the wine bottle. We both reach for the red, my hand over hers. We stay like that, the closest we've ever been. At the same time we remove our hands.

"Go ahead, take it." It is the chivalrous thing to do.

"No, you take it."

"Please take it."

"No, you."

Here we are bickering like an old married couple. Except the comfort cushion of shared years is not present. Taking a knife, I split the red into two halves. We settle on the half closest to us. Two strong-willed people sharing a unique time together. It is understood that it has no future. That night we share each other with a passion that could never be recreated. It is our goodbye.

Chapter 89

Alan Cohen is no dummy. He has underlings leak selected information to the media. The public is getting educated and scared. The pressure it creates has to help his case. The bad guys have no excuse for hurting innocent lives. Pet owners soon form their own lobbying groups. Hopefully, this case will get national attention. Alan has a feeling some top executive at a major network must have a dog and be concerned. Press the right button and the big doors open. As I said, Alan Cohen is no dummy. I can see him playing for a high federal position down the road.

Vito and Catherine have regular meetings concerning the case. I become the occasional consultant. It suits me. The trial is in six weeks. Pretty quick for wheels of justice. The power of the press. The towel man gives me a call. He compliments my coolness under fire. He wants to know if he can use me for a consultant in some of his work. Sure, why not?

Catherine moves her stuff to another Marriott in town. Her place is still off-limits until the trial is over.

Chapter 90

Before I know it, the next morning is here, and I am walking over the bridge with my yoga mat in hand. Entering the gym, I view the building where the Bruins and Celtics played their terrible losing seasons. Everything goes in cycles. If I just can figure out how professional sports fits into nature's evolution.

Entering the yoga studio is like seeing an old friend. Except the class fee went up one dollar. There are five women with mats down against the back wall. I open my mat in a slot between two ladies in meditative modes. Or maybe they aren't awake yet.

The instructor enters, moves to a far corner, faces the wall, and opens a book. After about ten minutes, the room is full of women of all ages, shapes, and sizes. The two men are unkempt and paunchy. No competition. I can't let it go. I see no familiar faces. Or bodies. The instructor is all business. No flow, just pose after pose. Sort of like gymnastics in a steaming room.

At the end, while we are all on our backs and exhausted, the instructor, Karen, offers this quote from Woody Allen, "Eighty percent of success is showing up."

Chew on that.

Chapter 91

One year later and the events of the immediate past are fading. I seem to remember what I want to. Don't we all do that?

The fall season is fading into winter. Leaves of brown and dark green hold on until the next rough wind. Routine, as always, is my pathway to peace. We are both on the couch facing the large window. With the leaves getting thinner, our view is of the morning crowd walking. Some alone, some with humans, some with dogs, some with all of the above.

"We're both getting older."

She just sighs, her head on my shoulder. Her body leans sweetly against me. Sharing each other has become our favorite and special moments.

Looking at her, I quietly say, "Don't worry about the grey hair, it happens to all of us."

Her dark eyes express more than she can say.

I don't even know how old she is. She will never tell me even when I told her the big "sixty" is staring me in the face. Her tongue licks my ear, and she slides down the couch; it is time for a belly rub. Life without her would be tough. I try not to think about it.

I am about to slide into one of those introspective moments that some might describe as mild depression. She doesn't let me. Jumping off the couch, a quick shake, and Fern is ready for a walk. Good timing, we both need to get out. Meeting at my door, she waits with leash in mouth as I zip my old green ski jacket. Dressing is easy these days, jeans or khakis, sweater or sweater.

Down the steps, no more stale old cigar smoke. He moved out, and a young couple who are saving the earth moved in. The only smell from their place is an occasional joint.

Fern and I pay our respects to the memorial on Bunker Hill and follow the usual pattern. I have many friends during these walks; they say hi, never getting beyond the superficial. That's exactly what I want. My favorite season is the end of fall. It just is. Fern's coat is thickening up; she looks tougher.

Back in my place, I brew and drink my third round of coffee. Reluctantly, I check my messages.

"Hey, call. What the fuck is going on with you?" Vito is still trying to rekindle what was before.

No way. Not interested. I hit the Erase button. From the little contact I have with the police, it seems as if he is happy. Every so often the cops will pay me for a consult on a case. They will tell me what is up with Vito. I never see him; he transferred to another part of town. The word was that he sold the condo he and his ex-wife lived in. Being Boston, he made a nice profit. I was happy for him. Maybe he got his car washed.

He hooked up with the attorney, Patty Quinn. He lost twenty pounds. I never figured any woman would affect him like that. He is renting a fancy apartment in some high-rise overlooking the Charles. I have a feeling they are renting each other as well. Buying is such a commitment. He gained legal custody of Bowser. One cop taking care of another. I have to admit, I miss all the canines being together. It just worked. How often does that happen in life?

Lamar went south. Literally. He is living in a condo in a gated community in Florida. Alone. He took early retirement with medical benefits. The deal was good; he put the time in with the force and was injured on the job. I hope it isn't just a cover.

That deal didn't work out for Gord.

Andrew Dodge called me a few times. I consulted when the case was right for me. It was fun; he is a straight-up kind of guy. No bullshit. And he pays twice as much as the cops. Fun money for fun. I am still trying to figure out what "fun" is. My investment broker sees the checks.

Oh, the case went well. Sam got life with no parole, Isabella got fifteen years, and Axelrod is living under a different name in New Mexico.

My personal life is very personal. Besides Fern, it is just me and me. I wonder why I furnished the place with so many chairs. They are mostly empty.

* * *

Walking in the first light snow of the year to my morning workout, I stop and look at the little flakes hitting the water. They touch and melt into the moving river. They wet my Red Sox cap.

I miss seeing Aleni, the former yoga teacher. She's married and lives in San Francisco. Every damn thing changes. Who says change is good?

Thirty-pound dumbbells in each hand, I move my arms up to exercise my shoulders. This morning it is shoulders and abs. I look good; the cut is back. I nod at the regulars on machines and benches. First names only, the unwritten rules of a real gym, it's not a social club. I sign on with a trainer twice a week. Looking at his shaved head and beard could scare the hell out of you. He's a nice guy and knows his stuff. Because of him, I'm reaching a higher level of fitness than I've ever had. I know I'm addicted to exercise. So what? It's nice to have activities to turn your brain off.

My ex-wife used to tell me that as I age, I lose whatever social skills I had. OK. I never hear from her. Working out helps me forget the e-mail I got this morning. It was from Catherine. She is back in Florida and has her own consulting agency. She works with the FDA and private pharmaceutical companies. She has the best of both worlds. She is living her dream. The e-mail just said, "Hi. How are you?" Then she went on about her company and said I should check her Web site. Is this just networking? Even if it is, it forces me to lift heavier weights in order to have a new pain cover an old one.

* * *

Walking back over the bridge with the green Dartmouth sweatshirt's hood covering my wet head, I am seeing quick shadows of people. The little Greek café two blocks from my place has my seat by the door. Entering from the cold, the humid warmth feels great as I lift the *Boston Globe* from the chair that makes it mine. The owner always leaves it for me.

George, the owner, comes over and asks the question even though he knows the answer, "The usual?"

I nod. I have a big green mug with black coffee and a shot of espresso warming and charging me for the next few hours. Nobody makes it this good. Smell, texture, and always in the same mug. I know the mug; I memorized the chips in the porcelain.

The sports section is loaded with articles on how the new young players and the older players acquired by trades are going to make the Celtics and Bruins contenders. Hope springs eternal. That's better than reality.

Fueled by the fresh caffeine, I just about jog to my place. Fern is waiting on the other side of the door. Going down the steps, her pace is slower than three months ago. Being a gradual change, I didn't think about it or didn't want to. Maybe my pace is slowing down too. Another reason not to keep old contacts. I hate it when they tell me how good I look. What does that say about all the other times they just said "hi"?

The afternoon blends into a quiet continuum of food shopping and reading. I hardly noticed anything on my evening dog walk. The blending of my days is starting to become homogenized. Dinner time is approaching, and I place the fresh veggies and eggs on the counter for preparation. The greens are washed, chopped, and in a large glass bowl. The eggs enter the boiling water. My protein for the evening. I stopped worrying about the evils of cholesterol a long time ago. While fishing out the hard-boiled eggs from the water, I feel a strange kinship with them. Under an illusion of softness, I am becoming pretty hard-boiled myself. Another dinner alone.

Of course, Fern is there, but she never answers my questions. Looking at the bowl of greens and the three steaming protein capsules, I say, "Time to go out." At least I don't answer myself. My in-house dinner finds its way to the fridge.

I am walking to the Warren Tavern. I wore old khakis and a faded green turtleneck that I've known for a long time. My Red Sox cap is a given. My leather jacket is closed to my neck to keep the damp wind from hitting flesh.

Opening the door to the Tavern after a brisk walk, smelling the chef's work only confirms that I made the right decision to dine out. As I remembered, the hour I am present is prime time. I work my way over to the bar. Sitting between two guys with Red Sox caps on, I order.

"Harpoon?"

"We have it on draft. What size?"

"Mug."

The bartender, with his dark red apron and Red Sox cap, is the catcher. We just need a first baseman to complete the infield. The TV is blasting some sports, reporters yelling at each other. Nobody is listening. Sipping my fresh Harpoon IPA Ale, I look around the restaurant. Every table looks occupied. I hate eating at the bar. I look around a second time. My new surveillance technique, learned from my buddies on the force. I don't look at the people; I just check out their plates. It doesn't look good.

"You going to order?" The bartender looks at me while pouring a scotch for the guy sitting to my right.

"Another few minutes." He is down the other end of the bar by the time I complete my answer.

Halfway through the beer, he is looking at me again. Either it is a refill or a meal. I came here for a meal. "Hamburger, no bun and—"

He writes it down and is off placing it wherever orders are placed before I have time to negotiate no fries and extra veggies. I'll deal. I feel not very cool sitting there next to two strangers who totally ignore me. I need company.

"Tough season for the Bruins. Early, but they're not winning. I think it's the defense."

My two bar mates just stare ahead like I was talking to myself. I was. Before I have time to feel sorry for myself, my meal is in front of me.

"Refill?"

I finish the final third of the mug, and another takes its place. So here I am, sitting at a bar between two strangers who are cold warm-blooded bookends. I make an initial incision in the hamburger. It is just right. The taste test confirms it.

This is ridiculous, good food and ignoring company. I would have been better off staying home.

Before my next bite, I take another survey of the room. I spot a possible empty chair in the smaller of the two dining rooms. A woman is sitting at a table for two in the room where my odyssey started. Actually, it is the same table. She sits with her back to the window. I note the curtains still haven't been replaced. Her forest green cloth jacket and black wool cap are on the chair next to her. The thick straight dark hair is tied back, giving her a classic, proper look. Pale skin contrasts sharply with her hair. Small black-framed eyeglasses hang from her neck and rests on a dark fine wool sweater that is just short of being a turtleneck.

It is hard for me to take my eyes off her. She looks like she is in her mid-forties. She opens a book. She is drinking a glass of red wine. I munch on a forbidden fry and watch her take the first bite of salad. I think there are shrimp on top. Her fork never leaves her left hand. She has to be European. I saw that in a spy movie once. An American was outed as a spy at a restaurant because he switched his fork from left to right as he ate.

I always told my patients if they weren't happy where they were they should move. It was time to follow my own advice.

"Excuse me, it's so crowded at the bar, may I sit down?" There I am with my dinner in one hand, beer in the other, and still dressed with coat and hat, asking a stranger if I can have dinner with her. If she says no, I have nowhere to go.

My place at the bar is taken by a young guy. He buys a round for his new neighbors, and they share in all sorts of conversation. I guess I missed the boat on that one. If this woman says no, I eat standing up. Of course, it could be packaged and taken home. I'm thinking of cold fries or staring at an attractive woman eating her salad. She looks up and makes eye contact. I know I am being evaluated, and I have no CV in hand, just my dinner and drink. With one quick movement, her hand empties the chair, and her jacket and cap are hanging on the peg behind her.

"Thanks. I appreciate it."

I slide my plate on the table and place the mug down next to it. My jacket and cap are on the peg next to hers. Sitting down, I realize I have no knife and fork. I look around for some help. She sits back and is observing me as if I am the evening's entertainment. Maybe she is some psych professor at Harvard observing how sixtyish males handle stress in public places. A young man with a pitcher of water is headed in our direction.

"Excuse me." He stops. "I just sat down with my meal and—" All I see is his back, and in one minute he is placing a fork, knife, and napkin on the table in front of me.

"Thanks." This is said to his back.

I look at her; her fork is down, and she is staring at me. "I don't want to intrude on your privacy but—"

"Do not worry; in my country this is normal." She is French. The accent is classic. She continues, "Please, eat your meal." She is giving me permission to eat my hot meal while it was hot.

I take her advice. I am attacking an all-American hamburger while my "partner" is slowly acknowledging her salad as she turns the pages of her book. We don't speak to each other. I try to see what she is reading, but the angle of the book distorts the title in my line of vision. The fact that it is in French also makes it a tough call.

The carnivore content, I watch my intellectual vegetarian French tablemate read. Being American, I have to talk. Being me, living with a canine, I need a human conversation once in a while. The accent just makes it more interesting. Being me, how could I not talk with a beautiful woman whom I don't know?

"Excuse me, are you enjoying Boston?"

She slowly puts her book down and looks at me. She marks her place with a postcard that has a picture of Fenway Park. "Yes, I do enjoy Boston."

Pointing at her book, I say, "Have you been there?"

She backs her head away reflexively and gets a defensive look about her. Picking the soft cover book up and placing it closer to me, she says, "*The Challenges of Interpreting Modern Art in Design and Literature,* by Simon C. Barral."

"I was talking about Fenway Park. You know the postcard. Your bookmark."

"What is it when you say '*book mark*'?" She picks up her book as if to look for a significant mark.

"The card inside to mark where you have read. The picture on the card is of Fenway Park."

Very seriously, she opens the book and slowly removes the card. A nail file takes its place. Studying the picture, she says, "This is an important building?"

"A very important building."

"It is historic?"

"Very historic."

Once again she studies the picture and then flips it over to learn it was built in the early twentieth century. "How can this be historic, it is still new?"

"Ted Williams played there."

"Who is Ted Williams, a famous president?"

The waiter, the same young fellow who gave me the means to eat, pops up next to us. "Coffee, desert?"

Without looking at the waiter, the postcard has her total attention, she answers, "Coffee."

"Same." I don't ask for decaf; it is going to be a long night. I just have that feeling. I will have to get to know her before I review the history of baseball. "How many days have you been in Boston?"

"I have been here for three months."

"That is a long vacation."

"It is work; I am a visiting professor at Harvard."

"My name is Adam."

"I am Segolene. I am called Sego."

"Is this your first time here?"

"No. Two years ago I was teaching here for six months. I do the same now." She noticed me looking at the ring on her left hand. "My husband is teaching in a medical school in Lyon. We think it is good, every two years we have time to ourselves."

What do I say? I teach you baseball; you teach me history of modern art. I glance at my watch, time to walk Fern. The crowd is mostly leaving, and there is no line at the door.

"Refills?" The waiter resurfaces.

She speaks, "No."

Or maybe it is "none." Sounds the same to me. I offer a simple "no." I add a quick, "Check, please."

Both of our credit cards are on the table. We receive separate bills and place the cards on each bill, respectively. She picks up her large purse and moves her hands as if searching for lost keys. I am only half right.

"You OK?"

"I can't find my keys or my cell phone." She searches with the other hand. She stops and looks at me with a glimpse of vulnerability.

"Were you in a hurry when you left your place?"

"Yes, the taxi was waiting, and I just ran to the elevator." A pensive look, almost calm, maybe an expression of defeat, takes over her demeanor. "I left them on the kitchen table."

We handled the checks and both stand up to leave.

"Look, I have to walk my dog. I'll give you my phone; you can call a friend to help you."

"Thank you."

She is as tall as me, and we walk at the same pace. Standing up, she reveals the build of a runner.

"You like dogs?"

"Yes, I have one back in France."

"What breed?"

"Doberman. Yours?"

"A mix of many."

Is this deja vu all over again? Nothing much is said during the walk to my place. When we walk up the steps into the park, I don't offer the significance of the site. I don't feel like teaching American history tonight. Standing in front of the large oak outside door I turn to her.

"I can bring down my cell phone, or you can come up and use it."

"Thank you. I'd like to come up. May I use the WC?"

"Follow me."

Walking up the staircase, I miss the stale cigar smoke. I don't know why, but it gave the place a homey, lived-in feel. Of course, everybody else felt they were being subjected to carcinogens. The events of last year give me a confidence with this new woman. Or maybe I just don't care.

"She is so cute."

The two ladies are on the floor, and Fern is getting her belly rubbed. So Sego is truly a dog person. Good start. But she's married. She had thrown her large purse down against the couch before she sat down with Fern. I notice it is open.

She stands up and looks at me. "The bathroom?"

"Down the hall, first door on the left."

That's where I showered, and my dirty underwear and wet towel are piled on the floor against the tub. I wasn't counting on company. The door closes, and I glance at the open purse. Something shiny catches my eye. Fern is sitting by the pantry where I store her treats. She'll have to wait. Walking toward her purse, I recognize it isn't in the sight line from the hallway.

The newfound cop in me is very curious. I stand over the purse's opening and look directly at the shining object. It is a badge. It is on the inside of a black leather folding carrier with an ID facing the badge. I can't figure out what is written on the badge. It isn't new, and the letters are a bit blurry. It looks like initials for some organization. The ID is different. The letters are readable, and a picture is above the name. The image shows lighter hair, but it is her picture.

Badges like this aren't issued for academic careers. Especially in Europe where they take authority seriously. I look twice at the ID. I can hear running water from the bathroom. I'm not sure if there is talking that is also coming from the other side of the door. I don't know why, but I glance at the kitchen and notice my cell phone isn't on the countertop.

I am tempted to pull out the ID from the purse and study it, but the risk seems not worth it. Oh, the name under the picture is Jacqueline Lemaire.

* * *

Before I have much time to think, Sego, or whoever she is, is in the hallway wearing a big smile.

"Thanks for your phone; I made a few calls with no luck."

"No luck?"

"I left messages wherever I called."

She sits down on the couch. The same couch where Fern and I share the Boston sports world. Fern just sits and looks at the woman. She is as curious as I am. I don't know what to say. Standing and looking at her, my mind is racing in all sorts of directions. None familiar. Then again, I am in denial. This can't be happening again? I'm either doing nothing or the exciting unknown is sitting in my living room.

Sego/Jacqueline looks at me and says, "Do you have any wine?"

I remember that I have a California pinot noir in a drawer. Vito gave it to me for putting him up last year. I open it, pour it in one of the two wineglasses I own, and crack open a beer for myself.

After drinking half of her glass, she looks me directly in the eye. She undoes her bun and lets hair flow over her shoulders. She leans back on the couch and smiles. I notice her perfectly aligned teeth. A nice color white, not the fried-bleach look.

Quietly she says, "May I stay the night?"

I feel like I am fishing and hooked a fish bigger than the boat.

"I have to make a call."

I grab the phone and go into the study where Vito camped out for a few months. I dial the number he gave me if ever I needed him. I cannot erase the look on his face as he said that to me. It was "Kid, you never know."

I ignored it at the time. I dial. It rings. What the hell am I going to say to him? The ringing stops.

"Hello." It is said with quiet authority.

It is Lamar.